BORDERS.

CLASSICS

GUY DE MAUPASSANT

The Necklace

and Other Stories

Translated by Albert M. C. McMaster,
A. E. Henderson, Charlotte Garstin Quesada,
and others

BORDERS.
CLASSICS

Please direct sales or editorial inquiries to:
BordersTradeBookInventoryQuestions@bordersgroupinc.com

This edition is published by
Borders Classics, an imprint of Borders Group, Inc.,
by special arrangement with
Ann Arbor Media Group, LLC
2500 South State Street, Ann Arbor, MI 48104

Dust jacket copy by Kip Keller
Production team: Mae Barnard, Tina Budzinski, Lori Holland,
Denise Kennedy, Steven Moore, Kathie Radenbaugh,
and Rhonda Welton

Printed and bound in the United States of America
by Edwards Brothers, Inc.

ISBN 1-58726-168-5

07   06   05   04   10 9 8 7 6 5 4 3 2 1

CONTENTS

The Necklace

The girl was one of those pretty and charming young creatures who sometimes are born, as if by a slip of fate, into a family of clerks. She had no dowry, no expectations, no way of being known, understood, loved, married by any rich and distinguished man; so she let herself be married to a little clerk of the Ministry of Public Instruction.

She dressed plainly because she could not dress well, but she was unhappy as if she had really fallen from a higher station; since with women there is neither caste nor rank, for beauty, grace and charm take the place of family and birth. Natural ingenuity, instinct for what is elegant, a supple mind are their sole hierarchy, and often make of women of the people the equals of the very greatest ladies.

Mathilde suffered ceaselessly, feeling herself born to enjoy all delicacies and all luxuries. She was distressed at the poverty of her dwelling, at the bareness of the walls, at the shabby chairs, the ugliness of the curtains. All those things, of which another woman of her rank would never even have been conscious, tortured her and made her angry. The sight of the little Breton peasant who did her humble housework aroused in her despairing regrets and bewildering dreams. She thought of silent antechambers hung with Oriental tapestry, illumined by tall bronze candelabra, and of two great footmen in knee breeches who sleep in the big armchairs, made drowsy by the oppressive heat of the stove. She thought of long reception halls hung with ancient silk, of the dainty cabinets containing priceless curiosities and of the little coquettish perfumed reception rooms made for chatting at five o'clock with intimate friends, with men famous and sought after, whom all women envy and whose attention they all desire.

When she sat down to dinner, before the round table covered with a tablecloth in use three days, opposite her husband, who uncovered the soup tureen and declared with a delighted air, "Ah, the good soup! I don't know anything better than that," she thought of dainty dinners, of shining silverware, of tapestry that peopled the walls with ancient personages and with strange birds flying in the midst of a fairy forest; and she thought of delicious dishes served on marvelous plates and of the whispered gallantries to which you listen with a sphinx-like smile while you are eating the pink meat of a trout or the wings of a quail.

She had no gowns, no jewels, nothing. And she loved nothing but that. She felt made for that. She would have liked so much to please, to be envied, to be charming, to be sought after.

She had a friend, a former schoolmate at the convent, who was rich, and whom she did not like to go to see anymore because she felt so sad when she came home.

But one evening her husband reached home with a triumphant air and holding a large envelope in his hand.

"There," said he, "there is something for you."

She tore the paper quickly and drew out a printed card which bore these words:

> The Minister of Public Instruction and Madame Georges Ramponneau request the honor of M. and Madame Loisel's company at the palace of the Ministry on Monday evening, January 18th.

Instead of being delighted, as her husband had hoped, she threw the invitation on the table crossly, muttering: "What do you wish me to do with that?"

"Why, my dear, I thought you would be glad. You never go out, and this is such a fine opportunity. I had great trouble to get it. Everyone wants to go; it is very select, and they are not giving many invitations to clerks. The whole official world will be there."

She looked at him with an irritated glance and said impatiently: "And what do you wish me to put on my back?"

He had not thought of that. He stammered: "Why, the gown you go to the theatre in. It looks very well to me."

He stopped, distracted, seeing that his wife was weeping. Two great tears ran slowly from the corners of her eyes toward the corners of her mouth.

"What's the matter? What's the matter?" he answered.

By a violent effort she conquered her grief and replied in a calm voice, while she wiped her wet cheeks: "Nothing. Only I have no gown, and, therefore, I can't go to this ball. Give your card to some colleague whose wife is better equipped than I am."

He was in despair. He resumed: "Come, let us see, Mathilde. How much would it cost, a suitable gown, which you could use on other occasions—something very simple?"

She reflected several seconds, making her calculations and wondering also what sum she could ask without drawing on herself an immediate refusal and a frightened exclamation from the economical clerk.

Finally she replied hesitating: "I don't know exactly, but I think I could manage it with four hundred francs."

He grew a little pale, because he was laying aside just that amount to buy a gun and treat himself to a little shooting next summer on the plain of Nanterre, with several friends who went to shoot larks there of a Sunday.

But he said: "Very well. I will give you four hundred francs. And try to have a pretty gown."

The day of the ball drew near and Madame Loisel seemed sad, uneasy, anxious. Her frock was ready, however. Her husband said to her one evening: "What is the matter? Come, you have seemed very queer these last three days."

And she answered: "It annoys me not to have a single piece of jewelry, not a single ornament, nothing to put on. I shall look poverty-stricken. I would almost rather not go at all."

"You might wear natural flowers," said her husband. "They're very stylish at this time of year. For ten francs you can get two or three magnificent roses."

She was not convinced. "No; there's nothing more humiliating than to look poor among other women who are rich."

"How stupid you are!" her husband cried. "Go look up your friend, Madame Forestier, and ask her to lend you some jewels. You're intimate enough with her to do that."

She uttered a cry of joy: "True! I never thought of it."

The next day she went to her friend and told her of her distress.

Madame Forestier went to a wardrobe with a mirror, took out a large jewel box, brought it back, opened it and said to Madame Loisel: "Choose, my dear."

She saw first some bracelets, then a pearl necklace, then a Venetian gold cross set with precious stones, of admirable workmanship. She tried on the ornaments before the mirror, hesitated and could not make up her mind to part with them, to give them back. She kept asking: "Haven't you any more?"

"Why, yes. Look further; I don't know what you like."

Suddenly she discovered, in a black satin box, a superb diamond necklace, and her heart throbbed with an immoderate desire. Her hands trembled as she took it. She fastened it round her throat, out-side her high-necked waist, and was lost in ecstasy at her reflection in the mirror.

Then she asked, hesitating, filled with anxious doubt: "Will you lend me this, only this?"

"Why, yes, certainly."

She threw her arms round her friend's neck, kissed her passion-ately, then fled with her treasure.

The night of the ball arrived. Madame Loisel was a great success. She was prettier than any other woman present, elegant, graceful, smiling and wild with joy. All the men looked at her, asked her name, sought to be introduced. All the attachés of the Cabinet wished to waltz with her. She was remarked by the minister himself.

She danced with rapture, with passion, intoxicated by pleasure, forgetting all in the triumph of her beauty, in the glory of her success, in a sort of cloud of happiness comprised of all this homage, admira-tion, these awakened desires and of that sense of triumph which is so sweet to woman's heart.

She left the ball about four o'clock in the morning. Her husband had been sleeping since midnight in a little deserted anteroom with three other gentlemen whose wives were enjoying the ball.

He threw over her shoulders the wraps he had brought, the modest wraps of common life, the poverty of which contrasted with the el-egance of the ball dress. She felt this and wished to escape so as not to be remarked by the other women, who were enveloping themselves in costly furs.

Loisel held her back, saying: "Wait a bit. You will catch cold out-side. I will call a cab."

But she did not listen to him and rapidly descended the stairs. When they reached the street they could not find a carriage and began to look for one, shouting after the cabmen passing at a distance.

They went toward the Seine in despair, shivering with cold. At last they found on the quay one of those ancient night cabs which, as though they were ashamed to show their shabbiness during the day, are never seen round Paris until after dark.

It took them to their dwelling in the Rue des Martyrs, and sadly they mounted the stairs to their flat. All was ended for her. As to him, he reflected that he must be at the ministry at ten o'clock that morning.

She removed her wraps before the glass so as to see herself once more in all her glory. But suddenly she uttered a cry. She no longer had the necklace around her neck!

"What is the matter with you?" demanded her husband, already half undressed.

She turned distractedly toward him. "I have—I have—I've lost Madame Forestier's necklace," she cried.

He stood up, bewildered. "What!—how? Impossible!"

They looked among the folds of her skirt, of her cloak, in her pockets, everywhere, but did not find it.

"You're sure you had it on when you left the ball?" he asked.

"Yes, I felt it in the vestibule of the minister's house."

"But if you had lost it in the street we should have heard it fall. It must be in the cab."

"Yes, probably. Did you take his number?"

"No. And you—didn't you notice it?"

"No."

They looked, thunderstruck, at each other. At last Loisel put on his clothes.

"I shall go back on foot," said he, "over the whole route, to see whether I can find it."

He went out. She sat waiting on a chair in her ball dress, without strength to go to bed, overwhelmed, without any fire, without a thought.

Her husband returned about seven o'clock. He had found nothing.

He went to police headquarters, to the newspaper offices to offer a reward; he went to the cab companies—everywhere, in fact, whither he was urged by the least spark of hope.

She waited all day, in the same condition of mad fear before this terrible calamity.

Loisel returned at night with a hollow, pale face. He had discovered nothing.

"You must write to your friend," said he, "that you have broken the clasp of her necklace and that you are having it mended. That will give us time to turn round."

She wrote at his dictation.

At the end of a week they had lost all hope. Loisel, who had aged five years, declared: "We must consider how to replace that ornament."

The next day they took the box that had contained it and went to the jeweler whose name was found within. He consulted his books.

"It was not I, madame, who sold that necklace; I must simply have furnished the case."

Then they went from jeweler to jeweler, searching for a necklace like the other, trying to recall it, both sick with chagrin and grief.

They found, in a shop at the Palais Royal, a string of diamonds that seemed to them exactly like the one they had lost. It was worth forty thousand francs. They could have it for thirty-six.

So they begged the jeweler not to sell it for three days yet. And they made a bargain that he should buy it back for thirty-four thousand francs, in case they should find the lost necklace before the end of February.

Loisel possessed eighteen thousand francs which his father had left him. He would borrow the rest.

He did borrow, asking a thousand francs of one, five hundred of another, five louis here, three louis there. He gave notes, took up ruinous obligations, dealt with usurers and all the race of lenders. He compromised all the rest of his life, risked signing a note without even knowing whether he could meet it; and, frightened by the trouble yet to come, by the black misery that was about to fall upon him, by the prospect of all the physical privations and moral tortures that he was to suffer, he went to get the new necklace, laying upon the jeweler's counter thirty-six thousand francs.

When Madame Loisel took back the necklace Madame Forestier said to her with a chilly manner: "You should have returned it sooner; I might have needed it."

She did not open the case, as her friend had so much feared. If she had detected the substitution, what would she have thought, what would she have said? Would she not have taken Madame Loisel for a thief?

Thereafter Madame Loisel knew the horrible existence of the needy. She bore her part, however, with sudden heroism. That dreadful debt must be paid. She would pay it. They dismissed their servant; they changed their lodgings; they rented a garret under the roof.

She came to know what heavy housework meant and the odious cares of the kitchen. She washed the dishes, using her dainty fingers and rosy nails on greasy pots and pans. She washed the soiled linen, the shirts and the dishcloths, which she dried upon a line; she carried the slops down to the street every morning and carried up the water, stopping for breath at every landing. And dressed like a woman of the people, she went to the fruiterer, the grocer, the butcher, a basket on her arm, bargaining, meeting with impertinence, defending her miserable money, sou by sou.

Every month they had to meet some notes, renew others, obtain more time.

Her husband worked evenings, making up a tradesman's accounts, and late at night he often copied manuscript for five sous a page.

This life lasted ten years.

At the end of ten years they had paid everything, everything, with the rates of usury and the accumulations of the compound interest.

Madame Loisel looked old now. She had become the woman of impoverished households—strong and hard and rough. With frowsy hair, skirts askew and red hands, she talked loud while washing the floor with great swishes of water. But sometimes, when her husband was at the office, she sat down near the window and she thought of that gay evening of long ago, of that ball where she had been so beautiful and so admired.

What would have happened if she had not lost that necklace? Who knows? who knows? How strange and changeful is life! How small a thing is needed to make or ruin us!

But one Sunday, having gone to take a walk in the Champs-Élysées to refresh herself after the labors of the week, she suddenly perceived a woman who was leading a child. It was Madame Forestier, still young, still beautiful, still charming.

Madame Loisel felt moved. Should she speak to her? Yes, certainly. And now that she had paid, she would tell her all about it. Why not?

She went up. "Good day, Jeanne."

The other, astonished to be familiarly addressed by this plain goodwife, did not recognize her at all and stammered: "But—madame!—I do not know—You must have mistaken."

"No. I am Mathilde Loisel."

Her friend uttered a cry. "Oh, my poor Mathilde! How you are changed!"

"Yes, I have had a pretty hard life, since I last saw you, and great poverty—and that because of you!"

"Of me! How so?"

"Do you remember that diamond necklace you lent me to wear at the ministerial ball?"

"Yes. Well?"

"Well, I lost it."

"What do you mean? You brought it back."

"I brought you back another exactly like it. And it has taken us ten years to pay for it. You can understand that it was not easy for us, for us who had nothing. At last it is ended, and I am very glad."

Madame Forestier had stopped. "You say that you bought a necklace of diamonds to replace mine?"

"Yes. You never noticed it, then! They were very similar." And she smiled with a joy that was at once proud and ingenuous.

Madame Forestier, deeply moved, took her hands. "Oh, my poor Mathilde! Why, my necklace was paste! It was worth at most only five hundred francs!"

Ball of Fat

For several days in succession fragments of a defeated army had passed through the town. They were mere disorganized bands, not disciplined forces. The men wore long, dirty beards and tattered uniforms; they advanced in listless fashion, without a flag, without a leader. All seemed exhausted, worn out, incapable of thought or resolve, marching on-ward merely by force of habit, and dropping to the ground with fa-tigue the moment they halted. One saw, in particular, many enlisted men, peaceful citizens, men who lived quietly on their income, bend-ing beneath the weight of their rifles; and little active volunteers, eas-ily frightened but full of enthusiasm, as eager to attack as they were ready to take to flight; and amid these, a sprinkling of red-breeched soldiers, the pitiful remnant of a division cut down in a great battle; somber artillerymen, side by side with nondescript foot-soldiers; and, here and there, the gleaming helmet of a heavy-footed dragoon who had difficulty in keeping up with the quicker pace of the soldiers of the line. Legions of irregulars with high-sounding names—"Avengers of Defeat," "Citizens of the Tomb," "Brethren in Death"—passed in their turn, looking like banditti. Their leaders, former drapers or grain merchants, or tallow or soap chandlers—warriors by force of circum-stances, officers by reason of their mustachios or their money—cov-ered with weapons, flannel and gold lace, spoke in an impressive manner, discussed plans of campaign, and behaved as though they alone bore the fortunes of dying France on their braggart shoulders; though, in truth, they frequently were afraid of their own men—scoun-drels often brave beyond measure, but pillagers and debauchees.

Rumor had it that the Prussians were about to enter Rouen.

The members of the National Guard, who for the past two months had been reconnoitering with the utmost caution in the neighboring woods, occasionally shooting their own sentinels, and making ready for fight whenever a rabbit rustled in the undergrowth, had now re-turned to their homes. Their arms, their uniforms, all the death-deal-ing paraphernalia with which they had terrified all the milestones along the highroad for eight miles round, had suddenly and marvelously disappeared.

The last of the French soldiers had just crossed the Seine on their way to Pont-Audemer, through Saint-Sever and Bourg-Achard, and in their rear the vanquished general, powerless to do aught with the forlorn remnants of his army, himself dismayed at the final overthrow of a nation accustomed to victory and disastrously beaten despite its legendary bravery, walked between two orderlies.

Then a profound calm, a shuddering, silent dread, settled on the city. Many a round-paunched citizen, emasculated by years devoted to business, anxiously awaited the conquerors, trembling lest his roasting-jacks or kitchen knives should be looked upon as weapons.

Life seemed to have stopped short; the shops were shut, the streets deserted. Now and then an inhabitant, awed by the silence, glided swiftly by in the shadow of the walls. The anguish of suspense made men even desire the arrival of the enemy.

In the afternoon of the day following the departure of the French troops, a number of uhlans, coming no one knew whence, passed rapidly through the town. A little later on, a black mass descended St. Catherine's Hill, while two other invading bodies appeared respectively on the Darnetal and the Boisguillaume roads. The advance guards of the three corps arrived at precisely the same moment at the Square of the Hôtel de Ville, and the German army poured through all the adjacent streets, its battalions making the pavement ring with their firm, measured tread.

Orders shouted in an unknown, guttural tongue rose to the windows of the seemingly dead, deserted houses; while behind the fast-closed shutters eager eyes peered forth at the victors-masters now of the city, its fortunes, and its lives, by "right of war." The inhabitants, in their darkened rooms, were possessed by that terror which follows in the wake of cataclysms, of deadly upheavals of the earth, against which all human skill and strength are vain. For the same thing happens whenever the established order of things is upset, when security no longer exists, when all those rights usually protected by the law of man or of Nature are at the mercy of unreasoning, savage force. The earthquake crushing a whole nation under falling roofs; the flood let loose, and engulfing in its swirling depths the corpses of drowned peasants, along with dead oxen and beams torn from shattered houses; or the army, covered with glory, murdering those who defend themselves, making prisoners of the rest, pillaging in the name of the Sword, and giving thanks to God to the thunder of cannon—all these are appalling scourges, which destroy all belief in eternal justice, all that confidence we have been taught to feel in the protection of Heaven and the reason of man.

Small detachments of soldiers knocked at each door, and then disappeared within the houses; for the vanquished saw they would have to be civil to their conquerors.

At the end of a short time, once the first terror had subsided, calm was again restored. In many houses the Prussian officer ate at the same table with the family. He was often well-bred, and, out of politeness, expressed sympathy with France and repugnance at being compelled to take part in the war. This sentiment was received with gratitude; besides, his protection might be needful some day or other. By the exercise of tact the number of men quartered in one's house might be reduced; and why should one provoke the hostility of a person on whom one's whole welfare depended? Such conduct would savor less of bravery than of fool-hardiness. And foolhardiness is no longer a failing of the citizens of Rouen as it was in the days when their city earned renown by its heroic defenses. Last of all—final argument based on the national politeness—the folk of Rouen said to one another that it was only right to be civil in one's own house, provided there was no public exhibition of familiarity with the foreigner. Out of doors, therefore, citizen and soldier did not know each other; but in the house both chatted freely, and each evening the German remained a little longer warming himself at the hospitable hearth.

Even the town itself resumed by degrees its ordinary aspect. The French seldom walked abroad, but the streets swarmed with Prussian soldiers. Moreover, the officers of the Blue Hussars, who arrogantly dragged their instruments of death along the pavements, seemed to hold the simple townsmen in but little more contempt than did the French cavalry officers who had drunk at the same cafes the year before.

But there was something in the air, a something strange and subtle, an intolerable foreign atmosphere like a penetrating odor—the odor of invasion. It permeated dwellings and places of public resort, changed the taste of food, made one imagine one's self in far-distant lands, amid dangerous, barbaric tribes.

The conquerors exacted money, much money. The inhabitants paid what was asked; they were rich. But the wealthier a Norman trades-man becomes, the more he suffers at having to part with anything that belongs to him, at having to see any portion of his substance pass into the hands of another.

Nevertheless, within six or seven miles of the town, along the course of the river as it flows onward to Croisset, Dieppedalle and Biessart, boatmen and fishermen often hauled to the surface of the water the body of a German, bloated in his uniform, killed by a blow from knife or club, his head crushed by a stone, or perchance pushed from some bridge into the stream below. The mud of the river-bed swallowed up these obscure acts of vengeance—savage, yet legitimate; these unrecorded deeds of bravery; these silent attacks fraught with greater danger than battles fought in broad day, and surrounded, moreover, with no halo of romance. For hatred of the foreigner ever arms a few intrepid souls, ready to die for an idea.

At last, as the invaders, though subjecting the town to the strictest discipline, had not committed any of the deeds of horror with which they had been credited while on their triumphal march, the people grew bolder, and the necessities of business again animated the breasts of the local merchants. Some of these had important commercial interests at Havre—occupied at present by the French army—and wished to attempt to reach that port by overland route to Dieppe, taking the boat from there.

Through the influence of the German officers whose acquaintance they had made, they obtained a permit to leave town from the general in command.

A large four-horse coach having, therefore, been engaged for the journey, and ten passengers having given in their names to the proprietor, they decided to start on a certain Tuesday morning before daybreak, to avoid attracting a crowd.

The ground had been frozen hard for some time-past, and about three o'clock on Monday afternoon—large black clouds from the north shed their burden of snow uninterruptedly all through that evening and night.

At half-past four in the morning the travelers met in the courtyard of the Hôtel de Normandie, where they were to take their seats in the coach.

They were still half asleep, and shivering with cold under their wraps. They could see one another but indistinctly in the darkness, and the mountain of heavy winter wraps in which each was swathed made them look like a gathering of obese priests in their long cassocks. But two men recognized each other, a third accosted them, and the three began to talk. "I am bringing my wife," said one. "So am I." "And I, too." The first speaker added: "We shall not return to Rouen, and if the Prussians approach Havre we will cross to England." All three, it turned out, had made the same plans, being of similar disposition and temperament.

Still the horses were not harnessed. A small lantern carried by a stable-boy emerged now and then from one dark doorway to disappear immediately in another. The stamping of horses' hoofs, deadened by the dung and straw of the stable, was heard from time to time, and from inside the building issued a man's voice, talking to the animals and swearing at them. A faint tinkle of bells showed that the harness was being got ready; this tinkle soon developed into a continuous jingling, louder or softer according to the movements of the horse, sometimes stopping altogether, then breaking out in a sudden peal accompanied by a pawing of the ground by an iron-shod hoof.

The door suddenly closed. All noise ceased. The frozen townsmen were silent; they remained motionless, stiff with cold.

A thick curtain of glistening white flakes fell ceaselessly to the ground; it obliterated all outlines, enveloped all objects in an icy mantle of foam; nothing was to be heard throughout the length and breadth of the silent, winter-bound city save the vague, nameless rustle of falling snow—a sensation rather than a sound—the gentle mingling of light atoms which seemed to fill all space, to cover the whole world.

The man reappeared with his lantern, leading by a rope a melancholy-looking horse, evidently being led out against his inclination. The hostler placed him beside the pole, fastened the traces, and spent some time in walking round him to make sure that the harness was all right; for he could use only one hand, the other being engaged in holding the lantern. As he was about to fetch the second horse he noticed the motionless group of travelers, already white with snow, and said to them: "Why don't you get inside the coach? You'd be under shelter, at least."

This did not seem to have occurred to them, and they at once took his advice. The three men seated their wives at the far end of the coach, then got in themselves; lastly the other vague, snow-shrouded forms clambered to the remaining places without a word.

The floor was covered with straw, into which the feet sank. The ladies at the far end, having brought with them little copper foot-warmers heated by means of a kind of chemical fuel, proceeded to light these, and spent some time in expatiating in low tones on their advantages, saying over and over again things which they had all known for a long time.

At last, six horses instead of four having been harnessed to the diligence, on account of the heavy roads, a voice outside asked: "Is everyone there?" To which a voice from the interior replied: "Yes," and they set out.

The vehicle moved slowly, slowly, at a snail's pace; the wheels sank into the snow; the entire body of the coach creaked and groaned; the horses slipped, puffed, steamed, and the coachman's long whip cracked incessantly, flying hither and thither, coiling up, then flinging out its length like a slender serpent, as it lashed some rounded flank, which instantly grew tense as it strained in further effort.

But the day grew apace. Those light flakes which one traveler, a native of Rouen, had compared to a rain of cotton fell no longer. A murky light filtered through dark, heavy clouds, which made the country more dazzlingly white by contrast, a whiteness broken sometimes by a row of tall trees spangled with hoarfrost, or by a cottage roof hooded in snow.

Within the coach the passengers eyed one another curiously in the dim light of dawn.

Right at the back, in the best seats of all, Monsieur and Madame Loiseau, wholesale wine merchants of the Rue Grand-Pont, slumbered opposite each other. Formerly clerk to a merchant who had failed in business, Loiseau had bought his master's interest, and made a fortune for himself. He sold very bad wine at a very low price to the retail-dealers in the country, and had the reputation, among his friends and acquaintances, of being a shrewd rascal a true Norman, full of quips and wiles. So well established was his character as a cheat that, in the mouths of the citizens of Rouen, the very name of Loiseau became a byword for sharp practice.

Above and beyond this, Loiseau was noted for his practical jokes of every description—his tricks, good or ill-natured; and no one could mention his name without adding at once: "He's an extraordinary man—Loiseau." He was undersized and potbellied, had a florid face with grayish whiskers.

His wife—tall, strong, determined, with a loud voice and decided manner—represented the spirit of order and arithmetic in the business house which Loiseau enlivened by his jovial activity.

Beside them, dignified in bearing, belonging to a superior caste, sat Monsieur Carre-Lamadon, a man of considerable importance, a king in the cotton trade, proprietor of three spinning-mills, officer of the Legion of Honor, and member of the General Council. During the whole time the Empire was in the ascendancy he remained the chief of the well-disposed Opposition, merely in order to command a higher value for his devotion when he should rally to the cause which he meanwhile opposed with "courteous weapons," to use his own expression.

Madame Carre-Lamadon, much younger than her husband, was the consolation of all the officers of good family quartered at Rouen. Pretty, slender, graceful, she sat opposite her husband, curled up in her furs, and gazing mournfully at the sorry interior of the coach.

Her neighbors, the Comte and Comtesse Hubert de Breville, bore one of the noblest and most ancient names in Normandy. The count, a nobleman advanced in years and of aristocratic bearing, strove to enhance by every artifice of the toilet, his natural resemblance to King Henry IV, who, according to a legend of which the family were inordinately proud, had been the favored lover of a de Breville lady, and father of her child—the frail one's husband having, in recognition of this fact, been made a count and governor of a province.

A colleague of Monsieur Carre-Lamadon in the General Council, Count Hubert represented the Orléanist party in his department. The story of his marriage with the daughter of a small ship-owner at Nantes had always remained more or less of a mystery. But as the countess had an air of unmistakable breeding, entertained faultlessly, and was even supposed to have been loved by a son of Louis-Philippe, the nobility vied with one another in doing her honor, and her drawing-room remained the most select in the whole countryside—the only one which retained the old spirit of gallantry, and to which access was not easy.

The fortune of the Brevilles, all in real estate, amounted, it was said, to five hundred thousand francs a year.

These six people occupied the farther end of the coach, and represented Society—with an income—the strong, established society of good people with religion and principle.

It happened by chance that all the women were seated on the same side; and the countess had, moreover, as neighbors two nuns, who spent the time in fingering their long rosaries and murmuring paternosters and aves. One of them was old, and so deeply pitted with smallpox that she looked for all the world as if she had received a charge of shot full in the face. The other, of sickly appearance, had a pretty but wasted countenance, and a narrow, consumptive chest, sapped by that devouring faith which is the making of martyrs and visionaries.

A man and woman, sitting opposite the two nuns, attracted all eyes.

The man—a well-known character—was Cornudet, the democrat, the terror of all respectable people. For the past twenty years his big red beard had been on terms of intimate acquaintance with the tankards of all the republican cafes. With the help of his comrades and brethren he had dissipated a respectable fortune left him by his father, an old-established confectioner, and he now impatiently awaited the Republic, that he might at last be rewarded with the post he had earned by his revolutionary orgies. On the fourth of September—possibly as the result of a practical joke—he was led to believe that he had been appointed prefect; but when he attempted to take up the duties of the position the clerks in charge of the office refused to recognize his authority, and he was compelled in consequence to retire. A good sort of fellow in other respects, inoffensive and obliging, he had thrown himself zealously into the work of making an organized defense of the town. He had had pits dug in the level country, young forest trees felled, and traps set on all the roads; then at the approach of the enemy, thoroughly satisfied with his preparations, he had hastily returned to the town. He thought he might now do more good at Havre, where new entrenchments would soon be necessary.

The woman, who belonged to the courtesan class, was celebrated for an embonpoint unusual for her age, which had earned her the nickname "Boule de Suif" (Ball of Fat). Short and round, fat as a pig, with puffy fingers constricted at the joints, looking like rows of short sausages; with a shiny, tightly-stretched skin and an enormous bust filling out the bodice of her dress, she was yet attractive and much sought after, owing to her fresh and pleasing appearance. Her face was like a crimson apple, a peony-bud just bursting into bloom; she had two magnificent dark eyes, fringed with thick, heavy lashes, which cast a shadow into their depths; her mouth was small, ripe, kissable, and was furnished with the tiniest of white teeth.

As soon as she was recognized the respectable matrons of the party began to whisper among themselves, and the words "hussy" and "public scandal" were uttered so loudly that Boule de Suif raised her head. She forthwith cast such a challenging, bold look at her neighbors that a sudden silence fell on the company, and all lowered their eyes, with the exception of Loiseau, who watched her with evident interest.

But conversation was soon resumed among the three ladies, whom the presence of this girl had suddenly drawn together in the bonds of friendship—one might almost say in those of intimacy. They decided that they ought to combine, as it were, in their dignity as wives in face of this shameless hussy; for legitimized love always despises its easygoing brother.

The three men, also, brought together by a certain conservative instinct awakened by the presence of Cornudet, spoke of money matters in a tone expressive of contempt for the poor. Count Hubert related the losses he had sustained at the hands of the Prussians, spoke of the cattle which had been stolen from him, the crops which had been ruined, with the easy manner of a nobleman who was also a tenfold millionaire, and whom such reverses would scarcely inconvenience for a single year. Monsieur Carre-Lamadon, a man of wide experience in the cotton industry, had taken care to send six hundred thousand francs to England as provision against the rainy day he was always anticipating. As for Loiseau, he had managed to sell to the French commissariat department all the wines he had in stock, so that the state now owed him a considerable sum, which he hoped to receive at Havre.

And all three eyed one another in friendly, well-disposed fashion. Although of varying social status, they were united in the brotherhood of money—in that vast freemasonry made up of those who possess, who can jingle gold wherever they choose to put their hands into their breeches' pockets.

The coach went along so slowly that at ten o'clock in the morning it had not covered twelve miles. Three times the men of the party got out and climbed the hills on foot. The passengers were becoming uneasy, for they had counted on lunching at Tôtes, and it seemed now as if they would hardly arrive there before nightfall. Everyone was eagerly looking out for an inn by the roadside, when, suddenly, the coach foundered in a snowdrift, and it took two hours to extricate it.

As appetites increased, their spirits fell; no inn, no wine shop could be discovered, the approach of the Prussians and the transit of the starving French troops having frightened away all business.

The men sought food in the farmhouses beside the road, but could not find so much as a crust of bread; for the suspicious peasant invariably hid his stores for fear of being pillaged by the soldiers, who, being entirely without food, would take violent possession of everything they found.

About one o'clock Loiseau announced that he positively had a big hollow in his stomach. They had all been suffering in the same way for some time, and the increasing gnawings of hunger had put an end to all conversation.

Now and then someone yawned, another followed his example, and each in turn, according to his character, breeding and social position, yawned either quietly or noisily, placing his hand before the gaping void whence issued breath condensed into vapor.

Several times Boule de Suif stooped, as if searching for something under her petticoats. She would hesitate a moment, look at her neighbors, and then quietly sit upright again. All faces were pale and drawn. Loiseau declared he would give a thousand francs for a knuckle of ham. His wife made an involuntary and quickly checked gesture of protest. It always hurt her to hear of money being squandered, and she could not even understand jokes on such a subject.

"As a matter of fact, I don't feel well," said the count. "Why did I not think of bringing provisions?" Each one reproached himself in similar fashion.

Cornudet, however, had a bottle of rum, which he offered to his neighbors. They all coldly refused except Loiseau, who took a sip, and returned the bottle with thanks, saying: "That's good stuff; it warms one up, and cheats the appetite." The alcohol put him in good humor, and he proposed they should do as the sailors did in the song: eat the fattest of the passengers. This indirect allusion to Boule de Suif shocked the respectable members of the party. No one replied; only Cornudet smiled. The two good sisters had ceased to mumble their rosary, and, with hands enfolded in their wide sleeves, sat motionless, their eyes steadfastly cast down, doubtless offering up as a sacrifice to Heaven the suffering it had sent them.

At last, at three o'clock, as they were in the midst of an apparently limitless plain, with not a single village in sight, Boule de Suif stooped quickly, and drew from underneath the seat a large basket covered with a white napkin.

From this she extracted first of all a small earthenware plate and a silver drinking cup, then an enormous dish containing two whole chickens cut into joints and imbedded in jelly. The basket was seen to contain other good things: pies, fruit, dainties of all sorts—provisions, in short, for a three days' journey, rendering their owner independent of wayside inns. The necks of four bottles protruded from among the food. She took a chicken wing, and began to eat it daintily, together with one of those rolls called in Normandy "Regence."

All looks were directed toward her. An odor of food filled the air, causing nostrils to dilate, mouths to water, and jaws to contract painfully. The scorn of the ladies for this disreputable female grew positively ferocious; they would have liked to kill her, or throw, her and her drinking cup, her basket, and her provisions, out of the coach into the snow of the road below.

But Loiseau's gaze was fixed greedily on the dish of chicken. He said: "Well, well, this lady had more forethought than the rest of us. Some people think of everything."

She looked up at him. "Would you like some, sir? It is hard to go on fasting all day."

He bowed. "Upon my soul, I can't refuse; I cannot hold out another minute. All is fair in war time, is it not, madame?" And, casting a glance on those around, he added: "At times like this it is very pleasant to meet with obliging people."

He spread a newspaper over his knees to avoid soiling his trousers, and, with a pocketknife he always carried, helped himself to a chicken leg coated with jelly, which he thereupon proceeded to devour.

Then Boule le Suif, in low, humble tones, invited the nuns to partake of her repast. They both accepted the offer unhesitatingly, and after a few stammered words of thanks began to eat quickly, without raising their eyes. Neither did Cornudet refuse his neighbor's offer, and, in combination with the nuns, a sort of table was formed by opening out the newspaper over the four pairs of knees.

Mouths kept opening and shutting, ferociously masticating and devouring the food. Loiseau, in his corner, was hard at work, and in low tones urged his wife to follow his example. She held out for a long time, but overstrained Nature gave way at last. Her husband, assuming his politest manner, asked their "charming companion" if he might be allowed to offer Madame Loiseau a small helping.

"Why, certainly, sir," she replied, with an amiable smile, holding out the dish.

When the first bottle of claret was opened some embarrassment was caused by the fact that there was only one drinking cup, but this was passed from one to another, after being wiped. Cornudet alone, doubtless in a spirit of gallantry, raised to his own lips that part of the rim which was still moist from those of his fair neighbor.

Then, surrounded by people who were eating, and well-nigh suffocated by the odor of food, the Comte and Comtesse de Breville and Monsieur and Madame Carre-Lamadon endured that hateful form of torture which has perpetuated the name of Tantalus. All at once the manufacturer's young wife heaved a sigh which made everyone turn and look at her; she was white as the snow without; her eyes closed, her head fell forward; she had fainted. Her husband, beside himself, implored the help of his neighbors. No one seemed to know what to do until the elder of the two nuns, raising the patient's head, placed Boule de Suif's drinking cup to her lips, and made her swallow a few drops of wine. The pretty invalid moved, opened her eyes, smiled, and declared in a feeble voice that she was all right again. But, to prevent a recurrence of the catastrophe, the nun made her drink a cupful of claret, adding: "It's just hunger—that's what is wrong with you."

Then Boule de Suif, blushing and embarrassed, stammered, looking at the four passengers who were still fasting: "Mon Dieu, if I might offer these ladies and gentlemen——"

She stopped short, fearing a snub. But Loiseau continued: "Hang it all, in such a case as this we are all brothers and sisters and ought to assist each other. Come, come, ladies, don't stand on ceremony, for goodness' sake! Do we even know whether we shall find a house in which to pass the night? At our present rate of going we shan't be at Tôtes till midday tomorrow."

They hesitated, no one daring to be the first to accept. But the count settled the question. He turned toward the abashed girl, and in his most distinguished manner said: "We accept gratefully, madame."

As usual, it was only the first step that cost. This Rubicon once crossed, they set to work with a will. The basket was emptied. It still contained a pâté de foie gras, a lark pie, a piece of smoked tongue, Crassane pears, Pont-Leveque gingerbread, fancy cakes, and a cup full of pickled gherkins and onions—Boule de Suif, like all women, being very fond of indigestible things.

They could not eat this girl's provisions without speaking to her. So they began to talk, stiffly at first; then, as she seemed by no means forward, with greater freedom. Mesdames de Breville and Carre-Lamadon, who were accomplished women of the world, were gracious and tactful. The countess especially displayed that amiable condescension characteristic of great ladies whom no contact with baser mortals can sully, and was absolutely charming. But the sturdy Madame Loiseau, who had the soul of a gendarme, continued morose, speaking little and eating much.

Conversation naturally turned on the war. Terrible stories were told about the Prussians, deeds of bravery were recounted of the French; and all these people who were fleeing themselves were ready to pay homage to the courage of their compatriots. Personal experiences soon followed, and Boule le Suif related with genuine emotion, and with that warmth of language not uncommon in women of her class and temperament, how it came about that she had left Rouen.

"I thought at first that I should be able to stay," she said. "My house was well stocked with provisions, and it seemed better to put up with feeding a few soldiers than to banish myself goodness knows where. But when I saw these Prussians it was too much for me! My blood boiled with rage; I wept the whole day for very shame. Oh, if only I had been a man! I looked at them from my window—the fat swine, with their pointed helmets!—and my maid held my hands to keep me from throwing my furniture down on them. Then some of them were quartered on me; I flew at the throat of the first one who entered. They are just as easy to strangle as other men! And I'd have been the death of that one if I hadn't been dragged away from him by my hair. I had to hide after that. And as soon as I could get an opportunity I left the place, and here I am."

She was warmly congratulated. She rose in the estimation of her companions, who had not been so brave; and Cornudet listened to her with the approving and benevolent smile of an apostle, the smile a priest might wear in listening to a devotee praising God; for long-bearded democrats of his type have a monopoly of patriotism, just as priests have a monopoly of religion. He held forth in turn, with dogmatic self-assurance, in the style of the proclamations daily pasted on the walls of the town, winding up with a specimen of stump oratory in which he reviled "that besotted fool of a Louis Napoleon."

But Boule de Suif was indignant, for she was an ardent Bonapartist. She turned as red as a cherry, and stammered in her wrath: "I'd just like to have seen you in his place—you and your sort! There would have been a nice mix-up. Oh, yes! It was you who betrayed that man. It would be impossible to live in France if we were governed by such rascals as you!"

Cornudet, unmoved by this tirade, still smiled a superior, contemptuous smile; and one felt that high words were impending, when the count interposed, and, not without difficulty, succeeded in calming the exasperated woman, saying that all sincere opinions ought to be respected. But the countess and the manufacturer's wife, imbued with the unreasoning hatred of the upper classes for the Republic, and instinct, moreover, with the affection felt by all women for the pomp and circumstance of despotic government, were drawn, in spite of themselves, toward this dignified young woman, whose opinions coincided so closely with their own.

The basket was empty. The ten people had finished its contents without difficulty amid general regret that it did not hold more. Conversation went on a little longer, though it flagged somewhat after the passengers had finished eating.

Night fell, the darkness grew deeper and deeper, and the cold made Boule de Suif shiver, in spite of her plumpness. So Madame de Breville offered her her foot-warmer, the fuel of which had been several times renewed since the morning, and she accepted the offer at once, for her feet were icy cold. Mesdames Carre-Lamadon and Loiseau gave theirs to the nuns.

The driver lighted his lanterns. They cast a bright gleam on a cloud of vapor which hovered over the sweating flanks of the horses, and on the roadside snow, which seemed to unroll as they went along in the changing light of the lamps.

All was now indistinguishable in the coach; but suddenly a movement occurred in the corner occupied by Boule de Suif and Cornudet; and Loiseau, peering into the gloom, fancied he saw the big, bearded democrat move hastily to one side, as if he had received a well-directed, though noiseless, blow in the dark.

Tiny lights glimmered ahead. It was Tôtes. The coach had been on the road eleven hours, which, with the three hours allotted the horses in four periods for feeding and breathing, made fourteen. It entered the town, and stopped before the Hôtel du Commerce.

The coach door opened; a well-known noise made all the travelers start; it was the clanging of a scabbard, on the pavement; then a voice called out something in German.

Although the coach had come to a standstill, no one got out; it looked as if they were afraid of being murdered the moment they left their seats. Thereupon the driver appeared, holding in his hand one of his lanterns, which cast a sudden glow on the interior of the coach, lighting up the double row of startled faces, mouths agape, and eyes wide open in surprise and terror.

Beside the driver stood in the full light a German officer, a tall young man, fair and slender, tightly encased in his uniform like a woman in her corset, his flat shiny cap, tilted to one side of his head, making him look like an English bellboy. His exaggerated mustache, long and straight and tapering to a point at either end in a single blond hair that could hardly be seen, seemed to weigh down the corners of his mouth and give a droop to his lips.

In Alsatian French he requested the travellers to alight, saying stiffly: "Kindly get down, ladies and gentlemen."

The two nuns were the first to obey, manifesting the docility of holy women accustomed to submission on every occasion. Next appeared the count and countess, followed by the manufacturer and his wife, after whom came Loiseau, pushing his larger and better half before him.

"Good day, sir," he said to the officer as he put his foot to the ground, acting on an impulse born of prudence rather than of politeness. The other, insolent like all in authority, merely stared without replying.

Boule de Suif and Cornudet, though near the door, were the last to alight, grave and dignified before the enemy. The stout girl tried to control herself and appear calm; the democrat stroked his long russet beard with a somewhat trembling hand. Both strove to maintain their dignity, knowing well that at such a time each individual is always looked upon as more or less typical of his nation; and, also, resenting the complaisant attitude of their companions, Boule de Suif tried to wear a bolder front than her neighbors, the virtuous women, while he, feeling that it was incumbent on him to set a good example, kept up the attitude of resistance which he had first assumed when he undertook to mine the high roads round Rouen.

They entered the spacious kitchen of the inn, and the German, having demanded the passports signed by the general in command, in which were mentioned the name, description and profession of each traveler, inspected them all minutely, comparing their appearance with the written particulars.

Then he said brusquely: "All right," and turned on his heel.

They breathed freely. All were still hungry; so supper was ordered. Half an hour was required for its preparation, and while two servants were apparently engaged in getting it ready the travelers went to look at their rooms. These all opened off a long corridor, at the end of which was a glazed door with a number on it.

They were just about to take their seats at table when the innkeeper appeared in person. He was a former horse-dealer—a large, asthmatic individual, always wheezing, coughing, and clearing his throat. Follenvie was his patronymic. He called: "Mademoiselle Elisabeth Rousset?"

Boule de Suif started, and turned round. "That is my name."

"Mademoiselle, the Prussian officer wishes to speak to you immediately."

"To me?"

"Yes; if you are Mademoiselle Elisabeth Rousset." She hesitated, reflected a moment, and then declared roundly: "That may be; but I'm not going."

They moved restlessly around her; everyone wondered and speculated as to the cause of this order. The count approached: "You are wrong, madame, for your refusal may bring trouble not only on yourself but also on all your companions. It never pays to resist those in authority. Your compliance with this request cannot possibly be fraught with any danger; it has probably been made because some formality or other was forgotten."

All added their voices to that of the count; Boule de Suif was begged, urged, lectured, and at last convinced; everyone was afraid of the complications which might result from headstrong action on her part. She said finally: "I am doing it for your sakes, remember that!"

The countess took her hand. "And we are grateful to you."

She left the room. All waited for her return before commencing the meal. Each was distressed that he or she had not been sent for rather than this impulsive, quick-tempered girl, and each mentally rehearsed platitudes in case of being summoned also.

But at the end of ten minutes she reappeared breathing hard, crimson with indignation. "Oh! the scoundrel! the scoundrel!" she stammered.

All were anxious to know what had happened; but she declined to enlighten them, and when the count pressed the point, she silenced him with much dignity, saying: "No; the matter has nothing to do with you, and I cannot speak of it."

Then they took their places round a high soup tureen, from which issued an odor of cabbage. In spite of this coincidence, the supper was cheerful. The cider was good; the Loiseaus and the nuns drank it from motives of economy. The others ordered wine; Cornudet demanded beer. He had his own fashion of uncorking the bottle and making the beer foam, gazing at it as he inclined his glass and then raised it to a position between the lamp and his eye that he might judge of its color. When he drank, his great beard, which matched the color of his favorite beverage, seemed to tremble with affection; his eyes positively squinted in the endeavor not to lose sight of the beloved glass, and he looked for all the world as if he were fulfilling the only function for which he was born. He seemed to have established in his mind an affinity between the two great passions of his life—pale ale and revolution—and assuredly he could not taste the one without dreaming of the other.

Monsieur and Madame Follenvie dined at the end of the table. The man, wheezing like a broken-down locomotive, was too short-winded to talk when he was eating. But the wife was not silent a moment; she told how the Prussians had impressed her on their arrival, what they did, what they said; execrating them in the first place because they cost her money, and in the second because she had two sons in the army. She addressed herself principally to the countess, flattered at the opportunity of talking to a lady of quality.

Then she lowered her voice, and began to broach delicate subjects. Her husband interrupted her from time to time, saying: "You would do well to hold your tongue, Madame Follenvie."

But she took no notice of him, and went on: "Yes, madame, these Germans do nothing but eat potatoes and pork, and then pork and potatoes. And don't imagine for a moment that they are clean! No, indeed! And if only you saw them drilling for hours, indeed for days, together; they all collect in a field, then they do nothing but march backward and forward, and wheel this way and that. If only they would cultivate the land, or remain at home and work on their high roads! Really, madame, these soldiers are of no earthly use! Poor people have to feed and keep them, only in order that they may learn how to kill! True, I am only an old woman with no education, but when I see them wearing themselves out marching about from morning till night, I say to myself: When there are people who make discoveries that are of use to people, why should others take so much trouble to do harm? Really, now, isn't it a terrible thing to kill people, whether they are Prussians, or English, or Poles, or French? If we revenge ourselves on anyone who injures us we do wrong, and are punished for it; but when our sons are shot down like partridges, that is all right, and decorations are given to the man who kills the most. No, indeed, I shall never be able to understand it."

Cornudet raised his voice: "War is a barbarous proceeding when we attack a peaceful neighbor, but it is a sacred duty when undertaken in defense of one's country."

The old woman looked down: "Yes; it's another matter when one acts in self-defense; but would it not be better to kill all the kings, seeing that they make war just to amuse themselves?"

Cornudet's eyes kindled. "Bravo, citizens!" he said.

Monsieur Carré-Lamadon was reflecting profoundly. Although an ardent admirer of great generals, the peasant woman's sturdy common sense made him reflect on the wealth which might accrue to a country by the employment of so many idle hands now maintained at a great expense, of so much unproductive force, if they were employed in those great industrial enterprises which it will take centuries to complete.

But Loiseau, leaving his seat, went over to the innkeeper and began chatting in a low voice. The big man chuckled, coughed, sputtered; his enormous carcass shook with merriment at the pleasantries of the other; and he ended by buying six casks of claret from Loiseau to be delivered in spring, after the departure of the Prussians.

The moment supper was over everyone went to bed, worn out with fatigue.

But Loiseau, who had been making his observations on the sly, sent his wife to bed, and amused himself by placing first his ear, and then his eye, to the bedroom keyhole, in order to discover what he called "the mysteries of the corridor."

At the end of about an hour he heard a rustling, peeped out quickly, and caught sight of Boule de Suif, looking more rotund than ever in a dressing-gown of blue cashmere trimmed with white lace. She held a candle in her hand, and directed her steps to the numbered door at the end of the corridor. But one of the side doors was partly opened, and when, at the end of a few minutes, she returned, Cornudet, in his shirt-sleeves, followed her. They spoke in low tones, then stopped short. Boule de Suif seemed to be stoutly denying him admission to her room. Unfortunately, Loiseau could not at first hear what they said; but toward the end of the conversation they raised their voices, and he caught a few words. Cornudet was loudly insistent.

"How silly you are! What does it matter to you?" he said.

She seemed indignant, and replied: "No, my good man, there are times when one does not do that sort of thing; besides, in this place it would be shameful."

Apparently he did not understand, and asked the reason. Then she lost her temper and her caution, and, raising her voice still higher, said: "Why? Can't you understand why? When there are Prussians in the house! Perhaps even in the very next room!"

He was silent. The patriotic shame of this wanton, who would not suffer herself to be caressed in the neighborhood of the enemy, must have roused his dormant dignity, for after bestowing on her a simple kiss he crept softly back to his room. Loiseau, much edified, capered round the bedroom before taking his place beside his slumbering spouse.

Then silence reigned throughout the house. But soon there arose from some remote part—it might easily have been either cellar or attic—a stertorous, monotonous, regular snoring, a dull, prolonged rumbling, varied by tremors like those of a boiler under pressure of steam. Monsieur Follenvie had gone to sleep.

As they had decided on starting at eight o'clock the next morning, everyone was in the kitchen at that hour; but the coach, its roof covered with snow, stood by itself in the middle of the yard, without either horses or driver. They sought the latter in the stables, coach-houses and barns, but in vain. So the men of the party resolved to scour the country for him, and sallied forth. They found themselves in the square, with the church at the farther side, and to right and left low-roofed houses where there were some Prussian soldiers. The first soldier they saw was peeling potatoes. The second, farther on, was washing out a barber's shop. Another, bearded to the eyes, was fondling a crying infant, and dandling it on his knees to quiet it; and the stout peasant women, whose men-folk were for the most part at the war, were, by means of signs, telling their obedient conquerors what work they were to do: chop wood, prepare soup, grind coffee; one of them even was doing the washing for his hostess, an infirm old grandmother.

The count, astonished at what he saw, questioned the beadle who was coming out of the presbytery. The old man answered: "Oh, those men are not at all a bad sort; they are not Prussians, I am told; they come from somewhere farther off, I don't exactly know where. And they have all left wives and children behind them; they are not fond of war either, you may be sure! I am sure they are mourning for the men where they come from, just as we do here; and the war causes them just as much unhappiness as it does us. As a matter of fact, things are not so very bad here just now, because the soldiers do no harm, and work just as if they were in their own homes. You see, sir, poor folk always help one another; it is the great ones of this world who make war."

Cornudet indignant at the friendly understanding established between conquerors and conquered, withdrew, preferring to shut himself up in the inn.

"They are re-peopling the country," jested Loiseau.

"They are undoing the harm they have done," said Monsieur Carre-Lamadon gravely.

But they could not find the coach driver. At last he was discovered in the village cafe, fraternizing cordially with the officer's orderly.

"Were you not told to harness the horses at eight o'clock?" demanded the count.

"Oh, yes; but I've had different orders since."

"What orders?"

"Not to harness at all."

"Who gave you such orders?"

"Why, the Prussian officer."

"But why?"

"I don't know. Go and ask him. I am forbidden to harness the horses, so I don't harness them—that's all."

"Did he tell you so himself?"

"No, sir; the innkeeper gave me the order from him."

"When?"

"Last evening, just as I was going to bed."

The three men returned in a very uneasy frame of mind.

They asked for Monsieur Follenvie, but the servant replied that on account of his asthma he never got up before ten o'clock. They were strictly forbidden to rouse him earlier, except in case of fire.

They wished to see the officer, but that also was impossible, although he lodged in the inn. Monsieur Follenvie alone was authorized to interview him on civil matters. So they waited. The women returned to their rooms, and occupied themselves with trivial matters.

Cornudet settled down beside the tall kitchen fireplace, before a blazing fire. He had a small table and a jug of beer placed beside him, and he smoked his pipe—a pipe which enjoyed among democrats a consideration almost equal to his own, as though it had served its country in serving Cornudet. It was a fine meerschaum, admirably colored to a black the shade of its owner's teeth, but sweet-smelling, gracefully curved, at home in its master's hand, and completing his physiognomy. And Cornudet sat motionless, his eyes fixed now on the dancing flames, now on the froth which crowned his beer; and after each draught he passed his long, thin fingers with an air of satisfaction through his long, greasy hair, as he sucked the foam from his mustache.

Loiseau, under pretence of stretching his legs, went out to see if he could sell wine to the country dealers. The count and the manufacturer began to talk politics. They forecast the future of France. One believed in the Orleans dynasty, the other in an unknown savior—a hero who should rise up in the last extremity: a du Guesclin, perhaps a Joan of Arc? or another Napoleon Bonaparte? Ah! if only the Prince Imperial were not so young! Cornudet, listening to them, smiled like a man who holds the keys of destiny in his hands. His pipe perfumed the whole kitchen.

As the clock struck ten, Monsieur Follenvie appeared. He was immediately surrounded and questioned, but could only repeat, three or four times in succession, and without variation, the words: "The officer said to me, just like this: 'Monsieur Follenvie, you will forbid them to harness up the coach for those travelers tomorrow. They are not to start without an order from me. You hear? That is sufficient.'"

Then they asked to see the officer. The count sent him his card, on which Monsieur Carre-Lamadon also inscribed his name and titles. The Prussian sent word that the two men would be admitted to see him after his luncheon—that is to say, about one o'clock.

The ladies reappeared, and they all ate a little, in spite of their anxiety. Boule de Suif appeared ill and very much worried.

They were finishing their coffee when the orderly came to fetch the gentlemen.

Loiseau joined the other two; but when they tried to get Cornudet to accompany them, by way of adding greater solemnity to the occasion, he declared proudly that he would never have anything to do with the Germans, and, resuming his seat in the chimney corner, he called for another jug of beer.

The three men went upstairs, and were ushered into the best room in the inn, where the officer received them lolling at his ease in an armchair, his feet on the mantelpiece, smoking a long porcelain pipe, and enveloped in a gorgeous dressing-gown, doubtless stolen from the deserted dwelling of some citizen destitute of taste in dress. He neither rose, greeted them, nor even glanced in their direction. He afforded a fine example of that insolence of bearing which seems natural to the victorious soldier.

After the lapse of a few moments he said in his halting French: "What do you want?"

"We wish to start on our journey," said the count.

"No."

"May I ask the reason of your refusal?"

"Because I don't choose."

"I would respectfully call your attention, monsieur, to the fact that your general in command gave us a permit to proceed to Dieppe; and I do not think we have done anything to deserve this harshness at your hands."

"I don't choose—that's all. You may go."

They bowed, and retired.

The afternoon was wretched. They could not understand the caprice of this German, and the strangest ideas came into their heads. They all congregated in the kitchen, and talked the subject to death, imagining all kinds of unlikely things. Perhaps they were to be kept as hostages—but for what reason? or to be extradited as prisoners of war? or possibly they were to be held for ransom? They were panic-stricken at this last supposition. The richest among them were the most alarmed, seeing themselves forced to empty bags of gold into the insolent soldier's hands in order to buy back their lives. They racked their brains for plausible lies whereby they might conceal the fact that they were rich, and pass themselves off as poor—very poor. Loiseau took off his watch chain, and put it in his pocket. The approach of night increased their apprehension. The lamp was lighted, and as it wanted yet two hours to dinner Madame Loiseau proposed a game of trente et un. It would distract their thoughts. The rest agreed, and Cornudet himself joined the party, first putting out his pipe for politeness' sake.

The count shuffled the cards, dealt, and Boule de Suif had thirty-one to start with; soon the interest of the game assuaged the anxiety of the players. But Cornudet noticed that Loiseau and his wife were in league to cheat.

They were about to sit down to dinner when Monsieur Follenvie appeared, and in his grating voice announced: "The Prussian officer sends to ask Mademoiselle Elisabeth Rousset if she has changed her mind yet."

Boule de Suif stood still, pale as death. Then, suddenly turning crimson with anger, she gasped out: "Kindly tell that scoundrel, that

cur, that carrion of a Prussian, that I will never consent—you understand?—never, never, never!"

The fat innkeeper left the room. Then Boule de Suif was surrounded, questioned, entreated on all sides to reveal the mystery of
her visit to the officer. She refused at first; but her wrath soon got the
better of her.

"What does he want? He wants to make me his mistress!" she cried.

No one was shocked at the word, so great was the general indignation. Cornudet broke his jug as he banged it down on the table. A
loud outcry arose against this base soldier. All were furious. They drew
together in common resistance against the foe, as if some part of the
sacrifice exacted of Boule de Suif had been demanded of each. The
count declared, with supreme disgust, that those people behaved like
ancient barbarians. The women, above all, manifested a lively and
tender sympathy for Boule de Suif. The nuns, who appeared only at
meals, cast down their eyes, and said nothing.

They dined, however, as soon as the first indignant outburst had
subsided; but they spoke little and thought much.

The ladies went to bed early; and the men, having lighted their
pipes, proposed a game of écarté, in which Monsieur Follenvie was
invited to join, the travelers hoping to question him skillfully as to the
best means of vanquishing the officer's obduracy. But he thought of
nothing but his cards, would listen to nothing, reply to nothing, and
repeated, time after time: "Attend to the game, gentlemen! attend to
the game!" So absorbed was his attention that he even forgot to expec-
torate. The consequence was that his chest gave forth rumbling sounds
like those of an organ. His wheezing lungs struck every note of the
asthmatic scale, from deep, hollow tones to a shrill, hoarse piping
resembling that of a young cock trying to crow.

He refused to go to bed when his wife, overcome with sleep, came
to fetch him. So she went off alone, for she was an early bird, always
up with the sun; while he was addicted to late hours, ever ready to
spend the night with friends. He merely said: "Put my eggnog by the
fire," and went on with the game. When the other men saw that nothing was to be got out of him they declared it was time to retire, and
each sought his bed.

They rose fairly early the next morning, with a vague hope of being
allowed to start, a greater desire than ever to do so, and a terror at
having to spend another day in this wretched little inn.

Alas! the horses remained in the stable, the driver was invisible.

They spent their time, for want of something better to do, in wandering round the coach.

Luncheon was a gloomy affair; and there was a general coolness toward Boule de Suif, for night, which brings counsel, had somewhat modified the judgment of her companions. In the cold light of the morning they almost bore a grudge against the girl for not having secretly sought out the Prussian, that the rest of the party might receive a joyful surprise when they awoke. What could be simpler?

Besides, who would have been the wiser? She might have saved appearances by telling the officer that she had taken pity on their distress. Such a step would be of so little consequence to her.

But no one as yet confessed to such thoughts.

In the afternoon, seeing that they were all bored to death, the count proposed a walk in the neighborhood of the village. Each one wrapped himself up well, and the little party set out, leaving behind only Cornudet, who preferred to sit over the fire, and the two nuns, who were in the habit of spending their day in the church or at the presbytery.

The cold, which grew more intense each day, almost froze the noses and ears of the pedestrians, their feet began to pain them so that each step was a penance, and when they reached the open country it looked so mournful and depressing in its limitless mantle of white that they all hastily retraced their steps, with bodies benumbed and hearts heavy.

The four women walked in front, and the three men followed a little in their rear.

Loiseau, who saw perfectly well how matters stood, asked suddenly "if that trollop were going to keep them waiting much longer in this godforsaken spot." The count, always courteous, replied that they could not exact so painful a sacrifice from any woman, and that the first move must come from herself. Monsieur Carre-Lamadon remarked that if the French, as they talked of doing, made a counter-attack by way of Dieppe, their encounter with the enemy must inevitably take place at Tôtes. This reflection made the other two anxious.

"Supposing we escape on foot?" said Loiseau.

The count shrugged his shoulders.

"How can you think of such a thing, in this snow? And with our wives? Besides, we should be pursued at once, overtaken in ten minutes, and brought back as prisoners at the mercy of the soldiery."

This was true enough; they were silent.

The ladies talked of dress, but a certain constraint seemed to prevail among them.

Suddenly, at the end of the street, the officer appeared. His tall, wasp-like, uniformed figure was outlined against the snow which bounded the horizon, and he walked, knees apart, with that motion peculiar to soldiers, who are always anxious not to soil their carefully polished boots.

He bowed as he passed the ladies, then glanced scornfully at the men, who had sufficient dignity not to raise their hats, though Loiseau made a movement to do so.

Boule de Suif flushed crimson to the ears, and the three married women felt unutterably humiliated at being met thus by the soldier in company with the girl whom he had treated with such scant ceremony.

Then they began to talk about him, his figure, and his face. Madame Carre-Lamadon, who had known many officers and judged them as a connoisseur, thought him not at all bad-looking; she even regretted that he was not a Frenchman, because in that case he would have made a very handsome hussar, with whom all the women would assuredly have fallen in love.

When they were once more within doors they did not know what to do with themselves. Sharp words even were exchanged apropos of the merest trifles. The silent dinner was quickly over, and each one went to bed early in the hope of sleeping, and thus killing time.

They came down next morning with tired faces and irritable tempers; the women scarcely spoke to Boule de Suif.

A church bell summoned the faithful to a baptism. Boule de Suif had a child being brought up by peasants at Yvetot. She did not see him once a year, and never thought of him; but the idea of the child who was about to be baptized induced a sudden wave of tenderness for her own, and she insisted on being present at the ceremony.

As soon as she had gone out, the rest of the company looked at one another and then drew their chairs together; for they realized that they must decide on some course of action. Loiseau had an inspiration: he proposed that they should ask the officer to detain Boule de Suif only, and to let the rest depart on their way.

Monsieur Follenvie was entrusted with this commission, but he returned to them almost immediately. The German, who knew human nature, had shown him the door. He intended to keep all the travelers until his condition had been complied with.

Whereupon Madame Loiseau's vulgar temperament broke bounds.

"We're not going to die of old age here!" she cried. "Since it's that vixen's trade to behave so with men I don't see that she has any right to refuse one more than another. I may as well tell you she took any lovers she could get at Rouen—even coachmen! Yes, indeed, madame—the coachman at the prefecture! I know it for a fact, for he buys his wine of us. And now that it is a question of getting us out of a difficulty she puts on virtuous airs, the drab! For my part, I think this officer has behaved very well. Why, there were three others of us, any one of whom he would undoubtedly have preferred. But no, he contents himself with the girl who is common property. He respects married women. Just think. He is master here. He had only to say: 'I wish it!' and he might have taken us by force, with the help of his soldiers."

The two other women shuddered; the eyes of pretty Madame Carre-Lamadon glistened, and she grew pale, as if the officer were indeed in the act of laying violent hands on her.

The men, who had been discussing the subject among themselves, drew near. Loiseau, in a state of furious resentment, was for delivering up "that miserable woman," bound hand and foot, into the enemy's power. But the count, descended from three generations of ambassadors, and endowed, moreover, with the lineaments of a diplomat, was in favor of more tactful measures.

"We must persuade her," he said.

Then they laid their plans.

The women drew together; they lowered their voices, and the discussion became general, each giving his or her opinion. But the conversation was not in the least coarse. The ladies, in particular, were adepts at delicate phrases and charming subtleties of expression to describe the most improper things. A stranger would have understood none of their allusions, so guarded was the language they employed. But, seeing that the thin veneer of modesty with which every woman of the world is furnished goes but a very little way below the surface, they began rather to enjoy this unedifying episode, and at bottom were hugely delighted—feeling themselves in their element, furthering the schemes of lawless love with the gusto of a gourmand cook who prepares supper for another.

Their gaiety returned of itself, so amusing at last did the whole business seem to them. The count uttered several rather risky witticisms, but so tactfully were they said that his audience could not help smiling. Loiseau in turn made some considerably broader jokes, but no one took offence; and the thought expressed with such brutal directness by his wife was uppermost in the minds of all: "Since it's the girl's trade, why should she refuse this man more than another?" Dainty Madame Carre-Lamadon seemed to think even that in Boule de Suif's place she would be less inclined to refuse him than another.

The blockade was as carefully arranged as if they were investing a fortress. Each agreed on the role which he or she was to play, the arguments to be used, the maneuvers to be executed. They decided on the plan of campaign, the stratagems they were to employ, and the surprise attacks which were to reduce this human citadel and force it to receive the enemy within its walls.

But Cornudet remained apart from the rest, taking no share in the plot.

So absorbed was the attention of all that Boule de Suif's entrance was almost unnoticed. But the count whispered a gentle "Hush!" which made the others look up. She was there. They suddenly stopped talking, and a vague embarrassment prevented them for a few moments from addressing her. But the countess, more practiced than the others in the wiles of the drawing-room, asked her: "Was the baptism interesting?"

The girl, still under the stress of emotion, told what she had seen and heard, described the faces, the attitudes of those present, and even the appearance of the church. She concluded with the words: "It does one good to pray sometimes."

Until lunch time the ladies contented themselves with being pleasant to her, so as to increase her confidence and make her amenable to their advice.

As soon as they took their seats at table the attack began. First they opened a vague conversation on the subject of self-sacrifice. Ancient examples were quoted: Judith and Holofernes; then, irrationally enough, Lucrece and Sextus; Cleopatra and the hostile generals whom she reduced to abject slavery by a surrender of her charms. Next was recounted an extraordinary story, born of the imagination of these ignorant millionaires, which told how the matrons of Rome seduced Hannibal, his lieutenants, and all his mercenaries at Capua. They held up to admiration all those women who from time to time have arrested the victorious progress of conquerors, made of their bodies a field of battle, a means of ruling, a weapon; who have vanquished by their heroic caresses hideous or detested beings, and sacrificed their chastity to vengeance and devotion.

All was said with due restraint and regard for propriety, the effect

heightened now and then by an outburst of forced enthusiasm calculated to excite emulation.

A listener would have thought at last that the one role of woman
on earth was a perpetual sacrifice of her person, a continual abandon-
ment of herself to the caprices of a hostile soldiery.

The two nuns seemed to hear nothing, and to be lost in thought.
Boule de Suif also was silent.

During the whole afternoon she was left to her reflections. But
instead of calling her "madame" as they had done hitherto, her companions addressed her simply as "mademoiselle," without exactly knowing why, but as if desirous of making her descend a step in the esteem
she had won, and forcing her to realize her degraded position.

Just as soup was served, Monsieur Follenvie reappeared, repeating
his phrase of the evening before:

"The Prussian officer sends to ask if Mademoiselle Elisabeth Rousset
has changed her mind."

Boule de Suif answered briefly: "No, monsieur."

But at dinner the coalition weakened. Loiseau made three unfortunate remarks. Each was cudgeling his brains for further examples of
self-sacrifice, and could find none, when the countess, possibly without ulterior motive, and moved simply by a vague desire to do homage
to religion, began to question the elder of the two nuns on the most
striking facts in the lives of the saints. Now, it fell out that many of
these had committed acts which would be crimes in our eyes, but the
Church readily pardons such deeds when they are accomplished for
the glory of God or the good of mankind. This was a powerful argument, and the countess made the most of it. Then, whether by reason
of a tacit understanding, a thinly veiled act of complaisance such as
those who wear the ecclesiastical habit excel in, or whether merely as
the result of sheer stupidity—a stupidity admirably adapted to further
their designs—the old nun rendered formidable aid to the conspira-
tor. They had thought her timid; she proved herself bold, talkative,
bigoted. She was not troubled by the ins and outs of casuistry; her
doctrines were as iron bars; her faith knew no doubt; her conscience
no scruples. She looked on Abraham's sacrifice as natural enough, for
she herself would not have hesitated to kill both father and mother if
she had received a divine order to that effect; and nothing, in her
opinion, could displease our Lord, provided the motive were praise-
worthy. The countess, putting to good use the consecrated authority
of her unexpected ally, led her on to make a lengthy and edifying

paraphrase of that axiom enunciated by a certain school of moralists: "The end justifies the means."

"Then, sister," she asked, "you think God accepts all methods, and pardons the act when the motive is pure?"

"Undoubtedly, madame. An action reprehensible in itself often derives merit from the thought which inspires it."

And in this wise they talked on, fathoming the wishes of God, predicting His judgments, describing Him as interested in matters which assuredly concern Him but little.

All was said with the utmost care and discretion, but every word uttered by the holy woman in her nun's garb weakened the indignant resistance of the courtesan. Then the conversation drifted somewhat, and the nun began to talk of the convents of her order, of her Superior, of herself, and of her fragile little neighbor, Sister St. Nicephore. They had been sent for from Havre to nurse the hundreds of soldiers who were in hospitals, stricken with smallpox. She described these wretched invalids and their malady. And, while they themselves were detained on their way by the caprices of the Prussian officer, scores of Frenchmen might be dying, whom they would otherwise have saved! For the nursing of soldiers was the old nun's specialty; she had been in the Crimea, in Italy, in Austria; and as she told the story of her campaigns she revealed herself as one of those holy sisters of the fife and drum who seem designed by nature to follow camps, to snatch the wounded from amid the strife of battle, and to quell with a word, more effectually than any general, the rough and insubordinate troopers—a masterful woman, her seamed and pitted face itself an image of the devastations of war.

No one spoke when she had finished for fear of spoiling the excellent effect of her words.

As soon as the meal was over the travelers retired to their rooms, whence they emerged the following day at a late hour of the morning.

Luncheon passed off quietly. The seed sown the preceding evening was being given time to germinate and bring forth fruit.

In the afternoon the countess proposed a walk; then the count, as had been arranged beforehand, took Boule de Suif's arm, and walked with her at some distance behind the rest.

He began talking to her in that familiar, paternal, slightly contemptuous tone which men of his class adopt in speaking to women like her, calling her "my dear child," and talking down to her from the height of his exalted social position and stainless reputation. He came straight to the point.

"So you prefer to leave us here, exposed like yourself to all the violence which would follow on a repulse of the Prussian troops, rather than consent to surrender yourself, as you have done so many times in your life?"

The girl did not reply.

He tried kindness, argument, sentiment. He still bore himself as count, even while adopting, when desirable, an attitude of gallantry, and making pretty—nay, even tender—speeches. He exalted the service she would render them, spoke of their gratitude; then, suddenly, speaking familiarly:

"And you know, sweetie, he could boast then of having made a conquest of a pretty girl such as he won't often find in his own country."

Boule de Suif did not answer, and joined the rest of the party.

As soon as they returned she went to her room, and was seen no more. The general anxiety was at its height. What would she do? If she still resisted, how awkward for them all!

The dinner hour struck; they waited for her in vain. At last Monsieur Follenvie entered, announcing that Mademoiselle Rousset was not well, and that they might sit down to table. They all pricked up their ears. The count drew near the innkeeper, and whispered: "Is it all right?"

"Yes."

Out of regard for propriety he said nothing to his companions, but merely nodded slightly toward them. A great sigh of relief went up from all breasts; every face was lighted up with joy.

"By God!" shouted Loiseau, "I'll stand champagne all round if there's any to be found in this place." And great was Madame Loiseau's dismay when the proprietor came back with four bottles in his hands. They had all suddenly become talkative and merry; a lively joy filled all hearts. The count seemed to perceive for the first time that Madame Carre-Lamadon was charming; the manufacturer paid compliments to the countess. The conversation was animated, sprightly, witty, and, although many of the jokes were in the worst possible taste, all the company were amused by them, and none offended—indignation being dependent, like other emotions, on surroundings. And the mental atmosphere had gradually become filled with gross imaginings and unclean thoughts.

At dessert even the women indulged in discreetly worded allusions. Their glances were full of meaning; they had drunk much. The count, who even in his moments of relaxation preserved a dignified demeanor, hit on a much-appreciated comparison of the condition of things with the termination of a winter spent in the icy solitude of the North Pole and the joy of shipwrecked mariners who at last perceive a southward track opening out before their eyes.

Loiseau, fairly in his element, rose to his feet, holding aloft a glass of champagne. "I drink to our deliverance!" he shouted.

All stood up, and greeted the toast with acclamation. Even the two good sisters yielded to the solicitations of the ladies, and consented to moisten their lips with the foaming wine, which they had never before tasted. They declared it was like effervescent lemonade, but with a pleasanter flavor.

"It is a pity," said Loiseau, "that we have no piano; we might have had a quadrille."

Cornudet had not spoken a word or made a movement; he seemed plunged in serious thought, and now and then tugged furiously at his great beard, as if trying to add still further to its length. At last, toward midnight, when they were about to separate, Loiseau, whose gait was far from steady, suddenly slapped him on the back, saying thickly: "You're not jolly tonight; why are you so silent, old man?"

Cornudet threw back his head, cast one swift and scornful glance over the assemblage, and answered: "I tell you all, you have done an infamous thing!" He rose, reached the door, and repeating "Infamous!" disappeared.

A chill fell on all. Loiseau himself looked foolish and disconcerted for a moment, but soon recovered his aplomb, and, writhing with laughter, exclaimed: "Really, you are all too green for anything!"

Pressed for an explanation, he related the "mysteries of the corridor," whereat his listeners were hugely amused. The ladies could hardly contain their delight. The count and Monsieur Carre-Lamadon laughed till they cried. They could scarcely believe their ears.

"What! you are sure? He wanted——"

"I tell you I saw it with my own eyes."

"And she refused?"

"Because the Prussian was in the next room!"

"Surely you are mistaken?"

"I swear I'm telling you the truth."

The count was choking with laughter. The manufacturer held his sides. Loiseau continued: "So you may well imagine he doesn't think this evening's business at all amusing."

And all three began to laugh again, choking, coughing, almost ill with merriment.

Then they separated. But Madame Loiseau, who was nothing if not spiteful, remarked to her husband as they were on the way to bed that "that stuck-up little minx of a Carre-Lamadon had laughed out of the wrong side of her mouth all evening."

"You know," she said, "when women run after uniforms it's all the same to them whether the men who wear them are French or Prussian. It's perfectly sickening!"

The next morning the snow showed dazzling white under a clear winter sun. The coach, ready at last, waited before the door; while a flock of white pigeons, with pink eyes spotted in the centers with black, puffed out their white feathers and walked sedately between the legs of the six horses, picking at the steaming manure.

The driver, wrapped in his sheepskin coat, was smoking a pipe on the box, and all the passengers, radiant with delight at their approaching departure, were putting up provisions for the remainder of the journey.

They were waiting only for Boule de Suif. At last she appeared.

She seemed rather shamefaced and embarrassed, and advanced with timid step toward her companions, who with one accord turned aside as if they had not seen her. The count, with much dignity, took his wife by the arm, and removed her from the unclean contact.

The girl stood still, stupefied with astonishment; then, plucking up courage, accosted the manufacturer's wife with a humble "Good-morning, madame," to which the other replied merely with a slight arid insolent nod, accompanied by a look of outraged virtue. Everyone suddenly appeared extremely busy, and kept as far from Boule de Suif as if their skirts had been infected with some deadly disease. Then they hurried to the coach, followed by the despised courtesan, who, arriving last of all, silently took the place she had occupied during the first part of the journey.

The rest seemed neither to see nor to know her—all save Madame Loiseau, who, glancing contemptuously in her direction, remarked, half aloud, to her husband: "What a mercy I am not sitting beside that creature!"

The lumbering vehicle started on its way, and the journey began afresh.

At first no one spoke. Boule de Suif dared not even raise her eyes. She felt at once indignant with her neighbors, and humiliated at having yielded to the Prussian into whose arms they had so hypocritically cast her.

But the countess, turning toward Madame Carre-Lamadon, soon broke the painful silence: "I think you know Madame d'Etrelles?"

"Yes; she is a friend of mine."

"Such a charming woman!"

"Delightful! Exceptionally talented, and an artist to the fingertips. She sings marvelously and draws to perfection."

The manufacturer was chatting with the count, and amid the clatter of the window-panes a word of their conversation was now and then distinguishable: "Shares—maturity—premium—time-limit."

Loiseau, who had abstracted from the inn the timeworn pack of cards, thick with the grease of five years' contact with half-wiped-off tables, started a game of bezique with his wife.

The good sisters, taking up simultaneously the long rosaries hanging from their waists, made the sign of the cross, and began to mutter in unison interminable prayers, their lips moving ever more and more swiftly, as if they sought which should outdistance the other in the race of orisons; from time to time they kissed a medal, and crossed themselves anew, then resumed their rapid and unintelligible murmur.

Cornudet sat still, lost in thought.

At the end of three hours Loiseau gathered up the cards, and remarked that he was hungry.

His wife thereupon produced a parcel tied with string, from which she extracted a piece of cold veal. This she cut into neat, thin slices, and both began to eat.

"We may as well do the same," said the countess. The rest agreed, and she unpacked the provisions which had been prepared for herself, the count, and the Carre-Lamadons. In one of those oval dishes, the lids of which are decorated with an earthenware hare, by way of showing that a game pie lies within, was a succulent delicacy consisting of the brown flesh of the game larded with streaks of bacon and flavored with other meats chopped fine. A solid wedge of Gruyere cheese, which had been wrapped in a newspaper, bore the imprint "News Item" on its rich, oily surface.

The two good sisters brought to light a hunk of sausage smelling strongly of garlic; and Cornudet, plunging both hands at once into the capacious pockets of his loose overcoat, produced from one four hard-boiled eggs and from the other a crust of bread. He removed the shells, threw them into the straw beneath his feet, and began to devour the eggs, letting morsels of the bright yellow yolk fall in his mighty beard, where they looked like stars.

Boule de Suif, in the haste and confusion of her departure, had not thought of anything, and, stifling with rage, she watched all these people placidly eating. At first, ill-suppressed wrath shook her whole person, and she opened her lips to shriek the truth at them, to overwhelm them with a volley of insults; but she could not utter a word, so choked was she with indignation.

No one looked at her, no one thought of her. She felt herself swallowed up in the scorn of these virtuous creatures, who had first sacrificed, then rejected her as a thing useless and unclean. Then she remembered her big basket full of the good things they had so greedily devoured: the two chickens coated in jelly, the pies, the pears, the four bottles of claret; and her fury broke forth like a cord that is overstrained, and she was on the verge of tears. She made terrible efforts at self-control, drew herself up, swallowed the sobs which choked her; but the tears rose nevertheless, shone at the brink of her eyelids, and soon two heavy drops coursed slowly down her cheeks. Others followed more quickly, like water filtering from a rock, and fell, one after another, on her rounded bosom. She sat upright, with a fixed expression, her face pale and rigid, hoping desperately that no one saw her give way.

But the countess noticed that she was weeping, and with a sign drew her husband's attention to the fact. He shrugged his shoulders, as if to say: "Well, what of it? It's not my fault." Madame Loiseau chuckled triumphantly, and murmured: "She's weeping for shame."

The two nuns had betaken themselves once more to their prayers, first wrapping the remainder of their sausage in paper.

Then Cornudet, who was digesting his eggs, stretched his long legs under the opposite seat, threw himself back, folded his arms, smiled like a man who had just thought of a good joke, and began to whistle the "Marseillaise."

The faces of his neighbors clouded; the popular air evidently did not find favor with them; they grew nervous and irritable, and seemed ready to howl as a dog does at the sound of a barrel-organ. Cornudet saw the discomfort he was creating, and whistled the louder; sometimes he even hummed the words:

Amour sacre de la patrie,
Conduis, soutiens, nos bras vengeurs,
Liberte, liberte cherie,
Combats avec tes defenseurs!

The coach progressed more swiftly, the snow being harder now; and all the way to Dieppe, during the long, dreary hours of the journey, first in the gathering dusk, then in the thick darkness, raising his voice above the rumbling of the vehicle, Cornudet continued with fierce obstinacy his vengeful and monotonous whistling, forcing his weary and exasperated hearers to follow the song from end to end, to recall every word of every line, as each was repeated over and over again with untiring persistency.

And Boule de Suif still wept, and sometimes a sob she could not restrain was heard in the darkness between two verses of the song.

Indiscretion

They had loved each other before marriage with a pure and lofty love. They had first met on the seashore. He had thought this young girl charming, as she passed by with her light-colored parasol and her dainty dress amid the marine landscape against the horizon. He had loved her, blond and slender, in these surroundings of blue ocean and spacious sky. He could not distinguish the tenderness which this budding woman awoke in him from the vague and powerful emotion which the fresh salt air and the grand scenery of surf and sunshine and waves aroused in his soul.

She, on the other hand, had loved him because he courted her, because he was young, rich, kind, and attentive. She had loved him because it is natural for young girls to love men who whisper sweet nothings to them.

So, for three months, they had lived side by side, and hand in hand. The greeting which they exchanged in the morning before the bath, in the freshness of the morning, or in the evening on the sand, under the stars, in the warmth of a calm night, whispered low, very low, already had the flavor of kisses, though their lips had never met.

Each dreamed of the other at night, each thought of the other on awaking, and, without yet having voiced their sentiments, each longed for the other, body and soul.

After marriage their love descended to earth. It was at first a tireless, sensuous passion, then exalted tenderness composed of tangible poetry, more refined caresses, and new and foolish inventions. Every glance and gesture was an expression of passion.

But, little by little, without even noticing it, they began to get tired of each other. Love was still strong, but they had nothing more to reveal to each other, nothing more to learn from each other, no new tale of endearment, no unexpected outburst, no new way of expressing the well-known, oft-repeated verb.

They tried, however, to rekindle the dwindling flame of the first love. Every day they tried some new trick or desperate attempt to bring back to their hearts the uncooled ardor of their first days of married life. They tried moonlight walks under the trees, in the sweet warmth of the summer evenings: the poetry of mist-covered beaches; the excitement of public festivals.

One morning Henriette said to Paul: "Will you take me to a cafe for dinner?"

"Certainly, dearie."

"To some well-known cafe?"

"Of course!"

He looked at her with a questioning glance, seeing that she was thinking of something which she did not wish to tell.

She went on: "You know, one of those cafes—oh, how can I explain myself?—a sporty cafe!"

He smiled: "Of course, I understand—you mean in one of the cafes which are commonly called bohemian."

"Yes, that's it. But take me to one of the big places, one where you are known, one where you have already supped—no—dined—well, you know—I—I—oh! I will never dare say it!"

"Go ahead, dearie. Little secrets should no longer exist between us."

"No, I dare not."

"Go on; don't be prudish. Tell me."

"Well, I—I—I want to be taken for your sweetheart—there! and I want the boys, who do not know that you are married, to take me for such; and you too—I want you to think that I am your sweetheart for one hour, in that place which must hold so many memories for you. There! And I will play that I am your sweetheart. It's awful, I know—I am abominably ashamed, I am as red as a peony. Don't look at me!"

He laughed, greatly amused, and answered: "All right, we will go tonight to a very swell place where I am well known."

Toward seven o'clock they went up the stairs of one of the big cafes on the Boulevard, he, smiling, with the look of a conqueror, she, timid, veiled, delighted. They were immediately shown to one of the luxurious private dining-rooms, furnished with four large armchairs and a red plush couch. The head waiter entered and brought them the menu. Paul handed it to his wife.

"What do you want to eat?"

"I don't care; order whatever is good."

After handing his coat to the waiter, he ordered dinner and champagne. The waiter looked at the young woman and smiled. He took the order and murmured: "Will Monsieur Paul have his champagne sweet or dry?"

"Dry, very dry."

Henriette was pleased to hear that this man knew her husband's name. They sat on the couch, side by side, and began to eat.

Ten candles lighted the room and were reflected in the mirrors all around them, which seemed to increase the brilliancy a thousandfold. Henriette drank glass after glass in order to keep up her courage, although she felt dizzy after the first few glasses. Paul, excited by the memories which returned to him, kept kissing his wife's hands. His eyes were sparkling.

She was feeling strangely excited in this new place, restless, pleased, a little guilty, but full of life. Two waiters, serious, silent, accustomed to seeing and forgetting everything, to entering the room only when it was necessary and to leaving it when they felt they were intruding, were silently flitting hither and thither.

Toward the middle of the dinner, Henriette was well under the influence of champagne. She was prattling along fearlessly, her cheeks flushed, her eyes glistening. "Come, Paul; tell me everything."

"What, sweetheart?"

"I don't dare tell you."

"Go on!"

"Have you loved many women before me?"

He hesitated, a little perplexed, not knowing whether he should hide his adventures or boast of them.

She continued: "Oh please tell me. How many have you loved?"

"A few."

"How many?"

"I don't know. How do you expect me to know such things?"

"Haven't you counted them?"

"Of course not."

"Then you must have loved a good many!"

"Perhaps."

"About how many? Just tell me about how many."

"But I don't know, dearest. Some years a good many, and some years only a few."

"How many a year, did you say?"

"Sometimes twenty or thirty, sometimes only four or five."

"Oh! that makes more than a hundred in all!"

"Yes, just about."

"Oh! I think that is dreadful!"

"Why dreadful?"

"Because it's dreadful when you think of it—all those women—and always—always the same thing. Oh! it's dreadful, just the same—more than a hundred women!"

He was surprised that she should think that dreadful, and answered with the air of superiority which men take with women when they wish to make them understand that they have said something foolish: "That's funny! If it is dreadful to have a hundred women, it's dreadful to have one."

"Oh, no, not at all!"

"Why not?"

"Because with one woman you have a real bond of love which attaches you to her, while with a hundred women it's not the same at all. There is no real love. I don't understand how a man can associate with such women."

"But they are all right."

"No, they can't be!"

"Yes, they are!"

"Oh, stop; you disgust me!"

"But then, why did you ask me how many sweethearts I had had?"

"Because——"

"That's no reason!"

"What were they—actresses, little shopgirls, or society women?"

"A few of each."

"It must have been rather monotonous toward the last."

"Oh, no; it's amusing to change."

She remained thoughtful, staring at her champagne glass. It was full—she drank it in one gulp; then putting it back on the table, she threw her arms around her husband's neck and murmured in his ear: "Oh! how I love you, sweetheart! how I love you!"

He threw his arms around her in a passionate embrace. A waiter, who was just entering, backed out, closing the door discreetly. In about five minutes the headwaiter came back, solemn and dignified, bringing the fruit for dessert. She was once more holding between her fingers a full glass, and gazing into the amber liquid as though seeking unknown things. She murmured in a dreamy voice: "Yes, it must be fun!"

Mademoiselle Fifi

Major Graf von Farlsberg, the Prussian commandant, was reading his newspaper as he lay back in a great easy-chair, with his booted feet on the beautiful marble mantelpiece where his spurs had made two holes, which had grown deeper every day during the three months that he had been in the chateau of Uville.

A cup of coffee was smoking on a small inlaid table, which was stained with liqueur, burned by cigars, notched by the penknife of the victorious officer, who occasionally would stop while sharpening a pencil, to jot down figures, or to make a drawing on it, just as it took his fancy.

When he had read his letters and the German newspapers, which his orderly had brought him, he got up, and after throwing three or four enormous pieces of green wood on the fire, for these gentlemen were gradually cutting down the park in order to keep themselves warm, he went to the window. The rain was descending in torrents, a regular Normandy rain, which looked as if it were being poured out by some furious person, a slanting rain, opaque as a curtain, which formed a kind of wall with diagonal stripes, and which deluged everything, a rain such as one frequently experiences in the neighborhood of Rouen, which is the watering-pot of France.

For a long time the officer looked at the sodden turf and at the swollen Andelle beyond it, which was overflowing its banks; he was drumming a waltz with his fingers on the window-panes, when a noise made him turn round. It was his second in command, Captain Baron von Kelweinstein.

The major was a giant, with broad shoulders and a long, fan-like beard, which hung down like a curtain to his chest. His whole solemn person suggested the idea of a military peacock, a peacock who was carrying his tail spread out on his breast. He had cold, gentle blue eyes, and a scar from a swordcut, which he had received in the war with Austria; he was said to be an honorable man, as well as a brave officer.

The captain, a short, red-faced man, was tightly belted in at the waist, his hair was cropped quite close to his head, and in certain lights he almost looked as if he had been rubbed over with phosphorus. He had lost two front teeth one night, though he could not quite remember how, and this sometimes made him speak unintelligibly, and he had a bald patch on top of his head surrounded by a fringe of curly, bright golden hair, which made him look like a monk.

The commandant shook hands with him and drank his cup of coffee (the sixth that morning), while he listened to his subordinate's report of what had occurred; and then they both went to the window and declared that it was a very unpleasant outlook. The major, who was a quiet man, with a wife at home, could accommodate himself to everything; but the captain, who led a fast life, who was in the habit of frequenting low resorts, and enjoying women's society, was angry at having to be shut up for three months in that wretched hole.

There was a knock at the door, and when the commandant said, "Come in," one of the orderlies appeared, and by his mere presence announced that breakfast was ready. In the dining-room they met three other officers of lower rank—a lieutenant, Otto von Grossling, and two sub-lieutenants, Fritz Schönberg and Baron von Eyrick, a very short, fair-haired man, who was proud and brutal toward men, harsh toward prisoners and as explosive as gunpowder.

Since he had been in France his comrades had called him nothing but Mademoiselle Fifi. They had given him that nickname on account of his dandified style and small waist, which looked as if he wore corsets; of his pale face, on which his budding mustache scarcely showed, and on account of the habit he had acquired of employing the French expression "Fi, fi donc," which he pronounced with a slight whistle when he wished to express his sovereign contempt for persons or things.

The dining-room of the chateau was a magnificent long room, whose fine old mirrors, that were cracked by pistol bullets, and whose Flemish tapestry, which was cut to ribbons, and hanging in rags in places from swordcuts, told too well what Mademoiselle Fifi's occupation was during his spare time.

There were three family portraits on the walls; a steel-clad knight, a cardinal and a judge, who were all smoking long porcelain pipes, which had been inserted into holes in the canvas, while a lady in a long, pointed waist proudly exhibited a pair of enormous mustaches, drawn with charcoal. The officers ate their breakfast almost in silence in that mutilated room, which looked dull in the rain and melancholy in its dilapidated condition, although its old oak floor had become as solid as the stone floor of an inn.

When they had finished eating and were smoking and drinking, they began, as usual, to berate the dull life they were leading. The bottles of brandy and of liqueur passed from hand to hand, and all sat back in their chairs and took repeated sips from their glasses, scarcely removing from their mouths the long, curved stems, which terminated in china bowls, painted in a manner to delight a Hottentot.

As soon as their glasses were empty they filled them again, with a gesture of resigned weariness, but Mademoiselle Fifi emptied his every minute, and a soldier immediately gave him another. They were enveloped in a cloud of strong tobacco smoke, and seemed to be sunk in a state of drowsy, stupid intoxication, that condition of stupid intoxication of men who have nothing to do, when suddenly the baron sat up and said: "Heavens! This cannot go on; we must think of something to do." And on hearing this, Lieutenant Otto and Sub-lieutenant Fritz, who preeminently possessed the serious, heavy German countenance, said: "What, captain?"

He thought for a few moments and then replied: "What? Why, we must get up some entertainment, if the commandant will allow us." "What sort of an entertainment, captain?" the major asked, taking his pipe out of his mouth. "I will arrange all that, commandant," the baron said. "I will send Le Devoir to Rouen, and he will bring back some ladies. I know where they can be found. We will have supper here, as all the materials are at hand and; at least, we shall have a jolly evening."

Graf von Farlsberg shrugged his shoulders with a smile: "You must surely be mad, my friend."

But all the other officers had risen and surrounded their chief, saying: "Let the captain have his way, commandant; it is terribly dull here." And the major ended by yielding. "Very well," he replied, and the baron immediately sent for Le Devoir. He was an old non-commissioned officer, who had never been seen to smile, but who carried out all the orders of his superiors to the letter, no matter what they might be. He stood there, with an impassive face, while he received the baron's instructions, and then went out, and five minutes later a large military wagon, covered with tarpaulin, galloped off as fast as four horses could draw it in the pouring rain. The officers all seemed to awaken from their lethargy, their looks brightened, and they began to talk.

Although it was raining as hard as ever, the major declared that it was not so dark, and Lieutenant von Grossling said with conviction that the sky was clearing up, while Mademoiselle Fifi did not seem to be able to keep still. He got up and sat down again, and his bright eyes seemed to be looking for something to destroy. Suddenly, looking at the lady with the mustaches, the young fellow pulled out his revolver and said: "You shall not see it." And without leaving his seat he aimed, and with two successive bullets cut out both the eyes of the portrait.

"Let us make a mine!" he then exclaimed, and the conversation was suddenly interrupted, as if they had found some fresh and powerful subject of interest. The mine was his invention, his method of destruction, and his favorite amusement.

When he left the chateau, the lawful owner, Comte Fernand d'Amoys d'Uville, had not had time to carry away or to hide anything except the plate, which had been stowed away in a hole made in one of the walls. As he was very rich and had good taste, the large drawing-room, which opened into the dining-room, looked like a gallery in a museum, before his precipitate flight.

Expensive oil paintings, water colors and drawings hung against the walls, while on the tables, on the hanging shelves and in elegant glass cupboards there were a thousand ornaments: small vases, statuettes, groups of Dresden china and grotesque Chinese figures, old ivory and Venetian glass, which filled the large room with their costly and fantastic array.

Scarcely anything was left now; not that the things had been stolen, for the major would not have allowed that, but Mademoiselle Fifi would every now and then have a mine, and on those occasions all the officers thoroughly enjoyed themselves for five minutes. The little marquis went into the drawing-room to get what he wanted, and he brought back a small, delicate china teapot, which he filled with gunpowder, and carefully introduced a piece of punk through the spout. This he lighted and took his infernal machine into the next room, but he came back immediately and shut the door. The Germans all stood expectant, their faces full of childish, smiling curiosity, and as soon as the explosion had shaken the chateau, they all rushed in at once.

Mademoiselle Fifi, who got in first, clapped his hands in delight at the sight of a terra-cotta Venus, whose head had been blown off, and each picked up pieces of porcelain and wondered at the strange shape of the fragments, while the major was looking with a paternal eye at the large drawing-room, which had been wrecked after the fashion of a Nero, and was strewn with the fragments of works of art. He went out first and said with a smile: "That was a great success this time."

But there was such a cloud of smoke in the dining-room, mingled with the tobacco smoke, that they could not breathe, so the commandant opened the window, and all the officers, who had returned for a last glass of cognac, went up to it.

The moist air blew into the room, bringing with it a sort of powdery spray, which sprinkled their beards. They looked at the tall trees which were dripping with rain, at the broad valley which was covered with mist, and at the church spire in the distance, which rose up like a gray point in the beating rain.

The bells had not rung since their arrival. That was the only resistance which the invaders had met with in the neighborhood. The parish priest had not refused to take in and to feed the Prussian soldiers; he had several times even drunk a bottle of beer or claret with the hostile commandant, who often employed him as a benevolent intermediary; but it was no use to ask him for a single stroke of the bells; he would sooner have allowed himself to be shot. That was his way of protesting against the invasion, a peaceful and silent protest, the only one, he said, which was suitable to a priest, who was a man of mildness, and not of blood; and everyone, for twenty-five miles round, praised Abbe Chantavoine's firmness and heroism in venturing to proclaim the public mourning by the obstinate silence of his church bells.

The whole village, enthusiastic at his resistance, was ready to back up their pastor and to risk anything, for they looked upon that silent protest as the safeguard of the national honor. It seemed to the peasants that thus they deserved better of their country than Belfort and Strassburg, that they had set an equally valuable example, and that the name of their little village would become immortalized by that; but, with that exception, they refused their Prussian conquerors nothing.

The commandant and his officers laughed among themselves at this inoffensive courage, and as the people in the whole country round showed themselves obliging and compliant toward them, they willingly tolerated their silent patriotism. Little Baron Wilhelm alone would have liked to have forced them to ring the bells. He was very angry at his superior's politic compliance with the priest's scruples, and every day begged the commandant to allow him to sound "ding-dong, ding-dong," just once, only just once, just by way of a joke. And he asked it in the coaxing, tender voice of some loved woman who is bent on obtaining her wish, but the commandant would not yield, and to console himself, Mademoiselle Fifi made a mine in the Chateau d'Uville.

The five men stood there together for five minutes, breathing in the moist air, and at last Lieutenant Fritz said with a laugh: "The ladies will certainly not have fine weather for their drive." Then they separated, each to his duty, while the captain had plenty to do in arranging for the dinner.

When they met again toward evening they began to laugh at seeing each other as spick and span and smart as on the day of a grand review. The commandant's hair did not look so gray as it was in the morning, and the captain had shaved, leaving only his mustache, which made him look as if he had a streak of fire under his nose.

In spite of the rain, they left the window open, and one of them went to listen from time to time; and at a quarter past six the baron said he heard a rumbling in the distance. They all rushed down, and presently the wagon drove up at a gallop with its four horses steaming and blowing, and splashed with mud to their girths. Five women dismounted, five handsome girls whom a comrade of the captain, to whom Le Devoir had presented his card, had selected with care.

They had not required much pressing, as they had got to know the Prussians in the three months during which they had had to do with them, and so they resigned themselves to the men as they did to the state of affairs.

They went at once into the dining-room, which looked still more dismal in its dilapidated condition when it was lighted up; while the table covered with choice dishes, the beautiful china and glass, and the plate, which had been found in the hole in the wall where its owner had hidden it, gave it the appearance of a bandits' inn, where they were supping after committing a robbery in the place. The captain was radiant, and put his arm round the women as if he were familiar with them; and when the three young men wanted to appropriate one each, he opposed them authoritatively, reserving to himself the right to apportion them justly, according to their several ranks, so as not to offend the higher powers. Therefore, to avoid all discussion, jarring, and suspicion of partiality, he placed them all in a row according to height, and addressing the tallest, he said in a voice of command:

"What is your name?" "Pamela," she replied, raising her voice. And then he said: "Number One, called Pamela, is adjudged to the commandant." Then, having kissed Blondina, the second, as a sign of proprietorship, he proffered stout Amanda to Lieutenant Otto; Eva, "the Tomato," to Sub-lieutenant Fritz, and Rachel, the shortest of them all, a very young, dark girl, with eyes as black as ink—a Jewess, whose snub nose proved the rule which allots hooked noses to all her race—to the youngest officer, frail Count Wilhelm d'Eyrick.

They were all pretty and plump, without any distinctive features, and all had a similarity of complexion and figure.

The three young men wished to carry off their prizes immediately, under the pretext that they might wish to freshen their faces; but the captain wisely opposed this, for he said they were quite fit to sit down to dinner, and his experience in such matters carried the day. There were only many kisses, expectant kisses.

Suddenly Rachel choked, and began to cough until the tears came into her eyes, while smoke came through her nostrils. Under pretence of kissing her, the count had blown a whiff of tobacco into her mouth. She did not fly into a rage and did not say a word, but she looked at her tormentor with latent hatred in her dark eyes.

They sat down to dinner. The commandant seemed delighted; he made Pamela sit on his right, and Blondina on his left, and said, as he unfolded his table napkin: "That was a delightful idea of yours, captain."

Lieutenants Otto and Fritz, who were as polite as if they had been with fashionable ladies, rather intimidated their guests, but Baron von Kelweinstein beamed, made obscene remarks and seemed on fire with his crown of red hair. He paid the women compliments in French of the Rhine, and sputtered out gallant remarks, only fit for a low pothouse, from between his two broken teeth.

They did not understand him, however, and their intelligence did not seem to be awakened until he uttered foul words and broad expressions, which were mangled by his accent. Then they all began to laugh at once like crazy women and fell against each other, repeating the words, which the baron then began to say all wrong, in order that he might have the pleasure of hearing them say dirty things. They gave him as much of that stuff as he wanted, for they were drunk after the first bottle of wine, and resuming their usual habits and manners, they kissed the officers to right and left of them, pinched their arms, uttered wild cries, drank out of every glass and sang French couplets and bits of German songs which they had picked up in their daily intercourse with the enemy.

Soon the men themselves became very unrestrained, shouted and broke the plates and dishes, while the soldiers behind them waited on them stolidly. The commandant was the only one who kept any restraint upon himself.

Mademoiselle Fifi had taken Rachel on his knee, and, getting excited, at one moment he kissed the little black curls on her neck and at another he pinched her furiously and made her scream, for he was seized by a species of ferocity, and tormented by his desire to hurt her. He often held her close to him and pressed a long kiss on the Jewess' rosy mouth until she lost her breath, and at last he bit her until a stream of blood ran down her chin and on to her bodice.

For the second time she looked him full in the face, and as she bathed the wound, she said: "You will have to pay for, that!" But he merely laughed a hard laugh and said: "I will pay."

At dessert champagne was served, and the commandant rose, and in the same voice in which he would have drunk to the health of the Empress Augusta, he drank: "To our ladies!" And a series of toasts began, toasts worthy of the lowest soldiers and of drunkards, mingled with obscene jokes, which were made still more brutal by their ignorance of the language. They got up, one after the other, trying to say something witty, forcing themselves to be funny, and the women, who were so drunk that they almost fell off their chairs, with vacant looks and clammy tongues applauded madly each time.

The captain, who no doubt wished to impart an appearance of gallantry to the orgy, raised his glass again and said: "To our victories over hearts," and, thereupon Lieutenant Otto, who was a species of bear from the Black Forest, jumped up, inflamed and saturated with drink, and suddenly seized by an access of alcoholic patriotism, he cried: "To our victories over France!"

Drunk as they were, the women were silent, but Rachel turned round, trembling, and said: "See here, I know some Frenchmen in whose presence you would not dare say that." But the little count, still holding her on his knee, began to laugh, for the wine had made him very merry, and said: "Ha! ha! ha! I have never met any of them myself. As soon as we show ourselves, they run away!" The girl, who was in a terrible rage, shouted into his face: "You are lying, you dirty scoundrel!"

For a moment he looked at her steadily with his bright eyes upon her, as he had looked at the portrait before he destroyed it with bullets from his revolver, and then he began to laugh: "Ah! yes, talk about them, my dear! Should we be here now if they were brave?" And, getting excited, he exclaimed: "We are the masters! France belongs to us!" She made one spring from his knee and threw herself into her chair, while he arose, held out his glass over the table and repeated: "France and the French, the woods, the fields and the houses of France belong to us!"

The others, who were quite drunk, and who were suddenly seized by military enthusiasm, the enthusiasm of brutes, seized their glasses, and shouting, "Long live Prussia!" they emptied them at a draught.

The girls did not protest, for they were reduced to silence and were afraid. Even Rachel did not say a word, as she had no reply to make. Then the little marquis put his champagne glass, which had just been refilled, on the head of the Jewess and exclaimed: "All the women in France belong to us also!"

At that she got up so quickly that the glass upset, spilling the amber-colored wine on her black hair as if to baptize her, and broke into a hundred fragments, as it fell to the floor. Her lips trembling, she defied the looks of the officer, who was still laughing, and stammered out in a voice choked with rage:

"That—that—that—is not true—for you shall not have the women of France!"

He sat down again so as to laugh at his ease; and, trying to speak with the Parisian accent, he said: "She is good, very good! Then why did you come here, my dear?" She was thunderstruck and made no reply for a moment, for in her agitation she did not understand him at first, but as soon as she grasped his meaning she said to him indignantly and vehemently: "I! I! I am not a woman, I am only a strumpet, and that is all that Prussians want."

Almost before she had finished he slapped her full in the face; but as he was raising his hand again, as if to strike her, she seized a small dessert knife with a silver blade from the table and, almost mad with rage, stabbed him right in the hollow of his neck. Something that he was going to say was cut short in his throat, and he sat there with his mouth half open and a terrible look in his eyes.

All the officers shouted in horror and leaped up tumultuously; but, throwing her chair between the legs of Lieutenant Otto, who fell down at full length, she ran to the window, opened it before they could seize her and jumped out into the night and the pouring rain.

In two minutes Mademoiselle Fifi was dead, and Fritz and Otto drew their swords and wanted to kill the women, who threw themselves at their feet and clung to their knees. With some difficulty the major stopped the slaughter and had the four terrified girls locked up in a room under the care of two soldiers, and then he organized the pursuit of the fugitive as carefully as if he were about to engage in a skirmish, feeling quite sure that she would be caught.

The table, which had been cleared immediately, now served as a bed on which to lay out the lieutenant, and the four officers stood at the windows, rigid and sobered with the stern faces of soldiers on duty, and tried to pierce through the darkness of the night amid the steady torrent of rain. Suddenly a shot was heard and then another, a long way off; and for four hours they heard from time to time near or distant reports and rallying cries, strange words of challenge, uttered in guttural voices.

In the morning they all returned. Two soldiers had been killed and three others wounded by their comrades in the ardor of that chase and in the confusion of that nocturnal pursuit, but they had not caught Rachel.

Then the inhabitants of the district were terrorized, the houses were turned topsy-turvy, the country was scoured and beaten up, over and over again, but the Jewess did not seem to have left a single trace of her passage behind her.

When the general was told of it he gave orders to hush up the affair, so as not to set a bad example to the army, but he severely censured the commandant, who in turn punished his inferiors. The general had said: "One does not go to war in order to amuse one's self and to caress prostitutes." Graf von Farlsberg, in his exasperation, made up his mind to have his revenge on the district, but as he required a pretext for showing severity, he sent for the priest and ordered him to have the bell tolled at the funeral of Baron von Eyrick.

Contrary to all expectation, the priest showed himself humble and most respectful, and when Mademoiselle Fifi's body left the Chateau d'Uville on its way to the cemetery, carried by soldiers, preceded, surrounded and followed by soldiers who marched with loaded rifles, for the first time the bell sounded its funeral knell in a lively manner, as if a friendly hand were caressing it. At night it rang again, and the next day, and every day; it rang as much as anyone could desire. Sometimes even it would start at night and sound gently through the darkness, seized with a strange joy, awakened one could not tell why. All the peasants in the neighborhood declared that it was bewitched, and nobody except the priest and the sacristan would now go near the church tower. And they went because a poor girl was living there in grief and solitude and provided for secretly by those two men.

She remained there until the German troops departed, and then one evening the priest borrowed the baker's cart and himself drove his prisoner to Rouen. When they got there he embraced her, and she quickly went back on foot to the establishment from which she had come, where the proprietress, who thought that she was dead, was very glad to see her.

A short time afterward a patriot who had no prejudices, and who liked her because of her bold deed, and who afterward loved her for herself, married her and made her a lady quite as good as many others.

A Duel

The war was over. The Germans occupied France. The whole country was pulsating like a conquered wrestler beneath the knee of his victorious opponent.

The first trains from Paris, distracted, starving, despairing Paris, were making their way to the new frontiers, slowly passing through the country districts and the villages. The passengers gazed through the windows at the ravaged fields and burned hamlets. Prussian soldiers, in their black helmets with brass spikes, were smoking their pipes astride their chairs in front of the houses which were still left standing. Others were working or talking just as if they were members of the families. As you passed through the different towns you saw entire regiments drilling in the squares, and, in spite of the rumble of the carriage-wheels, you could every moment hear the hoarse words of command.

M. Dubuis, who during the entire siege had served as one of the National Guard in Paris, was going to join his wife and daughter, whom he had prudently sent away to Switzerland before the invasion.

Famine and hardship had not diminished his big paunch so characteristic of the rich, peace-loving merchant. He had gone through the terrible events of the past year with sorrowful resignation and bitter complaints at the savagery of men. Now that he was journeying to the frontier at the close of the war, he saw the Prussians for the first time, although he had done his duty on the ramparts and mounted guard on many a cold night.

He stared with mingled fear and anger at those bearded armed men, installed all over French soil as if they were at home, and he felt in his soul a kind of fever of impotent patriotism, at the same time also the great need of that new instinct of prudence which since then has never left us. In the same railway carriage were two Englishmen, who had come to the country as sightseers and were gazing about them with looks of quiet curiosity. They were both also stout, and kept chatting in their own language, sometimes referring to their guidebook, and reading aloud the names of the places indicated.

Suddenly the train stopped at a little village station, and a Prussian officer jumped up with a great clatter of his saber on the double footboard of the railway carriage. He was tall, wore a tight-fitting uniform, and had whiskers up to his eyes. His red hair seemed to be on fire, and his long mustache, of a paler hue, stuck out on both sides of his face, which it seemed to cut in two.

The Englishmen at once began staring at him with smiles of newly awakened interest, while M. Dubuis made a show of reading a newspaper. He sat concealed in his corner like a thief in presence of a gendarme.

The train started again. The Englishmen went on chatting and looking out for the exact scene of different battles; and all of a sudden, as one of them stretched out his arm toward the horizon as he pointed out a village, the Prussian officer remarked in French, extending his long legs and lolling backward: "I killed a dozen Frenchmen in that village and took more than a hundred prisoners."

The Englishmen, quite interested, immediately asked: "Ha! and what is the name of this village?"

The Prussian replied: "Pharsbourg." He added: "We caught those French scoundrels by the ears."

And he glanced toward M. Dubuis, laughing conceitedly into his mustache.

The train rolled on, still passing through hamlets occupied by the victorious army. German soldiers could be seen along the roads, on the edges of fields, standing in front of gates or chatting outside cafes. They covered the soil like African locusts.

The officer said, with a wave of his hand: "If I had been in command, I'd have taken Paris, burned everything, killed everybody. No more France!"

The Englishman, through politeness, replied simply: "Ah, yes."

He went on: "In twenty years all Europe, all of it, will belong to us. Prussia is more than a match for all of them."

The Englishmen, getting uneasy, no longer replied. Their faces, which had become impassive, seemed made of wax behind their long whiskers. Then the Prussian officer began to laugh. And still, lolling back, he began to sneer. He sneered at the downfall of France, insulted the prostrate enemy; he sneered at Austria, which had been recently conquered; he sneered at the valiant but fruitless defense of the departments; he sneered at the Garde Mobile and at the useless artillery. He announced that Bismarck was going to build a city of iron with the captured cannon. And suddenly he placed his boots against the thigh of M. Dubuis, who turned away his eyes, reddening to the roots of his hair.

The Englishmen seemed to have become indifferent to all that was going on, as if they were suddenly shut up in their own island, far from the din of the world.

The officer took out his pipe, and looking fixedly at the Frenchman, said: "You haven't any tobacco, have you?"

M. Dubuis replied: "No, monsieur."

The German resumed: "You might go and buy some for me when the train stops." And he began laughing afresh as he added: "I'll give you the price of a drink."

The train whistled, and slackened its pace. They passed a station that had been burned down; and then they stopped altogether.

The German opened the carriage door, and, catching M. Dubuis by the arm, said: "Go and do what I told you—quick, quick!"

A Prussian detachment occupied the station. Other soldiers were standing behind wooden gratings, looking on. The engine was getting up steam before starting off again. Then M. Dubuis hurriedly jumped on the platform, and, in spite of the warnings of the station master, dashed into the adjoining compartment.

He was alone! He tore open his waistcoat, his heart was beating so rapidly, and, gasping for breath, he wiped the perspiration from his forehead.

The train drew up at another station. And suddenly the officer appeared at the carriage door and jumped in, followed close behind by the two Englishmen, who were impelled by curiosity. The German sat facing the Frenchman, and, laughing still, said: "You did not want to do what I asked you?"

M. Dubuis replied: "No, monsieur."

The train had just left the station.

The officer said: "I'll cut off your mustache to fill my pipe with."

And he put out his hand toward the Frenchman's face.

The Englishmen stared at them, retaining their previous impassive manner.

The German had already pulled out a few hairs, and was still tugging at the mustache, when M. Dubuis, with a back stroke of his hand, flung aside the officer's arm, and, seizing him by the collar, threw him down on the seat. Then, excited to a pitch of fury, his temples swollen and his eyes glaring, he kept throttling the officer with one hand, while with the other clenched he began to strike him violent blows in the face. The Prussian struggled, tried to draw his sword, to clinch with his adversary, who was on top of him. But M. Dubuis crushed him with his enormous weight and kept punching him without taking breath or knowing where his blows fell. Blood flowed down the face of the German, who, choking and with a rattling in his throat, spat out his broken teeth and vainly strove to shake off this infuriated man who was killing him.

The Englishmen had got on their feet and came closer in order to see better. They remained standing, full of mirth and curiosity, ready to bet for, or against, either combatant.

Suddenly M. Dubuis, exhausted by his violent efforts, rose and resumed his seat without uttering a word.

The Prussian did not attack him, for the savage assault had terrified and astonished the officer as well as causing him suffering. When he was able to breathe freely, he said: "Unless you give me satisfaction with pistols I will kill you."

M. Dubuis replied: "Whenever you like. I'm quite ready."

The German said: "Here is the town of Strasbourg. I'll get two officers to be my seconds, and there will be time before the train leaves the station."

M. Dubuis, who was puffing as hard as the engine, said to the Englishmen: "Will you be my seconds?" They both answered together: "Oh, yes!"

And the train stopped.

In a minute the Prussian had found two comrades, who brought pistols, and they made their way toward the ramparts.

The Englishmen were continually looking at their watches, shuffling their feet and hurrying on with the preparations, uneasy lest they should be too late for the train.

M. Dubuis had never fired a pistol in his life.

They made him stand twenty paces away from his enemy. He was asked: "Are you ready?"

While he was answering, "Yes, monsieur," he noticed that one of the Englishmen had opened his umbrella in order to keep off the rays of the sun.

A voice gave the signal: "Fire!"

M. Dubuis fired at random without delay, and he was amazed to see the Prussian opposite him stagger, lift up his arms and fall forward, dead. He had killed the officer.

One of the Englishmen exclaimed: "Ah!" He was quivering with delight, with satisfied curiosity and joyous impatience. The other, who still kept his watch in his hand, seized M. Dubuis' arm and hurried him in double-quick time toward the station, his fellow-countryman marking time as he ran beside them, with closed fists, his elbows at his sides, "One, two; one, two!"

And all three, running abreast rapidly, made their way to the station like three grotesque figures in a comic newspaper.

The train was on the point of starting. They sprang into their carriage. Then the Englishmen, taking off their traveling caps, waved them three times over their heads, exclaiming: "Hip! hip! hurrah!"

And gravely, one after the other, they extended their right hands to M. Dubuis and then went back and sat down in their own corner.

Mother Sauvage

Fifteen years had passed since I was at Virelogne. I returned there in the autumn to shoot with my friend Serval, who had at last rebuilt his chateau, which the Prussians had destroyed.

I loved that district. It is one of those delightful spots which have a sensuous charm for the eyes. You love it with a physical love. We, whom the country enchants, keep tender memories of certain springs, certain woods, certain pools, certain hills seen very often which have stirred us like joyful events. Sometimes our thoughts turn back to a corner in a forest, or the end of a bank, or an orchard filled with flowers, seen but a single time on some bright day, yet remaining in our hearts like the image of certain women met in the street on a spring morning in their light, gauzy dresses, leaving in soul and body an unsatisfied desire which is not to be forgotten, a feeling that you have just passed by happiness.

At Virelogne I loved the whole countryside, dotted with little woods and crossed by brooks which sparkled in the sun and looked like veins carrying blood to the earth. You fished in them for crawfish, trout and eels. Divine happiness! You could bathe in places and you often found snipe among the high grass which grew along the borders of these small water courses.

I was stepping along light as a goat, watching my two dogs running ahead of me, Serval, a hundred meters to my right, was beating a field of lucerne. I turned round by the thicket which forms the boundary of the wood of Sandres and I saw a cottage in ruins.

Suddenly I remembered it as I had seen it the last time, in 1869: neat, covered with vines, with chickens before the door. What is sadder than a dead house, with its skeleton standing bare and sinister?

I also recalled that inside its doors, after a very tiring day, the good woman had given me a glass of wine to drink and that Serval had told me the history of its people. The father, an old poacher, had been killed by the gendarmes. The son, whom I had once seen, was a tall, dry fellow who also passed for a fierce slayer of game. People called them "the Savages."

Was that a name or a nickname?

I called to Serval. He came up with his long strides like a crane.

I asked him: "What became of those people?" This was his story:

When war was declared, the son Sauvage, who was then thirty-three years old, enlisted, leaving his mother alone in the house. People did not pity the old woman very much because she had money; they knew it.

She remained entirely alone in that isolated dwelling, so far from the village, on the edge of the wood. She was not afraid, however, being of the same strain as the men folk—a hardy old woman, tall and thin, who seldom laughed and with whom one never jested. The women of the fields laugh but little in any case, that is men's business. But they themselves have sad and narrowed hearts, leading a melancholy, gloomy life. The peasants imbibe a little noisy merriment at the tavern, but their helpmates always have grave, stern countenances. The muscles of their faces have never learned the motions of laughter.

Mother Sauvage continued her ordinary existence in her cottage, which was soon covered by the snows. She came to the village once a week to get bread and a little meat. Then she returned to her house. As there was talk of wolves, she went out with a gun upon her shoulder—her son's gun, rusty and with the butt worn by the rubbing of the hand—and she was a strange sight, the tall "Savage," a little bent, going with slow strides over the snow, the muzzle of the piece extending beyond the black headdress, which confined her head and imprisoned her white hair, which no one had ever seen.

One day a Prussian force arrived. It was billeted upon the inhabitants, according to the property and resources of each. Four were allotted to the old woman, who was known to be rich.

They were four great fellows with fair complexion, blond beards and blue eyes, who had not grown thin in spite of the fatigue which they had endured already and who also, though in a conquered country, had remained kind and gentle. Alone with this aged woman, they showed themselves full of consideration, sparing her, as much as they could, all expense and fatigue. They could be seen, all four of them, making their toilet at the well in their shirt-sleeves in the gray dawn, splashing with great swishes of water their pink-white northern skin, while Mother Sauvage went and came, preparing their soup. They would be seen cleaning the kitchen, rubbing the tiles, splitting wood, peeling potatoes, doing up all the housework like four good sons around their mother.

But the old woman thought always of her own son, so tall and thin, with his hooked nose and his brown eyes and his heavy mustache which made a roll of black hair upon his lip. She asked every day of each of the soldiers who were installed beside her hearth: "Do you know where the 23rd French marching regiment was sent? My boy is in it."

They invariably answered, "No, we don't know, don't know a thing at all." And, understanding her pain and her uneasiness—they who had mothers, too, there at home—they rendered her a thousand little services. She loved them well, moreover, her four enemies, since the peasantry have no patriotic hatred; that belongs to the upper class alone. The humble, those who pay the most because they are poor and because every new burden crushes them down; those who are killed in masses, who make the true cannon's prey because they are so many; those, in fine, who suffer most cruelly the atrocious miseries of war because they are the feeblest and offer least resistance—they hardly understand at all those bellicose ardors, that excitable sense of honor or those pretended political combinations which in six months exhaust two nations, the conqueror with the conquered.

They said in the district, in speaking of the Germans of Mother Sauvage: "There are four who have found a soft place."

Now, one morning, when the old woman was alone in the house, she observed, far off on the plain, a man coming toward her dwelling. Soon she recognized him; it was the postman to distribute the letters. He gave her a folded paper and she drew out of her case the spectacles which she used for sewing. Then she read:

MADAME SAUVAGE:

This letter is to inform you of sad news. Your boy Victor was killed yesterday by a shell which almost cut him in two. I was nearby, as we stood next each other in the company, and he told me about you and asked me to let you know on the same day if anything happened to him.

I took his watch, which was in his pocket, to bring it back to you when the war is done.

CESAIRE RIVOT,
Soldier of the 2d class, March.
Reg. no. 23.

The letter was dated three weeks back.

She did not cry at all. She remained motionless, so overcome and stupefied that she did not even suffer as yet. She thought: "There's

Victor killed now." Then little by little the tears came to her eyes and the sorrow filled her heart. Her thoughts came, one by one, dreadful, torturing. She would never kiss him again, her child, her big boy, never again! The gendarmes had killed the father, the Prussians had killed the son. He had been cut in two by a cannon ball. She seemed to see the thing, the horrible thing: the head falling, the eyes open, while he chewed the corner of his big mustache as he always did in moments of anger.

What had they done with his body afterward? If they had only let her have her boy back as they had brought back her husband—with the bullet in the middle of the forehead!

But she heard a noise of voices. It was the Prussians returning from the village. She hid her letter very quickly in her pocket, and she received them quietly, with her ordinary face, having had time to wipe her eyes.

They were laughing, all four, delighted, for they brought with them a fine rabbit—stolen, doubtless—and they made signs to the old woman that there was to be something good to eat.

She set herself to work at once to prepare breakfast, but when it came to killing the rabbit, her heart failed her. And yet it was not the first. One of the soldiers struck it down with a blow of his fist behind the ears.

The beast once dead, she skinned the red body, but the sight of the blood which she was touching, and which covered her hands, and which she felt cooling and coagulating, made her tremble from head to foot, and she kept seeing her big boy cut in two, bloody, like this still palpitating animal.

She sat down at table with the Prussians, but she could not eat, not even a mouthful. They devoured the rabbit without bothering themselves about her. She looked at them sideways, without speaking, her face so impassive that they perceived nothing.

All of a sudden she said: "I don't even know your names, and here's a whole month that we've been together." They understood, not without difficulty, what she wanted, and told their names.

That was not sufficient; she had them written for her on a paper, with the addresses of their families, and, resting her spectacles on her great nose, she contemplated that strange handwriting, then folded the sheet and put it in her pocket, on top of the letter which told her of the death of her son.

When the meal was ended she said to the men: "I am going to work for you."

And she began to carry up hay into the loft where they slept.

They were astonished at her taking all this trouble; she explained to them that thus they would not be so cold; and they helped her. They heaped the stacks of hay as high as the straw roof, and in that manner they made a sort of great chamber with four walls of fodder, warm and perfumed, where they should sleep splendidly.

At dinner one of them was worried to see that Mother Sauvage still ate nothing. She told him that she had pains in her stomach. Then she kindled a good fire to warm herself, and the four Germans ascended to their lodging-place by the ladder which served them every night for this purpose.

As soon as they closed the trapdoor the old woman removed the ladder, then opened the outside door noiselessly and went back to look for more bundles of straw, with which she filled her kitchen. She went barefoot in the snow, so softly that no sound was heard. From time to time she listened to the sonorous and unequal snoring of the four soldiers who were fast asleep.

When she judged her preparations to be sufficient, she threw one of the bundles into the fireplace, and when it was alight she scattered it over all the others. Then she went outside again and looked.

In a few seconds the whole interior of the cottage was illumined with a brilliant light and became a frightful brasier, a gigantic fiery furnace, whose glare streamed out of the narrow window and threw a glittering beam upon the snow.

Then a great cry issued from the top of the house; it was a clamor of men shouting heartrending calls of anguish and of terror. Finally the trapdoor having given way, a whirlwind of fire shot up into the loft, pierced the straw roof, rose to the sky like the immense flame of a torch, and all the cottage flared.

Nothing more was heard therein but the crackling of the fire, the cracking of the walls, the falling of the rafters. Suddenly the roof fell in and the burning carcass of the dwelling hurled a great plume of sparks into the air, amid a cloud of smoke.

The country, all white, lit up by the fire, shone like a cloth of silver tinted with red.

A bell, far off, began to toll.

The old "Savage" stood before her ruined dwelling, armed with her gun, her son's gun, for fear one of those men might escape.

When she saw that it was ended, she threw her weapon into the brasier. A loud report followed.

People were coming, the peasants, the Prussians.

They found the woman seated on the trunk of a tree, calm and satisfied.

A German officer, but speaking French like a son of France, demanded: "Where are your soldiers?"

She reached her bony arm toward the red heap of fire which was almost out and answered with a strong voice: "There!"

They crowded round her. The Prussian asked: "How did it take fire?"

"It was I who set it on fire."

They did not believe her, they thought that the sudden disaster had made her crazy. While all pressed round and listened, she told the story from beginning to end, from the arrival of the letter to the last shriek of the men who were burned with her house, and never omitted a detail.

When she had finished, she drew two pieces of paper from her pocket, and, in order to distinguish them by the last gleams of the fire, she again adjusted her spectacles. Then she said, showing one: "That, that is the death of Victor." Showing the other, she added, indicating the red ruins with a bend of the head: "Here are their names, so that you can write home." She quietly held a sheet of paper out to the officer, who held her by the shoulders, and she continued: "You must write how it happened, and you must say to their mothers that it was I who did that, Victoire Simon, the Savage! Do not forget."

The officer shouted some orders in German. They seized her, they threw her against the walls of her house, still hot. Then twelve men drew quickly up before her, at twenty paces. She did not move. She had understood; she waited.

An order rang out, followed instantly by a long report. A belated shot went off by itself, after the others.

The old woman did not fall. She sank as though they had cut off her legs.

The Prussian officer approached. She was almost cut in two, and in her withered hand she held her letter bathed with blood.

My friend Serval added: "It was by way of reprisal that the Germans destroyed the chateau of the district, which belonged to me."

I thought of the mothers of those four fine fellows burned in that house and of the horrible heroism of that other mother shot against the wall.

And I picked up a little stone, still blackened by the flames.

This Business of Latin

This business of Latin that has been dinned into our ears for some time past recalls to my mind a story—a story of my youth.

I was finishing my studies with a teacher, in a big central town, at the Institution Robineau, celebrated through the entire province for the special attention paid there to the study of Latin.

For the past ten years, the Robineau Institute beat the imperial lycée of the town at every competitive examination, and all the colleges of the subprefecture, and these constant successes were due, they said, to an usher, a simple usher, M. Piquedent, or rather Père Piquedent.

He was one of those middle-aged men quite gray, whose real age it is impossible to tell, and whose history we can guess at first glance. Having entered as an usher at twenty into the first institution that presented itself so that he could proceed to take first his degree of Master of Arts and afterward the degree of Doctor of Laws, he found himself so enmeshed in this routine that he remained an usher all his life. But his love for Latin did not leave him and harassed him like an unhealthy passion. He continued to read the poets, the prose writers, the historians, to interpret them and penetrate their meaning, to comment on them with a perseverance bordering on madness.

One day, the idea came into his head to oblige all the students in his class to answer him in Latin only; and he persisted in this resolution until at last they were capable of sustaining an entire conversation with him just as they would in their mother tongue. He listened to them, as a leader of an orchestra listens to his musicians rehearsing, and striking his desk every moment with his ruler, he exclaimed:

"Monsieur Lefrere, Monsieur Lefrere, you are committing a solecism! You forget the rule.

"Monsieur Plantel, your way of expressing yourself is altogether French and in no way Latin. You must understand the genius of a language. Look here, listen to me."

Now, it came to pass that the pupils of the Institution Robineau carried off, at the end of the year, all the prizes for composition, translation, and Latin conversation.

Next year, the principal, a little man, as cunning as an ape, whom he resembled in his grinning and grotesque appearance, had had printed on his programs, on his advertisements, and painted on the door of his institution: "Latin Studies a Specialty. Five first prizes carried off in the five classes of the lycée. Two honor prizes at the general examinations in competition with all the lycées and colleges of France."

For ten years the Institution Robineau triumphed in the same fashion. Now my father, allured by these successes, sent me as a day pupil to Robineau's—or, as we called it, Robinetto or Robinettino's—and made me take special private lessons from Père Piquedent at the rate of five francs per hour, out of which the usher got two francs and the principal three francs. I was then eighteen, and was in the philosophy class.

These private lessons were given in a little room looking out on the street. It so happened that Père Piquedent, instead of talking Latin to me, as he did when teaching publicly in the institution, kept telling me his troubles in French. Without relations, without friends, the poor man conceived an attachment to me, and poured out his misery to me.

He had never for the last ten or fifteen years chatted confidentially with anyone. "I am like an oak in a desert," he said; "sicut quercus in solitudine."

The other ushers disgusted him. He knew nobody in the town, since he had no time to devote to making acquaintances.

"Not even the nights, my friend, and that is the hardest thing on me. The dream of my life is to have a room with my own furniture, my own books, little things that belong to myself and which others may not touch. And I have nothing of my own, nothing except my trousers and my frock-coat, nothing, not even my mattress and my pillow! I have not four walls to shut myself up in, except when I come to give a lesson in this room. Do you see what this means—a man forced to spend his life without ever having the right, without ever finding the time, to shut himself up all alone, no matter where, to think, to reflect, to work, to dream? Ah! my dear boy, a key, the key of a door which one can lock—this is happiness, mark you, the only happiness!

"Here, all day long, teaching all those restless rogues, and during the night the dormitory with the same restless rogues snoring. And I have to sleep in the bed at the end of two rows of beds occupied by these youngsters whom I must look after. I can never be alone, never! If I go out I find the streets full of people, and, when I am tired of walking, I go into some cafe crowded with smokers and billiard play-ers. I tell you what, it is the life of a galley slave."

I said, "Why did you not take up some other line, Monsieur Piquedent?"

He exclaimed, "What, my little friend? I am not a shoemaker, or a joiner, or a hatter, or a baker, or a hairdresser. I only know Latin, and I have no diploma which would enable me to sell my knowledge at a high price. If I were a doctor I would sell for a hundred francs what I now sell for a hundred sous; and I would supply it probably of an inferior quality, for my title would be enough to sustain my reputa-tion."

Sometimes he would say to me: "I have no rest in life except in the hours spent with you. Don't be afraid! you'll lose nothing by that. I'll make it up to you in the classroom by making you speak twice as much Latin as the others."

One day, I grew bolder, and offered him a cigarette. He stared at me in astonishment at first, then he gave a glance toward the door. "If anyone were to come in, my dear boy?"

"Well, let us smoke at the window," said I.

And we went and leaned our elbows on the windowsill looking on the street, holding concealed in our hands the little rolls of tobacco. Just opposite to us was a laundry. Four women in loose white waists were passing hot, heavy irons over the linen spread out before them, from which a warm steam arose.

Suddenly, another, a fifth, carrying on her arm a large basket which made her stoop, came out to take the customers their shirts, their handkerchiefs, and their sheets. She stopped on the threshold as if she were already fatigued; then, she raised her eyes, smiled as she saw us smoking, flung at us, with her left hand, which was free, the sly kiss characteristic of a free-and-easy working-woman, and went away at a slow place, dragging her feet as she went.

She was a woman of about twenty, small, rather thin, pale, rather pretty, with a roguish air and laughing eyes beneath her ill-combed fair hair.

Père Piquedent, affected, began murmuring: "What an occupation for a woman! Really a trade only fit for a horse."

And he spoke with emotion about the misery of the people. He had a heart which swelled with lofty democratic sentiment, and he referred to the fatiguing pursuits of the working class with phrases borrowed from Jean-Jacques Rousseau, and with sobs in his throat.

Next day, as we were leaning our elbows on the same window sill, the same woman perceived us and cried out to us: "Good day, scholars!" in a comical sort of tone, while she made a contemptuous gesture with her hands.

I flung her a cigarette, which she immediately began to smoke. And the four other ironers rushed out to the door with outstretched hands to get cigarettes also.

And each day a friendly intercourse was established between the working women of the pavement and the idlers of the boarding school.

Père Piquedent was really a comical sight. He trembled at being noticed, for he might lose his position; and he made timid and ridiculous gestures, quite a theatrical display of love signals, to which the women responded with a regular fusillade of kisses.

A perfidious idea came into my mind. One day, on entering our room, I said to the old usher in a low tone: "You would not believe it, Monsieur Piquedent, I met the little washerwoman! You know the one I mean, the woman who had the basket, and I spoke to her!"

He asked, rather worried at my manner: "What did she say to you?"

"She said to me—why, she said she thought you were very nice. The fact of the matter is, I believe, I believe, that she is a little in love with you." I saw that he was growing pale.

"She is laughing at me, of course. These things don't happen at my age," he replied.

I said gravely: "How is that? You are all right."

As I felt that my trick had produced its effect on him, I did not press the matter. But every day I pretended that I had met the little laundress and that I had spoken to her about him, so that in the end he believed me, and sent her ardent and earnest kisses.

Now it happened that one morning, on my way to the boarding school, I really came across her. I accosted her without hesitation, as if I had known her for the last ten years.

"Good day, mademoiselle. Are you quite well?"

"Very well, monsieur, thank you."

"Will you have a cigarette?"

"Oh! not in the street."

"You can smoke it at home."

"In that case, I will."

"Let me tell you, mademoiselle, there's something you don't know."

"What is that, monsieur?"

"The old gentleman—my old professor, I mean—"

"Père Piquedent?"

"Yes, Père Piquedent. So you know his name?"

"Faith, I do! What of that?"

"Well, he is in love with you!"

She burst out laughing wildly, and exclaimed: "You are only fooling."

"Oh no, I am not fooling! He keeps talking of you all through the lesson. I bet that he'll marry you!"

She ceased laughing. The idea of marriage makes every girl serious. Then she repeated, with an incredulous air: "This is nonsense!"

"I swear to you, it's true."

She picked up her basket which she had laid down at her feet. "Well, we'll see," she said. And she went away.

Presently when I had reached the boarding school, I took Père Piquedent aside, and said: "You must write to her; she is infatuated with you."

And he wrote a long letter, tenderly affectionate, full of phrases and circumlocutions, metaphors and similes, philosophy and academic gallantry; and I took on myself the responsibility of delivering it to the young woman.

She read it with gravity, with emotion; then she murmured: "How well he writes! It is easy to see he has got education! Does he really mean to marry me?"

I replied intrepidly: "Faith, he has lost his head about you!"

"Then he must invite me to dinner on Sunday at the Île des Fleurs."

I promised that she should be invited.

Père Piquedent was much touched by everything I told him about her. I added: "She loves you, Monsieur Piquedent, and I believe her to be a decent girl. It is not right to lead her on and then abandon her."

He replied in a firm tone: "I hope I, too, am a decent man, my friend."

I confess I had at the time no plan. I was playing a practical joke, a schoolboy joke, nothing more. I had been aware of the simplicity of the old usher, his innocence and his weakness. I amused myself without asking myself how it would turn out. I was eighteen, and I had been for a long time looked upon at the lycée as a sly practical joker.

So it was agreed that Père Piquedent and I should set out in a hack for the ferry of Queue de Vache, that we should there pick up Angele, and that I should take them into my boat, for in those days I was fond of boating. I would then bring them to the Île des Fleurs, where the three of us would dine. I had inflicted myself on them, the better to enjoy my triumph, and the usher, consenting to my arrangement, proved clearly that he was losing his head by thus risking the loss of his position.

When we arrived at the ferry, where my boat had been moored since morning, I saw in the grass, or rather above the tall weeds of the bank, an enormous red parasol, resembling a monstrous wild poppy. Beneath the parasol was the little laundress in her Sunday clothes. I was surprised. She was really pretty, though pale; and graceful, though with a rather suburban grace.

Père Piquedent raised his hat and bowed. She put out her hand toward him, and they stared at one another without uttering a word. Then they stepped into my boat, and I took the oars. They were seated side by side near the stern.

The usher was the first to speak. "This is nice weather for a row in a boat."

She murmured, "Oh, yes."

She dipped her hand into the water, skimming the surface, making a thin, transparent film like a sheet of glass, which made a soft plashing along the side of the boat.

When they were in the restaurant, she took it on herself to speak, and ordered dinner, fried fish, a chicken, and salad; then she led us on toward the isle, which she knew perfectly.

After this, she was gay, romping, and even rather tantalizing.

Until dessert, no question of love arose. I had treated them to champagne, and Père Piquedent was tipsy. Herself slightly the worse, she called out to him: "Monsieur Piquenez."

He said abruptly: "Mademoiselle, Monsieur Raoul has communicated my sentiments to you."

She became as serious as a judge. "Yes, monsieur."

"What is your reply?"

"We never reply to these questions!"

He puffed with emotion, and went on: "Well, will the day ever come that you will like me?"

She smiled. "You big stupid! You are very nice."

"In short, mademoiselle, do you think that, later on, we might—"

She hesitated a second; then in a trembling voice she said: "Do you mean to marry me when you say that? For on no other condition, you know."

"Yes, mademoiselle!"

"Well, that's all right, Monsieur Piquedent!"

It was thus that these two silly creatures promised marriage to each other through the trick of a young scamp. But I did not believe that it was serious, nor, indeed, did they, perhaps.

"You know, I have nothing, not four sous," she said.

He stammered, for he was as drunk as Silenus: "I have saved five thousand francs."

She exclaimed triumphantly: "Then we can set up in business?"

He became restless. "In what business?"

"What do I know? We shall see. With five thousand francs we could do many things. You don't want me to go and live in your boarding school, do you?"

He had not looked forward so far as this, and he stammered in great perplexity: "What business could we set up in? That would not do, for all I know is Latin!"

She reflected in her turn, passing in review all her business ambitions. "You could not be a doctor?"

"No, I have no diploma."

"Or a chemist?"

"No more than the other."

She uttered a cry of joy. She had discovered it. "Then we'll buy a grocer's shop! Oh! what luck! we'll buy a grocer's shop. Not on a big scale, of course; with five thousand francs one does not go far."

He was shocked at the suggestion. "No, I can't be a grocer. I am—I am—too well known: I only know Latin, that is all I know."

But she poured a glass of champagne down his throat. He drank it and was silent.

We got back into the boat. The night was dark, very dark. I saw clearly, however, that he had caught her by the waist, and that they were hugging each other again and again.

It was a frightful catastrophe. Our escapade was discovered, with the result that Père Piquedent was dismissed. And my father, in a fit of anger, sent me to finish my course of philosophy at Ribaudet's school.

Six months later I took my degree of Bachelor of Arts. Then I went to study law in Paris, and did not return to my native town till two years later.

At the corner of the Rue de Serpent a shop caught my eye. Over the door were the words: "Colonial Products—Piquedent"; then underneath, so as to enlighten the most ignorant: "Grocery."

I exclaimed: "Quantum mutatus ab illo!"

Piquedent raised his head, left his female customer, and rushed toward me with outstretched hands.

"Ah! my young friend, my young friend, here you are! What luck! what luck!"

A beautiful woman, very plump, abruptly left the cashier's desk and flung herself on my breast. I had some difficulty in recognizing her, she had grown so stout.

I asked: "So then, you're doing well?"

Piquedent had gone back to weigh the groceries. "Oh very well, very well, very well. I have cleared three thousand francs this year!"

"And what about Latin, Monsieur Piquedent?"

"Oh, good heavens! Latin, Latin, Latin—you see it does not keep the pot boiling!"

Miss Harriet

There were seven of us in a coach, four women and three men; one of the latter sat on the box seat beside the coachman. We were ascending, at a snail's pace, the winding road up the steep cliff along the coast.

Setting out from Etretat at break of day in order to visit the ruins of Tancarville, we were still half asleep, benumbed by the fresh air of the morning. The women especially, who were little accustomed to these early excursions, half opened and closed their eyes every moment, nodding their heads or yawning, quite insensible to the beauties of the dawn.

It was autumn. On both sides of the road stretched the bare fields, yellowed by the stubble of wheat and oats which covered the soil like a beard that had been badly shaved. The moist earth seemed to steam. Larks were singing high up in the air, while other birds piped in the bushes.

The sun rose at length in front of us, bright red on the plane of the horizon, and in proportion as it ascended, growing clearer from minute to minute, the country seemed to awake, to smile, to shake itself like a young girl leaving her bed in her white robe of vapor. The Comte d'Etraille, who was seated on the box, cried: "Look! look! a hare!" and he extended his arm toward the left, pointing to a patch of clover. The animal scurried along, almost hidden by the clover, only its large ears showing. Then it swerved across a furrow, stopped, started off again at full speed, changed its course, stopped anew, uneasy, spying out every danger, uncertain what route to take, when suddenly it began to run with great bounds, disappearing finally in a large patch of beet-root. All the men had waked up to watch the course of the animal.

René Lamanoir exclaimed: "We are not at all gallant this morning," and; regarding his neighbor, the little Baroness de Serennes, who struggled against sleep, he said to her in a low tone: "You are thinking of your husband, baroness. Reassure yourself; he will not return before Saturday, so you have still four days."

She answered with a sleepy smile: "How stupid you are!" Then, shaking off her torpor, she added: "Now, let somebody say something to make us laugh. You, Monsieur Chenal, who have the reputation of having had more love affairs than the Duc de Richelieu, tell us a love story in which you have played a part; anything you like."

Leon Chenal, an old painter, who had once been very handsome, very strong, very proud of his physique and very popular with women, took his long white beard in his hand and smiled. Then, after a few moments' reflection, he suddenly became serious.

"Ladies, it will not be an amusing tale, for I am going to relate to you the saddest love affair of my life, and I sincerely hope that none of my friends may ever pass through a similar experience.

"I was twenty-five years of age and was pillaging along the coast of Normandy. I call 'pillaging' wandering about, with a knapsack on one's back, from inn to inn, under the pretext of making studies and sketching landscapes. I knew nothing more enjoyable than that happy-go-lucky wandering life, in which one is perfectly free, without shackles of any kind, without care, without preoccupation, without thinking even of the morrow. One goes in any direction one pleases, without any guide save his fancy, without any counselor save his eyes. One stops because a running brook attracts one, because the smell of potatoes frying tickles one's olfactories on passing an inn. Sometimes it is the perfume of clematis which decides one in his choice or the roguish glance of the servant at an inn. Do not despise me for my affection for these rustics. These girls have a soul as well as senses, not to mention firm cheeks and fresh lips; while their hearty and willing kisses have the flavor of wild fruit. Love is always love, come whence it may. A heart that beats at your approach, an eye that weeps when you go away are things so rare, so sweet, so precious that they must never be despised.

"I have had rendezvous in ditches full of primroses, behind the cow stable, and in barns among the straw, still warm from the heat of the day. I have recollections of coarse gray cloth covering supple peasant skin and regrets for simple, frank kisses, more delicate in their unaffected sincerity than the subtle favors of charming and distinguished women.

"But what one loves most amid all these varied adventures is the country, the woods, the rising of the sun, the twilight, the moonlight. These are, for the painter, honeymoon trips with Nature. One is alone with her in that long and quiet association. You go to sleep in the fields, amid marguerites and poppies, and when you open your eyes in the full glare of the sunlight you descry in the distance the little village with its pointed clock tower which sounds the hour of noon.

"You sit down by the side of a spring which gushes out at the foot of an oak, amid a growth of tall, slender weeds, glistening with life. You go down on your knees, bend forward and drink that cold, pellucid water which wets your mustache and nose; you drink it with a physical pleasure, as though you kissed the spring, lip to lip. Sometimes, when you find a deep hole along the course of these tiny brooks, you plunge in quite naked, and you feel on your skin, from head to foot, as it were, an icy and delicious caress, the light and gentle quivering of the stream.

"You are gay on the hills, melancholy on the edge of ponds, inspired when the sun is setting in an ocean of blood-red clouds and casts red reflections on the river. And at night, under the moon, which passes across the vault of heaven, you think of a thousand strange things which would never have occurred to your mind under the brilliant light of day.

"So, in wandering through the same country where we are this year, I came to the little village of Benouville, on the cliff between Yport and Etretat. I came from Fécamp, following the coast, a high coast as straight as a wall, with its projecting chalk cliffs descending perpendicularly into the sea. I had walked since early morning on the short grass, smooth and yielding as a carpet, that grows on the edge of the cliff. And, singing lustily, I walked with long strides, looking sometimes at the slow circling flight of a gull with its white curved wings outlined on the blue sky, sometimes at the brown sails of a fishing bark on the green sea. In short, I had passed a happy day, a day of liberty and of freedom from care.

"A little farmhouse where travelers were lodged was pointed out to me, a kind of inn, kept by a peasant woman, which stood in the center of a Norman courtyard surrounded by a double row of beeches.

"Leaving the coast, I reached the hamlet, which was hemmed in by great trees, and I presented myself at the house of Mother Lecacheur.

"She was an old, wrinkled, and stern peasant woman, who seemed always to receive customers under protest, with a kind of defiance.

"It was the month of May. The spreading apple trees covered the court with a shower of blossoms which rained unceasingly both upon people and upon the grass.

"I said: 'Well, Madame Lecacheur, have you a room for me?'

"Astonished to find that I knew her name, she answered: 'That depends; everything is let, but all the same I can find out.'

"In five minutes we had come to an agreement, and I deposited my bag upon the earthen floor of a rustic room, furnished with a bed, two chairs, a table and a washbowl. The room looked into the large, smoky kitchen, where the lodgers took their meals with the people of the farm and the landlady, who was a widow.

"I washed my hands, after which I went out. The old woman was making a chicken fricassee for dinner in the large fireplace in which hung the iron pot, black with smoke.

"'You have travelers, then, at the present time?' said I to her.

"She answered in an offended tone of voice: 'I have a lady, an English lady, who has reached years of maturity. She occupies the other room.'

"I obtained, by means of an extra five sous a day, the privilege of dining alone out in the yard when the weather was fine.

"My place was set outside the door, and I was beginning to gnaw the lean limbs of the Normandy chicken, to drink the clear cider, and to munch the hunk of white bread, which was four days old but excellent.

"Suddenly the wooden gate which gave on the highway was opened, and a strange lady directed her steps toward the house. She was very thin, very tall, so tightly enveloped in a red Scotch plaid shawl that one might have supposed she had no arms, if one had not seen a long hand appear just above the hips, holding a white tourist umbrella. Her face was like that of a mummy, surrounded with curls of gray hair, which tossed about at every step she took and made me think, I know not why, of a pickled herring in curl papers. Lowering her eyes, she passed quickly in front of me and entered the house.

"That singular apparition cheered me. She undoubtedly was my neighbor, the English lady of mature age of whom our hostess had spoken.

"I did not see her again that day. The next day, when I had settled myself to commence painting at the end of that beautiful valley which you know and which extends as far as Etretat, I perceived, on lifting my eyes suddenly, something singular standing on the crest of the cliff, one might have said a pole decked out with flags. It was she. On seeing me, she suddenly disappeared. I reentered the house at midday for lunch and took my seat at the general table, so as to make the acquaintance of this odd character. But she did not respond to my polite advances, was insensible even to my little attentions. I poured out water for her persistently, I passed her the dishes with great eagerness. A slight, almost imperceptible, movement of the head and an English word, murmured so low that I did not understand it, were her only acknowledgments.

"I ceased occupying myself with her, although she had disturbed my thoughts.

"At the end of three days I knew as much about her as did Madame Lecacheur herself.

"She was called Miss Harriet. Seeking out a secluded village in which to pass the summer, she had been attracted to Benouville some six months before and did not seem disposed to leave it. She never spoke at table, ate rapidly, reading all the while a small book of Protestant propaganda. She gave a copy of it to everybody. The curé himself had received no fewer than four copies, conveyed by an urchin to whom she had paid two sous commission. She said sometimes to our hostess abruptly, without preparing her in the least for the declaration: 'I love the Savior more than anything. I admire Him in all creation; I adore Him in all nature; I carry Him always in my heart.'

"And she would immediately present the old woman with one of her tracts which were destined to convert the universe.

"In the village she was not liked. In fact, the schoolmaster having pronounced her an atheist, a kind of stigma attached to her. The curé, who had been consulted by Madame Lecacheur, responded: 'She is a heretic, but God does not wish the death of the sinner, and I believe her to be a person of pure morals.'

"These words, 'atheist,' 'heretic,' words which no one can precisely define, cast doubts into some minds. It was asserted, however, that this Englishwoman was rich and that she had passed her life in traveling through every country in the world because her family had cast her off. Why had her family cast her off? Because of her impiety, of course!

"She was, in fact, one of those people of exalted principles; one of those opinionated puritans, of which England produces so many; one of those good and insupportable old maids who haunt the tables d'hôte of every hotel in Europe, who spoil Italy, poison Switzerland, render the charming cities of the Mediterranean uninhabitable, carry everywhere their fantastic manias their manners of petrified vestals, their indescribable toilets and a certain odor of India rubber which makes one believe that at night they are slipped into a rubber casing.

"Whenever I caught sight of one of these individuals in a hotel I fled like the birds that see a scarecrow in a field.

"This woman, however, appeared so very singular that she did not displease me.

"Madame Lecacheur, instinctively hostile to everything that was not rustic, felt in her narrow soul a kind of hatred for the ecstatic declarations of the old maid. She had found a phrase by which to describe her, a term of contempt that rose to her lips, called forth by I know not what confused and mysterious mental ratiocination. She said: 'That woman is a demoniac.' This epithet, applied to that aus-tere and sentimental creature, seemed to me irresistibly droll. I myself never called her anything now but 'the demoniac,' experiencing a sin-gular pleasure in pronouncing aloud this word on perceiving her.

"One day I asked Mother Lecacheur: 'Well, what is our demoniac about today?'

"To which my rustic friend replied with a shocked air: 'What do you think, sir? She picked up a toad which had had its paw crushed and carried it to her room and has put it in her washbasin and ban-daged it as if it were a man. If that is not profanation I should like to know what is!'

"On another occasion, when walking along the shore she bought a large fish which had just been caught, simply to throw it back into the sea again. The sailor from whom she had bought it, although she paid him handsomely, now began to swear, more exasperated, indeed, than if she had put her hand into his pocket and taken his money. For more than a month he could not speak of the circumstance without becoming furious and denouncing it as an outrage. Oh, yes! She was indeed a demoniac, this Miss Harriet, and Mother Lecacheur must have had an inspiration in thus christening her.

"The stable boy, who was called Sapeur because he had served in Africa in his youth, entertained other opinions. He said with a rogu-ish air: 'She is an old hag who has seen life.'

"If the poor woman had but known!

"The little kind-hearted Céleste did not wait upon her willingly, but I was never able to understand why. Probably her only reason was that she was a stranger, of another race; of a different tongue and of another religion. She was, in fact, a demoniac!

"She passed her time wandering about the country, adoring and seeking God in nature. I found her one evening on her knees in a cluster of bushes. Having discovered something red through the leaves,

I brushed aside the branches, and Miss Harriet at once rose to her feet, confused at having been found thus, fixing on me terrified eyes like those of an owl surprised in open day.

"Sometimes, when I was working among the rocks, I would suddenly descry her on the edge of the cliff like a lighthouse signal. She would be gazing in rapture at the vast sea glittering in the sunlight and the boundless sky with its golden tints. Sometimes I would distinguish her at the end of the valley, walking quickly with her elastic English step, and I would go toward her, attracted by I know not what, simply to see her illuminated visage, her dried-up, ineffable features, which seemed to glow with inward and profound happiness.

"I would often encounter her also in the corner of a field, sitting on the grass under the shadow of an apple tree, with her little religious pamphlet lying open on her knee while she gazed out at the distance.

"I could not tear myself away from that quiet country neighborhood, to which I was attached by a thousand links of love for its wide and peaceful landscape. I was happy in this sequestered farm, far removed from everything, but in touch with the earth, the good, beautiful, green earth. And—must I avow it?—there was, besides, a little curiosity which retained me at the residence of Mother Lecacheur. I wished to become acquainted a little with this strange Miss Harriet and to know what transpires in the solitary souls of those wandering old Englishwomen.

"We became acquainted in a rather singular manner. I had just finished a study which appeared to me to be worth something, and so it was, as it sold for ten thousand francs fifteen years later. It was as simple, however, as two and two make four and was not according to academic rules. The whole right side of my canvas represented a rock, an enormous rock, covered with sea-wrack, brown, yellow and red, across which the sun poured like a stream of oil. The light fell upon the rock as though it were aflame without the sun, which was at my back, being visible. That was all. A first bewildering study of blazing, gorgeous light.

"On the left was the sea, not the blue sea, the slate-colored sea, but a sea of jade, greenish, milky and solid beneath the deep-colored sky.

"I was so pleased with my work that I danced from sheer delight as I carried it back to the inn. I would have liked the whole world to see it at once. I can remember that I showed it to a cow that was browsing by the wayside, exclaiming as I did so: 'Look at that, my ancient beauty; you will not often see its like again.'

"When I had reached the house I immediately called out to Mother Lecacheur, shouting with all my might: 'Hullo there! Mrs. Landlady, come here and look at this.'

"The rustic approached and looked at my work with her stupid eyes which distinguished nothing and could not even tell whether the picture represented an ox or a house.

"Miss Harriet just then came home, and she passed behind me just as I was holding out my canvas at arm's length, exhibiting it to our landlady. The demoniac could not help but see it, for I took care to exhibit the thing in such a way that it could not escape her notice. She stopped abruptly and stood motionless, astonished. It was her rock which was depicted, the one which she climbed to dream away her time undisturbed.

"She uttered a British 'Aoh,' which was at once so accentuated and so flattering that I turned round to her, smiling, and said: 'This is my latest study, mademoiselle.'

"She murmured rapturously, comically and tenderly: 'Oh monsieur, you understand nature as a living thing.'

"I colored and was more touched by that compliment than if it had come from a queen. I was captured, conquered, vanquished. I could have embraced her, upon my honor.

"I took my seat at table beside her as usual. For the first time she spoke, thinking aloud: 'Oh, I do love nature!'

"I passed her some bread, some water, some wine. She now accepted these with the little smile of a mummy. I then began to talk about the scenery.

"After the meal we rose from the table together and walked leisurely across the courtyard; then, attracted doubtless by the fiery glow which the setting sun cast over the surface of the sea, I opened the gate which led to the cliff, and we walked along side by side, as contented as two persons might be who have just learned to understand and penetrate each other's motives and feelings.

"It was one of those warm, soft evenings which impart a sense of ease to flesh and spirit alike. All is enjoyment, everything charms. The balmy air, laden with the perfume of grasses and the smell of seaweed, soothes the olfactory sense with its wild fragrance, soothes the palate with its sea savor, soothes the mind with its pervading sweetness.

"We were now walking along the edge of the cliff, high above the boundless sea which rolled its little waves below us at a distance of a hundred meters. And we drank in with open mouth and expanded chest that fresh breeze, briny from kissing the waves, that came from the ocean and passed across our faces.

"Wrapped in her plaid shawl, with a look of inspiration as she faced the breeze, the Englishwoman gazed fixedly at the great sun ball as it descended toward the horizon. Far off in the distance a three-master in full sail was outlined on the blood-red sky and a steamship, somewhat nearer, passed along, leaving behind it a trail of smoke on the horizon. The red sun globe sank slowly lower and lower and presently touched the water just behind the motionless vessel, which, in its dazzling effulgence, looked as though framed in a flame of fire. We saw it plunge, grow smaller and disappear, swallowed up by the ocean.

"Miss Harriet gazed in rapture at the last gleams of the dying day. She seemed longing to embrace the sky, the sea, the whole land-scape. She murmured: 'Aoh! I love—I love——' I saw a tear in her eye. She continued: 'I wish I were a little bird, so that I could mount up into the firmament.'

"She remained standing as I had often before seen her, perched on the cliff, her face as red as her shawl. I should have liked to have sketched her in my album. It would have been a caricature of ecstasy.

"I turned away so as not to laugh.

"I then spoke to her of painting as I would have done to a fellow artist, using the technical terms common among the devotees of the profession. She listened attentively, eagerly seeking to divine the mean-ing of the terms, so as to understand my thoughts. From time to time she would exclaim: 'Oh, I understand, I understand. It is very interest-ing.'

"We returned home.

"The next day, on seeing me, she approached me, cordially hold-ing out her hand; and we at once became firm friends.

"She was a good creature who had a kind of soul on springs, which became enthusiastic at a bound. She lacked equilibrium like all women who are spinsters at the age of fifty. She seemed to be preserved in a pickle of innocence, but her heart still retained something very youth-ful and inflammable. She loved both nature and animals with a fer-vor, a love like old wine fermented through age, with a sensuous love that she had never bestowed on men.

"One thing is certain, that the sight of a bitch nursing her puppies, a mare roaming in a meadow with a foal at its side, a bird's nest full of young ones, screaming, with their open mouths and their enormous heads, affected her perceptibly. Poor, solitary, sad, wandering beings! I love you ever since I became acquainted with Miss Harriet.

"I soon discovered that she had something she would like to tell me, but dare not, and I was amused at her timidity. When I started out in the morning with my knapsack on my back, she would accompany me in silence as far as the end of the village, evidently struggling to find words with which to begin a conversation. Then she would leave me abruptly and walk away quickly with her springy step.

"One day, however, she plucked up courage: 'I would like to see how you paint pictures. Are you willing? I have been very curious.' And she blushed as if she had said something very audacious.

"I conducted her to the bottom of the Petit-Val, where I had begun a large picture.

"She remained standing behind me, following all my gestures with concentrated attention. Then, suddenly, fearing perhaps that she was disturbing me, she said: 'Thank you,' and walked away.

"But she soon became more friendly, and accompanied me every day, her countenance exhibiting visible pleasure. She carried her camp stool under her arm, not permitting me to carry it. She would remain there for hours, silent and motionless, following with her eyes the point of my brush, in its every movement. When I obtained unexpectedly just the effect I wanted by a dash of color put on with the palette knife, she involuntarily uttered a little 'Ah!' of astonishment, of joy, of admiration. She had the most tender respect for my canvases, an almost religious respect for that human reproduction of a part of nature's work divine. My studies appeared to her a kind of religious pictures, and sometimes she spoke to me of God, with the idea of converting me.

"Oh, he was a queer, good-natured being, this God of hers! He was a sort of village philosopher without any great resources and without great power, for she always figured him to herself as inconsolable over injustices committed under his eyes, as though he were powerless to prevent them.

"She was, however, on excellent terms with him, affecting even to be the confidante of his secrets and of his troubles. She would say: 'God wills' or 'God does not will,' just like a sergeant announcing to a recruit: 'The colonel has commanded.'

"At the bottom of her heart she deplored my ignorance of the intentions of the Eternal, which she endeavored to impart to me.

"Almost every day I found in my pockets, in my hat when I lifted it from the ground, in my paintbox, in my polished shoes, standing in front of my door in the morning, those little pious tracts which she no doubt received directly from Paradise.

"I treated her as one would an old friend, with unaffected cordiality. But I soon perceived that she had changed somewhat in her manner, though, for a while, I paid little attention to it.

"When I was painting, whether in my valley or in some country lane, I would see her suddenly appear with her rapid, springy walk. She would then sit down abruptly, out of breath, as though she had been running or were overcome by some profound emotion. Her face would be red, that English red which is denied to the people of all other countries; then, without any reason, she would turn ashy pale and seem about to faint away. Gradually, however, her natural color would return and she would begin to speak.

"Then, without warning, she would break off in the middle of a sentence, spring up from her seat and walk away so rapidly and so strangely that I was at my wits' end to discover whether I had done or said anything to displease or wound her.

"I finally came to the conclusion that those were her normal manners, somewhat modified no doubt in my honor during the first days of our acquaintance.

"When she returned to the farm, after walking for hours on the windy coast, her long curls often hung straight down, as if their springs had been broken. This had hitherto seldom given her any concern, and she would come to dinner without embarrassment all disheveled by her sister, the breeze.

"But now she would go to her room and arrange the untidy locks, and when I would say, with familiar gallantry—which, however, always offended her—'You are as beautiful as a star today, Miss Harriet,' a blush would immediately rise to her cheeks, the blush of a young girl, a girl of fifteen.

"Then she would suddenly become quite reserved and cease coming to watch me paint. I thought, 'This is only a fit of temper; it will blow over.' But it did not always blow over, and when I spoke to her she would answer me either with affected indifference or with sullen annoyance.

"She became by turns rude, impatient, and nervous. I never saw her now except at meals, and we spoke but little. I concluded at length that I must have offended her in some way, and, accordingly, I said to her one evening: 'Miss Harriet, why is it that you do not act toward me as before? What have I done to displease you? You are causing me much pain!'

"She replied in a most comical tone of anger: 'I am just the same with you as before. It is not true, not true,' and she ran upstairs and shut herself up in her room.

"Occasionally she would look at me in a peculiar manner. I have often said to myself since then that those who are condemned to death must look thus when they are informed that their last day has come. In her eye there lurked a species of insanity, an insanity at once mystical and violent; and even more, a fever, an aggravated longing, impatient and impotent, for the unattained and unattainable.

"Nay, it seemed to me there was also going on within her a struggle in which her heart wrestled with an unknown force that she sought to master, and even, perhaps, something else. But what do I know? What do I know?

"It was indeed a singular revelation.

"For some time I had commenced to work, as soon as daylight appeared, on a picture the subject of which was as follows: A deep ravine, enclosed, surmounted by two thickets of trees and vines, extended into the distance and was lost, submerged in that milky vapor, in that cloud like cotton down that sometimes floats over valleys at daybreak. And at the extreme end of that heavy, transparent fog one saw, or, rather, surmised, that a couple of human beings were approaching, a human couple, a youth and a maiden, their arms interlaced, embracing each other, their heads inclined toward each other, their lips meeting. A first ray of the sun, glistening through the branches, pierced that fog of the dawn, illuminated it with a rosy reflection just behind the rustic lovers, framing their vague shadows in a silvery background. It was well done; yes, indeed, well done.

"I was working on the declivity which led to the Valley of Etretat. On this particular morning I had, by chance, the sort of floating vapor which I needed. Suddenly something rose up in front of me like a phantom; it was Miss Harriet. On seeing me she was about to flee. But I called after her, saying: 'Come here, come here, mademoiselle. I have a nice little picture for you.'

"She came forward, though with seeming reluctance. I handed her my sketch. She said nothing, but stood for a long time, motionless, looking at it, and suddenly she burst into tears. She wept spasmodically, like men who have striven hard to restrain their tears, but who can do so no longer and abandon themselves to grief, though still resisting. I sprang to my feet, moved at the sight of a sorrow I did not comprehend, and I took her by the hand with an impulse of brusque affection, a true French impulse which acts before it reflects.

"She let her hands rest in mine for a few seconds, and I felt them quiver as if all her nerves were being wrenched. Then she withdrew her hands abruptly, or, rather, snatched them away.

"I recognized that tremor, for I had felt it, and I could not be deceived. Ah! the love tremor of a woman, whether she be fifteen or fifty years of age, whether she be of the people or of society, goes so straight to my heart that I never have any hesitation in understanding it!

"Her whole frail being had trembled, vibrated, been overcome. I knew it. She walked away before I had time to say a word, leaving me as surprised as if I had witnessed a miracle and as troubled as if I had committed a crime.

"I did not go in to breakfast. I went to take a turn on the edge of the cliff, feeling that I would just as much weep as laugh, looking on the adventure as both comic and deplorable and my position as ridiculous, believing her unhappy enough to go insane.

"I asked myself what I ought to do. It seemed best for me to leave the place, and I immediately resolved to do so.

"Somewhat sad and perplexed, I wandered about until dinnertime and entered the farmhouse just when the soup had been served up.

"I sat down at the table as usual. Miss Harriet was there, eating away solemnly, without speaking to anyone, without even lifting her eyes. Her manner and expression were, however, the same as usual.

"I waited patiently till the meal had been finished, when, turning toward the landlady, I said: 'Well, Madame Lecacheur, it will not be long now before I shall have to take my leave of you.'

"The good woman, at once surprised and troubled, replied in her drawling voice: 'My dear sir, what is it you say? You are going to leave us after I have become so accustomed to you?'

"I glanced at Miss Harriet out of the corner of my eye. Her countenance did not change in the least. But Céleste, the little servant, looked up at me. She was a fat girl, of about eighteen years of age, rosy, fresh, as strong as a horse, and possessing the rare attribute of cleanliness. I had kissed her at odd times in out-of-the-way corners, after the manner of travelers—nothing more.

"The dinner being at length over, I went to smoke my pipe under the apple trees, walking up and down from one end of the enclosure to the other. All the reflections which I had made during the day, the

strange discovery of the morning, that passionate and grotesque attachment for me, the recollections which that revelation had suddenly
called up, recollections at once charming and perplexing, perhaps also
that look which the servant had cast on me at the announcement of
my departure—all these things, mixed up and combined, put me now
in a reckless humor, gave me a tickling sensation of kisses on the lips
and in my veins a something which urged me on to commit some
folly.

"Night was coming on, casting its dark shadows under the trees,
when I descried Céleste, who had gone to fasten up the poultry yard
at the other end of the enclosure. I darted toward her, running so
noiselessly that she heard nothing, and as she got up from closing the
small trapdoor by which the chickens got in and out, I clasped her in
my arms and rained on her coarse, fat face a shower of kisses. She
struggled, laughing all the time, as she was accustomed to do in such
circumstances. Why did I suddenly loose my grip of her? Why did I at
once experience a shock? What was it that I heard behind me?

"It was Miss Harriet, who had come upon us, who had seen us and
who stood in front of us motionless as a specter. Then she disappeared
in the darkness.

"I was ashamed, embarrassed, more desperate at having been thus
surprised by her than if she had caught me committing some criminal act.

"I slept badly that night. I was completely unnerved and haunted
by sad thoughts. I seemed to hear loud weeping, but in this I was no
doubt deceived. Moreover, I thought several times that I heard someone walking up and down in the house and opening the hall door.

"Toward morning I was overcome by fatigue and fell asleep. I got
up late and did not go downstairs until the late breakfast, being still in
a bewildered state, not knowing what kind of expression to put on.

"No one had seen Miss Harriet. We waited for her at table, but she
did not appear. At length Mother Lecacheur went to her room. The
Englishwoman had gone out. She must have set out at break of day, as
she was wont to do, in order to see the sun rise.

"Nobody seemed surprised at this, and we began to eat in silence.

"The weather was hot, very hot, one of those broiling, heavy days
when not a leaf stirs. The table had been placed out of doors, under
an apple tree, and from time to time Sapeur had gone to the cellar to
draw a jug of cider, everybody was so thirsty. Céleste brought the dishes
from the kitchen, a ragout of mutton with potatoes, a cold rabbit and

a salad. Afterward she placed before us a dish of strawberries, the first of the season.

"As I wished to wash and freshen these, I begged the servant to go and draw me a pitcher of cold water.

"In about five minutes she returned, declaring that the well was dry. She had lowered the pitcher to the full extent of the cord and had touched the bottom, but on drawing the pitcher up again it was empty. Mother Lecacheur, anxious to examine the thing for herself, went and looked down the hole. She returned, announcing that one could see clearly something in the well, something altogether unusual. But this no doubt was bundles of straw, which a neighbor had thrown in out of spite.

"I wished to look down the well also, hoping I might be able to clear up the mystery, and I perched myself close to the brink. I perceived indistinctly a white object. What could it be? I then conceived the idea of lowering a lantern at the end of a cord. When I did so the yellow flame danced on the layers of stone and gradually became clearer. All four of us were leaning over the opening, Sapeur and Céleste having now joined us. The lantern rested on a black-and-white indistinct mass, singular, incomprehensible. Sapeur exclaimed:

"'It is a horse. I see the hoofs. It must have got out of the meadow during the night and fallen in headlong.'

"But suddenly a cold shiver froze me to the marrow. I first recognized a foot, then a leg sticking up; the whole body and the other leg were completely under water.

"I stammered out in a loud voice, trembling so violently that the lantern danced hither and thither over the slipper: 'It is a woman! Who—who—can it be? It is Miss Harriet!'

"Sapeur alone did not manifest horror. He had witnessed many such scenes in Africa.

"Mother Lecacheur and Céleste began to utter piercing screams and ran away.

"But it was necessary to recover the corpse of the dead woman. I attached the young man securely by the waist to the end of the pulley rope and lowered him very slowly, watching him disappear in the darkness. In one hand he held the lantern and a rope in the other. Soon I recognized his voice, which seemed to come from the center of the earth, saying: 'Stop!'

"I then saw him fish something out of the water. It was the other leg. He then bound the two feet together and shouted anew: 'Haul up!'

"I began to wind up, but I felt my arms crack, my muscles twitch, and I was in terror lest I should let the man fall to the bottom. When his head appeared at the brink I asked: 'Well?' as if I expected he had a message from the drowned woman.

"We both got on the stone slab at the edge of the well and from opposite sides we began to haul up the body.

"Mother Lecacheur and Céleste watched us from a distance, concealed from view behind the wall of the house. When they saw issuing from the hole the black slippers and white stockings of the drowned person they disappeared.

"Sapeur seized the ankles, and we drew up the body of the poor woman. The head was shocking to look at, being bruised and lacerated, and the long gray hair, out of curl forevermore, hanging down tangled and disordered.

"'In the name of all that is holy! how lean she is,' exclaimed Sapeur in a contemptuous tone.

"We carried her into the room, and as the women did not put in an appearance I, with the assistance of the stable lad, dressed the corpse for burial.

"I washed her disfigured face. Under the touch of my finger an eye was slightly opened and regarded me with that pale, cold look, that terrible look of a corpse which seems to come from the beyond. I braided as well as I could her disheveled hair and with my clumsy hands arranged on her head a novel and singular coiffure. Then I took off her dripping wet garments, baring, not without a feeling of shame, as though I had been guilty of some profanation, her shoulders and her chest and her long arms, as slim as the twigs of a tree.

"I next went to fetch some flowers, poppies, bluets, marguerites and fresh, sweet-smelling grass with which to strew her funeral couch.

"I then had to go through the usual formalities, as I was alone to attend to everything. A letter found in her pocket, written at the last moment, requested that her body be buried in the village in which she had passed the last days of her life. A sad suspicion weighed on my heart. Was it not on my account that she wished to be laid to rest in this place?

"Toward evening all the female gossips of the locality came to view the remains of the defunct, but I would not allow a single person to enter. I wanted to be alone, and I watched beside her all night.

"I looked at the corpse by the flickering light of the candles, at this unhappy woman, unknown to us all, who had died in such a lamentable manner and so far away from home. Had she left no friends, no relations behind her? What had her infancy been? What had been her life? Whence had she come thither alone, a wanderer, lost like a dog driven from home? What secrets of sufferings and of despair were sealed up in that unprepossessing body, in that poor body whose outward appearance had driven from her all affection, all love?

"How many unhappy beings there are! I felt that there weighed upon that human creature the eternal injustice of implacable nature! It was all over with her, without her ever having experienced, perhaps, that which sustains the greatest outcasts to wit, the hope of being loved once! Otherwise why should she thus have concealed herself, fled from the face of others? Why did she love everything so tenderly and so passionately, everything living that was not a man?

"I recognized the fact that she believed in a God, and that she hoped to receive compensation from the latter for all the miseries she had endured. She would now disintegrate and become, in turn, a plant. She would blossom in the sun, the cattle would browse on her leaves, the birds would bear away the seeds, and through these changes she would become again human flesh. But that which is called the soul had been extinguished at the bottom of the dark well. She suffered no longer. She had given her life for that of others yet to come.

"Hours passed away in this silent and sinister communion with the dead. A pale light at length announced the dawn of a new day; then a red ray streamed in on the bed, making a bar of light across the coverlet and across her hands. This was the hour she had so much loved. The awakened birds began to sing in the trees.

"I opened the window to its fullest extent and drew back the curtains that the whole heavens might look in upon us, and, bending over the icy corpse, I took in my hands the mutilated head and slowly, without terror or disgust, I imprinted a kiss, a long kiss, upon those lips which had never before been kissed."

Leon Chenal remained silent. The women wept. We heard on the box seat the Count d'Atraille blowing his nose from time to time. The coachman alone had gone to sleep. The horses, who no longer felt the sting of the whip, had slackened their pace and moved along slowly. The coach, hardly advancing at all, seemed suddenly torpid, as if it had been freighted with sorrow.

Monsieur Parent

George's father was sitting in an iron chair, watching his little son with concentrated affection and attention, as little George piled up the sand into heaps during one of their walks. He would take up the sand with both hands, make a mound of it, and put a chestnut leaf on top. His father saw no one but him in that public park full of people.

The sun was just disappearing behind the roofs of the Rue Saint-Lazare, but still shed its rays obliquely on that little, overdressed crowd. The chestnut trees were lighted up by its yellow rays, and the three fountains before the lofty porch of the church had the appearance of liquid silver.

Monsieur Parent, accidentally looking up at the church clock, saw that he was five minutes late. He got up, took the child by the arm, shook his dress, which was covered with sand, wiped his hands, and led him in the direction of the Rue Blanche. He walked quickly, so as not to get in after his wife, and the child could not keep up with him. He took him up and carried him, though it made him pant when he had to walk up the steep street. He was a man of forty, already turning gray, and rather stout. At last he reached his house. An old servant who had brought him up, one of those trusted servants who are the tyrants of families, opened the door to him.

"Has madame come in yet?" he asked anxiously.

The servant shrugged her shoulders: "When have you ever known madame to come home at half-past six, monsieur?"

"Very well; all the better; it will give me time to change my things, for I am very warm."

The servant looked at him with angry and contemptuous pity. "Oh, I can see that well enough," she grumbled. "You are covered with perspiration, monsieur. I suppose you walked quickly and carried the child, and only to have to wait until half-past seven, perhaps, for madame. I have made up my mind not to have dinner ready on time. I shall get it for eight o'clock, and if you have to wait, I cannot help it; roast meat ought not to be burnt!"

Monsieur Parent pretended not to hear, but went into his own room, and as soon as he got in, locked the door, so as to be alone, quite alone. He was so used now to being abused and badly treated that he never thought himself safe except when he was locked in.

What could he do? To get rid of Julie seemed to him such a formidable thing to do that he hardly ventured to think of it, but it was just as impossible to uphold her against his wife, and before another month the situation would become unbearable between the two. He remained sitting there, with his arms hanging down, vaguely trying to discover some means to set matters straight, but without success. He said to himself: "It is lucky that I have George; without him I should be very miserable."

Just then the clock struck seven, and he started up. Seven o'clock, and he had not even changed his clothes. Nervous and breathless, he undressed, put on a clean shirt, hastily finished his toilet, as if he had been expected in the next room for some event of extreme importance, and went into the drawing-room, happy at having nothing to fear. He glanced at the newspaper, went and looked out of the window, and then sat down again, when the door opened, and the boy came in, washed, brushed, and smiling. Parent took him up in his arms and kissed him passionately; then he tossed him into the air, and held him up to the ceiling, but soon sat down again, as he was tired with all his exertion. Then, taking George on his knee, he made him ride horseback. The child laughed and clapped his hands and shouted with pleasure, as did his father, who laughed until his big stomach shook, for it amused him almost more than it did the child.

Parent loved him with all the heart of a weak, resigned, ill-used man. He loved him with mad bursts of affection, with caresses and with all the bashful tenderness which was hidden in him, and which had never found an outlet, even at the early period of his married life, for his wife had always shown herself cold and reserved.

Just then Julie came to the door, with a pale face and glistening eyes, and said in a voice which trembled with exasperation: "It is half-past seven, monsieur."

Parent gave an uneasy and resigned look at the clock and replied: "Yes, it certainly is half-past seven."

"Well, my dinner is quite ready now."

Seeing the storm which was coming, he tried to turn it aside. "But did you not tell me when I came in that it would not be ready before eight?"

"Eight! what are you thinking of? You surely do not mean to let the child dine at eight o'clock? It would ruin his stomach. Just suppose that he only had his mother to look after him! She cares a great deal about her child. Oh, yes, we will speak about her; she is a mother! What a pity it is that there should be any mothers like her!"

Parent thought it was time to cut short a threatened scene. "Julie," he said, "I will not allow you to speak like that of your mistress. You understand me, do you not? Do not forget it in the future."

The old servant, who was nearly choked with surprise, turned and went out, slamming the door so violently after her that the lusters on the chandelier rattled, and for some seconds it sounded as if a number of little invisible bells were ringing in the drawing-room.

Eight o'clock struck, the door opened, and Julie came in again. She had lost her look of exasperation, but now she put on an air of cold and determined resolution, which was still more formidable.

"Monsieur," she said, "I served your mother until the day of her death, and I have attended to you from your birth until now, and I think it may be said that I am devoted to the family."

She waited for a reply, and Parent stammered: "Why, yes, certainly, my good Julie."

"You know quite well," she continued, "that I have never done anything for the sake of money, but always for your sake; that I have never deceived you nor lied to you, that you have never had to find fault with me."

"Certainly, my good Julie."

"Very well, then, monsieur; it cannot go on any longer like this. I have said nothing, and left you in your ignorance, out of respect and admiration for you, but it is too much, and everyone in the neighborhood is laughing at you. Everybody knows about it, and so I must tell you also, although I do not like to repeat it. The reason why madame comes in at any time she chooses is that she is doing abominable things."

He seemed stupefied and not to understand, and could only stammer out: "Hold your tongue; you know I have forbidden you——"

But she interrupted him with irresistible resolution. "No, monsieur, I must tell you everything now. For a long time madame has been carrying on with Monsieur Limousin. I have seen them kiss scores of times behind the door. Ah! you may be sure that if Monsieur Limousin had been rich, madame would never have married Monsieur Parent. If you remember how the marriage was brought about, you would understand the matter from beginning to end."

Parent had risen, and stammered out, his face livid: "Hold your tongue! Hold your tongue, or——"

She went on, however: "No, I mean to tell you everything. She married you from self-interest, and she deceived you from the very first day. It was all settled between them beforehand. You need only reflect for a few moments to understand it, and then, as she was not satisfied with having married you, as she did not love you, she has made your life miserable, so miserable that it has almost broken my heart when I have seen it."

He walked up and down the room with hands clenched, repeating: "Hold your tongue, hold your tongue——" For he could find nothing else to say. The old servant, however, would not yield; she seemed resolved on everything.

George, who had been at first astonished and then frightened at those angry voices, began to utter shrill screams, and remained behind his father, with his face puckered up and his mouth open, roaring.

His son's screams exasperated Parent, and filled him with rage and courage. He rushed at Julie with both arms raised, ready to strike her, exclaiming: "Ah! you wretch. You will drive the child out of his senses." He already had his hand on her, when she screamed in his face:

"Monsieur, you may beat me if you like, me who raised you, but that will not prevent your wife from deceiving you, or alter the fact that your child is not yours——"

He stopped suddenly, let his arms fall, and remained standing opposite to her, so overwhelmed that he could understand nothing more.

"You need only to look at the child," she added, "to know who the father is! He is the very image of Monsieur Limousin. You need only look at his eyes and forehead. Why, even a blind man could see that!"

He had taken her by the shoulders, and was now shaking her with all his might. "Viper, viper!" he said. "Go out the room, viper! Go out, or I shall kill you! Go out! Go out!"

And with a desperate effort he threw her into the next room. She fell across the table, which was laid for dinner, breaking the glasses. Then, rising to her feet, she put the table between her master and herself. While he was pursuing her, in order to take hold of her again, she flung terrible words at him:

"You need only go out this evening after dinner, and come in again immediately, and you will see! You will see whether I have been lying! Just try it, and you will see." She had reached the kitchen door and escaped, but he ran after her, up the back stairs to her bedroom, into which she had locked herself, and knocking at the door, he said:

"You will leave my house this very instant!"

"You may be certain of that, monsieur," was her reply. "In an hour's time I shall not be here any longer."

He then went slowly downstairs again, holding on to the banister so as not to fall, and went back to the drawing-room, where little George was sitting on the floor, crying. He fell into a chair, and looked at the child with dull eyes. He understood nothing, knew nothing more; he felt dazed, stupefied, mad, as if he had just fallen on his head, and he scarcely even remembered the dreadful things the servant had told him. Then, by degrees, his mind, like muddy water, became calmer and clearer, and the abominable revelations began to work in his heart.

He was no longer thinking of George. The child was quiet now and sitting on the carpet; but, seeing that no notice was being taken of him, he began to cry. His father ran to him, took him in his arms, and covered him with kisses. His child remained to him, at any rate! What did the rest matter? He held him in his arms and pressed his lips to his light hair, and, relieved and composed, he whispered:

"George—my little George—my dear little George——" But he suddenly remembered what Julie had said! Yes, she had said that he was Limousin's child. Oh! it could not be possible, surely. He could not believe it, could not doubt, even for a moment, that he was his own child. It was one of those low scandals which spring from servants' brains! And he repeated: "George—my dear little George." The youngster was quiet again, now that his father was fondling him.

Parent felt the warmth of the little chest penetrate through his clothes, and it filled him with love, courage, and happiness; that gentle warmth soothed him, fortified him and saved him. Then he put the small, curly head away from him a little, and looked at it affectionately, still repeating: "George! Oh, my little George!" But suddenly he thought:

"Suppose he were to resemble Limousin, after all!" He looked at him with haggard, troubled eyes, and tried to discover whether there was any likeness in his forehead, in his nose, mouth, or cheeks. His thoughts wandered as they do when a person is going mad, and his child's face changed in his eyes, and assumed a strange look and improbable resemblances.

The hall bell rang. Parent gave a bound as if a bullet had gone through him. "There she is," he said. "What shall I do?" And he ran and locked himself up in his room, to have time to bathe his eyes. But in a few moments another ring at the bell made him jump again, and then he remembered that Julie had left, without the housemaid knowing it, and so nobody would go to open the door. What was he to do? He went himself, and suddenly he felt brave, resolute, ready for dissimulation and the struggle. The terrible blow had matured him in a few moments. He wished to know the truth, he desired it with the rage of a timid man, and with the tenacity of an easy-going man who has been exasperated.

Nevertheless, he trembled. Does one know how much excited cowardice there often is in boldness? He went to the door with furtive steps, and stopped to listen; his heart beat furiously. Suddenly, however, the noise of the bell over his head startled him like an explosion. He seized the lock, turned the key, and opening the door, saw his wife and Limousin standing before him on the stairs.

With an air of astonishment, which also betrayed a little irritation, she said:

"So you open the door now? Where is Julie?"

His throat felt tight and his breathing was labored as he tried to reply, without being able to utter a word.

"Are you dumb?" she continued. "I asked you where Julie is?"

"She—she—has—gone——" he managed to stammer.

His wife began to get angry. "What do you mean 'gone'? Where has she gone? Why?"

By degrees he regained his coolness. He felt an intense hatred rise up in him for that insolent woman who was standing before him.

"Yes, she has gone altogether. I sent her away."

"You have sent away Julie? Why, you must be mad."

"Yes, I sent her away because she was insolent, and because—because she was mstreating the child."

"Julie?"

"Yes—Julie."

"What was she insolent about?"

"About you."

"About me?"

"Yes, because the dinner was burnt, and you did not come in."

"And she said——"

"She said—offensive things about you—which I ought not—which I could not listen to——"

"What did she, say?"

"There's no point repeating them."

"I want to hear them."

"She said it was unfortunate for a man like me to be married to a woman like you, unpunctual, careless, disorderly, a bad mother, and a bad wife."

The young woman had gone into the anteroom, followed by Limousin, who did not say a word at this unexpected state of things. She shut the door quickly, threw her cloak on a chair, and going straight up to her husband, she stammered out: "You say? You say? That I am—"

Very pale and calm, he replied: "I say nothing, my dear. I am simply repeating what Julie said to me, as you wanted to know what it was, and I wish you to remark that I dismissed her just on account of what she said."

She trembled with a violent longing to tear out his beard and scratch his face. In his voice and manner she felt that he was asserting his position as master. Although she had nothing to say by way of reply, she tried to assume the offensive by saying something unpleasant. "I suppose you have had dinner?" she asked.

"No, I waited for you."

She shrugged her shoulders impatiently. "It is very stupid of you to wait after half-past seven," she said. "You might have guessed that I was detained, that I had a good many things to do, visits and shopping."

And then, suddenly, she felt that she wanted to explain how she had spent her time, and told him in abrupt, haughty words that, having to buy some furniture in a shop a long distance off, very far off, in the Rue de Rennes, she had met Limousin at past seven o'clock on the Boulevard Saint-Germain, and that then she had gone with him to have something to eat in a restaurant, as she did not like to go to one by herself, although she was faint with hunger. That was how she had dined with Limousin, if it could be called dining, for they had only some soup and half a chicken, as they were in a great hurry to get back.

Parent replied simply: "Well, you were quite right. I am not finding fault with you."

Then Limousin, who, had not spoken till then, and who had been half hidden behind Henriette, came forward and put out his hand, saying: "Are you well?"

Parent took his hand, and shaking it gently, replied: "Yes, I am very well."

But the young woman had felt a reproach in her husband's last words. "'Finding fault'! Why do you speak of finding fault? One might think that you meant to imply something."

"Not at all," he replied, by way of excuse. "I simply meant that I was not at all anxious although you were late, and that I did not find fault with you for it."

She, however, took the high hand, and tried to find a pretext for a quarrel. "Although I was late? One might really think that it was one o'clock in the morning, and that I spent my nights away from home."

"Certainly not, my dear. I said late because I could find no other word. You said you should be back at half-past six, and you returned at half-past eight. That was surely being late. I understand it perfectly well. I am not at all surprised, even. But—but—I can hardly use any other word."

"But you pronounce them as if I had been out all night."

"Oh, no—oh, no!"

She saw that he would yield on every point, and she was going into her own room, when at last she noticed that George was screaming, and then she asked, with some feeling: "What is the matter with the child?"

"I told you that Julie had been rather unkind to him."

"What has the wretch been doing to him?"

"Oh nothing much. She gave him a push, and he fell down."

She wanted to see her child, and ran into the dining room, but stopped short at the sight of the table covered with spilt wine, with broken decanters and glasses and overturned saltcellars. "Who did all that mischief?" she asked.

"It was Julie, who——" But she interrupted him furiously:

"That is too much, really! Julie speaks of me as if I were a shameless woman, beats my child, breaks my plates and dishes, turns my house upside down, and it appears that you think it all quite natural."

"Certainly not, as I have got rid of her."

"Really! You have got rid of her! But you ought to have had her arrested. In such cases, one ought to call in the Commissary of Police!"

"But—my dear—I really could not. There was no reason. It would have been very difficult——"

She shrugged her shoulders disdainfully. "There! you will never be anything but a poor, wretched fellow, a man without a will, without any firmness or energy. Ah! she must have said some nice things to you, your Julie, to make you dismiss her like that. I should like to have been here for a minute, only for a minute." Then she opened the drawing-room door and ran to George, took him into her arms and kissed him, and said: "Georgie, what is it, my darling, my pretty one, my treasure?"

Then, suddenly turning to another idea, she said: "But the child has had no dinner? You have had nothing to eat, my pet?"

"No, mamma."

Then she again turned furiously upon her husband. "Why, you must be mad, utterly mad! It is half-past eight, and George has had no dinner!"

He excused himself as best he could, for he had nearly lost his wits through the overwhelming scene and the explanation, and felt crushed by this ruin of his life. "But, my dear, we were waiting for you, as I did not wish to dine without you. As you come home late every day, I expected you every moment."

She threw her bonnet, which she had kept on till then, into an easy-chair, and in an angry voice she said: "It is really intolerable to have to do with people who can understand nothing, who can divine nothing and do nothing by themselves. So, I suppose, if I were to come in at twelve o'clock at night, the child would have had nothing to eat? Just as if you could not have understood that, as it was after half-past seven, I was prevented from coming home, that I had met with some hindrance!"

Parent trembled, for he felt that his anger was getting the upper hand, but Limousin interposed, and turning toward the young woman, said:

"My dear friend, you, are altogether unjust. Parent could not guess that you would come here so late, as you never do so, and then, how could you expect him to get over the difficulty all by himself, after having sent away Julie?"

But Henriette was very angry, and replied: "Well, at any rate, he must get over the difficulty himself, for I will not help him," she replied. "Let him settle it!" And she went into her own room, quite forgetting that her child had not had anything to eat.

Limousin immediately set to work to help his friend. He picked up the broken glasses which strewed the table and took them out, replaced the plates and knives and forks, and put the child into his high-chair, while Parent went to look for the chambermaid to wait at table. The girl came in, in great astonishment, as she had heard nothing in

George's room, where she had been working. She soon, however, brought in the soup, a burnt leg of mutton, and mashed potatoes.

Parent sat by the side of the child, very much upset and distressed at all that had happened. He gave the boy his dinner, and endeavored to eat something himself, but he could only swallow with an effort, as his throat felt paralyzed. By degrees he was seized with an insane desire to look at Limousin, who was sitting opposite to him, making bread pellets, to see whether George was like him, but he did not venture to raise his eyes for some time. At last, however, he made up his mind to do so, and gave a quick, sharp look at the face which he knew so well, although he almost fancied that he had never examined it carefully. It looked so different to what he had imagined. From time to time he looked at Limousin, trying to recognize a likeness in the smallest lines of his face, in the slightest features, and then he looked at his son, under the pretext of feeding him.

Two words were sounding in his ears: "His father! his father! his father!" They buzzed in his temples at every beat of his heart. Yes, that man, that tranquil man who was sitting on the other side of the table, was, perhaps, the father of his son, of George, of his little George. Parent left off eating; he could not swallow any more. A terrible pain, one of those attacks of pain which make men scream, roll on the ground, and bite the furniture, was tearing at his entrails, and he felt inclined to take a knife and plunge it into his stomach. He started when he heard the door open. His wife came in.

"I am hungry," she said; "aren't you, Limousin?"

He hesitated a little, and then said: "Yes, I am, upon my word." She had the leg of mutton brought in again. Parent asked himself "Have they had dinner? Or are they late because they have had a lovers' tryst?"

They both ate with a very good appetite. Henriette was very calm, but laughed and joked. Her husband watched her furtively. She had on a pink tea-gown trimmed with white lace, and her fair head, her white neck and her plump hands stood out from that coquettish and perfumed dress as though it were a seashell edged with foam.

What fun they must be making of him, if he had been their dupe since the first day! Was it possible to make a fool of a man, of a worthy man, because his father had left him a little money? Why could one not see into people's souls? How was it that nothing revealed to upright hearts the deceits of infamous hearts? How was it that voices had the same sound for adoring as for lying? Why was a false, deceptive look the same as a sincere one? And he watched them, waiting to catch a gesture, a word, an intonation. Then suddenly he thought: "I will surprise them this evening," and he said:

"My dear, as I have dismissed Julie, I will see about getting another girl this very evening. I will go at once to procure one by tomorrow morning, so I may not be in until late."

"Very well," she replied; "go. I shall not stir from here. Limousin will keep me company. We will wait for you." Then, turning to the maid, she said: "You had better put George to bed, and then you can clear away and go up to your room."

Parent had got up; he was unsteady on his legs, dazed and bewildered, and saying, "I shall see you again later on," he went out, holding on to the wall, for the floor seemed to roll like a ship. George had been carried out by his nurse, while Henriette and Limousin went into the drawing-room.

As soon as the door was shut, Limousin said: "You must be mad, surely, to torment your husband as you do?"

She immediately turned on him: "Ah! Do you know that I think the habit you have got into lately, of looking upon Parent as a martyr, is very unpleasant?"

Limousin threw himself into an easy-chair and crossed his legs. "I am not setting him up as a martyr in the least, but I think that, in our situation, it is ridiculous to defy this man as you do, from morning till night."

She took a cigarette from the mantelpiece, lighted it, and replied: "But I do not defy him; quite the contrary. Only he irritates me by his stupidity, and I treat him as he deserves."

Limousin continued impatiently: "What you are doing is very foolish! I am only asking you to treat your husband gently, because we both need him to trust us. I think that you ought to see that."

They were close together: he, tall, dark, with long whiskers and the rather vulgar manners of a good-looking man who is very well satisfied with himself; she, small, fair, and pink, a little Parisian, born in the back room of a shop, half cocotte and half bourgeoise, brought up to entice customers to the store by her glances, and married, in consequence, to a simple, unsophisticated man, who saw her outside the door every morning when he went out and every evening when he came home.

"But do you not understand, you great fool," she said, "that I hate him exactly because he married me, because he bought me, in fact;

because everything that he says and does, everything that he thinks, acts on my nerves? He exasperates me every moment by his stupidity, which you call his kindness; by his dullness, which you call his confidence, and then, above all, because he is my husband, instead of you. I feel him between us, although he does not interfere with us much. And then—and then! No, it is, after all, too idiotic of him not to guess anything! I wish he would, at any rate, be a little jealous. There are moments when I feel inclined to say to him: 'Do you not see, you stupid creature, that Paul is my lover?' It is quite incomprehensible that you cannot understand how hateful he is to me, how he irritates me. You always seem to like him, and you shake hands with him cordially. Men are very extraordinary at times."

"One must know how to dissimulate, my dear."

"It is not a question of dissimulation, but of feeling. One might think that, when you men deceive one another, you like each other better on that account, while we women hate a man from the moment that we have betrayed him."

"I do not see why one should hate an excellent fellow because one is friendly with his wife."

"You do not see it? You do not see it? You, all of you, are wanting in refinement of feeling. However, that is one of those things which one feels and cannot express. And then, moreover, one ought not. No, you would not understand; it is quite useless! You men have no delicacy of feeling."

And smiling, with the gentle contempt of an impure woman, she put both her hands on his shoulders and held up her lips to him. He stooped down and clasped her closely in his arms, and their lips met. And as they stood in front of the mantel mirror, another couple exactly like them embraced behind the clock.

They had heard nothing, neither the noise of the key nor the creaking of the door, but suddenly Henriette, with a loud cry, pushed Limousin away, and they saw Parent looking at them, livid with rage, without his shoes on and his hat over his forehead. He looked at each, one after the other, with a quick glance and without moving his head. He appeared beside himself. Then, without saying a word, he threw himself on Limousin, seized him as if he were going to strangle him, and flung him into the opposite corner of the room so violently that the other lost his balance, and, beating the air with his hand, struck his head violently against the wall.

When Henriette saw that her husband was going to murder her

lover, she threw herself on Parent, seized him by the neck, and digging her ten delicate, rosy fingers into his neck, she squeezed him so tightly, with all the vigor of a desperate woman, that the blood spurted out under her nails, and she bit his shoulder, as if she wished to tear it with her teeth. Parent, half-strangled and choking, loosened his hold on Limousin in order to shake off his wife, who was hanging to his neck. Putting his arms round her waist, he flung her also to the other end of the drawing-room.

Then, as his passion was short-lived, like that of most good-tempered men, and his strength was soon exhausted, he remained standing between the two, panting, worn out, not knowing what to do next. His brutal fury had expended itself in that effort, like the froth of a bottle of champagne, and his unwonted energy ended in a gasping for breath. As soon as he could speak, however, he said: "Go away—both of you—immediately! Go away!"

Limousin remained motionless in his corner, against the wall, too startled to understand anything as yet, too frightened to move a finger; while Henriette, with her hands resting on a small, round table, her head bent forward, her hair hanging down, the bodice of her dress unfastened, waited like a wild animal that is about to spring. Parent continued in a stronger voice: "Go away immediately. Get out of the house!"

His wife, however, seeing that he had got over his first exasperation, grew bolder, drew herself up, took two steps toward him, and, grown almost insolent, she said: "Have you lost your head? What is the matter with you? What is the meaning of this unjustifiable violence?"

But he turned toward her, and raising his fist to strike her, he stammered out: "Oh—oh—this is too much, too much! I heard everything! Everything—do you understand? Everything! You wretch—you wretch! You are two wretches! Get out of the house, both of you! Immediately, or I shall kill you! Leave the house!"

She saw that it was all over, and that he knew everything; that she could not prove her innocence, and that she must comply. But all her impudence had returned to her, and her hatred for the man, which was aggravated now, drove her to audacity, made her feel the need of bravado, and of defying him, and she said in a clear voice: "Come, Limousin; as he is going to turn me out of doors, I will go to your lodgings with you."

But Limousin did not move, and Parent, in a fresh access of rage, cried out: "Go, will you? Go, you wretches! Or else—or else——" He seized a chair and whirled it over his head.

Henriette walked quickly across the room, took her lover by the arm, dragged him from the wall, to which he appeared fixed, and led him toward the door, saying: "Do come, my friend—you see that the man is mad. Do come!"

As she went out she turned round to her husband, trying to think of something that she could do, something that she could invent to wound him to the heart as she left the house, and an idea struck her, one of those venomous, deadly ideas in which all a woman's perfidy shows itself, and she said resolutely: "I am going to take my child with me."

Parent was stupefied, and stammered: "Your—your child? You dare to talk of 'your' child? You venture—you venture to ask for your child— after—after——Oh, oh, that is too much! Go, you vile creature! Go!"

She went up to him again, almost smiling, almost avenged already, and defying him, standing close to him, and face to face, she said: "I want my child, and you have no right to keep him, because he is not yours—do you understand? He is not yours! He is Limousin's!"

And Parent cried out in bewilderment: "You lie—you lie—worthless woman!"

But she continued: "You fool! Everybody knows it except you. I tell you, this is his father. You need only look at him to see it."

Parent staggered backward, and then he suddenly turned round, took a candle, and rushed into the next room; returning almost immediately, carrying little George wrapped up in his bedclothes. The child, who had been suddenly awakened, was crying from fright. Parent threw him into his wife's arms, and then, without speaking, he pushed her roughly out toward the stairs, where Limousin was waiting, from motives of prudence.

Then he shut the door again, double-locked and bolted it, but had scarcely got back into the drawing-room when he fell to the floor at full length.

Parent lived alone, quite alone. During the five weeks that followed their separation, the feeling of surprise at his new life prevented him from thinking much. He had resumed his bachelor life, his habits of lounging about, and took his meals at a restaurant, as he had done formerly. As he wished to avoid any scandal, he gave his wife an allowance, which was arranged by their lawyers. By degrees, however, the thought of the child began to haunt him. Often, when he was at home alone at night, he suddenly thought he heard George calling out "Papa," and his heart would begin to beat, and he would get up quickly and open the door, to see whether by chance the child might have returned, as dogs or pigeons do. Why should a child have less instinct than an animal? On finding that he was mistaken, he would sit down in his armchair again and think of the boy. He would think of him for hours and whole days. It was not only a moral, but still more a physical obsession, a nervous longing to kiss him, to hold and fondle him, to take him on his knees and dance him. He felt the child's little arms around his neck, his little mouth pressing a kiss on his beard, his soft hair tickling his cheeks, and the remembrance of all those childish ways made him suffer as a man might for some beloved woman who has left him. Twenty or a hundred times a day he asked himself the question whether he was or was not George's father, and almost before he was in bed every night he recommenced the same series of despairing questionings.

He especially dreaded the darkness of the evening, the melancholy feeling of the twilight. Then a flood of sorrow invaded his heart, a torrent of despair which seemed to overwhelm him and drive him mad. He was as afraid of his own thoughts as men are of criminals, and he fled before them as one does from wild beasts. Above all things, he feared his empty, dark, horrible dwelling and the deserted streets, in which, here and there, a gas lamp flickered, where the isolated foot passenger whom one hears in the distance seems to be a night prowler, and makes one walk faster or slower, according to whether he is coming toward you or following you.

And in spite of himself, and by instinct, Parent went in the direction of the broad, well-lighted, populous streets. The light and the crowd attracted him, occupied his mind and distracted his thoughts, and when he was tired of walking aimlessly about among the moving crowd, when he saw the foot passengers becoming more scarce and the pavements less crowded, the fear of solitude and silence drove him into some large cafe full of drinkers and of light. He went there as flies go to a candle, and he would sit down at one of the little round tables and ask for a "bock," which he would drink slowly, feeling uneasy every time a customer got up to go. He would have liked to take him by the arm, hold him back, and beg him to stay a little longer, so much did he dread the time when the waiter should come up to him and say sharply: "Come, monsieur, it is closing time!"

He thus got into the habit of going to the beer houses, where the

continual elbowing of the drinkers brings you in contact with a familiar and silent public, where the heavy clouds of tobacco smoke lull
disquietude, while the heavy beer dulls the mind and calms the heart.
He almost lived there. He was scarcely up before he went there to find
people to distract his glances and his thoughts, and soon, as he felt
too lazy to move, he took his meals there.

After every meal, during more than an hour, he sipped three or
four small glasses of brandy, which stupefied him by degrees, and then
his head drooped on his chest, he shut his eyes, and went to sleep.
Then, awaking, he raised himself on the red velvet seat, straightened
his waistcoat, pulled down his cuffs, and took up the newspapers again,
though he had already seen them in the morning, and read them all
through again, from beginning to end. Between four and five o'clock
he went for a walk on the boulevards, to get a little fresh air, as he used
to say, and then came back to the seat which had been reserved for
him, and asked for his absinthe. He would talk to the regular customers whose acquaintance he had made. They discussed the news of the
day and political events, and that carried him on till dinner time; and
he spent the evening as he had the afternoon, until it was time to
close. That was a terrible moment for him when he was obliged to go
out into the dark, into his empty room full of dreadful recollections,
of horrible thoughts, and of mental agony. He no longer saw any of
his old friends, none of his relatives, nobody who might remind him
of his past life. But as his apartments were a hell to him, he took a
room in a large hotel, a good room on the ground floor, so as to see
the passersby. He was no longer alone in that great building. He felt
people swarming round him, he heard voices in the adjoining rooms,
and when his former sufferings tormented him too much at the sight
of his bed, which was turned down, and of his solitary fireplace, he
went out into the wide passages and walked up and down them like a
sentinel, before all the closed doors, and looked sadly at the shoes
standing in couples outside them, women's little boots by the side of
men's thick ones, and he thought that, no doubt, all these people
were happy, and were sleeping in their warm beds. Five years passed
thus; five miserable years. But one day, when he was taking his usual
walk between the Madeleine and the Rue Drouot, he suddenly saw a
lady whose bearing struck him. A tall gentleman and a child were with
her, and all three were walking in front of him. He asked himself
where he had seen them before, when suddenly he recognized a move-

ment of her hand; it was his wife, his wife with Limousin and his child, his little George.

His heart beat as if it would suffocate him, but he did not stop, for he wished to see them, and he followed them. They looked like a family of the better middle-class. Henriette was leaning on Paul's arm, and speaking to him in a low voice, and looking at him sideways occasionally. Parent got a side view of her and recognized her pretty features, the movements of her lips, her smile, and her coaxing glances. But the child chiefly took up his attention. How tall and strong he was! Parent could not see his face, but only his long, fair curls. That tall boy with bare legs, who was walking by his mother's side like a little man, was George. He saw them suddenly, all three, as they stopped in front of a shop. Limousin had grown very gray, had aged and was thinner; his wife, on the contrary, was as young-looking as ever, and had grown stouter. George he would not have recognized, he was so different from what he had been formerly.

They went on again and Parent followed them. He walked on quickly, passed them, and then turned round, so as to meet them face to face. As he passed the child he felt a mad longing to take him into his arms and run off with him, and he knocked against him as if by accident. The boy turned round and looked at the clumsy man angrily, and Parent hurried away, shocked, hurt, and pursued by that look. He went off like a thief, seized with a horrible fear lest he should have been seen and recognized by his wife and her lover. He went to his cafe without stopping, and fell breathless into his chair. That evening he drank three absinthes. For four months he felt the pain of that meeting in his heart. Every night he saw the three again, happy and tranquil, father, mother, and child walking on the boulevard before going in to dinner, and that new vision effaced the old one. It was another matter, another hallucination now, and also a fresh pain. Little George, his little George, the child he had so much loved and so often kissed, disappeared in the far distance, and he saw a new one, like a brother of the first, a little boy with bare legs, who did not know him! He suffered terribly at that thought. The child's love was dead; there was no bond between them; the child would not have held out his arms when he saw him. He had even looked at him angrily.

Then, by degrees he grew calmer, his mental torture diminished, the image that had appeared to his eyes and which haunted his nights became more indistinct and less frequent. He began once more to live nearly like everybody else, like all those idle people who drink beer off marble-topped tables and wear out their clothes on the threadbare velvet of the couches.

He grew old amid the smoke from pipes, lost his hair under the gas lights, looked upon his weekly bath, on his fortnightly visit to the barber's to have his hair cut, and on the purchase of a new coat or hat as an event. When he got to his cafe in a new hat he would look at himself in the glass for a long time before sitting down, and take it off and put it on again several times, and at last ask his friend, the lady at the bar, who was watching him with interest, whether she thought it suited him.

Two or three times a year he went to the theatre, and in the summer he sometimes spent his evenings at one of the open-air concerts in the Champs-Élysées. And so the years followed each other slow, monotonous, and short, because they were quite uneventful.

He very rarely now thought of the dreadful drama which had wrecked his life; for twenty years had passed since that terrible evening. But the life he had led since then had worn him out. The landlord of his cafe would often say to him: "You ought to pull yourself together a little, Monsieur Parent; you should get some fresh air and go into the country. I assure you that you have changed very much within the last few months." And when his customer had gone out he used to say to the barmaid: "That poor Monsieur Parent is booked for another world; it is bad never to get out of Paris. Advise him to go out of town for a day occasionally; he has confidence in you. Summer will soon be here; that will put him straight."

And she, full of pity and kindness for such a regular customer, said to Parent every day: "Come, monsieur, make up your mind to get a little fresh air. It is so charming in the country when the weather is fine. Oh, if I could, I would spend my life there!"

By degrees he was seized with a vague desire to go just once and see whether it was really as pleasant there as she said, outside the walls of the great city. One morning he said to her: "Do you know where one can get a good luncheon in the neighborhood of Paris?"

"Go to the Terrace at Saint-Germain; it is delightful there!"

He had been there formerly, just when he became engaged. He made up his mind to go there again, and he chose a Sunday, for no special reason, but merely because people generally do go out on Sundays, even when they have nothing to do all the week; and so one Sunday morning he went to Saint-Germain. He felt low-spirited and vexed at having yielded to that new longing, and at having broken through his usual habits. He was thirsty; he would have liked to get out at every station and sit down in the cafe which he saw outside and drink a bock or two, and then take the first train back to Paris. The journey seemed very long to him. He could remain sitting for whole days, as long as he had the same motionless objects before his eyes, but he found it very trying and fatiguing to remain sitting while he was being whirled along, and to see the whole country fly by, while he himself was motionless.

However, he found the Seine interesting every time he crossed it. Under the bridge at Chatou he saw some small boats going at great speed under the vigorous strokes of the bare-armed oarsmen, and he thought: "There are some fellows who are certainly enjoying themselves!" The train entered the tunnel just before you get to the station at Saint-Germain, and presently stopped at the platform. Parent got out, and walked slowly, for he already felt tired, toward the Terrace, with his hands behind his back, and when he got to the iron balustrade, stopped to look at the distant horizon. The immense plain spread out before him vast as the sea, green and studded with large villages, almost as populous as towns. The sun bathed the whole landscape in its full, warm light. The Seine wound like an endless serpent through the plain, flowed round the villages and along the slopes. Parent inhaled the warm breeze, which seemed to make his heart young again, to enliven his spirits, and to vivify his blood, and said to himself: "Why, it is delightful here."

Then he went on a few steps, and stopped again to look about him. The utter misery of his existence seemed to be brought into full relief by the intense light which inundated the landscape. He saw his twenty years of cafe life—dull, monotonous, heartbreaking. He might have traveled as others did, have gone among foreigners, to unknown countries beyond the sea, have interested himself somewhat in everything which other men are passionately devoted to, in arts and science; he might have enjoyed life in a thousand forms, that mysterious life which is either charming or painful, constantly changing, always inexplicable and strange. Now, however, it was too late. He would go on drinking bock after bock until he died, without any family, without friends, without hope, without any curiosity about anything, and he was seized with a feeling of misery and a wish to run away, to hide himself in Paris, in his cafe and his lethargy! All the thoughts, all the dreams, all the desires which are dormant in the slough of stagnating hearts had reawakened, brought to life by those rays of sunlight on the plain.

Parent felt that if he were to remain there any longer he should lose his reason, and he made haste to get to the Pavilion Henri IV for lunch, to try and forget his troubles under the influence of wine and alcohol, and at any rate to have someone to speak to.

He took a small table in one of the arbors, from which one can see all the surrounding country, ordered his lunch, and asked to be served at once. Then some more people arrived and sat down at tables near him. He felt more comfortable; he was no longer alone. Three persons were eating luncheon near him. He looked at them two or three times without seeing them clearly, as one looks at total strangers. Suddenly a woman's voice sent a shiver through him which seemed to penetrate to his very marrow. "George," it said, "will you carve the chicken?"

And another voice replied: "Yes, mamma."

Parent looked up, and he understood; he guessed immediately who those people were! He should certainly not have known them again. His wife had grown quite white and very stout, an elderly, serious, respectable lady, and she held her head forward as she ate for fear of spotting her dress, although she had a table napkin tucked under her chin. George had become a man. He had a slight beard, that uneven and almost colorless beard which adorns the cheeks of youths. He wore a high hat, a white waistcoat, and a monocle, because it looked swell, no doubt. Parent looked at him in astonishment. Was that George, his son? No, he did not know that young man; there could be nothing in common between them. Limousin had his back to him, and was eating; with his shoulders rather bent.

All three of them seemed happy and satisfied; they came and took luncheon in the country at well-known restaurants. They had had a calm and pleasant existence, a family existence in a warm and comfortable house, filled with all those trifles which make life agreeable, with affection, with all those tender words which people exchange continually when they love each other. They had lived thus, thanks to him, Parent, on his money, after having deceived him, robbed him, ruined him! They had condemned him, the innocent, simple-minded, jovial man, to all the miseries of solitude, to that abominable life which he had led, between the pavement and a bar-room, to every mental torture and every physical misery! They had made him a useless, aimless being, a waif in the world, a poor old man without any pleasures, any prospects, expecting nothing from anybody or anything. For him, the world was empty, because he loved nothing in the world. He might go among other nations, or go about the streets, go into all the houses in Paris, open every room, but he would not find inside any door the beloved face, the face of wife or child which smiles when it sees you. This idea worked upon him more than any other, the idea of a door which one opens, to see and to embrace somebody behind it.

And that was the fault of those three wretches! The fault of that worthless woman, of that infamous friend, and of that tall, light-haired lad who put on insolent airs. Now he felt as angry with the child as he did with the other two. Was he not Limousin's son? Would Limousin have kept him and loved him otherwise? Would not Limousin very quickly have got rid of the mother and of the child if he had not felt sure that it was his, positively his? Does anybody bring up other people's children? And now they were there, quite close to him, those three who had made him suffer so much.

Parent looked at them, irritated and excited at the recollection of all his sufferings and of his despair, and was especially exasperated at their placid and satisfied looks. He felt inclined to kill them, to throw his siphon of seltzer water at them, to split open Limousin's head as he every moment bent it over his plate, raising it again immediately.

He would have his revenge now, on the spot, as he had them under his hand. But how? He tried to think of some means, he pictured such dreadful things as one reads of in the newspapers occasionally, but could not hit on anything practical. And he went on drinking to excite himself, to give himself courage not to allow such an opportunity to escape him, as he might never have another.

Suddenly an idea struck him, a terrible idea; and he left off drinking to mature it. He smiled as he murmured: "I have them, I have them! We will see; we will see!"

They finished their luncheon slowly, conversing with perfect unconcern. Parent could not hear what they were saying, but he saw their quiet gestures. His wife's face especially exasperated him. She had assumed a haughty air, the air of a comfortable, devout woman, of an unapproachable, devout woman, sheathed in principles, ironclad in virtue. They paid their bill and got up from table. Parent then noticed Limousin. He might have been taken for a retired diplomat, for he looked a man of great importance, with his soft white whiskers, the tips of which touched his coat collar.

They walked away. Parent rose and followed them. First they went up and down the terrace, and calmly admired the landscape, and then they went into the forest. Parent followed them at a distance, hiding himself so as not to excite their suspicion too soon.

Parent came up to them by degrees, breathing hard with emotion and fatigue, for he was unused to walking now. He soon came up to them, but was seized with fear, an inexplicable fear, and he passed them, so as to turn round and meet them face to face. He walked on, his heart beating, feeling that they were just behind him now, and he said to himself: "Come, now is the time. Courage! courage! Now is the moment!"

He turned round. They were all three sitting on the grass, at the foot of a huge tree, and were still chatting. He made up his mind, and walked back rapidly; stopping in front of them in the middle of the road, he said abruptly, in a voice broken by emotion: "It is I! Here I am! I suppose you did not expect me?"

They all three stared at this man, who seemed to be insane.

He continued: "One would suppose that you did not know me again. Just look at me! I am Parent, Henri Parent. You thought it was all over, and that you would never see me again. Ah! but here I am once more, you see, and now we will have an explanation."

Henriette, terrified, hid her face in her hands, murmuring: "Oh! Good heavens!"

Seeing this stranger, who seemed to be threatening his mother, George sprang up, ready to seize him by the collar. Limousin, thunderstruck, looked in horror at this apparition, who, after gasping for breath, continued: "So now we will have an explanation; the proper moment has come! Ah! you deceived me, you condemned me to the life of a convict, and you thought that I should never catch you!"

The young man took him by the shoulders and pushed him back. "Are you mad?" he asked. "What do you want? Go on your way immediately, or I shall give you a thrashing!"

"What do I want?" replied Parent. "I want to tell you who these people are."

George, however, was in a rage, and shook him; and was even going to strike him.

"Let me go," said Parent. "I am your father. There, see whether they recognize me now, the wretches!"

The young man, thunderstruck, unclenched his fists and turned toward his mother. Parent, as soon as he was released, approached her.

"Well," he said, "tell him yourself who I am! Tell him that my name is Henri Parent, that I am his father because his name is George

Parent, because you are my wife, because you are all three living on my money, on the allowance of ten thousand francs which I have allowed you since I drove you out of my house. Will you tell him also why I drove you out? Because I surprised you with this beggar, this wretch, your lover! Tell him what I was, an honorable man, whom you married for money, and whom you deceived from the very first day. Tell him who you are, and who I am——"

He stammered and gasped for breath in his rage. The woman exclaimed in a heartrending voice:

"Paul, Paul, stop him; make him be quiet! Do not let him say this before my son!"

Limousin had also risen to his feet. He said in a very low voice: "Hold your tongue! Hold your tongue! Do you understand what you are doing?"

"I quite know what I am doing," resumed Parent, "and that is not all. There is one thing that I will know, something that has tormented me for twenty years." Then, turning to George, who was leaning against a tree in consternation, he said:

"Listen to me. When she left my house she thought it was not enough to have deceived me, but she also wanted to drive me to despair. You were my only consolation, and she took you with her, swearing that I was not your father, but, that he was your father. Was she lying? I do not know. I have been asking myself the question for the last twenty years." He went close up to her, tragic and terrible, and, pulling away her hands, with which she had covered her face, he continued:

"Well, now! I call upon you to tell me which of us two is the father of this young man; he or I, your husband or your lover. Come! Come! tell us."

Limousin rushed at him. Parent pushed him back, and, sneering in his fury, he said: "Ah! you are brave now! You are braver than you were that day when you ran downstairs because you thought I was going to murder you. Very well! If she will not reply, tell me yourself. You ought to know as well as she. Tell me, are you this young fellow's father? Come on! Come on, tell me!"

He turned to his wife again. "If you will not tell me, at any rate tell your son. He is a man, now, and he has the right to know who his father is. I do not know, and I never did know, never, never! I cannot tell you, my boy."

He seemed to be losing his senses; his voice grew shrill and he worked his arms about as if he had an epileptic fit. "Come on! . . . Give me an answer. She does not know . . . I'll bet you that she does not know . . . no . . . she does not know, by Jove! Ha! ha! ha! Nobody knows . . . nobody . . . How can one know such things? You will not know either, my boy, you will not know anymore than I do . . . never. . . . Look here . . . Ask her you will find that she does not know . . . I do not know either . . . nor does he, nor do you, nobody knows. You can choose . . . You can choose . . . yes, you can choose him or me . . . Choose.

"Good evening . . . It is all over. If she makes up her mind to tell you, you will come and let me know, will you not? I am living at the Hôtel des Continents . . . I should be glad to know . . . Good evening . . . I hope you will enjoy yourselves very much. . . ."

And he went away gesticulating, talking to himself under the tall trees, in the quiet, the cool air, which was full of the fragrance of growing plants. He did not turn round to look at them, but went straight on, walking under the stimulus of his rage, under a storm of passion, with that one fixed idea in his mind. All at once he found himself outside the station. A train was about to start and he got in. During the journey his anger calmed down, he regained his senses and returned to Paris, astonished at his own boldness, full of aches and pains as if he had broken some bones. Nevertheless, he went to have a bock at his brewery.

When she saw him come in, Mademoiselle Zoë asked in surprise: "What! back already? are you tired?"

"Yes—yes, I am tired . . . very tired . . . You know, when one is not used to going out. . . . I've had enough of it. I shall not go to the country again. It would have been better to have stayed here. In the future, I shall not stir abroad."

She could not persuade him to tell her about his little excursion, much as she wished to.

For the first time in his life, he got thoroughly drunk that night, and had to be carried home.

In the Spring

With the first day of spring, when the awakening earth puts on its garment of green, and the warm, fragrant air fans our faces and fills our lungs and appears even to penetrate to our hearts, we experience a vague, undefined longing for freedom, for happiness, a desire to run, to wander aimlessly, to breathe in the spring. The previous winter having been unusually severe, this spring feeling was like a form of intoxication in May, as if there were an overabundant supply of sap.

One morning on waking I saw from my window the blue sky glowing in the sun above the neighboring houses. The canaries hanging in the windows were singing loudly, and so were the servants on every floor; a cheerful noise rose up from the streets, and I went out, my spirits as bright as the day, to go—I did not exactly know where. Everybody I met seemed to be smiling; an air of happiness appeared to pervade everything in the warm light of returning spring. One might almost have said that a breeze of love was blowing through the city, and the sight of the young women whom I saw in the streets in their morning toilets, in the depths of whose eyes there lurked a hidden tenderness, and who walked with languid grace, filled my heart with agitation.

Without knowing how or why, I found myself on the banks of the Seine. Steamboats were starting for Suresnes, and suddenly I was seized by an unconquerable desire to take a walk through the woods. The deck of the Mouche was covered with passengers, for the sun in early spring draws one out of the house, in spite of themselves, and everybody moves about, goes and comes and talks to his neighbor.

I had a girl neighbor; a little work-girl, no doubt, who possessed the true Parisian charm: a little head, with light curly hair, which looked like a shimmer of light as it danced in the wind, came down to her ears, and descended to the nape of her neck, where it became such fine, light-colored down that one could scarcely see it, but felt an irresistible desire to shower kisses on it.

Under my persistent gaze, she turned her head toward me, and then immediately looked down, while a slight crease at the side of her mouth, that was ready to break out into a smile, also showed a fine, silky, pale down which the sun was gilding a little.

The calm river grew wider; the atmosphere was warm and perfectly still, but a murmur of life seemed to fill all space.

My neighbor raised her eyes again, and this time, as I was still looking at her, she smiled decidedly. She was charming, and in her passing glance I saw a thousand things, which I had hitherto been ignorant of, for I perceived unknown depths, all the charm of tenderness, all the poetry which we dream of, all the happiness which we are continually in search of. I felt an insane longing to open my arms and to carry her off somewhere, so as to whisper the sweet music of words of love into her ears.

I was just about to address her when somebody touched me on the shoulder, and as I turned round in some surprise, I saw an ordinary-looking man, who was neither young nor old, and who gazed at me sadly.

"I should like to speak to you," he said.

I made a grimace, which he no doubt saw, for he added: "It is a matter of importance."

I got up, therefore, and followed him to the other end of the boat and then he said: "Monsieur, when winter comes, with its cold, wet and snowy weather, your doctor says to you constantly: 'Keep your feet warm, guard against chills, colds, bronchitis, rheumatism and pleurisy.' Then you are very careful, you wear flannel, a heavy greatcoat and thick shoes, but all this does not prevent you from passing two months in bed. But when spring returns, with its leaves and flowers, its warm, soft breezes and its smell of the fields, all of which causes you vague disquiet and causeless emotion, nobody says to you: 'Monsieur, beware of love! It is lying in ambush everywhere; it is watching for you at every corner; all its snares are laid, all its weapons are sharpened, all its guiles are prepared! Beware of love! Beware of love! It is more dangerous than brandy, bronchitis or pleurisy! It never forgives and makes everybody commit irreparable follies.' Yes, monsieur, I say that the French government ought to put large public notices on the walls, with these words: 'Return of spring. French citizens, beware of love!' just as they put: 'Beware of paint.' However, as the government will not do this, I must supply its place, and I say to you: 'Beware of love!' for it is just going to seize you, and it is my duty to inform you of it, just as in Russia they inform anyone that his nose is frozen."

I was much astonished at this individual, and assuming a dignified manner, I said: "Really, monsieur, you appear to me to be interfering in a matter which is no concern of yours."

He made an abrupt movement and replied: "Ah! monsieur, monsieur! If I see that a man is in danger of being drowned at a dangerous spot, ought I to let him perish? So just listen to my story and you will see why I ventured to speak to you like this.

"It was about this time last year that it occurred. But, first of all, I must tell you that I am a clerk in the Admiralty, where our chiefs, the commissioners, take their gold lace as quill-driving officials seriously, and treat us like forecastle men on board a ship. Well, from my office I could see a small bit of blue sky and the swallows, and I felt inclined to dance among my portfolios.

"My yearning for freedom grew so intense that, in spite of my repugnance, I went to see my chief, a short, bad-tempered man, who was always in a rage. When I told him that I was not well, he looked at me and said: 'I do not believe it, monsieur, but be off with you! Do you think that any office can operate with clerks like you?' I started at once and went down the Seine. It was a day like this, and I took the Mouche, to go as far as Saint-Cloud. Ah! what a good thing it would have been if my chief had refused me permission to leave the office that day!

"I seemed to myself to expand in the sun. I loved everything—the steamer, the river, the trees, the houses and my fellow-passengers. I felt inclined to kiss something, no matter what; it was love, laying its snare. Presently, at the Trocadéro, a girl, with a small parcel in her hand, came on board and sat down opposite me. She was decidedly pretty, but it is surprising, monsieur, how much prettier women seem to us when the day is fine at the beginning of the spring. Then they have an intoxicating charm, something quite peculiar about them. It is just like drinking wine after cheese.

"I looked at her and she also looked at me, but only occasionally, as that girl did at you, just now; but at last, by dint of looking at each other constantly, it seemed to me that we knew each other well enough to enter into conversation, and I spoke to her and she replied. She was decidedly pretty and nice and she intoxicated me, monsieur!

"She got out at Saint-Cloud, and I followed her. She went and delivered her parcel, and when she returned the boat had just started. I walked by her side, and the warmth of the air made us both sigh. 'It would be very nice in the woods,' I said. 'Indeed, it would!' she replied. 'Shall we go there for a walk, mademoiselle?'

"She gave me a quick upward look, as if to see exactly what I was like, and then, after a little hesitation, she accepted my proposal, and soon we were there, walking side by side. Under the foliage, which was still rather sparse, the tall, thick, bright green grass was inundated by the sun, and the air was full of insects that were also making love to one another, and birds were singing in all directions. My companion began to jump and to run, intoxicated by the air and the smell of the country, and I ran and jumped, following her example. How silly we are at times, monsieur!

"Then she sang unrestrainedly a thousand things, opera airs and the song of Musette! The song of Musette! How poetical it seemed to me, then! I almost cried over it. Ah! Those silly songs make us lose our heads; and, believe me, never marry a woman who sings in the country, especially if she sings the song of Musette!

"She soon grew tired, and sat down on a grassy slope, and I sat at her feet and took her hands, her little hands, that were so marked with the needle, and that filled me with emotion. I said to myself: 'These are the sacred marks of toil.' Oh! monsieur, do you know what those sacred marks of toil mean? They mean all the gossip of the work-room, the whispered scandal, the mind soiled by all the filth that is talked; they mean lost chastity, foolish chatter, all the wretchedness of their everyday life, all the narrowness of ideas which belongs to women of the lower orders, combined to their fullest extent in the girl whose fingers bear the sacred marks of toil.

"Then we looked into each other's eyes for a long while. Oh! what power a woman's eye has! How it agitates us, how it invades our very being, takes possession of us, and dominates us! How profound it seems, how full of infinite promises! People call that looking into each other's souls! Oh! monsieur, what humbug! If we could see into each other's souls, we should be more careful of what we did. However, I was captivated and was crazy about her and tried to take her into my arms, but she said: 'Paws off!' Then I knelt down and opened my heart to her and poured out all the affection that was suffocating me. She seemed surprised at my change of manner and gave me a sidelong glance, as if to say, 'Ah! so that is the way women make a fool of you, old fellow! Very well, we will see.'

"In love, monsieur, we are always novices, and women artful dealers.

"No doubt I could have had her, and I saw my own stupidity later, but what I wanted was not a woman's person, it was love, it was the ideal. I was sentimental, when I ought to have been using my time to a better purpose.

"As soon as she had had enough of my declarations of affection, she got up, and we returned to Saint-Cloud, and I did not leave her until we got to Paris; but she had looked so sad as we were returning, that at last I asked her what was the matter. 'I am thinking,' she replied, 'that this has been one of those days of which we have only a few in life.' My heart beat so that it felt as if it would break my ribs.

"I saw her on the following Sunday, and the next Sunday, and every Sunday. I took her to Bougival, Saint-Germain, Maisons-Lafitte, Poissy; to every suburban resort of lovers.

"The little jade, in turn, pretended to love me, until, at last, I altogether lost my head, and three months later I married her.

"What can you expect, monsieur, when a man is a clerk, living alone, without any relations, or anyone to advise him? One says to oneself: 'How sweet life would be with a wife!'

"And so one gets married and she calls you names from morning till night, understands nothing, knows nothing, chatters continually, sings the song of Musette at the top of her voice (oh! that song of Musette, how tired one gets of it!); quarrels with the charcoal dealer, tells the janitor all her domestic problems, confides all the secrets of her bedroom to the neighbor's servant, discusses her husband with the tradespeople, and has her head so stuffed with stupid stories, with idiotic superstitions, with extraordinary ideas and monstrous prejudices, that I—for what I have said applies more particularly to myself— shed tears of discouragement every time I talk to her."

He stopped, as he was rather out of breath and very much moved, and I looked at him, for I felt pity for this poor, artless devil, and I was just going to give him some sort of answer, when the boat stopped. We were at Saint-Cloud.

The little woman who had so taken my fancy rose from her seat in order to land. She passed close to me, and gave me a sidelong glance and a furtive smile, one of those smiles that drive you wild. Then she jumped on the landing-stage. I sprang forward to follow her, but my neighbor laid hold of my arm. I shook myself loose, however, whereupon he seized the skirt of my coat and pulled me back, exclaiming: "You shall not go! you shall not go!" in such a loud voice that everybody turned round and laughed, and I remained standing motionless and furious, but without venturing to face scandal and ridicule, and the steamboat started.

The little woman on the landing-stage looked at me as I went off with an air of disappointment, while my persecutor rubbed his hands and whispered to me: "You must acknowledge that I have done you a great service."

Useless Beauty

1

About half-past five one afternoon at the end of June, when the sun was shining warm and bright into the large courtyard, a very elegant victoria with two beautiful black horses drew up in front of the mansion.

The Comtesse de Mascaret came down the steps just as her husband, who was coming home, appeared in the carriage entrance. He stopped for a few moments to look at his wife and turned rather pale. The countess was very beautiful, graceful and distinguished-looking, with her long oval face, her complexion like yellow ivory, her large gray eyes and her black hair; and she got into her carriage without looking at him, without even seeming to have noticed him, with such a particularly high-bred air, that the furious jealousy by which he had been devoured for so long again gnawed at his heart. He went up to her and said: "You are going for a drive?"

She merely replied disdainfully: "You can see I am!"

"In the Bois de Boulogne?"

"Most probably."

"May I come with you?"

"The carriage belongs to you."

Without being surprised at the tone in which she answered him, he got in and sat down by his wife's side and said: "Bois de Boulogne." The footman jumped up beside the coachman, and the horses as usual pranced and tossed their heads until they were in the street. Husband and wife sat side by side without speaking. He was thinking how to begin a conversation, but she maintained such an obstinately hard look that he did not venture to make the attempt. At last, however, he cunningly, accidentally as it were, touched the countess' gloved hand with his own, but she drew her arm away with a movement which was so expressive of disgust that he remained thoughtful, in spite of his usual authoritative and despotic character, and he said: "Gabrielle!"

"What do you want?"

"I think you are looking adorable."

She did not reply, but remained lying back in the carriage, looking like an irritated queen. By that time they were driving up the Champs-Élysées, toward the Arc de Triomphe. That immense monument, at the end of the long avenue, raised its colossal arch against the red sky and the sun seemed to be descending on it, showering fiery dust on it from the sky.

The stream of carriages, with dashes of sunlight reflected in the silver trappings of the harness and the glass of the lamps, flowed on in a double current toward the town and toward the Bois, and the Comte de Mascaret continued: "My dear Gabrielle!"

Unable to control herself any longer, she replied in an exasperated voice: "Oh! do leave me in peace, pray! I am not even allowed to have my carriage to myself now." He pretended not to hear her and continued: "You never have looked so pretty as you do today."

Her patience had come to an end, and she replied with irrepressible anger: "You are wrong to notice it, for I swear to you that I will never have anything to do with you in that way again."

The count was decidedly stupefied and upset, and, his violent nature gaining the upper hand, he exclaimed: "What do you mean by that?" in a tone that betrayed rather the brutal master than the lover. She replied in a low voice, so that the servants might not hear amid the deafening noise of the wheels: "Ah! What do I mean by that? What do I mean by that? Now I recognize you again! Do you want me to tell everything?"

"Yes."

"Everything that has weighed on my heart since I have been the victim of your terrible selfishness?"

He had grown red with surprise and anger and he growled between his closed teeth: "Yes, tell me everything."

He was a tall, broad-shouldered man, with a big red beard, a handsome man, a nobleman, a man of the world, who passed as a perfect husband and an excellent father, and now, for the first time since they had started, she turned toward him and looked him full in the face: "Ah! You will hear some disagreeable things, but you must know that I am prepared for everything, that I fear nothing, and you less than anyone today."

He also was looking into her eyes and was already shaking with rage as he said in a low voice: "You are mad."

"No, but I will no longer be the victim of the hateful penalty of maternity, which you have inflicted on me for eleven years! I wish to take my place in society as I have the right to do, as all women have the right to do."

He suddenly grew pale again and stammered: "I do not understand you."

"Oh! yes; you understand me well enough. It is now three months since I had my last child, and as I am still very beautiful, and as, in spite of all your efforts you cannot spoil my figure, as you just now perceived, when you saw me on the doorstep, you think it is time that I should think of having another child."

"But you are talking nonsense!"

"No, I am not, I am thirty, and I have had seven children, and we have been married eleven years, and you hope that this will go on for ten years longer, after which you will leave off being jealous."

He seized her arm and squeezed it, saying: "I will not allow you to talk to me like that any longer."

"And I shall talk to you till the end, until I have finished all I have to say to you, and if you try to prevent me, I shall raise my voice so that the two servants, who are on the box, may hear. I only allowed you to come with me for that object, for I have these witnesses who will oblige you to listen to me and to contain yourself, so now pay attention to what I say. I have always felt an antipathy to you, and I have always let you see it, for I have never lied, monsieur. You married me in spite of myself; you forced my parents, who were in embarrassed circumstances, to give me to you, because you were rich, and they obliged me to marry you in spite of my tears.

"So you bought me, and as soon as I was in your power, as soon as I had become your companion, ready to attach myself to you, to forget your coercive and threatening proceedings, in order that I might only remember that I ought to be a devoted wife and to love you as much as it might be possible for me to love you, you became jealous, you, as no man has ever been before, with the base, ignoble jealousy of a spy, which was as degrading to you as it was to me. I had not been married eight months when you suspected me of every perfidiousness, and you even told me so. What a disgrace! And as you could not prevent me from being beautiful and from pleasing people, from being called in drawing-rooms and also in the newspapers one of the most beautiful women in Paris, you tried everything you could think of to keep admirers from me, and you hit upon the abominable idea of making me spend my life in a constant state of motherhood, until the time should come when I should disgust every man. Oh, do not deny it. I did not understand it for some time, but then I guessed it. You even boasted about it to your sister, who told me of it, for she is fond of me and was disgusted at your boorish coarseness.

"Ah! Remember how you have behaved in the past! How for eleven years you have compelled me to give up all society and simply be a mother to your children. And then you would grow disgusted with me and I was sent into the country, the family chateau, among fields and meadows. And when I reappeared, fresh, pretty and unspoiled, still seductive and constantly surrounded by admirers, hoping that at last I should live a little more like a rich young society woman, you were seized with jealousy again, and you began once more to persecute me with that infamous and hateful desire from which you are suffering at this moment by my side. And it is not the desire of possessing me—for I should never have refused myself to you, but it is the wish to make me unsightly.

"And then that abominable and mysterious thing occurred which I was a long time in understanding (but I grew sharp by way of watching your thoughts and actions): You attached yourself to your children with all the security which they gave you while I bore them. You felt affection for them, with all your aversion to me, and in spite of your ignoble fears, which were momentarily allayed by your pleasure in seeing me lose my symmetry.

"Oh! how often have I noticed that joy in you! I have seen it in your eyes and guessed it. You loved your children as victories, and not because they were of your own blood. They were victories over me, over my youth, over my beauty, over my charms, over the compliments which were paid me and over those that were whispered around me without being paid to me personally. And you are proud of them, you make a parade of them, you take them out for drives in your break in the Bois de Boulogne and you give them donkey rides at Montmorency. You take them to theatrical matinees so that you may be seen in the midst of them, so that the people may say: 'What a kind father' and that it may be repeated——"

He had seized her wrist with savage brutality, and he squeezed it so violently that she was quiet and nearly cried out with the pain and he said to her in a whisper: "I love my children, do you hear? What you have just told me is disgraceful in a mother. But you belong to me; I am master—your master—I can exact from you what I like and when I like—and I have the law on my side."

He was trying to crush her fingers in the strong grip of his large, muscular hand, and she, livid with pain, tried in vain to free them from that vise which was crushing them. The agony made her breathe hard and the tears came into her eyes. "You see that I am the master and the stronger," he said.

When he somewhat loosened his grip, she asked him: "Do you think that I am a religious woman?"

He was surprised and stammered, "Yes."

"Do you think that I could lie if I swore to the truth of anything to you before an altar on which Christ's body is?"

"No."

"Will you go with me to some church?"

"What for?"

"You shall see. Will you?"

"If you absolutely wish it, yes."

She raised her voice and said: "Philippe!" And the coachman, bending down a little, without taking his eyes from his horses, seemed to turn his ear alone toward his mistress, who continued: "Drive to St. Philippe-du-Roule." And the victoria, which had reached the entrance of the Bois de Boulogne, returned to Paris.

Husband and wife did not exchange a word further during the drive, and when the carriage stopped before the church, Madame de Mascaret jumped out and entered it, followed by the count, a few yards distant. She went, without stopping, as far as the choir-screen, and falling on her knees at a chair, she buried her face in her hands. She prayed for a long time, and he, standing behind her could see that she was crying. She wept noiselessly, as women weep when they are in great, poignant grief. There was a kind of undulation in her body, which ended in a little sob, which was hidden and stifled by her fingers.

But the Comte de Mascaret thought that the situation was lasting too long, and he touched her on the shoulder. That contact recalled her to herself, as if she had been burned, and getting up, she looked straight into his eyes. "This is what I have to say to you. I am afraid of nothing, whatever you may do to me. You may kill me if you like. One of your children is not yours, and one only; that I swear to you before God, who hears me here. That was the only revenge that was possible for me in return for all your abominable masculine tyrannies, in return for the penal servitude of childbearing to which you have condemned me. Who was my lover? That you never will know! You may suspect everyone, but you never will find out. I gave myself to him, without love and without pleasure, only for the sake of betraying you, and he also made me a mother. Which is the child? That also you never will know. I have seven; try to find out! I intended to tell you this later, for one has not avenged oneself on a man by deceiving him, unless he knows it. You have driven me to confess it today. I have now finished."

She hurried through the church toward the open door, expecting to hear behind her the quick step of her husband whom she had defied and to be knocked to the ground by a blow of his fist, but she heard nothing and reached her carriage. She jumped into it at a bound, overwhelmed with anguish and breathless with fear. So she called out to the coachman: "Home!" and the horses set off at a quick trot.

2

The Comtesse de Mascaret was waiting in her room for dinnertime as a criminal sentenced to death awaits the hour of his execution. What was her husband going to do? Had he come home? Despotic, passionate, ready for any violence as he was, what was he meditating, what had he made up his mind to do? There was no sound in the house, and every moment she looked at the clock. Her maid had come and dressed her for the evening and had then left the room again. Eight o'clock struck and almost at the same moment there were two knocks at the door, and the butler came in and announced dinner.

"Has the count come in?"

"Yes, Madame la Comtesse. He is in the dining room."

For a little moment she felt inclined to arm herself with a small revolver which she had bought some time before, foreseeing the tragedy which was being rehearsed in her heart. But she remembered that all the children would be there, and she took nothing except a bottle of smelling salts. He rose somewhat ceremoniously from his chair. They exchanged a slight bow and sat down. The three boys with their tutor, Abbé Martin, were on her right and the three girls, with Miss Smith, their English governess, were on her left. The youngest child, who was only three months old, remained upstairs with his nurse.

The abbé said grace as usual when there was no company, for the children did not come down to dinner when guests were present. Then they began dinner. The countess, suffering from emotion, which she had not calculated upon, remained with her eyes cast down, while the count scrutinized now the three boys and now the three girls with an uncertain, unhappy expression, which traveled from one to the other. Suddenly pushing his wineglass from him, it broke, and the wine was spilt on the tablecloth, and at the slight noise caused by this little accident the countess started up from her chair; and for the first time they looked at each other. Then, in spite of themselves, in spite of the irritation of their nerves caused by every glance, they continued to exchange looks, rapid as pistol shots.

The abbé, who felt that there was some cause for embarrassment which he could not divine, attempted to begin a conversation and tried various subjects, but his useless efforts gave rise to no ideas and did not bring out a word. The countess, with feminine tact and obeying her instincts of a woman of the world, attempted to answer him two or three times, but in vain. She could not find words, in the perplexity of her mind, and her own voice almost frightened her in the silence of the large room, where nothing was heard except the slight sound of plates and knives and forks.

Suddenly her husband said to her, bending forward: "Here, amid your children, will you swear to me that what you told me just now is true?"

The hatred which was fermenting in her veins suddenly roused her, and replying to that question with the same firmness with which she had replied to his looks, she raised both her hands, the right pointing toward the boys and the left toward the girls, and said in a firm, resolute voice and without any hesitation: "On the head of my children, I swear that I have told you the truth."

He got up and throwing his table napkin on the table with a movement of exasperation, he turned round and flung his chair against the wall, and then went out without another word, while she, uttering a deep sigh, as if after a first victory, went on in a calm voice: "You must not pay any attention to what your father has just said, my darlings; he was very much upset a short time ago, but he will be all right again in a few days."

Then she talked with the abbé and Miss Smith and had tender, pretty words for all her children, those sweet, tender mother's ways which unfold little hearts.

When dinner was over she went into the drawing-room, all her children following her. She made the elder ones chatter, and when their bedtime came she kissed them for a long time and then went alone into her room.

She waited, for she had no doubt that the count would come, and she made up her mind then, as her children were not with her, to protect herself as a woman of the world as she would protect her life, and in the pocket of her dress she put the little loaded revolver which she had bought a few days previously. The hours went by, the hours struck, and every sound was hushed in the house. Only the cabs continued to rumble through the streets, but their noise was only heard vaguely through the shuttered and curtained windows.

She waited, full of nervous energy, without any fear of him now, ready for anything, and almost triumphant, for she had found means of torturing him continually during every moment of his life.

But the first gleam of dawn came in through the fringe at the bottom of her curtain without his having come into her room, and then she awoke to the fact, with much amazement, that he was not coming. Having locked and bolted her door, for greater security, she went to bed at last and remained there, with her eyes open, thinking and barely understanding it all, without being able to guess what he was going to do.

When her maid brought her tea she at the same time handed her a letter from her husband. He told her that he was going to undertake a longish journey and in a postscript added that his lawyer would provide her with any sums of money she might require for all her expenses.

<h1 style="text-align:center">3</h1>

It was at the opera, between two acts of *Robert the Devil*. In the stalls the men were standing up, with their hats on, their waistcoats cut very low so as to show a large amount of white shirt front, in which gold and jeweled studs glistened, and were looking at the boxes full of ladies in low dresses covered with diamonds and pearls, who were expanding like flowers in that illuminated hothouse, where the beauty of their faces and the whiteness of their shoulders seemed to bloom in order to be gazed at, amid the sound of the music and of human voices.

Two friends, with their backs to the orchestra, were scanning those rows of elegance, that exhibition of real or false charms, of jewels, of luxury and of pretension which displayed itself in all parts of the Grand Théâtre, and one of them, Roger de Salnis, said to his companion,

Bernard Grandin: "Just look how beautiful the Comtesse de Mascaret still is."

The older man in turn looked through his opera glasses at a tall lady in a box opposite. She appeared to be still very young, and her striking beauty seemed to attract all eyes in every corner of the house. Her pale complexion, of an ivory tint, gave her the appearance of a statue, while a small diamond coronet glistened on her black hair like a streak of light.

When he had looked at her for some time, Bernard Grandin replied with a jocular accent of sincere conviction: "You may well call her beautiful!"

"How old do you think she is?"

"Wait a moment. I can tell you exactly, for I have known her since she was a child and I saw her make her debut into society when she was quite a girl. She is . . . she is . . . thirty- . . . thirty-six."

"Impossible!"

"I am sure of it."

"She looks twenty-five."

"She has had seven children."

"Incredible."

"And what is more, they are all seven alive, as she is a very good mother. I occasionally go to the house, which is a very quiet and pleasant one, where one may see the phenomenon of the family in the midst of society."

"How very strange! And have there never been any rumors about her?"

"Never."

"But what about her husband? He is peculiar, is he not?"

"Yes and no. Very likely there has been a little drama between them, one of those little domestic dramas which one suspects, never finds out exactly, but guesses at pretty closely."

"What is it?"

"I do not know anything about it. Mascaret leads a very fast life now, after being a model husband. As long as he remained a good spouse he had a shocking temper, was crabby and easily took offence, but since he has been leading his present wild life he has become quite different. But one might surmise that he has some trouble, a worm gnawing somewhere, for he has aged very much."

Thereupon the two friends talked philosophically for some minutes about the secret, unknowable troubles which differences of character or perhaps physical antipathies, which were not perceived at first, give rise to in families, and then Roger de Salnis, who was still looking at Madame de Mascaret through his opera glasses, said: "It is almost unbelievable that that woman can have had seven children!"

"Yes, in eleven years; after which, when she was thirty, she refused to have any more, in order to take her place in society, which she seems likely to do for many years."

"Poor women!"

"Why do you pity them?"

"Why? Ah! my dear fellow, just consider! Eleven years in a condition of motherhood for such a woman! What a hell! All her youth, all her beauty, every hope of success, every poetical ideal of a brilliant life sacrificed to that abominable law of reproduction which turns the normal woman into a mere machine for bringing children into the world."

"What would you have? It is only Nature!"

"Yes, but I say that Nature is our enemy, that we must always fight against Nature, for she is continually dragging us back to an animal state. You may be sure that God has not put anything on this earth that is clean, pretty, elegant, or accessory to our ideal; the human brain has done it. It is man who has introduced a little grace, beauty, unknown charm and mystery into creation by singing about it, interpreting it, by admiring it as a poet, idealizing it as an artist and by explaining it through science, doubtless making mistakes, but finding ingenious reasons, hidden grace and beauty, unknown charm and mystery in the various phenomena of Nature. God created only coarse beings, full of the germs of disease, who, after a few years of bestial enjoyment, grow old and infirm, with all the ugliness and all the want of power of human decrepitude. He seems to have made them only in order that they may reproduce their species in an ignoble manner and then die like ephemeral insects. I said 'reproduce their species in an ignoble manner' and I adhere to that expression. What is there as a matter of fact more ignoble and more repugnant than that act of reproduction of living beings, against which all delicate minds always have revolted and always will revolt? Since all the organs which have been invented by this economical and malicious Creator serve two purposes, why did He not choose another method of performing that sacred mission, which is the noblest and the most exalted of all human functions? The mouth, which nourishes the body by means of material food, also diffuses abroad speech and thought. Our flesh renews itself of its own accord, while we are thinking about it. The olfactory organs, through which the vital air reaches the lungs, communicate all the perfumes of the world to the brain: the smell of flowers, of woods, of trees, of the sea. The ear, which enables us to communicate with our fellow men, has also allowed us to invent music, to create dreams, happiness, infinite and even physical pleasure by means of sound! But one might say that the cynical and cunning Creator wished to prohibit man from ever ennobling and idealizing his intercourse with women. Nevertheless man has found love, which is not a bad reply to that sly deity, and he has adorned it with so much poetry that woman often forgets the sensual part of it. Those among us who are unable to deceive themselves have invented vice and refined debauchery, which is another way of laughing at God and paying homage, immodest homage, to beauty.

"But the normal man begets children just like an animal coupled with another by law. Look at that woman! Is it not abominable to think that such a jewel, such a pearl, born to be beautiful, admired, fêted and adored, has spent eleven years of her life in providing heirs for the Comte de Mascaret?"

Bernard Grandin replied with a laugh: "There is a great deal of truth in all that, but very few people would understand you."

Salnis became more and more animated. "Do you know how I picture God myself?" he said. "As an enormous, creative organ beyond our ken, who scatters millions of worlds into space, just as one single fish would deposit its spawn in the sea. He creates because it is His function as God to do so, but He does not know what He is doing and is stupidly prolific in His work and is ignorant of the combinations of all kinds which are produced by His scattered germs. The human mind is a lucky little local, passing accident which was totally unforeseen, and condemned to disappear with this earth and to recommence perhaps here or elsewhere the same or different with fresh combinations of eternally new beginnings. We owe it to this little lapse of intelligence on His part that we are very uncomfortable in this world which was not made for us, which had not been prepared to receive us, to lodge and feed us or to satisfy reflecting beings, and we owe it to Him also that we have to struggle without ceasing against what are still called the designs of Providence, when we are really refined and civilized beings."

Grandin, who was listening to him attentively as he had long known the surprising outbursts of his imagination, asked him: "Then you believe that human thought is the spontaneous product of blind divine generation?"

"Naturally! A fortuitous function of the nerve centers of our brain, like the unforeseen chemical action due to new mixtures and similar also to a charge of electricity, caused by friction or the unexpected proximity of some substance, similar to all phenomena caused by the infinite and fruitful fermentation of living matter.

"But, my dear fellow, the truth of this must be evident to anyone who looks about him. If the human mind, ordained by an omniscient Creator, had been intended to be what it has become, exacting, inquiring, agitated, tormented—so different from mere animal thought and resignation—would the world which was created to receive the beings which we now are have been this unpleasant little park for small game, this salad patch, this wooded, rocky and spherical kitchen garden where your improvident Providence had destined us to live naked, in caves or under trees, nourished on the flesh of slaughtered animals, our brethren, or on raw vegetables nourished by the sun and the rain?

"But it is sufficient to reflect for a moment, in order to understand that this world was not made for such creatures as we are. Thought, which is developed by a miracle in the nerves of the cells in our brain, powerless, ignorant and confused as it is, and as it will always remain, makes all of us who are intellectual beings eternal and wretched exiles on earth.

"Look at this earth, as God has given it to those who inhabit it. Is it not visibly and solely made, planted and covered with forests for the sake of animals? What is there for us? Nothing. And for them, everything, and they have nothing to do but to eat or go hunting and eat each other, according to their instincts, for God never foresaw gentleness and peaceable manners; He only foresaw the death of creatures which were bent on destroying and devouring each other. Are not the quail, the pigeon and the partridge the natural prey of the hawk? the sheep, the stag and the ox that of the great flesh-eating animals, rather than meat to be fattened and served up to us with truffles, which have been unearthed by pigs for our special benefit?

"As to ourselves, the more civilized, intellectual and refined we are, the more we ought to conquer and subdue that animal instinct, which represents the will of God in us. And so, in order to mitigate our lot as brutes, we have discovered and made everything, beginning with houses, then exquisite food, sauces, sweetmeats, pastry, drink, stuffs, clothes, ornaments, beds, mattresses, carriages, railways and innumerable machines, besides arts and sciences, writing and poetry. Every ideal comes from us as do all the amenities of life, in order to make our existence as simple reproducers, for which divine Providence solely intended us, less monotonous and less hard.

"Look at this theatre. Is there not here a human world created by us, unforeseen and unknown to eternal fate, intelligible to our minds alone, a sensual and intellectual distraction, which has been invented solely by and for that discontented and restless little animal, man?

"Look at that woman, Madame de Mascaret. God intended her to live in a cave, naked or wrapped in the skins of wild animals. But is she not better as she is? But, speaking of her, does anyone know why and how her brute of a husband, having such a companion by his side, and especially after having been boorish enough to make her a mother seven times, has suddenly left her, to run after loose women?"

Grandin replied: "Oh, my dear fellow, this is probably the only reason. He found that raising a family was becoming too expensive, and from reasons of domestic economy he has arrived at the same principles which you lay down as a philosopher."

Just then the curtain rose for the third act, and they turned round, took off their hats and sat down.

4

The Comte and Comtesse Mascaret were sitting side by side in the carriage which was taking them home from the opera, without speaking; but suddenly the husband said to his wife: "Gabrielle!"

"What do you want?"

"Don't you think that this has lasted long enough?"

"What?"

"The horrible punishment to which you have condemned me for the last six years?"

"What do you want? I cannot help it."

"Then tell me which of them it is."

"Never."

"Think that I can no longer see my children or feel them round me, without having my heart burdened with this doubt? Tell me which of them it is, and I swear that I will forgive you and treat it like the others."

"I have not the right to do so."

"Do you not see that I can no longer endure this life, this thought which is wearing me out, or this question which I am constantly asking myself, this question which tortures me each time I look at them? It is driving me mad."

"Then you have suffered a great deal?" she said.

"Terribly. Should I, without that, have accepted the horror of living by your side, and the still greater horror of feeling and knowing that there is one among them whom I cannot recognize and who prevents me from loving the others?"

"Then you have really suffered very much?" she repeated.

And he replied in a constrained and sorrowful voice: "Yes, for do I not tell you every day that it is intolerable torture to me? Should I have remained in that house, near you and them, if I did not love them? Oh! You have behaved abominably toward me. All the affection of my heart I have bestowed upon my children, and that you know. I am for them a father of the olden time, as I was for you a husband of one of the families of old, for by instinct I have remained a natural man, a man of former days. Yes, I will confess it, you have made me terribly jealous, because you are a woman of another race, of another soul, with other requirements. Oh! I shall never forget the things you said to me, but from that day I troubled myself no more about you. I did not kill you, because then I should have had no means on earth of ever discovering which of our—of your children is not mine. I have waited, but I have suffered more than you would believe, for I can no longer venture to love them, except, perhaps, the two eldest; I no longer venture to look at them, to call them to me, to kiss them; I cannot take them on my knee without asking myself, 'Can it be this one?' I have been correct in my behavior toward you for six years, and even kind and complaisant. Tell me the truth, and I swear that I will do nothing unkind."

He thought, in spite of the darkness of the carriage, that he could perceive that she was moved, and feeling certain that she was going to speak at last, he said: "I beg you, I beseech you to tell me," he said.

"I have been more guilty than you think perhaps," she replied, "but I could no longer endure that life of continual motherhood, and I had only one means of driving you from me. I lied before God and I lied, with my hand raised to my children's head, for I never have wronged you."

He seized her arm in the darkness, and squeezing it as he had done on that terrible day of their drive in the Bois de Boulogne, he stammered: "Is that true?"

"It is true."

But, wild with grief, he said with a groan: "I shall have fresh doubts that will never end! When did you lie, the last time or now? How am I to believe you at present? How can one believe a woman after that? I shall never again know what I am to think. I would rather you had said to me, 'It is Jacques or it is Jeanne.'"

The carriage drove into the courtyard of the house and when it had drawn up in front of the steps the count alighted first, as usual, and offered his wife his arm to mount the stairs. As soon as they reached the first floor he said: "May I speak to you for a few moments longer?" And she replied, "I am quite willing."

They went into a small drawing-room and a footman, in some surprise, lighted the wax candles. As soon as he had left the room and they were alone the count continued: "How am I to know the truth? I have begged you a thousand times to speak, but you have remained dumb, impenetrable, inflexible, inexorable, and now today you tell me that you have been lying. For six years you have actually allowed me to believe such a thing! No, you are lying now, I do not know why, but out of pity for me, perhaps?"

She replied in a sincere and convincing manner: "If I had not done so, I should have had four more children in the last six years!"

"Can a mother speak like that?"

"Oh!" she replied, "I do not feel that I am the mother of children who never have been born; it is enough for me to be the mother of those that I have and to love them with all my heart. I am a woman of the civilized world, monsieur—we all are—and we are no longer, and we refuse to be, mere females to restock the earth."

She got up, but he seized her hands. "Only one word, Gabrielle. Tell me the truth!"

"I have just told you. I never have dishonored you."

He looked her full in the face, and how beautiful she was, with her gray eyes, like the cold sky. In her dark hair sparkled the diamond coronet, like a radiance. He suddenly felt, felt by a kind of intuition, that this grand creature was not merely a being destined to perpetuate the race, but the strange and mysterious product of all our complicated desires which have been accumulating in us for centuries but which have been turned aside from their primitive and divine object and have wandered after a mystic, imperfectly perceived and intangible beauty. There are some women like that, who blossom only for our dreams, adorned with every poetical attribute of civilization, with that ideal luxury, coquetry and esthetic charm which surround woman, a living statue that brightens our life.

Her husband remained standing before her, stupefied at his tardy and obscure discovery, confusedly hitting on the cause of his former jealousy and understanding it all very imperfectly, and at last he said: "I believe you, for I feel at this moment that you are not lying, and before I really thought that you were."

She put out her hand to him: "We are friends then?"

He took her hand and kissed it and replied: "We are friends. Thank you, Gabrielle."

Then he went out, still looking at her, and surprised that she was still so beautiful and feeling a strange emotion arising in him.

Madame Tellier's Establishment

1

They went there every evening about eleven o'clock, just as they would go to the club. Six or eight of them; always the same set, not fast men, but respectable tradesmen, and young men in government or some other employ, and they would drink their Chartreuse, and laugh with the girls, or else talk seriously with Madame Tellier, whom everybody respected, and then they would go home at twelve o'clock! The younger men would sometimes stay later.

It was a small, comfortable house painted yellow, at the corner of a street behind Saint Etienne's Church, and from the windows one could see the docks full of ships being unloaded, the big salt marsh, and, rising beyond it, the Virgin's Hill with its old gray chapel.

Madame Tellier, who came of a respectable family of peasant proprietors in the Eure, had taken up her profession just as she might have become a milliner or dressmaker. The prejudice which is so violent and deeply rooted in large towns does not exist in the country places in Normandy. The peasant says: "It is a paying business," and he sends his daughter to keep an establishment of this character just as he would send her to keep a girls' school.

She had inherited the house from an old uncle, to whom it had belonged. Monsieur and Madame Tellier, who had formerly been innkeepers near Yvetot, had immediately sold their house, as they thought that the business at Fécamp was more profitable, and they arrived one fine morning to assume the direction of the enterprise, which was declining on account of the proprietors' absence. They were good enough people in their way, and soon made themselves liked by their staff and their neighbors.

Monsieur died of apoplexy two years later, for as the new place kept him in idleness and without any exercise, he had grown excessively stout, and his health had suffered. Since she had been a widow, all the frequenters of the establishment made much of her; but people said that, personally, she was quite virtuous, and even the girls in the house could not discover anything against her. She was tall, stout, and affable, and her complexion, which had become pale in the dimness of her house, the shutters of which were scarcely ever opened, shone as if it had been varnished. She had a fringe of curly false hair, which gave her a juvenile look that contrasted strongly with the ripeness of her figure. She was always smiling and cheerful, and was fond of a joke, but there was a shade of reserve about her, which her occupation had not quite made her lose. Coarse words always shocked her, and when any young fellow who had been badly brought up called her establishment a vile name, she was angry and disgusted.

In a word, she had a refined mind, and although she treated her women as friends, yet she very frequently used to say that "she and they were not made of the same stuff."

Sometimes during the week she would hire a carriage and take some of her girls into the country, where they used to enjoy themselves on the grass by the side of the little river. They were like a lot of girls let out from school, and would run races and play childish games. They had a cold dinner on the grass, and drank cider, and went home at night with a delicious feeling of fatigue, and in the carriage they kissed Madame Tellier as their kind mother, who was full of goodness and complaisance.

The house had two entrances. At the corner there was a sort of taproom, which sailors and the lower orders frequented at night, and she had two girls whose special duty it was to wait on them with the assistance of Frédéric, a short, light-haired, beardless fellow, as strong as a horse. They set the half bottles of wine and the jugs of beer on the shaky marble tables before the customers, and then urged the men to drink.

The three other girls—there were only five of them—formed a kind of aristocracy, and they remained with the company on the first floor, unless they were wanted downstairs and there was nobody on the first floor. The Jupiter Room, where the tradesmen used to meet, was papered in blue, and embellished with a large drawing representing Leda and the swan. The room was reached by a winding staircase, through a narrow door opening on the street, and above this door a lantern enclosed in wire, such as one still sees in some towns, at the foot of the shrine of some saint, burned all night long.

The house, which was old and damp, smelled slightly of mildew. At times there was an odor of eau de Cologne in the passages, or sometimes from a half-open door downstairs the noisy mirth of the common men sitting and drinking rose to the first floor, much to the disgust of the gentlemen who were there. Madame Tellier, who was on friendly terms with her customers, did not leave the room, and took much interest in what was going on in the town, and they regularly told her all the news. Her serious conversation was a change from the ceaseless chatter of the three women; it was a rest from the obscene jokes of those stout individuals who every evening indulged in the commonplace debauchery of drinking a glass of liqueur in company with common women.

The names of the girls on the first floor were Fernande, Raphaele, and Rosa, the Jade. As the staff was limited, madame had endeavored that each member of it should be a pattern, an epitome of the feminine type, so that every customer might find as nearly as possible the realization of his ideal. Fernande represented the striking blonde; she was very tall, rather fat, and lazy; a country girl, who could not get rid of her freckles, and whose short, light, almost colorless, tow-like hair, like combed-out hemp, barely covered her head.

Raphaele, who came from Marseilles, played the indispensable part of the beautiful Jewess, and was thin, with high cheekbones covered with rouge, and black hair covered with pomade, which curled on her forehead. Her eyes would have been handsome, if the right one had not had a speck in it. Her Roman nose came down over a square jaw, where two false upper teeth contrasted strangely with the bad color of the rest.

Rosa was a little ball of fat, nearly all body, with very short legs, and from morning till night she sang songs, which were alternately risqué or sentimental, in a harsh voice; told silly, interminable tales, and only stopped talking in order to eat, and left off eating in order to talk; she was never still, and was active as a squirrel, in spite of her embonpoint and her short legs; her laugh, which was a torrent of shrill cries, resounded here and there, ceaselessly, in a bedroom, in the loft, in the cafe, everywhere, and all about nothing.

The two women on the ground floor—Lodise, who was nicknamed La Cocotte, and Flora, whom they called Balancoise, because she limped a little, the former always dressed as the Goddess of Liberty, with a tri-colored sash, and the other as a Spanish señorita, with a string of copper coins in her carroty hair, which jingled at every uneven step—looked like cooks dressed up for the carnival. They were like all other women of the lower orders, neither uglier nor betterlooking than they usually are.

They looked just like servants at an inn, and were generally called "the two pumps."

A jealous peace, which was, however, very rarely disturbed, reigned among these five women, thanks to Madame Tellier's conciliatory wisdom, and to her constant good humor, and the establishment, which was the only one of its kind in the little town, was very much frequented. Madame Tellier had succeeded in giving it such a respectable appearance, was so amiable and obliging to everybody, her good heart was so well known, that she was treated with a certain amount of consideration. The regular customers spent money on her, and were delighted when she was especially friendly toward them, and when they met during the day, they would say: "Until this evening, you know where," just as men say: "At the club, after dinner." In a word, Madame Tellier's house was somewhere to go to, and they very rarely missed their daily meetings there.

One evening toward the end of May, the first arrival, Monsieur Poulin, who was a timber merchant, and had been mayor, found the door shut. The lantern behind the grating was not lit; there was not a sound in the house; everything seemed dead. He knocked, gently at first, but then more loudly, but nobody answered the door. Then he went slowly up the street, and when he got to the market place he met Monsieur Duvert, the gunsmith, who was going to the same place, so they went back together, but did not meet with any better success. But suddenly they heard a loud noise, close to them, and on going round the house, they saw a number of English and French sailors, who were hammering at the closed shutters of the taproom with their fists.

The two tradesmen immediately made their escape, but a low "Psst!" stopped them; it was Monsieur Tournevau, the fish-curer, who had recognized them, and was trying to attract their attention. They told him what had happened, and he was all the more annoyed, as he was a married man and father of a family, and only went on Saturdays. That was his regular evening, and now he should be deprived of this dissipation for the whole week.

The three men went as far as the quay together, and on the way they met young Monsieur Philippe, the banker's son, who frequented the place regularly, and Monsieur Pinipesse, the tax collector, and they all returned to the Rue aux Juifs together, to make a last attempt. But the exasperated sailors were besieging the house, throwing stones at the shutters, and shouting, and the five first-floor customers went away as quickly as possible, and walked aimlessly about the streets.

Presently they met Monsieur Dupuis, the insurance agent, and then Monsieur Vasse, the judge of the Tribunal of Commerce, and they took a long walk, going to the pier first of all, where they sat down in a row on the granite parapet and watched the rising tide.

When the promenaders had sat there for some time, Monsieur Tournevau said: "This is not very amusing!"

"Decidedly not," Monsieur Pinipesse replied, and they started off to walk again.

After going through the street alongside the hill, they returned over the wooden bridge which crosses the Retenue, passed close to the railway, and came out again on the marketplace, when, suddenly, a quarrel arose between Monsieur Pinipesse and Monsieur Tournevau about an edible mushroom which one of them declared he had found in the neighborhood.

As they were out of temper already from having nothing to do, they would very probably have come to blows if the others had not interfered. Monsieur Pinipesse went off furious, and soon another altercation arose between the ex-mayor, Monsieur Poulin, and Monsieur Dupuis, the insurance agent, on the subject of the tax collector's salary and the profits which he might make. Insulting remarks were freely passing between them when a torrent of formidable cries was heard, and the body of sailors, who were tired of waiting so long outside a closed house, came into the square. They were walking arm in arm, two and two, and formed a long procession, and were shouting furiously. The townsmen hid themselves in a doorway, and the yelling crew disappeared in the direction of the abbey. For a long time they still heard the noise, which diminished like a storm in the distance, and then silence was restored. Monsieur Poulin and Monsieur Dupuis, who were angry with each other, went in different directions, without wishing each other good-bye.

The other four set off again, and instinctively went in the direction of Madame Tellier's establishment, which was still closed, silent, impenetrable. A quiet, but obstinate drunken man was knocking at the door of the lower room, and then stopped and called Frédéric, in a low voice, but finding that he got no answer, he sat down on the doorstep, and waited the course of events.

The others were just going to retire, when the noisy band of sailors reappeared at the end of the street. The French sailors were shouting the "Marseillaise," and the Englishmen "Rule Britannia." There was a general lurching against the wall, and then the drunken fellows went on their way toward the quay, where a fight broke out between the two nations, in the course of which an Englishman had his arm broken and a Frenchman his nose split.

The drunken man who had waited outside the door, was crying by that time, as drunken men and children cry when they are vexed, and the others went away. By degrees, calm was restored in the noisy town; here and there, at moments, the distant sound of voices could be heard, and then died away in the distance.

One man only was still wandering about, Monsieur Tournevau, the fish-curer, who was annoyed at having to wait until the following Saturday, and he hoped something would turn up, he did not know what; but he was exasperated at the police for thus allowing an establishment of such public utility, which they had under their control, to be closed.

He went back to it and examined the walls, trying to find out some reason, and on the shutter he saw a notice stuck up. He struck a wax match and read the following, in a large, uneven hand: "Closed on account of the Confirmation."

Then he went away, as he saw it was useless to remain, and left the drunken man lying on the pavement fast asleep, outside that inhospitable door.

The next day, all the regular customers, one after the other, found some reason for going through the street, with a bundle of papers under their arm to keep them in countenance, and with a furtive glance they all read that mysterious notice:

Closed on account of the Confirmation

2

Madame Tellier had a brother, who was a carpenter in their native place, Virville, in the Department of Eure. When she still kept the inn at Yvetot, she had stood godmother to that brother's daughter, who had received the name of Constance—Constance Rivet; she herself being a Rivet on her father's side. The carpenter, who knew that his sister was in a good position, did not lose sight of her, although they did not meet often, for they were both kept at home by their occupations, and lived a long way from each other. But as the girl was twelve years old, and going to be confirmed, he seized that opportunity to write to his sister, asking her to come and be present at the ceremony. Their old parents were dead, and as she could not well refuse her goddaughter, she accepted the invitation. Her brother, whose name was Joseph, hoped that by dint of showing his sister attention, she might be induced to make her will in the girl's favor, as she had no children of her own.

His sister's occupation did not trouble his scruples in the least, and, besides, nobody knew anything about it at Virville. When they spoke of her, they only said: "Madame Tellier is living in Fécamp," which might mean that she was living on her own private income. It was quite twenty leagues from Fécamp to Virville, and for a peasant, twenty leagues on land is as long a journey as crossing the ocean would be to city people. The people at Virville had never been further than Rouen, and nothing attracted the people from Fécamp to a village of five hundred houses in the middle of a plain, and situated in another department; at any rate, nothing was known about her business.

But the Confirmation was coming on, and Madame Tellier was in great embarrassment. She had no substitute, and did not at all care to leave her house, even for a day; for all the rivalries between the girls upstairs and those downstairs would infallibly break out. No doubt Frédéric would get drunk, and when he was in that state, he would knock anybody down for a mere word. At last, however, she made up her mind to take them all with her, with the exception of the man, to whom she gave a holiday until the next day but one.

When she asked her brother, he made no objection, but undertook to put them all up for a night, and so on Saturday morning the eight-o'clock express carried off Madame Tellier and her companions in a second-class carriage. As far as Beuzeville they were alone, and chattered like magpies, but at that station a couple got in. The man, an old peasant, dressed in a blue blouse with a turned-down collar, wide sleeves tight at the wrist, ornamented with white embroidery, wearing an old high hat with long nap, held an enormous green umbrella in one hand, and a large basket in the other, from which the heads of three frightened ducks protruded. The woman, who sat up stiffly in her rustic finery, had a face like a fowl, with a nose that was as pointed as a bill. She sat down opposite her husband and did not stir, as she was startled at finding herself in such smart company.

There was certainly an array of striking colors in the carriage. Madame Tellier was dressed in blue silk from head to foot, and had on a dazzling red imitation French cashmere shawl. Fernande was puffing

in a Scotch plaid dress, of which her companions had laced the bodice as tight as they could, forcing up her full bust, that was continually
heaving up and down. Raphaele, with a bonnet covered with feathers,
so that it looked like a bird's nest, had on a lilac dress with gold spots
on it, and there was something Oriental about it that suited her Jew-
ish face. Rosa had on a pink skirt with large flounces, and looked like
a very fat child, an obese dwarf; while the two Pumps looked as if they
had cut their dresses out of old flowered curtains dating from the
Restoration.

As soon as they were no longer alone in the compartment, the
ladies put on staid looks, and began to talk of subjects which might
give others a high opinion of them. But at Bolbeck a gentleman with
light whiskers, a gold chain, and wearing two or three rings, got in,
and put several parcels wrapped in oilcloth on the rack over his head.
He looked inclined for a joke, and seemed a good-hearted fellow.

"Are you ladies changing your quarters?" he said, and that question embarrassed them all considerably. Madame Tellier, however,
quickly regained her composure, and said sharply, to avenge the honor
of her corps:

"I think you might try and be polite!"

He excused himself, and said: "I beg your pardon, I ought to have
said your nunnery."

She could not think of a retort, so, perhaps thinking she had said
enough, madame gave him a dignified bow and compressed her lips.

Then the gentleman, who was sitting between Rosa and the old
peasant, began to wink knowingly at the ducks whose heads were sticking out of the basket, and when he felt that he had fixed the attention
of his public, he began to tickle them under the bills and spoke fun-
nily to them to make the company smile.

"We have left our little pond, quack! quack! to make the acquaintance of the little spit, qu-ack! qu-ack!"

The unfortunate creatures turned their necks away, to avoid his
caresses, and made desperate efforts to get out of their wicker prison,
and then, suddenly, all at once, uttered the most lamentable quacks
of distress. The women exploded with laughter. They leaned forward
and pushed each other, so as to see better; they were very much interested in the ducks, and the gentleman redoubled his airs, his wit, and
his teasing.

Rosa joined in, and leaning over her neighbor's legs, she kissed the
three animals on the head, and immediately all the girls wanted to

kiss them, in turn, and as they did so the gentleman took them on his knee, jumped them up and down and pinched their arms. The two peasants, who were even in greater consternation than their poultry, rolled their eyes as if they were possessed, without venturing to move, and their old wrinkled faces had not a smile, not a twitch.

Then the gentleman, who was a commercial traveler, offered the ladies suspenders by way of a joke, and taking up one of his packages, he opened it. It was a joke, for the parcel contained garters. There were blue silk, pink silk, red silk, violet silk, mauve silk garters, and the buckles were made of two gilt metal cupids embracing each other. The girls uttered exclamations of delight and looked at them with that gravity natural to all women when they are considering an article of dress. They consulted one another by their looks or in a whisper, and replied in the same manner, and Madame Tellier was longingly handling a pair of orange garters that were broader and more impos-ing looking than the rest; really fit for the mistress of such an estab-lishment.

The gentleman waited, for he had an idea. "Come, my kittens," he said, "you must try them on."

There was a torrent of exclamations, and they squeezed their petti-coats between their legs, but he quietly waited his time and said: "Well, if you will not try them on I shall pack them up again." And he added cunningly: "I offer any pair they like to those who will try them on."

But they would not, and sat up very straight and looked dignified.

But the two Pumps looked so distressed that he renewed his offer to them, and Flora, especially, visibly hesitated, and he insisted: "Come, my dear, a little courage! Just look at that lilac pair; it will suit your dress admirably."

That decided her, and pulling up her dress she showed a thick leg fit for a milkmaid, in a badly fitting, coarse stocking. The commercial traveler stooped down and fastened the garter. When he had done this, he gave her the lilac pair and asked: "Who next?"

"Me! Me!" they all shouted at once, and he began on Rosa, who uncovered a shapeless, round thing without any ankle, a regular "sau-sage of a leg," as Raphaele used to say.

Lastly, Madame Tellier herself put out her leg, a handsome, muscu-lar Norman leg, and in his surprise and pleasure, the commercial traveler gallantly took off his hat to salute that master calf, like a true French cavalier.

The two peasants, who were speechless from surprise, glanced sideways out of the corner of one eye, and they looked so exactly like fowls that the man with the light whiskers, when he sat up, said: "Co—co—ri—co" under their very noses, and that gave rise to another storm of amusement.

The old people got out at Motteville with their basket, their ducks and their umbrella, and they heard the woman say to her husband as they went away:

"They are no good and are off to that cursed place, Paris."

The funny commercial traveler himself got out at Rouen, after behaving so coarsely that Madame Tellier was obliged sharply to put him in his right place, and she added, as a moral: "This will teach us not to talk to the first comer."

At Oissel they changed trains, and at a little station further on Monsieur Joseph Rivet was waiting for them with a large cart with a number of chairs in it, drawn by a white horse.

The carpenter politely kissed all the ladies and then helped them into his conveyance.

Three of them sat on three chairs at the back, Raphaele, Madame Tellier and her brother on the three chairs in front, while Rosa, who had no seat, settled herself as comfortably as she could on tall Fernande's knees, and then they set off.

But the horse's jerky trot shook the cart so terribly that the chairs began to dance and threw the travelers about, to the right and to the left, as if they were dancing puppets, which made them scream and make horrible grimaces.

They clung on to the sides of the vehicle, their bonnets fell on their backs, over their faces and on their shoulders, and the white horse went on stretching out his head and holding out his little hairless tail like a rat's, with which he whisked his buttocks from time to time.

Joseph Rivet, with one leg on the shafts and the other doubled under him, held the reins with his elbows very high, and kept uttering a kind of clucking sound, which made the horse prick up its ears and go faster.

The green country extended on either side of the road, and here and there the colza in flower presented a waving expanse of yellow, from which arose a strong, wholesome, sweet and penetrating odor, which the wind carried to some distance.

The cornflowers showed their little blue heads amid the rye, and the women wanted to pick them, but Monsieur Rivet refused to stop.

Then, sometimes, a whole field appeared to be covered with blood, so thick were the poppies, and the cart, which looked as if it were filled with flowers of more brilliant hue, jogged on through fields bright with wild flowers, and disappeared behind the trees of a farm, only to reappear and to go on again through the yellow or green standing crops, which were studded with red or blue.

One o'clock struck as they drove up to the carpenter's door. They were tired out and pale with hunger, as they had eaten nothing since they left home. Madame Rivet ran out and made them alight, one after another, and kissed them as soon as they were on the ground, and she seemed as if she would never tire of kissing her sister-in-law, whom she apparently wanted to monopolize. They had lunch in the workshop, which had been cleared out for the next day's dinner.

The capital omelet, followed by boiled chitterlings and washed down with good hard cider, made them all feel comfortable.

Rivet had taken a glass so that he might drink with them, and his wife cooked, waited on them, brought in the dishes, took them out and asked each of them in a whisper whether they had everything they wanted. A number of boards standing against the walls and heaps of shavings that had been swept into the corners gave out a smell of planed wood, a smell of a carpenter's shop, that resinous odor which penetrates to the lungs.

They wanted to see the little girl, but she had gone to church and would not be back again until evening, so they all went out for a stroll in the country.

It was a small village, through which the highroad passed. Ten or a dozen houses on either side of the single street were inhabited by the butcher, the grocer, the carpenter, the innkeeper, the shoemaker and the baker.

The church was at the end of the street and was surrounded by a small churchyard, and four immense lime trees, which stood just outside the porch, shaded it completely. It was built of flint, in no particular style, and had a slate-roofed steeple. When you got past it, you were again in the open country, which was varied here and there by clumps of trees which hid the homesteads.

Rivet had given his arm to his sister, out of politeness, although he was in his working clothes, and was walking with her in a dignified manner. His wife, who was overwhelmed by Raphaele's gold-striped dress, walked between her and Fernande, and roly-poly Rosa was trotting behind with Louise and Flora, the Seesaw, who was limping along, quite tired out.

The inhabitants came to their doors, the children left off playing, and a window curtain would be raised, so as to show a muslin cap, while an old woman with a crutch, who was almost blind, crossed herself as if it were a religious procession, and they all gazed for a long time at those handsome ladies from town, who had come so far to be present at the confirmation of Joseph Rivet's little girl, and the carpenter rose very much in the public estimation.

As they passed the church they heard some children singing. Little shrill voices were singing a hymn, but Madame Tellier would not let them go in, for fear of disturbing the little cherubs.

After the walk, during which Joseph Rivet enumerated the principal landed proprietors, spoke about the yield of the land and the productiveness of the cows and sheep, he took his tribe of women home and installed them in his house, and as it was very small, they had to put them into the rooms, two and two.

Just for once Rivet would sleep in the workshop on the shavings; his wife was to share her bed with her sister-in-law, and Fernande and Raphaele were to sleep together in the next room. Louise and Flora were put into the kitchen, where they had a mattress on the floor, and Rosa had a little dark cupboard to herself at the top of the stairs, close to the loft, where the candidate for confirmation was to sleep.

When the little girl came in she was overwhelmed with kisses; all the women wished to caress her with that need of tender expansion, that habit of professional affection which had made them kiss the ducks in the railway carriage.

They each of them took her on their knees, stroked her soft, light hair and pressed her in their arms with vehement and spontaneous outbursts of affection, and the child, who was very good and religious, bore it all patiently.

As the day had been a fatiguing one for everybody, they all went to bed soon after dinner. The whole village was wrapped in that perfect stillness of the country, which is almost like a religious silence, and the girls, who were accustomed to the noisy evenings of their establishment, felt rather impressed by the perfect repose of the sleeping village, and they shivered, not with cold, but with those little shivers of loneliness which come over uneasy and troubled hearts.

As soon as they were in bed, two and two together, they clasped each other in their arms, as if to protect themselves against this feeling of the calm and profound slumber of the earth. But Rosa, who was alone in her little dark cupboard, felt a vague and painful emotion come over her.

She was tossing about in bed, unable to get to sleep, when she heard the faint sobs of a crying child close to her head, through the partition. She was frightened, and called out, and was answered by a weak voice, broken by sobs. It was the little girl, who was always used to sleeping in her mother's room, and who was afraid in her small attic.

Rosa was delighted, got up softly so as not to awaken anyone, and went and fetched the child. She took her into her warm bed, kissed her and pressed her to her bosom, lavished exaggerated manifestations of tenderness on her, and at last grew calmer herself and went to sleep. And till morning the candidate for confirmation slept with her head on Rosa's bosom.

At five o'clock the little church bell, ringing the Angelus, woke the women, who usually slept the whole morning long.

The villagers were up already, and the women went busily from house to house, carefully bringing short, starched muslin dresses or very long wax tapers tied in the middle with a bow of silk fringed with gold, and with dents in the wax for the fingers.

The sun was already high in the blue sky, which still had a rosy tint toward the horizon, like a faint remaining trace of dawn. Families of fowls were walking about outside the houses, and here and there a black cock, with a glistening breast, raised his head, which was crowned by his red comb, flapped his wings and uttered his shrill crow, which the other cocks repeated.

Vehicles of all sorts came from neighboring parishes, stopping at the different houses, and tall Norman women dismounted, wearing dark dresses, with kerchiefs crossed over the bosom, fastened with silver brooches a hundred years old.

The men had put on their blue smocks over their new frock-coats or over their old dress-coats of green-cloth, the two tails of which hung down below their blouses. When the horses were in the stable there was a double line of rustic conveyances along the road: carts, cabriolets, tilburies, wagonettes, traps of every shape and age, tipping forward on their shafts or else tipping backward with the shafts up in the air.

The carpenter's house was as busy as a bee-hive. The women, in dressing-jackets and petticoats, with their thin, short hair, which looked faded and worn, hanging down their backs, were busy dressing the child, who was standing quietly on a table, while Madame Tellier was directing the movements of her battalion. They washed her, did her hair, dressed her, and with the help of a number of pins, they arranged the folds of her dress and took in the waist, which was too large.

Then, when she was ready, she was told to sit down and not to move, and the women hurried off to get ready themselves.

The church bell began to ring again, and its tinkle was lost in the air, like a feeble voice which is soon drowned in space. The candidates came out of the houses and went toward the parochial building, which contained the two schools and the mansion house, and which stood quite at one end of the village, while the church was situated at the other.

The parents, in their very best clothes, followed their children, with embarrassed looks, and those clumsy movements of a body bent by toil.

The little girls disappeared in a cloud of muslin, which looked like whipped cream, while the lads, who looked like embryo waiters in a cafe and whose heads shone with pomatum, walked with their legs apart, so as not to get any dust or dirt on their black trousers.

It was something for a family to be proud of, when a large number of relatives, who had come from a distance, surrounded the child, and the carpenter's triumph was complete.

Madame Tellier's regiment, with its leader at its head, followed Constance; her father gave his arm to his sister, her mother walked by the side of Raphaele, Fernande with Rosa and Louise and Flora together, and thus they proceeded majestically through the village, like a general's staff in full uniform, while the effect on the village was startling.

At the school the girls ranged themselves under the Sister of Mercy and the boys under the schoolmaster, and they started off, singing a hymn as they went. The boys led the way, in two files, between the two rows of vehicles, from which the horses had been taken out, and the girls followed in the same order; and as all the people in the village had given the town ladies the precedence out of politeness, they came immediately behind the girls, and lengthened the double line of the procession still more, three on the right and three on the left, while their dresses were as striking as a display of fireworks.

When they went into the church the congregation grew quite excited. They pressed against each other, turned round and jostled one another in order to see, and some of the devout ones spoke almost aloud, for they were so astonished at the sight of those ladies whose dresses were more elaborate than the priest's vestments.

The mayor offered them his pew, the first one on the right, close to the choir, and Madame Tellier sat there with her sister-in-law, Fernande and Raphaele. Rosa, Louise and Flora occupied the second seat, in company with the carpenter.

The choir was full of kneeling children, the girls on one side and the boys on the other, and the long wax tapers which they held looked like lances pointing in all directions, and three men were standing in front of the lectern, singing as loud as they could.

They prolonged the syllables of the sonorous Latin indefinitely, holding on to "Amens" with interminable "a-a's," which the reed stop of the organ sustained in a monotonous, long-drawn-out tone.

A child's shrill voice took up the reply, and from time to time a priest sitting in a stall and wearing a biretta got up, muttered something and sat down again, while the three singers continued, their eyes fixed on the big book of plain chant lying open before them on the outstretched wings of a wooden eagle.

Then silence ensued and the service went on. Toward the close Rosa, with her head in both hands, suddenly thought of her mother, her village church and her first communion. She almost fancied that that day had returned, when she was so small and was almost hidden in her white dress, and she began to cry.

First of all she wept silently, and the tears dropped slowly from her eyes, but her emotion increased with her recollections, and she began to sob. She took out her pocket handkerchief, wiped her eyes and held it to her mouth, so as not to scream, but it was in vain. A sort of rattle escaped her throat, and she was answered by two other profound, heartbreaking sobs, for her two neighbors, Louise and Flora, who were kneeling near her, overcome by similar recollections, were sobbing by her side, amid a flood of tears; and as tears are contagious, Madame Tellier soon in turn found that her eyes were wet, and on turning to her sister-in-law, she saw that all the occupants of her seat were also crying.

Soon, throughout the church, here and there, a wife, a mother, a sister, seized by the strange sympathy of poignant emotion, and affected at the sight of those handsome ladies on their knees, shaken with sobs was moistening her cambric pocket handkerchief and pressing her beating heart with her left hand.

Just as the sparks from an engine will set fire to dry grass, so the tears of Rosa and of her companions infected the whole congregation in a moment. Men, women, old men and lads in new smocks were soon all sobbing, and something superhuman seemed to be hovering over their heads—a spirit, the powerful breath of an invisible and all powerful Being.

Suddenly a species of madness seemed to pervade the church, the noise of a crowd in a state of frenzy, a tempest of sobs and stifled cries. It came like gusts of wind which blow the trees in a forest, and the priest, paralyzed by emotion, stammered out incoherent prayers, without finding words, ardent prayers of the soul soaring to heaven.

The people behind him gradually grew calmer. The cantors, in all the dignity of their white surplices, went on in somewhat uncertain voices, and the reed stop itself seemed hoarse, as if the instrument had been weeping; the priest, however, raised his hand to command silence and went and stood on the chancel steps, when everybody was silent at once.

After a few remarks on what had just taken place, and which he attributed to a miracle, he continued, turning to the seats where the carpenter's guests were sitting; "I especially thank you, my dear sisters, who have come from such a distance, and whose presence among us, whose evident faith and ardent piety have set such a salutary example to all. You have edified my parish; your emotion has warmed all hearts; without you, this great day would not, perhaps, have had this really divine character. It is sufficient, at times, that there should be one chosen lamb, for the Lord to descend on His flock."

His voice failed him again, from emotion, and he said no more, but concluded the service.

They now left the church as quickly as possible; the children themselves were restless and tired with such a prolonged tension of the mind. The parents left the church by degrees to see about dinner.

There was a crowd outside, a noisy crowd, a babel of loud voices, where the shrill Norman accent was discernible. The villagers formed two ranks, and when the children appeared, each family took possession of their own.

The whole houseful of women caught hold of Constance, surrounded her and kissed her, and Rosa was especially demonstrative. At last she took hold of one hand, while Madame Tellier took the other, and Raphaele and Fernande held up her long muslin skirt, so that it might not drag in the dust; Louise and Flora brought up the rear with Madame Rivet; and the child, who was very silent and thoughtful, set off for home in the midst of this guard of honor.

Dinner was served in the workshop on long boards supported by trestles, and through the open door they could see all the enjoyment that was going on in the village. Everywhere they were feasting, and through every window were to be seen tables surrounded by people in their Sunday best, and a cheerful noise was heard in every house, while the men sat in their shirt-sleeves, drinking glass after glass of cider.

In the carpenter's house the gaiety maintained somewhat of an air of reserve, the consequence of the emotion of the girls in the morning, and Rivet was the only one who was in a jolly mood, and he was drinking to excess. Madame Tellier looked at the clock every moment, for, in order not to lose two days running, they must take the 3:55 train, which would bring them to Fécamp by dark.

The carpenter tried very hard to distract her attention, so as to keep his guests until the next day, but he did not succeed, for she never joked when there was business on hand, and as soon as they had had their coffee she ordered her girls to make haste and get ready, and then, turning to her brother, she said:

"You must put in the horse immediately," and she herself went to finish her last preparations.

When she came down again, her sister-in-law was waiting to speak to her about the child, and a long conversation took place, in which, however, nothing was settled. The carpenter's wife was artful and pretended to be very much affected, and Madame Tellier, who was holding the girl on her knee, would not pledge herself to anything definite, but merely gave vague promises—she would not forget her, there was plenty of time, and besides, they would meet again.

But the conveyance did not come to the door and the women did not come downstairs. Upstairs they even heard loud laughter, romping, little screams, and much clapping of hands, and so, while the carpenter's wife went to the stable to see whether the cart was ready, madame went upstairs.

Rivet, who was very drunk, was plaguing Rosa, who was half choking with laughter. Louise and Flora were holding him by the arms and trying to calm him, as they were shocked at his levity after that morning's ceremony; but Raphaele and Fernande were urging him on, writhing and holding their sides with laughter, and they uttered shrill cries at every rebuff the drunken fellow received.

The man was furious, his face was red, and he was trying to shake off the two women who were clinging to him, while he was pulling Rosa's skirt with all his might and stammering incoherently.

But Madame Tellier, who was very indignant, went up to her brother, seized him by the shoulders, and threw him out of the room with such violence that he fell against the wall in the passage, and a minute afterward they heard him pumping water on his head in the yard, and when he reappeared with the cart he was quite calm.

They started off in the same way as they had come the day before, and the little white horse started off with his quick, dancing trot. Under the hot sun, their fun, which had been checked during dinner, broke out again. The girls now were amused at the jolting of the cart, pushed their neighbors' chairs, and burst out laughing every moment.

There was a glare of light over the country, which dazzled their eyes, and the wheels raised two trails of dust along the highroad. Presently, Fernande, who was fond of music, asked Rosa to sing something, and she boldly struck up "The Fat Curé of Meudon," but Madame Tellier made her stop immediately, as she thought it a very unsuitable song for such a day, and she added: "Sing us something of Beranger's." And so, after a moment's hesitation, Rosa began Beranger's song, "The Grandmother," in her worn-out voice, and all the girls, and even Madame Tellier herself, joined in the chorus:

> How I regret
>   My dimpled arms,
>   My nimble legs,
>   And vanished charms!

"That is first rate," Rivet declared, carried away by the rhythm, and they shouted the refrain to every verse, while Rivet beat time on the shaft with his foot, and with the reins on the back of the horse, who, as if he himself were carried away by the rhythm, broke into a wild gallop, and threw all the women in a heap, one on top of the other, on the bottom of the conveyance.

They got up, laughing as if they were mad, and the song went on, shouted at the top of their voices, beneath the burning sky, among the ripening grain, to the rapid gallop of the little horse, who set off every time the refrain was sung, and galloped a hundred yards, to their great delight, while occasionally a stone-breaker by the roadside sat up and looked at the load of shouting females through his wire spectacles.

When they got out at the station, the carpenter said: "I am sorry you are going; we might have had some good times together." But Madame Tellier replied very sensibly: "Everything has its right time, and we cannot always be enjoying ourselves."

And then he had a sudden inspiration: "Look here, I will come and see you at Fécamp next month." And he gave Rosa a roguish and knowing look.

"Come," his sister replied, " be sensible; you may come if you like, but you are not to be up to any of your tricks."

He did not reply, and as they heard the whistle of the train, he immediately began to kiss them all. When it came to Rosa's turn, he tried to get to her mouth, which she, however, smiling with her lips closed, turned away from him each time by a rapid movement of her head to one side. He held her in his arms, but he could not attain his object, as his large whip, which he was holding in his hand and waving behind the girl's back in desperation, interfered with his movements.

"Passengers for Rouen, take your seats!" a guard cried, and they got in. There was a slight whistle, followed by a loud whistle from the engine, which noisily puffed out its first jet of steam, while the wheels began to turn a little with a visible effort, and Rivet left the station and ran along by the track to get another look at Rosa, and as the carriage passed him, he began to crack his whip and to jump, while he sang at the top of his voice:

> How I regret
>   My dimpled arms,
> My nimble legs,
>   And vanished charms.

And then he watched a white pocket-handkerchief, which somebody was waving, as it disappeared in the distance.

3

They slept the peaceful sleep of a quiet conscience, until they got to Rouen, and when they returned to the house, refreshed and rested, Madame Tellier could not help saying: "It was all very well, but I was longing to get home."

They hurried over their supper, and then, when they had put on their usual evening costume, waited for their regular customers, and the little colored lamp outside the door told the passersby that Madame Tellier had returned, and in a moment the news spread, nobody knew how or through whom.

Monsieur Philippe, the banker's son, even carried his friendliness so far as to send a special messenger to Monsieur Tournevau, who was in the bosom of his family.

The fish-curer had several cousins to dinner every Sunday, and they were having coffee, when a man came in with a letter in his hand. Monsieur Tournevau was much excited; he opened the envelope and grew pale; it contained only these words in pencil:

> The cargo of cod has been found; the ship has come into port; good business for you. Come immediately.

He felt in his pockets, gave the messenger two sous, and suddenly blushing to his ears, he said: "I must go out." He handed his wife the laconic and mysterious note, rang the bell, and when the servant came in, he asked her to bring him his hat and overcoat immediately. As soon as he was in the street, he began to hurry, and the way seemed to him to be twice as long as usual, in consequence of his impatience.

Madame Tellier's establishment had put on quite a holiday look. On the ground floor, a number of sailors were making a deafening noise, and Louise and Flora drank with one and the other, and were being called for in every direction at once.

The upstairs room was full by nine o'clock. Monsieur Vasse of the Tribunal of Commerce, Madame Tellier's regular but Platonic wooer, was talking to her in a corner in a low voice, and they were both smiling, as if they were about to come to an understanding.

Monsieur Poulin, the ex-mayor, was talking to Rosa, and she was running her hands through the old gentleman's white whiskers.

Tall Fernande was on the sofa, her feet on the coat of Monsieur Pinipesse, the tax collector, and leaning back against young Monsieur Philippe, her right arm around his neck, while she held a cigarette in her left hand.

Raphaele appeared to be talking seriously with Monsieur Dupuis, the insurance agent, and she finished by saying: "Yes, I will, yes."

Just then, the door opened suddenly, and Monsieur Tournevau came in, and was greeted with enthusiastic cries of "Long live

Tournevau!" And Raphaele, who was dancing alone up and down the room, went and threw herself into his arms. He seized her in a vigorous embrace and, without saying a word, lifted her up as if she had been a feather.

Rosa was chatting to the ex-mayor, kissing him and pulling; both his whiskers at the same time, in order to keep his head straight.

Fernande and Madame Tellier remained with the four men, and Monsieur Philippe exclaimed: "I will pay for some champagne; get three bottles, Madame Tellier." And Fernande gave him a hug, and whispered to him: "Play us a waltz, will you?" So he rose and sat down at the old piano in the corner, and managed to get a hoarse waltz out of the depths of the instrument.

The tall girl put her arms round the tax collector, Madame Tellier let Monsieur Vasse take her round the waist, and the two couples turned round, kissing as they danced. Monsieur Vasse, who had formerly danced in good society, waltzed with such elegance that Madame Tellier was quite captivated.

Frédéric brought the champagne; the first cork popped, and Monsieur Philippe played the introduction to a quadrille, through which the four dancers walked in society fashion, decorously, with propriety, deportment, bows and curtsies, and then they began to drink.

Monsieur Philippe next struck up a lively polka, and Monsieur Tournevau started off with the handsome Jewess, whom he held without letting her feet touch the ground. Monsieur Pinipesse and Monsieur Vasse had started off with renewed vigor, and from time to time one or other couple would stop to toss off a long draught of sparkling wine, and that dance was threatening to become never-ending, when Rosa opened the door.

"I want to dance," she exclaimed. And she caught hold of Monsieur Dupuis, who was sitting idle on the couch, and the dance began again.

But the bottles were empty. "I will pay for one," Monsieur Tournevau said. "So will I," Monsieur Vasse declared. "And I will do the same," Monsieur Dupuis remarked.

They all began to clap their hands, and it soon became a regular ball, and from time to time Louise and Flora ran upstairs quickly and had a few turns, while their customers downstairs grew impatient, and then they returned regretfully to the taproom. At midnight they were still dancing.

Madame Tellier let them amuse themselves while she had long private talks in corners with Monsieur Vasse, as if to settle the last details of something that had already been settled.

At last, at one o'clock, the two married men, Monsieur Tournevau and Monsieur Pinipesse, declared that they were going home, and wanted to pay. Nothing was charged for except the champagne, and that cost only six francs a bottle, instead of ten, which was the usual price, and when they expressed their surprise at such generosity, Madame Tellier, who was beaming, said to them: "We don't have a holiday every day."

The False Gems

M. Lantin had met the young woman at a soirée, at the home of the assistant chief of his bureau, and at first sight had fallen madly in love with her.

She was the daughter of a country physician who had died some months previously. She had come to live in Paris, with her mother, who visited much among her acquaintances, in the hope of making a favorable marriage for her daughter. They were poor and honest, quiet and unaffected.

The young girl was a perfect type of the virtuous woman whom every sensible young man dreams of one day winning for life. Her simple beauty had the charm of angelic modesty, and the imperceptible smile which constantly hovered about her lips seemed to be the reflection of a pure and lovely soul. Her praises resounded on every side. People were never tired of saying: "Happy the man who wins her love! He could not find a better wife."

Now M. Lantin enjoyed a snug little income of seven thousand francs, and, thinking he could safely assume the responsibilities of matrimony, proposed to this model young girl and was accepted.

He was unspeakably happy with her; she governed his household so cleverly and economically that they seemed to live in luxury. She lavished the most delicate attentions on her husband, coaxed and fondled him, and the charm of her presence was so great that six years after their marriage M. Lantin discovered that he loved his wife even more than during the first days of their honeymoon.

He only felt inclined to blame her for two things: her love of the theater, and a taste for false jewelry. Her friends (she was acquainted with some officers' wives) frequently procured for her a box at the theater, often for the first representations of the new plays; and her husband was obliged to accompany her, whether he willed or not, to these amusements, though they bored him excessively after a day's labor at the office.

After a time, M. Lantin begged his wife to get some lady of her acquaintance to accompany her. She was at first opposed to such an

arrangement; but, after much persuasion on his part, she finally consented—to the infinite delight of her husband.

Now, with her love for the theater came also the desire to adorn
her person. True, her costumes remained as before, simple, and in the
most correct taste; but she soon began to ornament her ears with
huge rhinestones which glittered and sparkled like real diamonds.
Around her neck she wore strings of false pearls, and on her arms
bracelets of imitation gold.

Her husband frequently remonstrated with her, saying:

"My dear, as you cannot afford to buy real diamonds, you ought to
appear adorned with your beauty and modesty alone, which are the
rarest ornaments of your sex."

But she would smile sweetly, and say:

"What can I do? I am so fond of jewelry. It is my only weakness.
We cannot change our natures."

Then she would roll the pearl necklaces around her fingers, and
hold up the bright gems for her husband's admiration, gently coaxing him:

"Look! are they not lovely? One would swear they were real."

M. Lantin would then answer, smilingly:

"You have bohemian tastes, my dear."

Often of an evening, when they were enjoying a tête-à-tête by the
fireside, she would place on the tea table the leather box containing
the "trash," as M. Lantin called it. She would examine the false gems
with a passionate attention as though they were in some way con-
nected with a deep and secret joy; and she often insisted on passing a
necklace around her husband's neck, and laughing heartily would
exclaim: "How droll you look!" Then she would throw herself into his
arms and kiss him affectionately.

One evening in winter she attended the opera, and on her return
was chilled through and through. The next morning she coughed,
and eight days later she died of inflammation of the lungs.

M. Lantin's despair was so great that his hair became white in one
month. He wept unceasingly; his heart was torn with grief, and his
mind was haunted by the remembrance, the smile, the voice—by every
charm of his beautiful, dead wife.

Time, the healer, did not assuage his grief. Often during office
hours, while his colleagues were discussing the topics of the day, his
eyes would suddenly fill with tears, and he would give vent to his grief
in heartrending sobs. Everything in his wife's room remained as be-

fore her decease; and here he was wont to seclude himself daily and think of her who had been his treasure—the joy of his existence.

But life soon became a struggle. His income, which in the hands of his wife had covered all household expenses, was now no longer sufficient for his own immediate wants; and he wondered how she could have managed to buy such excellent wines, and such rare delicacies, things which he could no longer procure with his modest resources.

He incurred some debts and was soon reduced to absolute poverty. One morning, finding himself without a centime in his pocket, he resolved to sell something, and, immediately, the thought occurred to him of disposing of his wife's paste jewels. He cherished in his heart a sort of rancor against the false gems. They had always irritated him in the past, and the very sight of them spoiled somewhat the memory of his lost darling.

To the last days of her life, she had continued to make purchases; bringing home new gems almost every evening. He decided to sell the heavy necklace which she seemed to prefer, and which, he thought, ought to be worth about six or seven francs; for although paste it was, nevertheless, of very fine workmanship.

He put it in his pocket and started out in search of a jeweler's shop. He entered the first one he saw, feeling a little ashamed to expose his misery, and also to offer such a worthless article for sale. "Sir," said he to the merchant, "I would like to know what this is worth." The man took the necklace, examined it, called his clerk and made some remarks in an undertone; then he put the ornament back on the counter, and looked at it from a distance to judge of the effect.

M. Lantin was annoyed by all this detail and was on the point of saying: "Oh! I know well enough it is not worth anything," when the jeweler said: "Sir, that necklace is worth from twelve to fifteen thousand francs; but I could not buy it unless you tell me now whence it comes."

The widower opened his eyes wide and remained gaping, not comprehending the merchant's meaning. Finally he stammered: "You say . . . are you sure?" The other replied dryly: "You can search elsewhere and see if anyone will offer you more. I consider it worth fifteen thousand at the most. Come back here if you cannot do better."

M. Lantin, beside himself with astonishment, took up the necklace and left the store. He wished time for reflection.

Once outside, he felt inclined to laugh, and said to himself: "The fool! Had I only taken him at his word! That jeweler cannot distinguish real diamonds from paste."

A few minutes after, he entered another store in the Rue de la Paix. As soon as the proprietor glanced at the necklace, he cried out:

"Ah, parbleu! I know it well; it was bought here."

M. Lantin was disturbed, and asked:

"How much is it worth?"

"Well, I sold it for twenty thousand francs. I am willing to take it back for eighteen thousand when you inform me, according to our legal formality, how it comes to be in your possession."

This time M. Lantin was dumfounded. He replied:

"But . . . but . . . examine it closely. Until this moment I was under the impression that it was paste."

Said the jeweler:

"What is your name, sir?"

"Lantin—I am in the employ of the Minister of the Interior. I live at No. 16 Rue des Martyrs."

The merchant looked through his books, found the entry, and said: "That necklace was sent to Mme. Lantin's address, 16 Rue des Martyrs, July 20, 1876."

The two men looked into each other's eyes—the widower speechless with astonishment, the jeweler scenting a thief. The latter broke the silence by saying:

"Will you leave this necklace here for twenty-four hours? I will give you a receipt."

"Certainly," answered M. Lantin, hastily. Then, putting the ticket in his pocket, he left the store.

He wandered aimlessly through the streets, his mind in a state of dreadful confusion. He tried to reason, to understand. His wife could not afford to purchase such a costly ornament. Certainly not. But, then, it must have been a present!—a present!—a present from whom? Why was it given her?

He stopped and remained standing in the middle of the street. A horrible doubt entered his mind—she? Then all the other gems must have been presents, too! The earth seemed to tremble beneath him— the tree before him was falling—throwing up his arms, he fell to the ground, unconscious. He recovered his senses in a pharmacy into which some passersby had taken him, and was then taken to his home. When he arrived he shut himself up in his room and wept until nightfall.

Finally, overcome with fatigue, he threw himself on the bed, where he passed an uneasy, restless night.

The following morning he arose and prepared to go to the office. It was hard to work after such a, shock. He sent a letter to his employer requesting to be excused. Then he remembered that he had to return to the jeweler's. He did not like the idea; but he could not leave the necklace with that man. So he dressed and went out.

It was a lovely day; a clear blue sky smiled on the busy city below, and men of leisure were strolling about with their hands in their pockets.

Observing them, M. Lantin said to himself: "The rich, indeed, are happy. With money it is possible to forget even the deepest sorrow. One can go where one pleases, and in travel find that distraction which is the surest cure for grief. Oh! if I were only rich!"

He began to feel hungry, but his pocket was empty. He again remembered the necklace. Eighteen thousand francs! Eighteen thousand francs! What a sum!

He soon arrived in the Rue de la Paix, opposite the jeweler's. Eighteen thousand francs! Twenty times he resolved to go in, but shame kept him back. He was hungry, however—very hungry, and had not a centime in his pocket. He decided quickly, ran across the street in order not to have time for reflection, and entered the store.

The proprietor immediately came forward, and politely offered him a chair; the clerks glanced at him knowingly.

"I have made inquiries, M. Lantin," said the jeweler, "and if you are still resolved to dispose of the gems, I am ready to pay you the price I offered."

"Certainly, sir," stammered M. Lantin.

Whereupon the proprietor took from a drawer eighteen large bills, counted and handed them to M. Lantin, who signed a receipt and with a trembling hand put the money into his pocket.

As he was about to leave the store, he turned toward the merchant, who still wore the same knowing smile, and lowering his eyes, said:

"I have—I have other gems which I have received from the same source. Will you buy them also?"

The merchant bowed: "Certainly, sir."

M. Lantin said gravely: "I will bring them to you." An hour later he returned with the gems.

The large diamond earrings were worth twenty thousand francs; the bracelets thirty-five thousand; the rings, sixteen thousand; a set of emeralds and sapphires, fourteen thousand; a gold chain with solitaire pendant, forty thousand—making the sum of one hundred and forty-three thousand francs.

The jeweler remarked, jokingly:

"There was a person who invested all her earnings in precious stones."

M. Lantin replied, seriously:

"It is merely another way of investing one's money."

That day he lunched at Voisin's and drank wine worth twenty francs a bottle. Then he hired a carriage and made a tour of the Bois, and as he scanned the various carriages with a contemptuous air he could hardly refrain from crying out to the occupants:

"I, too, am rich!—I am worth two hundred thousand francs."

Suddenly he thought of his employer. He drove up to the office, and entered gaily, saying:

"Sir, I have come to resign my position. I have just inherited three hundred thousand francs."

He shook hands with his former colleagues and confided to them some of his projects for the future; then he went off to dine at the Café Anglais.

He seated himself beside a gentleman of aristocratic bearing, and during the meal informed the latter confidentially that he had just inherited a fortune of four hundred thousand francs.

For the first time in his life he was not bored at the theater, and spent the remainder of the night in a mad frolic.

Six months afterward he married again. His second wife was a very virtuous woman, with a violent temper. She caused him much sorrow.

Bed No. 29

When Captain Epivent passed in the street all the ladies turned to look at him. He was the true type of a handsome officer of hussars. He was always on parade, always strutted a little and seemed preoccupied and proud of his leg, his figure, and his mustache. He had superb ones, it is true, a superb leg, figure, and mustache. The last-named was blond, very heavy, falling martially from his lip in a beautiful sweep the color of ripe wheat, carefully turned at the ends, and falling over both sides of his mouth in two powerful sprigs of hair cut square across. His waist was thin as if he wore a corset, while vigorous masculine chest, bulged and arched, spread itself above his waist. His leg was admirable, a gymnastic leg, the leg of a dancer whose muscular flesh outlined each movement under the clinging cloth of the red pantaloon.

He walked with muscles taut with feet and arms apart, and with the slightly balanced step of the cavalier, who knows how to make the most of his limbs and his carriage, and who seems a conqueror in a uniform, but looks commonplace in a mufti.

Like many other officers, Captain Epivent carried a civil costume badly. He had no air of elegance as soon as he was clothed in the gray or black of the shop clerk. But in his proper setting he was triumph. He had besides a handsome face, the nose thin and curved, blue eyes, and a good forehead. He was bald, without ever being able to comprehend why his hair had fallen off. He consoled himself with thinking that, with a heavy mustache, a head a little bald was not so bad.

He scorned everybody in general, with a difference in the degrees of his scorn.

In the first place, for him the middle class did not exist. He looked at them as he would look at animals, without according them more of his attention than he would give to sparrows or chickens. Officers, alone, counted in his world; but he did not have the same esteem for all officers. He only respected handsome men; an imposing presence, the true, military quality being first. A solider was a merry fellow, a devil, created for love and war, a man of brawn, muscle and hair, nothing more. He classed the generals of the French army according to their figure, their bearing, and the stern look of their faces. Bourbaki appeared to him the greatest warrior of modern times.

He often laughed at the officers of the line who were short and fat, and puffed while marching. And he had a special scorn for the poor recruits from the polytechnic schools, those thin, little men with spectacles, awkward and unskillful, who seemed as much made for a uniform as a wolf for saying mass, as he often asserted. He was indignant that they should be tolerated in the army, those abortions with the lank limbs, who marched like crabs, did not drink, ate little, and seemed to love equations better than pretty girls.

Captain Epivent himself had constant successes and triumphs with the fair sex.

Every time he took supper in company with a woman he thought himself certain of finishing the night with her upon the same mattress, and, if unsurmountable obstacles hindered that evening, his victory was sure at least the following day. His comrades did not like him to meet their mistresses, and the merchants in the shops, who had their pretty wives at the counter, knew him, feared him, and hated him desperately. When he passed, the merchants' wives in spite of themselves exchanged a look with him through the glass of the front windows; one of those looks that avail more than tender words, which contain an appeal and a response, a desire and an avowal. And the husbands, who turned away with a sort of instinct, returned brusquely, casting a furious look at the proud, arched silhouette of the officer. And, when the captain had passed, smiling and content with his impression, the merchants, handling with nervous hands the objects spread out before them, declared:

"There's a great dandy. When shall we stop feeding all these good-for-nothings who go dragging their tinware through the streets? For my part, I would rather be a butcher than a soldier. Then if there's blood on my table, it is the blood of beasts, at least. And he is useful, is the butcher; and the knife he carries has not killed men. I do not understand how these murderers are tolerated walking on the public streets, carrying with them their instruments of death. It is necessary to have them, I suppose, but at least, let them conceal themselves, and not dress up in masquerade, with their red breeches and blue coats. The executioner doesn't dress himself up, does he?"

The woman, without answering, would shrug her shoulders, while the husband, divining the gesture without seeing it, would cry:

"Anybody must be stupid to watch those fellows parade up and down."

Nevertheless, Captain Epivent's reputation for conquests was well established in the whole French army.

Now, in 1868, his regiment, the One Hundred and Second Hussars came into garrison at Rouen.

He was soon known in the town. He appeared every evening, toward five o'clock, upon the Boieldieu mall, to take his absinthe and coffee at the Comedy; and, before entering the establishment, he would always take a turn upon the promenade, to show his leg, his figure, and his moustaches.

The merchants of Rouen who also promenaded there with their hands behind their backs, preoccupied with business affairs, speaking in high and low voices, would sometimes throw him a glance and murmur:

"Egad! that's a handsome fellow!"

But when they knew him, they remarked:

"Look! Captain Epivent! But he's a rascal all the same!"

The women on meeting him had a very queer little movement of the head, a kind of shiver of modesty, as if they felt themselves grow weak or unclothed before him. They would lower their heads a little, with a smile upon their lips, as if they had a desire to be found charming and have a look from him. When he walked with a comrade the comrade never failed to murmur with jealous envy, each time that he saw the sport:

"The rascal of an Epivent has the chances!"

Among the licensed girls of the town it was a struggle, a race, to see who would carry him off. They all came at five o'clock, the officers' hour, to the Boieldieu mall, and dragged their skirts up and down the length of the walk, two by two, while the lieutenants, captains, and commanders, two by two, dragged their swords along the ground before entering the *café*.

One evening the beautiful Irma, the mistress, it was said, of M. Templier-Papon, the rich manufacturer, stopped her carriage in front of the Comedy and, getting out, made a pretense of buying some paper or some visiting cards of M. Paulard, the engraver, in order to pass before the officers' tables and cast a look at Captain Epivent which seemed to say: "When you will," so clearly that Colonel Prune, who was drinking the green liquor with his lieutenant-colonel, could not help muttering:

"Confound that fellow! He has the chances, that scamp!"

The remark of the Colonel was repeated, and Captain Epivent, moved by this approbation of his superior, passed the next day and many times after that under the windows of the beauty, in his most captivating attitude.

She saw him, showed herself, and smiled.

That same evening he was her lover.

They attracted attention, made an exhibition of their attachment, and mutually compromised themselves, both of them proud of their adventure.

Nothing was so talked of in town as the beautiful Irma and the officer. M. Templier-Papon alone was ignorant of their relation.

Captain Epivent beamed with glory; every instant he would say:

"Irma happened to say to me—Irma told me tonight—or, yesterday at dinner Irma said—"

For a whole year they walked with and displayed in Rouen this love like a flag taken from the enemy. He felt himself aggrandized by this conquest, envied, more sure of the future, surer of the decoration so much desired, for the eyes of all were upon him, and he was satisfied to find himself well in sight, instead of being forgotten.

But here war was declared, and the Captain's regiment was one of the first to be sent to the front. The adieux were lamentable. They lasted the whole night long.

Sword, red breeches, cap, and jacket were all overturned from the back of a chair upon the floor; robes, skirts, silk stockings, also fallen down, were spread around and mingled with the uniform in distress upon the carpet; the room upside down as if there had been a battle; Irma wild, her hair unbound, threw her despairing arms around the officer's neck, straining him to her; then, leaving him, rolled upon the floor, overturning the furniture, catching the fringes of the arm-chairs, biting their feet, while the Captain much moved, but not skill-ful at consolation, repeated:

"Irma, my little Irma, do not cry so, it is necessary."

He occasionally wiped a tear from the corner of his eye with the end of his finger. They separated at daybreak. She followed her lover in her carriage as far as the first stopping-place. Then she kissed him before the whole regiment at the moment of separation. They even found this very genteel, worthy, and very romantic; and the comrades pressed the Captain's hand and said to him:

"Confound you, rogue, she has a heart, all the same, the little one."

They seemed to see something patriotic in it.

The regiment was sorely proved during the campaign. The Captain conducted himself heroically and finally received the cross of honor. Then, the war ended, he returned to Rouen and the garrison.

Immediately upon his return he asked of news of Irma, but no one was able to give him anything exact. Some said she was married to a Prussian major. Others, that she had gone to her parents who were farmers in the suburbs of Yvetot.

He even sent his orderly to the mayor's office to consult the registry of deaths. The name of his mistress was not to be found.

He was very angry, which fact he paraded everywhere. He even took the enemy to task for his unhappiness, attributing to the Prussians, who had occupied Rouen, the disappearance of the young girl, declaring:

"In the next war, they shall pay well for it, the beggars!"

Then, one morning as he entered the mess-room at the breakfast hour, an old porter, in a blouse and an oilcloth cap, gave him a letter, which he opened and read:

My Dearie:
   I am in the hospital, very ill, very ill. Will you not come and see me? It would give me so much pleasure!
                                        Irma

The Captain grew pale and, moved with pity, declared:

"It's too bad! The poor girl! I will go there as soon as breakfast."

And during the whole time at the table, he told the officers that Irma was in the hospital and that he was going to see her that blessed morning. It must be the fault of those unspeakable Prussians. She had doubtless found herself alone without a sou, broken down with misery, for they must certainly have stolen her furniture.

"Ah! the dirty whelps."

Everybody listened with great excitement. Scarcely had he slipped his napkin in his wooden ring, when he rose and, taking his sword from the peg, and swelling out his chest to make him thin, hooked his belt and set out with hurried step to the city hospital.

But entrance to the hospital building, where he expected to enter immediately, was sharply refused him, and he was obliged to find his Colonel and explain his case to him in order to get a word from him to the director.

This man, after having kept the handsome Captain waiting some time in his anteroom, gave him an authorized pass and a cold and disapproving greeting.

Inside the door he felt himself constrained in this asylum of misery and suffering and death. A boy in the service showed him the way. He walked upon tiptoe, that he might make no noise, through the long corridors, where floated a slight, moist odor of illness and medicines. A murmur of voices alone disturbed the silence of the hospital.

At times, through an open door, the Captain perceived a dormitory, with its rows of beds whose clothes were raised by the forms of the bodies.

Some convalescents were seated in chairs at the foot of their couches, sewing, and clothed in the uniform gray cloth dress with white cap.

His guide suddenly stopped before one of these corridors filled with patients. He read on the door, in large letters: "Syphilis." The Captain started: then he felt that he was blushing. An attendant was preparing a medicine at a little wooden table at the door.

"I will show you," she said, "it is bed 29."

And she walked ahead of the officer. She indicated a bed: "There it is."

There was nothing to be seen but a bundle of bedclothes. Even the head was concealed under the coverlet. Everywhere faces were to be seen on the couches, pale faces, astonished at the sight of a uniform, the faces of women, young women and old women, but all seemingly plain and common in the humble, regulation garb.

The Captain, very much disturbed, supporting his sword in one hand and carrying his cap in the other, murmured:

"Irma."

There was a sudden motion in the bed and the face of his mistress appeared, but so changed, so tired, so thin, that he would scarcely have known it.

She gasped, overcome by emotion and then said:

"Albert!–Albert! It is you! Oh! I am so glad–so glad." And the tears ran down her cheeks.

The attendant brought a chair. "Be seated, sir," she said.

He sat down and looked at the pale, wretched countenance, so little like that of the beautiful, fresh girl he had left. Finally he said:

"What seems to be the matter with you?"

She replied, weeping: "You know well enough, it is written on the door." And she hid her eyes under the edge of the bedclothes.

Dismayed and ashamed, he continued:

"How have you caught it, my poor girl?"

She answered: "It was those beasts of Prussians. They took me almost by force and then poisoned me."

He found nothing to add. He looked at her and kept turning his cap around on his knees.

The other patients gazed at him, and he believed that he detected an odor of putrefaction, of contaminated flesh, in this corridor full of girls tainted with this ignoble, terrible malady.

She murmured: "I do not believe that I shall recover. The doctor says it is very serious."

Then she perceived the cross upon the officer's breast and cried:

"Oh! you have been honored; now I am content. How contented I am! If I could only embrace you!"

A shiver of fear and disgust ran along the Captain's skin at the thought of this kiss. He had a desire to make his escape, to be in the clear air and never see this woman again. He remained, however, not knowing how to make the adieux, and finally stammered:

"You took no care of yourself, then."

A flame flashed in Irma's eyes: "No, the desire to avenge myself came to me when I should have broken away from it. And I poisoned them too, all, all that I could. As long as there were any of them in Rouen, I had no thought for myself."

He declared, in a constrained tone in which there was a little note of gaiety: "So far, you have done some good."

Getting animated, and her cheekbones getting red, she answered:

"Oh! yes, there will more than one of them die from my fault. I tell you I had my vengeance."

Again he said, "So much the better." Then rising, he added, "Well, I must leave you now, because I have only time to meet my appointment with the Colonel—"

She showed much emotion, crying out: "Already! You leave me already! And when you have scarcely arrived!"

But he wished to go at any cost, and said:

"But you see that I came immediately; and it is absolutely necessary that I be at the Colonel's at the appointed time."

She asked: "Is it still Colonel Prune?"

"Still Colonel Prune. He was twice wounded."

She continued: "And your comrades? Have some of them been killed?"

"Yes. Saint-Timon, Savagnat, Poli, Saprival, Robert, De Courson,

Pasafil, Santal, Caravan, and Poivrin are dead. Sahel had an arm carried off and Courvoisin a leg amputated. Paquet lost his right eye."

She listened, much interested. Then suddenly she stammered:

"Will you kiss me, say? before you leave me; Madame Langlois is not there."

And, in spite of the disgust which came to his lips, he placed them against the wan forehead, while she, throwing her arms around him, scattered random kisses over his blue jacket.

Then she said: "You will come again? Say that you will come again— Promise me that you will."

"Yes, I promise."

"When, now. Can you come Thursday?"

"Yes, Thursday—"

"Thursday at two o'clock?"

"Yes, Thursday at two o'clock."

"You promise?"

"I promise."

"Adieu, my dearie."

"Adieu."

And he went away, confused by the staring glances of those in the dormitory, bending his tall form to make himself seem smaller. And when he was in the street he took a long breath.

That evening his comrades asked him: "Well, how is Irma?"

He answered in a constrained voice: "She has a trouble with the lungs; she is very ill."

But a little lieutenant, scenting something from his manner, went to headquarters, and, the next day, when the Captain went into mess he was welcomed by a volley of laughter and jokes. They had found vengeance at last.

It was learned further that Irma had made a spite marriage with the staff-major of the Prussians, that she had gone through the country on horseback with the colonel of the Blue Hussars, and many others, and that, in Rouen, she was no longer called anything but the "wife of the Prussians."

For eight days the Captain was the victim of his regiment. He received by post and by messenger, notes from those who can reveal the past and the future, circulars of specialists, and medicines, that nature of which was inscribed on the package.

And the Colonel, catching the drift of it, said in severe tone:

"Well, the Captain had a pretty acquaintance! I send him my compliments."

At the end of twelve days he was appealed to by another letter from Irma. He tore it up with rage and made no reply to it.

A week later she wrote him again that she was very ill and wished to see him to say farewell.

He did not answer.

After some days more he received a note from a chaplain of the hospital.

The girl Irma Pavolin is on her deathbed and begs you to come.

He dared not refuse to oblige the chaplain, but he entered the hospital with a heart swelling with wicked anger, with wounded vanity, and humiliation.

He found her scarcely changed at all and thought that she had deceived him. "What do you wish of me?" he asked.

"I wish to say farewell. It appears that I am near the end."

He did not believe it.

"Listen," said he, "you have made me the laughing stock of the regiment, and I do not wish it to continue."

She asked: "What have I done?"

He was irritated at not knowing how to answer. But he said:

"Is it nothing that I return here to be joked by everybody on your account?"

She looked at him with languid eyes, where shone a pale light of anger, and answered:

"What can I have done? I have not been genteel with you, perhaps! Is it because I have sometimes asked for something? But for you, I would have remained with M. Templier-Papon, and would not have found myself here today. No, you see, if anyone has reproaches to make it is not you."

He answered in a clear tone: "I have not made reproaches, but I cannot continue to come to see you, because your conduct with the Prussians has been the shame of the town."

She sat up, with a little shake, in the bed, as she replied:

"My conduct with the Prussians? But when I tell you that they took me, and when I tell you that if I took no thought of myself, it was because I wished to poison them! If I had wished to cure myself, it would not have been so difficult, I can tell you! But I wished to kill them, and I have killed them, come now! I have killed them!"

He remained standing: "In any case," said he, "it was a shame."

She had a kind of suffocation, and then replied:

"Why is it a shame for me to cause them to die and try to extermi-nate them, tell me? You did not talk that way when you used to come to my house in Jeanne-d'Arc street. Ah! it is a shame! You have not done as much, with your cross of honor! I deserve more merit than you, do you understand, more than you, for I have killed more Prussians than you!"

He stood stupefied before her trembling with indignation. He stam-mered: "Be still—you must—be still—because those things—I cannot al-low—anyone to touch upon—"

But she was not listening: "What harm have you done the Prussians? Would it ever have happened if you had kept them from coming to Rouen? Tell me! It is you who should stop and listen. And I have done more harm than you, I, yes, more harm to them than you, and I am going to die for it while you are singing songs and making yourself fine to inveigle women—"

Upon each bed a head was raised and all eyes looked at this man in uniform who stammered again:

"You must be still—more quiet—you know—"

But she would not be quiet. She cried out:

"Ah! yes, you are a pretty *poser!* I know you well. I know you. And I tell you that I have done them more harm than you—I—and that I have killed more than all your regiment together—come now, you coward."

He went away, in fact he fled, stretching his long legs as he passed between the two rows of beds where the syphilitic patients were be-coming excited. And he heard the gasping, stifled voice of Irma pur-suing him:

"More than you—yes—I have killed more than you—"

He tumbled down the staircase four steps at a time, and ran until he was shut fast in his room.

The next day he heard that she was dead.

My Uncle Jules

A white-haired old man begged us for alms. My companion, Joseph Davranche, gave him five francs. Noticing my surprised look, he said: "That poor unfortunate reminds me of a story which I shall tell you, the memory of which continually pursues me. Here it is:

"My family, which came originally from Havre, was not rich. We just managed to make both ends meet. My father worked hard, came home late from the office, and earned very little. I had two sisters.

"My mother suffered a good deal from our reduced circumstances, and she often had harsh words for her husband, veiled and sly reproaches. The poor man then made a gesture which used to distress me. He would pass his open hand over his forehead, as if to wipe away perspiration which did not exist, and he would answer nothing. I felt his helpless suffering. We economized on everything, and never would accept an invitation to dinner, so as not to have to return the courtesy. All our provisions were bought at bargain sales. My sisters made their own gowns, and long discussions would arise on the price of a piece of braid worth fifteen centimes a yard. Our meals usually consisted of soup and beef, prepared with every kind of sauce.

"They say it is wholesome and nourishing, but I should have preferred a change.

"I used to go through terrible scenes on account of lost buttons and torn trousers.

"Every Sunday, dressed in our best, we would take our walk along the breakwater. My father, in a frock coat, high hat and kid gloves, would offer his arm to my mother, decked out and beribboned like a ship on a holiday. My sisters, who were always ready first, would await the signal for leaving; but at the last minute someone always found a spot on my father's frock coat, and it had to be wiped away quickly with a rag moistened with benzine.

"My father, in his shirt-sleeves, his silk hat on his head, would await the completion of the operation, while my mother, putting on her spectacles, and taking off her gloves in order not to spoil them, would make haste.

"Then we set out ceremoniously. My sisters marched on ahead, arm in arm. They were of marriageable age and had to be displayed. I walked on the left of my mother and my father on her right. I remember the pompous air of my poor parents in these Sunday walks, their stern expression, their stiff walk. They moved slowly, with a serious expression, their bodies straight, their legs stiff, as if something of extreme importance depended upon their appearance.

"Every Sunday, when the big steamers were returning from unknown and distant countries, my father would invariably utter the same words: 'What a surprise it would be if Jules were on that one! Eh?'

"My uncle Jules, my father's brother, was the only hope of the family, after being its only fear. I had heard about him since childhood, and it seemed to me that I should recognize him immediately, knowing as much about him as I did. I knew every detail of his life up to the day of his departure for America, although this period of his life was spoken of only in hushed tones.

"It seems that he had led a bad life, that is to say, he had squandered a little money, which action, in a poor family, is one of the greatest crimes. With rich people a man who amuses himself only sows his wild oats. He is what is generally called a sport. But among needy families a boy who forces his parents to break into the capital becomes a good-for-nothing, a rascal, a scamp. And this distinction is just, although the action be the same, for consequences alone determine the seriousness of the act.

"Well, Uncle Jules had visibly diminished the inheritance on which my father had counted, after he had swallowed his own to the last penny. Then, according to the custom of the times, he had been shipped off to America on a freighter going from Havre to New York.

"Once there, my uncle began to sell something or other, and he soon wrote that he was making a little money and that he soon hoped to be able to indemnify my father for the harm he had done him. This letter caused a profound emotion in the family. Jules, who up to that time had not been worth his salt, suddenly became a good man, a kind-hearted fellow, true and honest like all the Davranches.

"One of the captains told us that he had rented a large shop and was doing an important business.

"Two years later a second letter came, saying: 'My dear Philippe, I am writing to tell you not to worry about my health, which is excellent. Business is good. I leave tomorrow for a long trip to South America. I may be away for several years without sending you any news.

If I shouldn't write, don't worry. When my fortune is made I shall return to Havre. I hope that it will not be too long and that we shall all live happily together. . . .'

"This letter became the gospel of the family. It was read on the slightest provocation, and it was shown to everybody.

"For ten years nothing was heard from Uncle Jules; but as time went on my father's hope grew, and my mother, also, often said: 'When that good Jules is here, our position will be different. There is one who knew how to get along!'

"And every Sunday, while watching the big steamers approaching from the horizon, pouring out a stream of smoke, my father would repeat his eternal question: 'What a surprise it would be if Jules were on that one! Eh?'

"We almost expected to see him waving his handkerchief and crying: 'Hey! Philippe!'

"Thousands of schemes had been planned on the strength of this expected return; we were even to buy a little house with my uncle's money—a little place in the country near Ingouville. In fact, I wouldn't swear that my father had not already begun negotiations.

"The elder of my sisters was then twenty-eight, the other twenty-six. They were not yet married, and that was a great grief to everyone.

"At last a suitor presented himself for the younger one. He was a clerk, not rich, but honorable. I have always been morally certain that Uncle Jules' letter, which was shown him one evening, had swept away the young man's hesitation and definitely decided him.

"He was accepted eagerly, and it was decided that after the wedding the whole family should take a trip to Jersey.

"Jersey is the ideal trip for poor people. It is not far; one crosses a strip of sea in a steamer and lands on foreign soil, as this little island belongs to England. Thus, a Frenchman, with a two hours' sail, can observe a neighboring people at home and study their customs.

"This trip to Jersey completely absorbed our ideas, was our sole anticipation, the constant thought of our minds.

"At last we left. I see it as plainly as if it had happened yesterday. The boat was getting up steam against the quay at Granville; my father, bewildered, was superintending the loading of our three pieces of baggage; my mother, nervous, had taken the arm of my unmarried sister, who seemed lost since the departure of the other one, like the last chicken of a brood; behind us came the bride and groom, who always stayed behind, a thing that often made me turn round.

"The whistle sounded. We got on board, and the vessel, leaving the breakwater, forged ahead through a sea as flat as a marble table. We watched the coast disappear in the distance, happy and proud, like all who do not travel much.

"My father was swelling out his chest in the breeze, beneath his frock coat, which had that morning been very carefully cleaned; and he spread around him that odor of benzine, which always made me recognize Sunday. Suddenly he noticed two elegantly dressed ladies to whom two gentlemen were offering oysters. An old, ragged sailor was opening them with his knife and passing them to the gentlemen, who would then offer them to the ladies. They ate them in a dainty manner, holding the shell on a fine handkerchief and advancing their mouths a little in order not to spot their dresses. Then they would drink the liquid with a rapid little motion and throw the shell overboard.

"My father was probably pleased with this delicate manner of eating oysters on a moving ship. He considered it good form, refined, and, going up to my mother and sisters, he asked: 'Would you like me to offer you some oysters?'

"My mother hesitated on account of the expense, but my two sisters immediately accepted. My mother said in a provoked manner: 'I am afraid that they will hurt my stomach. Offer the children some, but not too much, it would make them sick.' Then, turning toward me, she added: 'As for Joseph, he doesn't need any. Boys shouldn't be spoiled.'

"However, I remained beside my mother, finding this discrimination unjust. I watched my father as he pompously conducted my two sisters and his son-in-law toward the ragged old sailor.

"The two ladies had just left, and my father showed my sisters how to eat them without spilling the liquor. He even tried to give them an example, and seized an oyster. He attempted to imitate the ladies, and immediately spilled all the liquid over his coat. I heard my mother mutter: 'He would do far better to keep quiet.'

"But, suddenly, my father appeared to be worried; he retreated a few steps, stared at his family gathered around the old shell-opener, and quickly came toward us. He seemed very pale, with a peculiar look. In a low voice he said to my mother: 'It's extraordinary how that man opening the oysters looks like Jules.'

"Astonished, my mother asked: 'What Jules?'

"My father continued: 'Why, my brother. If I did not know that he was well off in America, I should think it was he.'

"Bewildered, my mother stammered: 'You are crazy! As long as you know that it is not he, why do you say such foolish things?'

"But my father insisted: 'Go on over and see, Clarisse! I would rather have you see with your own eyes.'

"She arose and walked to her daughters. I, too, was watching the man. He was old, dirty, wrinkled, and did not lift his eyes from his work.

"My mother returned. I noticed that she was trembling. She exclaimed quickly: 'I believe that it is him. Why don't you ask the captain? But be very careful that we don't have this rogue on our hands again!'

"My father walked away, but I followed him. I felt strangely moved.

"The captain—a tall, thin man, with blond whiskers—was walking along the bridge with an important air as if he were commanding the Indian mail steamer.

"My father addressed him ceremoniously, and questioned him about his profession, adding many compliments: 'What might be the importance of Jersey? What did it produce? What was the population? The customs? The nature of the soil?' etc., etc. Then: 'You have there an old shell opener who seems quite interesting. Do you know anything about him?'

"The captain, whom this conversation began to weary, answered dryly: 'He is some old French tramp whom I found last year in America, and I brought him back. It seems that he has some relatives in Havre, but that he doesn't wish to return to them because he owes them money. His name is Jules—Jules Darmanche, or Darvanche, or something like that. It seems that he was once rich over there, but you can see what's left of him now.'

"My father turned ashy pale and muttered, his throat contracted, his eyes haggard. 'Ah! ah! very well, very well. I'm not in the least surprised. Thank you very much, captain.'

"He went away, and the astonished sailor watched him disappear. He returned to my mother so upset that she said to him: 'Sit down; someone will notice that something is the matter.'

"He sank down on a bench and stammered: 'It's him! It's him!' Then he asked: 'What are we going to do?'

"She answered quickly: 'We must get the children out of the way. Since Joseph knows everything, he can go and get them. We must take good care that our son-in-law doesn't find out.'

"My father seemed absolutely bewildered. He murmured: 'What a catastrophe!'

"Suddenly growing furious, my mother exclaimed: 'I always thought that that thief never would do anything, and that he would drop down on us again! As if one could expect anything from a Davranche!'

"My father passed his hand over his forehead, as he always did when his wife reproached him. She added: 'Give Joseph some money so that he can pay for the oysters. All we need to top the climax would be to be recognized by that beggar. That would be very pleasant! Let's get down to the other end of the boat, and take care that that man doesn't come near us!'

"They gave me five francs and walked away.

"Astonished, my sisters were awaiting their father. I said that mamma had felt a sudden attack of sea-sickness, and I asked the shell-opener: 'How much do we owe you, monsieur?'

"I felt like laughing: he was my uncle! He answered: 'Two francs fifty.'

"I held out my five francs and he returned the change. I looked at his hand; it was a poor, wrinkled, sailor's hand, and I looked at his face, an unhappy old face. I said to myself: 'That is my uncle, the brother of my father, my uncle!'

"I gave him a ten-centime tip. He thanked me: 'God bless you, my young sir!'

"He spoke like a poor man receiving alms. I couldn't help thinking that he must have begged over there! My sisters looked at me, surprised at my generosity. When I returned the two francs to my father, my mother asked me in surprise: 'Was there three francs' worth? That is impossible.'

"I answered in a firm voice, 'I gave ten centimes as a tip.'

"My mother started, and, staring at me, she exclaimed: 'You must be crazy! Give ten centimes to that man, to that vagabond—'

"She stopped at a look from my father, who was pointing at his son-in-law. Then everybody was silent.

"Before us, on the distant horizon, a purple shadow seemed to rise out of the sea. It was Jersey.

"As we approached the breakwater a violent desire seized me once more to see my Uncle Jules, to be near him, to say to him something consoling, something tender. But as no one was eating any more oysters, he had disappeared, having probably gone below to the dirty hold that was the home of the poor wretch."

The Model

Curving like a crescent moon, the little town of Etretat, with its white cliffs, its white, shingly beach and its blue sea, lay in the sunlight at high noon one July day. At either extremity of this crescent its two "gates," the smaller to the right, the larger one at the left, stretched forth—one a dwarf and the other a colossal limb—into the water, and the bell tower, almost as tall as the cliff, wide below, narrowing at the top, raised its pointed summit to the sky.

On the sands beside the water a crowd was seated watching the bathers. On the terrace of the Casino another crowd, seated or walking, displayed beneath the brilliant sky a perfect flower patch of bright costumes, with red and blue parasols embroidered with large flowers in silk.

On the walk at the end of the terrace, other persons, the restful, quiet ones, were walking slowly, far from the dressy throng.

A young man, well known and celebrated as a painter, Jean Sumner, was walking with a dejected air beside a wheelchair in which sat a young woman, his wife. A manservant was gently pushing the chair, and the crippled woman was gazing sadly at the brightness of the sky, the gladness of the day, and the happiness of others.

They did not speak. They did not look at each other.

"Let us stop a while," said the young woman.

They stopped, and the painter sat down on a camp stool that the servant handed him.

Those who were passing behind the silent and motionless couple looked at them compassionately. A whole legend of devotion was attached to them. He had married her in spite of her infirmity, touched by her affection for him, it was said.

Not far from there, two young men were chatting, seated on a bench and looking out into the horizon.

"No, it is not true; I tell you that I am well acquainted with Jean Sumner."

"But then, why did he marry her? For she was a cripple when she married, was she not?"

"Just so. He married her . . . he married her . . . just as everyone marries, parbleu! because he was an idiot!"

"But why?"

"But why—but why, my friend? There is no why. People do stupid things just because they do stupid things. And, besides, you know very well that painters make a specialty of foolish marriages. They almost always marry models, former sweethearts, in fact, women of doubtful reputation, frequently. Why do they do this? Who can say? One would suppose that constant association with the general run of models would disgust them forever with that class of women. Not at all. After having posed them they marry them. Read that little book—so true, so cruel and so beautiful—by Alphonse Daudet: *Artists' Wives*.

"In the case of the couple you see over there, the accident occurred in a special and terrible manner. The little woman played a frightful comedy, or, rather, tragedy. She risked all to win all. Was she sincere? Did she love Jean? Shall we ever know? Who is able to determine precisely how much is put on and how much is real in the actions of a woman? They are always sincere in an eternal mobility of impressions. They are furious, criminal, devoted, admirable and base in obedience to intangible emotions. They tell lies incessantly without intention, without knowing or understanding why, and in spite of it all are absolutely frank in their feelings and sentiments, which they display by violent, unexpected, incomprehensible, foolish resolutions which overthrow our arguments, our customary poise and all our selfish plans. The unforeseenness and suddenness of their determinations will always render them undecipherable enigmas as far as we are concerned. We continually ask ourselves: 'Are they sincere? Are they pretending?'

"But, my friend, they are sincere and insincere at one and the same time, because it is their nature to be extremists in both and to be neither one nor the other.

"See the methods that even the best of them employ to get what they desire. They are complex and simple, these methods. So complex that we can never guess at them beforehand, and so simple that after having been victimized we cannot help being astonished and exclaiming: 'What! Did she make a fool of me so easily as that?'

"And they always succeed, old man, especially when it is a question of getting married.

"But this is Sumner's story:

"The little woman was a model, of course. She posed for him. She was pretty, very stylish-looking, and had a divine figure, it seems. He fancied that he loved her with his whole soul. That is another strange thing. As soon as one likes a woman one sincerely believes that they could not get along without her for the rest of their life. One knows that one has felt the same way before and that disgust invariably succeeded gratification; that in order to pass one's existence side by side with another there must be not a brutal, physical passion which soon dies out, but a sympathy of soul, temperament and temper. One should know how to determine in the enchantment to which one is subjected whether it proceeds from the physical, from a certain sensuous intoxication, or from a deep spiritual charm.

"Well, he believed himself in love; he made her no end of promises of fidelity, and was devoted to her.

"She was really attractive, gifted with that fashionable flippancy that little Parisians so readily affect. She chattered, babbled, made foolish remarks that sounded witty from the manner in which they were uttered. She used graceful gesture's which were calculated to attract a painter's eye. When she raised her arms, when she bent over, when she got into a carriage, when she held out her hand to you, her gestures were perfect and appropriate.

"For three months Jean never noticed that, in reality, she was like all other models.

"He rented a little house for her for the summer at Andresy.

"I was there one evening when for the first time doubts came into my friend's mind.

"As it was a beautiful evening we thought we would take a stroll along the bank of the river. The moon poured a flood of light on the trembling water, scattering yellow gleams along its ripples in the currents and all along the course of the wide, slow river.

"We strolled along the bank, a little enthused by that vague exaltation that these dreamy evenings produce in us. We would have liked to undertake some wonderful task, to love some unknown, deliciously poetic being. We felt ourselves vibrating with raptures, longings, strange aspirations. And we were silent, our beings pervaded by the serene and living coolness of the beautiful night, the coolness of the moonlight, which seemed to penetrate one's body, permeate it, soothe one's spirit, fill it with fragrance and steep it in happiness.

"Suddenly Josephine (that is her name) uttered an exclamation: 'Oh, did you see the big fish that jumped, over there?'

"He replied without looking, without thinking: 'Yes, dear.'

"She was angry. 'No, you did not see it, for your back was turned.'

"He smiled. 'Yes, that's true. It is so delightful that I am not thinking of anything.'

"She was silent, but at the end of a minute she felt as if she must say something and asked: 'Are you going to Paris tomorrow?'

"'I do not know,' he replied.

"She was annoyed again. 'Do you think it is very amusing to walk along without speaking? People talk unless they're stupid.'

"He did not reply. Then, feeling with her woman's instinct that she was going to make him angry, she began to sing a popular air that had harassed our ears and our minds for two years: 'Je regardais en fair. . . .'

"He murmured: 'Please keep quiet.'

"She replied angrily: 'Why do you wish me to keep quiet?'

"'You spoil the landscape for us!' he said.

"Then followed a scene—a hateful, idiotic scene, with unexpected reproaches, unsuitable recriminations, then tears. Nothing was left unsaid. They went back to the house. He had allowed her to talk without replying, enervated by the beauty of the scene and dumfounded by this storm of abuse.

"Three months later he strove wildly to free himself from those invincible and invisible bonds with which such a friendship chains our lives. She kept him under her influence, tyrannizing over him, making his life a burden to him. They quarreled continually, vituperating and finally fighting each other.

"He wanted to break with her at any cost. He sold all his canvases, borrowed money from his friends, realizing twenty thousand francs (he was not well known then), and left them for her one morning with a note of farewell.

"He came and took refuge with me.

"About three o'clock that afternoon there was a ring at the bell. I went to the door. A woman sprang toward me, pushed me aside, came in and went into my atelier. It was she!

"He had risen when he saw her coming.

"She threw the envelope containing the banknotes at his feet with a truly noble gesture and said in a quick tone: 'There's your money. I don't want it!'

"She was very pale, trembling and ready undoubtedly to commit any folly. As for him, I saw him grow pale also, pale with rage and exasperation, ready also perhaps to commit any violence.

"He asked: 'What do you want?'

"She replied: 'I do not choose to be treated like a casual pick-up. You implored me to accept you. I asked you for nothing. Keep me with you!'

"He stamped his foot. 'No, that's a little too much! If you think you are going—'

"I had seized his arm. 'Keep still, Jean . . . Let me settle it.'

"I went toward her and quietly, little by little, I began to reason with her, exhausting all the arguments that are used under similar circumstances. She listened to me, motionless, with a fixed gaze, obstinate and silent.

"Finally, not knowing what more to say, and seeing that there would be a scene, I thought of a last resort and said: 'He loves you still, my dear, but his family want him to marry someone else, so you understand—'

"She gave a start and exclaimed: 'Ah! Ah! Now I understand!' And turning toward him, she said: 'You are . . . you are going to get married?'

"He replied decidedly, 'Yes.'

"She took a step forward. 'If you marry, I will kill myself! Do you hear?'

"He shrugged his shoulders and replied: 'Well then, kill yourself!'

"She stammered out, almost choking with her violent emotion: 'What did you say? What did you say? What did you say? Say it again!'

"He repeated: 'Well then, kill yourself if you like!'

"With her face almost livid, she replied: 'Do not dare me! I will throw myself from the window!'

"He began to laugh, walked toward the window, opened it, and bowing with the gesture of one who desires to let someone else precede him, he said: 'This is the way. After you!'

"She looked at him for a second with terrible, wild, staring eyes. Then, taking a run as if she were going to jump a hedge in the country, she rushed past me and past him, jumped over the sill and disappeared.

"I shall never forget the impression made on me by that open window after I had seen that body pass through it to fall to the ground. It appeared to me suddenly to be as large as the heavens and as hollow as space. And I drew back instinctively, not daring to look at it, as though I feared I might fall out myself.

"Jean, dumfounded, stood motionless.

"They brought the poor girl in with both legs broken. She will never walk again.

"Jean, wild with remorse and also possibly touched with gratitude, made up his mind to marry her.

"There you have it, old man."

It was growing dusk. The young woman felt chilly and wanted to go home, and the servant wheeled the invalid chair in the direction of the village. The painter walked beside his wife, neither of them having exchanged a word for an hour.

In the Woods

As the mayor was about to sit down to breakfast, word was brought to him that the rural policeman, with two prisoners, was awaiting him at the town hall. He went there at once and found old Hochedur standing guard before a middle-class couple whom he was regarding with a severe expression on his face.

The man, a fat old fellow with a red nose and white hair, seemed utterly dejected; while the woman, a little roundabout individual with shining cheeks, looked at the official who had arrested them, with defiant eyes.

"What is it? What is it, Hochedur?"

The rural policeman made his deposition: He had gone out that morning at his usual time, in order to patrol his beat from the forest of Champioux as far as the boundaries of Argenteuil. He had not noticed anything unusual in the country except that it was a fine day, and that the wheat was doing well, when the son of old Bredel, who was going over his vines, called out to him: "Here, Papa Hochedur, go and have a look at the outskirts of the wood. In the first thicket you will find a pair of lovers who must be a hundred and thirty years old between them!"

He went in the direction indicated, entered the thicket, and there he heard words that made him suspect a flagrant breach of morality. Advancing, therefore, on his hands and knees as if to surprise a poacher, he had arrested the couple whom he found there.

The mayor looked at the culprits in astonishment, for the man was certainly sixty, and the woman fifty-five at least, and he began to question them, beginning with the man, who replied in such a weak voice that he could scarcely be heard.

"What is your name?"

"Nicholas Beaurain."

"Your occupation?"

"Haberdasher, in the Rue des Martyrs, in Paris."

"What were you doing in the wood?"

The haberdasher remained silent, with his eyes on his fat paunch, and his hands hanging at his sides, and the mayor continued: "Do you deny what the officer of the municipal authorities states?"

"No, monsieur."

"So you confess it?"

"Yes, monsieur."

"What have you to say in your defense?"

"Nothing, monsieur."

"Where did you meet the partner in your misdemeanor?"

"She is my wife, monsieur."

"Your wife?"

"Yes, monsieur."

"Then . . . then . . . you do not live together in Paris?"

"I beg your pardon, monsieur, but we are living together!"

"But in that case—you must be mad, altogether mad, my dear sir, to get caught playing lovers in the country at ten o'clock in the morning."

The haberdasher seemed ready to cry with shame, and he muttered: "It was she who enticed me! I told her it was very stupid, but once a woman gets something into her head—you know—you can't get it out."

The mayor, who liked a joke, smiled and replied: "In your case, the contrary ought to have happened. You would not be here, if she had had the idea only in her head."

Then Monsieur Beauain was seized with rage and turning to his wife, he said: "Do you see to what you have brought us with your poetry? And now we shall have to go before the courts at our age, for a breach of morals! And we shall have to shut up the shop, sell our good will, and go to some other neighborhood! That's what it has come to."

Madame Beaurain got up, and without looking at her husband, she explained herself without embarrassment, without useless modesty, and almost without hesitation. "Of course, monsieur, I know that we have made ourselves ridiculous. Will you allow me to plead my cause like an advocate, or rather like a poor woman? And I hope that you will be kind enough to send us home, and to spare us the disgrace of a prosecution.

"Years ago, when I was young, I made Monsieur Beaurain's acquaintance one Sunday in this neighborhood. He was employed in a draper's shop, and I was a saleswoman in a ready-made clothing establishment. I remember it as if it were yesterday. I used to come and spend Sundays here occasionally with a friend of mine, Rose Levèque, with whom I lived in the Rue Pigalle, and Rose had a sweetheart, while I had nobody. He used to bring us here, and one Saturday he told me laughing that he should bring a friend with him the next day. I quite understood what he meant, but I replied that it would be no good; for I was virtuous, monsieur.

"The next day we met Monsieur Beaurain at the railway station, and in those days he was good-looking, but I had made up my mind not to encourage him, and I did not. Well, we arrived at Bezons. It was a lovely day, the sort of day that touches your heart. When it is fine even now, just as it used to be formerly, I grow quite foolish, and when I am in the country I utterly lose my head. The green grass, the swallows flying so swiftly, the smell of the grass, the scarlet poppies, the daisies—all that makes me crazy. It is like champagne when one is not accustomed to it!

"Well, it was lovely weather, warm and bright, and it seemed to penetrate your body through your eyes when you looked and through your mouth when you breathed. Rose and Simon hugged and kissed each other every minute, and that gave me a queer feeling! Monsieur Beaurain and I walked behind them, without speaking much, for when people do not know each other, they do not find anything to talk about. He looked timid, and I liked to see his embarrassment. At last we got to the little wood; it was as cool as in a bath there, and we four sat down. Rose and her lover teased me because I looked rather stern, but you will understand that I could not be otherwise. And then they began to kiss and hug again, without restraining themselves any more than if we had not been there; and then they whispered together, and got up and went off among the trees, without saying a word. You may fancy what I looked like, alone with this young fellow whom I had just met for the first time. I felt so confused at seeing them go that it gave me courage, and I began to talk. I asked him what his business was, and he said he was a linen draper's assistant, as I told you just now. We talked for a few minutes, and that made him bold, and he wanted to take liberties with me, but I told him sharply to keep his hands to himself. Is not that true, Monsieur Beaurain?"

Monsieur Beaurain, who was looking at his feet in confusion, did not reply, and she continued: "Then he saw that I was virtuous, and he began to make flirt with me nicely, like an honorable man, and from that time he came every Sunday, for he was very much in love with me. I was very fond of him also, very fond of him! He was a good-looking fellow, formerly, and in short he married me the next September, and we started in business in the Rue des Martyrs.

"It was a hard struggle for many years, monsieur. Business did not prosper, and we could not afford many country excursions, and, besides, we had got out of the habit of them. One has other things in one's head, and thinks more of the cashbox than of pretty speeches when one is in business. We were growing old by degrees without perceiving it, like quiet people who do not think much about love. One does not regret anything as long as one does not notice what one has lost.

"And then, monsieur, business became better, and we were confident as to the future! Then, you see, I do not exactly know what went on in my mind, no, I really do not know, but I began to dream like a little boarding-school girl. The sight of the little carts full of flowers that are drawn about the streets made me cry; the smell of violets sought me out in my easy-chair, behind my cashbox, and made my heart beat! Then I would get up and go out on the doorstep to look at the blue sky between the roofs. When one looks up at the sky from the street, it looks like a river descending on Paris, winding as it flows, and the swallows pass to and fro in it like fish. These ideas are very silly at my age! But how can one help it, monsieur, when one has worked all one's life? A moment comes in which one perceives that one could have done something else, and that one regrets, oh! yes, one feels intense regret! Just think, for twenty years I might have gone and had kisses in the woods, like other women. I used to think how delightful it would be to lie under the trees and be in love with someone! And I thought of it every day and every night! I dreamed of the moonlight on the water, until I felt inclined to drown myself.

"I did not venture to speak to Monsieur Beaurain about this at first. I knew that he would make fun of me, and send me back to sell my needles and cotton! Then again, to speak the truth, Monsieur Beaurain never said much to me, but when I looked in the glass, I also understood quite well that I no longer appealed to anyone!

"Well, I made up my mind, and I suggested an excursion into the country, to the place where we had first become acquainted. He agreed without suspecting anything, and we arrived here this morning, about nine o'clock.

"I felt quite young again when I got among the wheat, for a woman's heart never grows old! And really, I no longer saw my husband as he is at present, but just as he was formerly! That I will swear to you, monsieur. As true as I am standing here, I went crazy. I began to kiss him, and he was more surprised than if I had tried to murder him. He kept saying to me: 'Why, you must be mad! You are mad this morning! What is the matter with you?' I did not listen to him, I only listened to my own heart, and I made him come into the wood with me. That is all. I have spoken the truth, Monsieur Mayor, the whole truth."

The mayor was a sensible man. He rose from his chair, smiled, and said: "Go in peace, madame, and next time you visit our woods, be more discreet."

The Piece of String

It was market day, and from everywhere around Goderville the peasants and their wives were coming toward the town. The men walked slowly, throwing the whole body forward at every step of their long, crooked legs. They were deformed from pushing the plough, which makes the left shoulder higher and bends their figures sideways; from reaping the grain, when they have to spread their legs so as to keep on their feet. Their starched blue blouses, glossy as though varnished, ornamented at collar and cuffs with a little embroidered design and blown out around their bony bodies, looked very much like balloons about to soar, whence issued two arms and two feet.

Some of these fellows dragged a cow or a calf at the end of a rope. And just behind the animal followed their wives, beating it over the back with a leaf-covered branch to hasten its pace, and carrying large baskets out of which protruded the heads of chickens or ducks. These women walked more quickly and energetically than the men with their erect, dried-up figures, adorned with scanty little shawls pinned over their flat chests, and their heads wrapped around with a white cloth, enclosing the hair and surmounted by a cap.

Now a char-a-banc passed by, jogging along behind a nag and shaking up strangely the two men on the seat, and the woman at the bottom of the cart who held fast to its sides to lessen the hard jolting.

In the marketplace at Goderville was a great crowd, a mingled multitude of men and beasts. The horns of cattle, the high, long-napped hats of wealthy peasants, and the headdresses of the women came to the surface of that sea. And the sharp, shrill, barking voices made a continuous, wild din, while above it occasionally rose a huge burst of laughter from the sturdy lungs of a merry peasant or a prolonged bellow from a cow tied fast to the wall of a house.

It all smelled of the stable, of milk, of hay and of perspiration, giving off that half-human, half-animal odor which is peculiar to country folks.

Maître Hauchecorne, of Breaute, had just arrived at Goderville and was making his way toward the square when he perceived on the ground a little piece of string. Maître Hauchecorne, economical as are all true Normans, reflected that everything was worth picking up which could be of any use, and he stooped down, but painfully, because he suffered from rheumatism. He took the bit of thin string from the ground and was carefully preparing to roll it up when he saw Maître Malandain, the harness maker, on his doorstep staring at him. They had once had a quarrel about a halter, and they had borne each other malice ever since. Maître Hauchecorne was overcome with a sort of shame at being seen by his enemy picking up a bit of string in the road. He quickly hid it beneath his blouse and then slipped it into his breeches pocket, then pretended to be still looking for something on the ground which he did not discover and finally went off toward the marketplace, his head bent forward and his body almost doubled in two by rheumatic pains.

He was at once lost in the crowd, which kept moving about slowly and noisily as it chaffered and bargained. The peasants examined the cows, went off, came back, always in doubt for fear of being cheated, never quite daring to decide, looking the seller square in the eye in the effort to discover the tricks of the man and the defect in the beast.

The women, having placed their great baskets at their feet, had taken out the poultry, which lay upon the ground, their legs tied together, with terrified eyes and scarlet combs.

They listened to propositions, maintaining their prices in a decided manner with an impassive face or perhaps deciding to accept the smaller price offered, suddenly calling out to the customer who was starting to go away: "All right, I'll let you have them, Maît' Anthime."

Then, little by little, the square became empty, and when the Angelus struck midday those who lived at a distance poured into the inns.

At Jourdain's the great room was filled with eaters, just as the vast court was filled with vehicles of every sort—wagons, gigs, chars-a-bancs, tilburies, innumerable vehicles that have no name, yellow with mud, misshapen, pieced together, raising their shafts to heaven like two arms, or it may be with their nose on the ground and their rear in the air.

Just opposite to where the diners were eating, the huge fireplace, with its bright flame, gave out a burning heat on the backs of those who sat at the right. Three spits were turning, loaded with chickens, pigeons, and with joints of mutton, and a delectable odor of roast meat and of gravy flowing over crisp brown skin arose from the hearth, kindled merriment, caused mouths to water.

All the aristocracy of the plough were eating there at Maît' Jourdain's, the innkeeper's, a dealer in horses also and a sharp fellow who had made a great deal of money in his day.

The dishes were passed round, were emptied, as were the jugs of yellow cider. Everyone told of his affairs, of his purchases and his sales. They exchanged news about the crops. The weather was good for greens, but too wet for grain.

Suddenly the drum began to beat in the courtyard before the house. Everyone, except some of the most indifferent, were on their feet at once and ran to the door, to the windows, their mouths full and napkins in their hand.

When the public crier had finished his drumbeat he called forth in a jerky voice, pausing in the wrong places: "Be it known to the inhabitants of Goderville and in general to all persons present at the market that there has been lost this morning on the Beuzeville road, between nine and ten o'clock, a black leather pocketbook containing five hundred francs and business papers. You are requested to return it to the mayor's office at once or to Maître Fortune Houlbreque, of Manneville. There will be a reward of twenty francs."

Then the man went away. They heard once more at a distance the dull beating of the drum and the faint voice of the crier. Then they all began to talk of this incident, reckoning up the chances Maître Houlbreque had of finding or of not finding his pocketbook again.

The meal went on. They were finishing their coffee when the corporal of gendarmes appeared on the threshold. He asked: "Is Maître Hauchecorne of Breaute here?"

Maître Hauchecorne, seated at the other end of the table answered: "Here I am, here I am." And he followed the corporal.

The mayor was waiting for him, seated in an armchair. He was the notary of the place, a tall, grave man of pompous speech. "Maître Hauchecorne," said he, "this morning on the Beuzeville road, you were seen to pick up the pocketbook lost by Maître Houlbreque of Manneville."

The countryman looked at the mayor in amazement frightened already at this suspicion that rested on him, he knew not why.

"I . . . I picked up that pocketbook?"

"Yes, you."

"I swear I don't even know anything about it."

"You were seen."

"I was seen . . . I? Who saw me?"

"M. Malandain, the harness-maker."

Then the old man remembered, understood, and, reddening with anger, said: "Ah! he saw me, did he, the rascal? He saw me picking up this string here, M'sieu Mayor." And fumbling at the bottom of his pocket, he pulled out the little end of string.

But the mayor incredulously shook his head: "You will not make me believe, Maître Hauchecorne, that M. Malandain, who is a man whose word can be relied on, has mistaken this string for a pocketbook."

The peasant, furious, raised his hand and spat on the ground beside him as if to attest his good faith, repeating:

"For all that, it is God's truth, M'sieu Mayor. There! On my soul's salvation, I repeat it."

The mayor continued: "After you picked up the object in question, you even looked about for some time in the mud to see if a piece of money had not dropped out of it."

The good man was choking with indignation and fear.

"How can they tell . . . how can they tell such lies as that to slander an honest man! How can they?"

His protestations were in vain; he was not believed.

He was confronted with M. Malandain, who repeated and sustained his testimony. They railed at one another for an hour. At his own request Maître Hauchecorne was searched. Nothing was found on him.

At last the mayor, much perplexed, sent him away, warning him that he would inform the public prosecutor and ask for guidance.

The news had spread. When he left the mayor's office the old man was surrounded, interrogated with a curiosity that was serious or mocking, as the case might be, but into which no indignation entered. And he began to tell the story of the string. They did not believe him. They laughed.

He passed on, buttonholed by everyone, himself buttonholing his acquaintances, beginning over and over again his tale and his protestations, showing his pockets turned inside out to prove that he had nothing in them.

They said to him: "You old rogue!"

He grew more and more angry, feverish, in despair at not being believed, and kept on telling his story.

The night came. It was time to go home. He left with three of his neighbors, to whom he pointed out the place where he had picked up the string, and all the way he talked of his adventure.

That evening he made the round of the village of Breaute for the purpose of telling everyone. He met only unbelievers.

He brooded over it all night long.

The next day, about one in the afternoon, Marius Paumelle, a farm-hand of Maître Breton, the market gardener at Ymauville, returned the pocketbook and its contents to Maître Holbreque of Manneville.

This man said, indeed, that he had found it on the road, but not knowing how to read, he had carried it home and given it to his master.

The news spread to the environs. Maître Hauchecorne was in-formed. He started off at once and began to relate his story with the sequel. He was triumphant.

"What grieved me," said he, "was not the thing itself, do you un-derstand, but it was being accused of lying. Nothing does you so much harm as being in disgrace for lying."

All day he talked of his adventure. He told it on the roads to the people who passed, at the cabaret to the people who drank and next Sunday when they came out of church. He even stopped strangers to tell them about it. He was easy now, and yet something worried him without his knowing exactly what it was. People had a joking manner while they listened. They did not seem convinced. He seemed to feel their remarks behind his back.

On Tuesday of the following week he went to market at Goderville, prompted solely by the need of telling his story.

Malandain, standing on his doorstep, began to laugh as he saw him pass. Why?

He accosted a farmer of Criquetot, who did not let him finish, and giving him a punch in the pit of the stomach cried in his face: "Oh, you great rogue!" Then he turned his heel upon him.

Maître Hauchecorne remained speechless and grew more and more uneasy. Why had they called him "great rogue"?

When seated at table in Jourdain's tavern he began again to ex-plain the whole affair.

A horse dealer of Montivilliers shouted at him: "Get out, get out, you old scamp! I know all about your old string."

Hauchecorne stammered: "But since they found it again, the pock-etbook. . . ."

But the other continued: "Hold your tongue, pops; there's one who finds it and there's another who returns it. And no one the wiser."

The farmer was speechless. He understood at last. They accused him of having had the pocketbook brought back by an accomplice, by a confederate.

He tried to protest. The whole table began to laugh.

He could not finish his dinner, and went away amid a chorus of jeers.

He went home indignant, choking with rage, with confusion, the more cast down since with his Norman craftiness he was, perhaps, capable of having done what they accused him of and even of boasting of it as a good trick. He was dimly conscious that it was impossible to prove his innocence, his craftiness being so well known. He felt himself struck to the heart by the injustice of the suspicion.

He began anew to tell his tale, lengthening his recital every day, each day adding new proofs, more energetic declarations and more sacred oaths, which he thought of, which he prepared in his hours of solitude, for his mind was entirely occupied with the story of the string. The more he denied it, the more artful his arguments, the less he was believed.

"Those are liars' proofs," they said behind his back.

He felt this. It preyed upon him and he exhausted himself in useless efforts. He was visibly wasting away.

Jokers would make him tell the story of "the piece of string" to amuse them, just as you make a soldier who has been on a campaign tell his version of a battle. His mind kept growing weaker and about the end of December he took to his bed.

He passed away early in January, and, in the ravings of death agony, he protested his innocence, repeating: "A little bit of string—a little bit of string. See, here it is, M'sieu Mayor."

The Devil

The peasant and the doctor stood on opposite sides of the bed, beside the old, dying woman. She was calm and resigned and her mind quite clear as she looked at them and listened to their conversation. She was going to die, and she did not rebel at it, for her time was come, as she was ninety-two.

The July sun streamed in at the window and the open door and cast its hot flames on the uneven brown clay floor, which had been stamped down by four generations of clodhoppers. The smell of the fields came in also, driven by the sharp wind and parched by the noontide heat. The grasshoppers chirped themselves hoarse, and filled the country with their shrill noise, which was like that of the wooden toys which are sold to children at fair time.

The doctor raised his voice and said: "Honoré, you cannot leave your mother in this state; she may die at any moment."

And the peasant, in great distress, replied: "But I must get in my wheat, for it has been lying on the ground a long time, and the weather is just right for it; what do you say about it, mother?" And the dying old woman, still tormented by her Norman avariciousness, replied yes with her eyes and her forehead, and thus urged her son to get in his wheat, and to leave her to die alone.

But the doctor got angry, and, stamping his foot, he said: "You are no better than a brute, do you hear, and I will not allow you to do it, do you understand? And if you must get in your wheat today, go and fetch Rapet's wife and make her look after your mother; I will have it, do you understand me? And if you do not obey me, I will let you die like a dog, when you are ill in your turn; do you hear?"

The peasant, a tall, thin fellow with slow movements, who was tormented by indecision, by his fear of the doctor and his fierce love of saving, hesitated, calculated, and stammered out: "How much does La Rapet charge for attending sick people?"

"How should I know?" the doctor cried. "That depends upon how long she is needed. Settle it with her, by Heaven! But I want her to be here within an hour, do you hear?"

So the man decided. "I will go for her," he replied; "don't get angry, doctor."

And the latter left, calling out as he went: "Be careful, be very careful, you know, for I do not joke when I am angry!"

As soon as they were alone the peasant turned to his mother and said in a resigned voice: "I will go and fetch La Rapet, as the man will have it. Don't worry till I get back."

And he went out in his turn.

La Rapet, who was an old washerwoman, watched the dead and the dying of the neighborhood, and then, as soon as she had sewn her customers into that linen cloth from which they would emerge no more, she went and took up her iron to smooth out the linen of the living. Wrinkled like a last year's apple, spiteful, envious, avaricious with a phenomenal avarice, bent double, as if she had been broken in half across the loins by the constant motion of passing the iron over the linen, one might have said that she had a kind of abnormal and cynical love of a death struggle. She never spoke of anything but of the people she had seen die, of the various kinds of deaths at which she had been present, and she related with the greatest minuteness details which were always similar, just as a sportsman recounts his luck.

When Honoré Bontemps entered her cottage, he found her preparing the starch for the collars of the women villagers, and he said: "Good evening; I hope you are doing well, Mother Rapet?"

She turned her head round to look at him, and said: "As usual, as usual, and you?"

"Oh! as for me, I am as well as I could wish, but my mother is not well."

"Your mother?"

"Yes, my mother!"

"What is the matter with her?"

"She is going to turn up her toes, that's what's the matter with her!"

The old woman took her hands out of the water and asked with sudden sympathy: "Is she as bad as all that?"

"The doctor says she will not last till morning."

"Then she certainly is very bad!"

Honoré hesitated, for he wanted to make a few preparatory remarks before coming to his proposition; but as he could hit upon nothing, he made up his mind suddenly.

"How much will you ask to stay with her till the end? You know that I am not rich, and I cannot even afford to keep a servant girl. It is just that which has brought my poor mother to this state—too much worry and fatigue! She did the work of ten, in spite of her ninety-two years. You don't find any made of that stuff nowadays!"

La Rapet answered gravely: "There are two prices: Forty sous by day and three francs by night for the rich, and twenty sous by day and forty by night for the others. You shall pay me the twenty and forty."

But the peasant reflected, for he knew his mother well. He knew how tenacious of life, how vigorous and unyielding she was, and she might last another week, in spite of the doctor's opinion; and so he said resolutely: "No, I would rather you would fix a price for the whole time until the end. I will take my chance, one way or the other. The doctor says she will die very soon. If that happens, so much the better for you, and so much the worse for her, but if she holds out till tomorrow or longer, so much the better for her and so much the worse for you!"

The nurse looked at the man in astonishment, for she had never treated a death as a speculation, and she hesitated, tempted by the idea of the possible gain, but she suspected that he wanted to play her a trick. "I can say nothing until I have seen your mother," she replied.

"Then come with me and see her."

She washed her hands, and went with him immediately.

They did not speak on the road; she walked with short, hasty steps, while he strode on with his long legs, as if he were crossing a brook at every step.

The cows lying down in the fields, overcome by the heat, raised their heads heavily and lowed feebly at the two passersby, as if to ask them for some green grass.

When they got near the house, Honoré Bontemps murmured: "Suppose it is all over?" And his unconscious wish that it might be so showed itself in the sound of his voice.

But the old woman was not dead. She was lying on her back, on her wretched bed, her hands covered with a purple cotton counterpane, horribly thin, knotty hands, like the claws of strange animals, like crabs, half closed by rheumatism, fatigue and the work of nearly a century which she had accomplished.

La Rapet went up to the bed and looked at the dying woman, felt her pulse, tapped her on the chest, listened to her breathing, and asked her questions, so as to hear her speak; and then, having looked at her for some time, she went out of the room, followed by Honoré. Her decided opinion was that the old woman would not last till night.

He asked: "Well?"

And the sick-nurse replied: "Well, she may last two days, perhaps three. You will have to give me six francs, everything included."

"Six francs! six francs!" he shouted. "Are you out of your mind? I tell you she cannot last more than five or six hours!" And they disputed angrily for some time, but as the nurse said she must go home, as the time was going by, and as his wheat would not come to the farmyard by itself, he finally agreed to her terms. "Very well, then, that is settled: six francs, including everything, until the corpse is taken out."

And he went away, with long strides, to his wheat lying on the ground under the hot sun that ripens the grain, while the sick-nurse went in again to the house.

She had brought some work with her, for she worked without cease by the side of the dead and dying, sometimes for herself, sometimes for the family that employed her as seamstress and paid her rather more in that capacity. Suddenly, she asked: "Have you received the last sacraments, Mother Bontemps?"

The old peasant woman shook her head, and La Rapet, who was very devout, got up quickly: "Good heavens, is it possible? I will go and fetch the curé"; and she rushed off to the parsonage so quickly that the urchins in the street thought some accident had happened when they saw her running.

The priest came immediately in his surplice, preceded by a choirboy who rang a bell to announce the passage of the Host through the parched and quiet country. Some men who were working at a distance took off their large hats and remained motionless until the white vestment had disappeared behind some farm buildings; the women who were making up the sheaves stood up to make the sign of the cross; the frightened black hens ran away along the ditch until they reached a well-known hole, through which they suddenly disappeared, while a foal which was tied in a meadow took fright at the sight of the surplice and began to gallop round and round, kicking out every now and then. The acolyte, in his red cassock, walked quickly, and the priest, with his head inclined toward one shoulder and his square biretta on his head, followed him, muttering some prayers; while last of all came La Rapet, bent almost double as if she wished to prostrate herself, as she walked with folded hands as they do in church.

Honoré saw them pass in the distance, and he asked: "Where is our priest going?" His man, who was more intelligent, replied: "He is taking the sacrament to your mother, of course!"

The peasant was not surprised, and said: "That may be," and went on with his work.

Mother Bontemps confessed, received absolution and communion, and the priest took his departure, leaving the two women alone in the suffocating room, while La Rapet began to look at the dying woman, and to ask herself whether it could last much longer.

The day was on the wane, and gusts of cooler air began to blow, causing a view of Epinal, which was fastened to the wall by two pins, to flap up and down; the scanty window curtains, which had formerly been white, but were now yellow and covered with fly specks, looked as if they were going to fly off, as if they were struggling to get away, like the old woman's soul.

Lying motionless, with her eyes open, she seemed to await with indifference that death which was so near and which yet delayed its coming. Her short breathing whistled in her constricted throat. It would stop altogether soon, and there would be one woman less in the world; no one would regret her.

At nightfall Honoré returned, and when he went up to the bed and saw that his mother was still alive, he asked: "How is she?" just as he had done formerly when she had been ailing, and then he sent La Rapet away, saying to her: "Tomorrow morning at five o'clock, without fail."

And she replied: "Tomorrow, at five o'clock."

She came at daybreak, and found Honoré eating his soup, which he had made himself before going to work, and the sick-nurse asked him: "Well, is your mother dead?"

"She is a little better, on the contrary," he replied, with a sly look out of the corner of his eyes. And he went out.

La Rapet, seized with anxiety, went up to the dying woman, who remained in the same state, lethargic and impassive, with her eyes open and her hands clutching the counterpane. The nurse perceived that this might go on thus for two days, four days, eight days, and her avaricious mind was seized with fear, while she was furious at the sly fellow who had tricked her, and at the woman who would not die.

Nevertheless, she began to work, and waited, looking intently at the wrinkled face of Mother Bontemps. When Honoré returned to breakfast he seemed quite satisfied and even in a bantering humor.

He was decidedly getting in his wheat under very favorable circumstances.

La Rapet was becoming exasperated; every minute now seemed to her so much time and money stolen from her. She felt a mad inclination to take this old woman, this, headstrong old fool, this obstinate old wretch, and to stop that short, rapid breath, which was robbing her of her time and money, by squeezing her throat a little. But then she reflected on the danger of doing so, and other thoughts came into her head; so she went up to the bed and said: "Have you ever seen the Devil?"

Mother Bontemps murmured: "No."

Then the sick-nurse began to talk and to tell her tales that were likely to terrify the weak mind of the dying woman. Some minutes before one dies the Devil appears, she said, to all who are in the death throes. He has a broom in his hand, a saucepan on his head, and he utters loud cries. When anybody sees him, all is over, and that person has only a few moments longer to live. She then enumerated all those to whom the Devil had appeared that year: Josephine Loisel, Eulalie Ratier, Sophie Padagnau, Séraphine Grospied.

Mother Bontemps, who had at last become disturbed in mind, moved about, wrung her hands, and tried to turn her head to look toward the end of the room. Suddenly La Rapet disappeared at the foot of the bed. She took a sheet out of the cupboard and wrapped herself up in it; she put the iron saucepan on her head, so that its three short bent feet rose up like horns, and she took a broom in her right hand and a tin pail in her left, which she threw up suddenly, so that it might fall to the ground noisily.

When it came down, it certainly made a terrible noise. Then, climbing upon a chair, the nurse lifted up the curtain which hung at the bottom of the bed, and showed herself, gesticulating and uttering shrill cries into the iron saucepan which covered her face, while she menaced the old peasant woman, who was nearly dead, with her broom.

Terrified, with an insane expression on her face, the dying woman made a superhuman effort to get up and escape; she even got her shoulders and chest out of bed; then she fell back with a deep sigh. All was over, and La Rapet calmly put everything back into its place: the broom into the corner by the cupboard the sheet inside it, the saucepan on the hearth, the pail on the floor, and the chair against the wall. Then, with professional movements, she closed the dead woman's large eyes, put a plate on the bed and poured some holy water into it, placing in it the twig of boxwood that had been nailed to the chest of drawers, and kneeling down, she fervently repeated the prayers for the dead, which she knew by heart, as a matter of business.

And when Honoré returned in the evening he found her praying, and he calculated immediately that she had made twenty sous out of him, for she had only spent three days and one night there, which made five francs altogether, instead of the six which he owed her.

The Dowry

The marriage of Maître Simon Lebrument with Mademoiselle Jeanne Cordier was a surprise to no one. Maître Lebrument had bought out the practice of Maître Papillon; naturally, he had to have money to pay for it; and Mademoiselle Jeanne Cordier had three hundred thousand francs clear in currency, and in bonds payable to bearer.

Maître Lebrument was a handsome man. He was stylish, although in a provincial way; but, nevertheless, he was stylish—a rare thing at Boutigny-le-Rebours.

Mademoiselle Cordier was graceful and fresh-looking, although a trifle awkward; nevertheless, she was a handsome girl, and one to be desired.

The marriage ceremony turned all Boutigny topsy-turvy. Everybody admired the young couple, who quickly returned home to domestic felicity, having decided simply to take a short trip to Paris, after a few days of retirement.

This téte-à-téte was delightful, Maître Lebrument having shown just the proper amount of delicacy. He had taken as his motto: "Everything comes to him who waits." He knew how to be at the same time patient and energetic. His success was rapid and complete.

After four days, Madame Lebrument adored her husband. She could not get along without him. She would sit on his knees, and taking him by the ears she would say: "Open your mouth and shut your eyes." He would open his mouth wide and partly close his eyes, and he would try to nip her fingers as she slipped some dainty between his teeth. Then she would give him a kiss, sweet and long, which would make chills run up and down his spine. And then, in his turn, he would not have enough caresses to please his wife from morning to night and from night to morning.

When the first week was over, he said to his young companion: "If you wish, we will leave for Paris next Tuesday. We will be like two lovers, we will go to the restaurants, the theaters, the concert halls, everywhere, everywhere!"

She was ready to dance for joy. "Oh! yes, yes. Let us go as soon as possible."

He continued: "And then, as we must forget nothing, ask your father to have your dowry ready; I shall pay Maître Papillon on this trip."

She answered: "All right: I will tell him tomorrow morning."

And he took her in his arms once more, to renew those sweet games of love which she had so enjoyed for the past week.

The following Tuesday, father-in-law and mother-in-law went to the station with their daughter and their son-in-law who were leaving for the capital.

The father-in-law said: "I tell you it is very imprudent to carry so much money about in a pocketbook." And the young lawyer smiled.

"Don't worry; I am accustomed to such things. You understand that, in my profession, I sometimes have as much as a million on me. In this manner, at least we avoid a great amount of red tape and delay. You needn't worry."

The conductor was crying: "All aboard for Paris!"

They scrambled into a car, where two old ladies were already seated.

Lebrument whispered into his wife's ear: "What a bother! I won't be able to smoke."

She answered in a low voice, "It annoys me too, but not on account of your cigar."

The whistle blew and the train started. The trip lasted about an hour, during which time they did not say very much to each other, as the two old ladies did not go to sleep.

As soon as they were in front of the Saint-Lazare Station, Maître Lebrument said to his wife: "Dearie, let us first go over to the Boulevard and get something to eat; then we can quietly return and get our trunk and bring it to the hotel."

She immediately assented. "Oh! yes. Let's eat at the restaurant. Is it far?"

He answered: "Yes, it's quite a distance, but we will take the omnibus."

She was surprised: "Why don't we take a cab?"

He began to scold her smilingly: "Is that the way you save money? A cab for a five minutes' ride at six cents a minute! You would deprive yourself of nothing."

"That's true," she said, a little embarrassed.

A big omnibus was passing by, drawn by three big horses, which were trotting along. Lebrument called out: "Conductor! Conductor!"

The heavy carriage stopped. And the young lawyer, pushing his wife, said to her quickly: "Go inside; I'm going up on top so that I may smoke at least one cigarette before lunch."

She had no time to answer. The conductor, who had seized her by the arm to help her up the step, pushed her inside, and she fell into a seat, bewildered, looking through the back window at the feet of her husband as he climbed up to the top of the vehicle.

And she sat there motionless, between a fat man who smelled of cheap tobacco and an old woman who smelled of garlic.

All the other passengers were lined up in silence—a grocer's boy, a young girl, a soldier, a gentleman with gold-rimmed spectacles and a big silk hat, two ladies with a self-satisfied and crabbed look that seemed to say: "We are riding in this thing, but we don't have to," two sisters of charity, and an undertaker. They looked like a collection of caricatures.

The jolting of the wagon made them wag their heads and the shaking of the wheels seemed to stupefy them—they all looked as though they were asleep.

The young woman remained motionless. "Why didn't he come inside with me?" she was saying to herself. An unaccountable sadness seemed to be hanging over her. He really need not have acted so.

The sisters motioned to the conductor to stop, and they got off one after the other, leaving in their wake the pungent smell of camphor. The bus started up and soon stopped again. And in got a cook, red-faced and out of breath. She sat down and placed her basket of provisions on her knees. A strong odor of dish-water filled the vehicle.

"It's further than I imagined," thought Jeanne.

The undertaker went out, and was replaced by a coachman who seemed to bring the atmosphere of the stable with him. The young girl had as a successor a messenger, the odor of whose feet showed that he was continually walking.

The lawyer's wife began to feel ill at ease, nauseated, ready to cry without knowing why.

Other persons left and others entered. The stage went on through interminable streets, stopping at stations and starting again.

"How far it is!" thought Jeanne. "I hope he hasn't gone to sleep! He has been so tired the last few days."

Little by little all the passengers left. She was left alone, all alone. The conductor cried: "Vaugirard!"

Seeing that she did not move, he repeated: "Vaugirard!"

She looked at him, understanding that he was speaking to her, as there was no one else there. For the third time the man said: "Vaugirard!"

Then she asked: "Where are we?"

He answered gruffly:

"We're at Vaugirard, of course! I have been yelling that for the last half hour!"

"Is it far from the Boulevard?" she said.

"Which boulevard?"

"The Boulevard des Italiens."

"We passed that a long time ago!"

"Would you mind telling my husband?"

"Your husband! Where is he?"

"On the top of the bus."

"On the top! There hasn't been anybody there for a long time."

She started, terrified.

"What? That's impossible! He got on with me. Look well! He must be there."

The conductor was becoming uncivil: "Come on, missy, you've talked enough! You can find ten men for everyone that you lose. Now run along. You'll find another one somewhere."

Tears were coming to her eyes. She insisted: "But, monsieur, you are mistaken; I assure you that you must be mistaken. He had a big portfolio under his arm."

The man began to laugh: "A big portfolio! Oh, yes! He got off at the Madeleine. He got rid of you, all right! Ha! ha! ha!"

The 'bus had stopped. She got out and, in spite of herself, she looked up instinctively to the roof. It was absolutely deserted.

Then she began to cry, and, without thinking that anybody was listening or watching her, she said out loud: "What is going to become of me?"

An inspector approached: "What's the matter?"

The conductor answered, in a bantering tone of voice: "It's a lady who got ditched by her husband during the trip."

The other continued: "Oh! that's nothing. You go about your business."

Then he turned on his heels and walked away.

She began to walk straight ahead, too bewildered, too crazed even to understand what had happened to her. Where was she to go? What could she do? What could have happened to him? How could he have made such a mistake? How could he have been so forgetful?

She had two francs in her pocket. To whom could she go? Suddenly she remembered her cousin Barral, one of the assistants in the offices of the Ministry of the Navy.

She had just enough to pay for a cab. She drove to his house. He met her just as he was leaving for his office. He was carrying a large portfolio under his arm, just like Lebrument.

She jumped out of the carriage. "Henri!" she cried.

He stopped, astonished: "Jeanne! Here—all alone! What are you doing? Where have you come from?"

Her eyes full of tears, she stammered: "My husband has just got lost!"

"Lost! Where?"

"On an omnibus."

"On an omnibus?"

Weeping, she told him her whole adventure.

He listened, thought, and then asked: "Was his mind clear this morning?"

"Yes."

"Good. Did he have much money with him?"

"Yes, he was carrying my dowry."

"Your dowry! All of it?"

"Yes, all of it—in order to pay for the practice that he bought."

"Well, my dear cousin, by this time your husband must be well on his way to Belgium."

She could not understand. She kept repeating: "My husband . . . you say. . . ."

"I say that he has disappeared with your . . . your capital—that's all!"

She stood there, a prey to conflicting emotions, sobbing. "Then he is . . . he is . . . he is a villain!"

And, faint from excitement, she leaned her head on her cousin's shoulder and wept.

As people were stopping to look at them, he pushed her gently into the vestibule of his house, and, supporting her with his arm around her waist, he led her up the stairs, and as his astonished servant opened the door, he ordered: "Sophie, run to the restaurant and get lunch for two. I am not going to the office today."

The Mask

There was a masquerade ball at the Elysée-Montmartre that evening. It was the "Mi-Careme," and the crowds were pouring into the brightly lighted passage that leads to the dance hall, like water flowing through the open lock of a canal. The loud roar of the orchestra, bursting like a storm of sound, shook the rafters, swelled through the whole neighborhood and awoke, in the streets and in the depths of the houses, an irresistible desire to jump, to get warm, to have fun, which slumbers within each human animal.

The patrons came from every quarter of Paris; there were people of all classes who love noisy pleasures, a little seedy and tinged with debauch. There were clerks and girls—girls of every description, some wearing common cotton, some the finest batiste; rich girls, covered with diamonds, and poor girls of sixteen, full of the desire to revel, to belong to men, to spend money. Elegant black evening suits, in search of fresh or faded but appetizing novelty, wandering through the excited crowds, looking, searching, while the masqueraders seemed moved above all by the desire for amusement. Already the far-famed quadrilles had attracted around them a curious crowd. The moving hedge which encircled the four dancers swayed in and out like a snake, sometimes nearer and sometimes farther away, according to the motions of the performers. The two women, whose lower limbs seemed to be attached to their bodies by rubber springs, were making wonderful and surprising motions with their legs. Their partners hopped and skipped about, waving their arms about. One could imagine their panting breath beneath their masks.

One of them, who had taken his place in the most famous quadrille, as substitute for an absent celebrity, the handsome "Songe-au-Gosse," was trying to keep up with the tireless "Arete-de-Veau" and was making strange, fancy steps that aroused the joy and sarcasm of the audience.

He was thin, dressed like a dandy, with a pretty varnished mask on his face. It had a curly blond mustache and a wavy wig. He looked like a wax figure from the Musée Grevin, like a strange and fantastic caricature of the charming young man of fashion plates, and he danced with visible effort, clumsily, with a comical impetuosity. He appeared rusty beside the others when he tried to imitate their gambols: he seemed overcome by rheumatism, as heavy as a great Dane playing with greyhounds. Mocking bravos encouraged him. And he, carried away with enthusiasm, jigged about with such frenzy that suddenly, carried away by a wild spurt, he pitched head foremost into the living wall formed by the audience, which opened up before him to allow him to pass, then closed around the inanimate body of the dancer, stretched out on his face.

Some men picked him up and carried him away, calling for a doctor. A gentleman stepped forward, young and elegant, in well-fitting evening clothes, with large pearl studs. "I am a professor of the Faculty of Medicine," he said in a modest voice. He was allowed to pass, and he entered a small room full of little cardboard boxes, where the still-lifeless dancer had been stretched out on some chairs. The doctor at first wished to take off the mask, but he noticed that it was attached in a complicated manner, with a perfect network of small metal wires which cleverly bound it to his wig and covered the whole head. Even the neck was imprisoned in a false skin that continued the chin and was painted the color of flesh, being attached to the collar of the shirt.

All this had to be cut with strong scissors. When the physician had slit open this surprising arrangement, from the shoulder to the temple, he opened this armor and found the face of an old man, worn out, thin, and wrinkled. The surprise among those who had brought in this seemingly young dancer was so great that no one laughed, no one said a word.

All were watching this sad face as he lay on the straw chairs, his eyes closed, his face covered with white hair, some long, falling from the forehead over the face, others short, growing around the face and the chin, and beside this poor head, that pretty little, neat varnished, smiling mask.

The man regained consciousness after being inanimate for a long time, but he still seemed to be so weak and sick that the physician feared some dangerous complication. He asked: "Where do you live?"

The old dancer seemed to be making an effort to remember, and then he mentioned the name of the street, which no one knew. He was asked for more definite information about the neighborhood. He answered with a great slowness, indecision and difficulty, which revealed his upset state of mind. The physician continued:

"I will take you home myself."

Curiosity had overcome him to find out who this strange dancer, this phenomenal jumper might be. Soon the two rolled away in a cab to the other side of Montmartre.

They stopped before a high building of poor appearance. They went up a winding staircase. The doctor held to the banister, which was so grimy that the hand stuck to it, and he supported the dizzy old man, whose forces were beginning to return. They stopped at the fourth floor.

The door at which they had knocked was opened by an old woman, neat looking, with a white nightcap enclosing a thin face with sharp features, one of those good, rough faces of a hard-working and faithful woman. She cried out: "For goodness sake! What's the matter?"

He told her the whole story in a few words. She became reassured and even calmed the physician himself by telling him that the same thing had happened many times. She said: "He must be put to bed, monsieur, that is all. Let him sleep and tomorrow he will be all right."

The doctor continued: "But he can hardly speak."

"Oh! that's just a little drink, nothing more; he has eaten no dinner, in order to be nimble, and then he took a few absinthes in order to work himself up to the proper pitch. You see, drink gives strength to his legs, but it stops his thoughts and words. He is too old to dance as he does. Really, his lack of common sense is enough to drive one mad!"

The doctor, surprised, insisted: "But why does he dance like that at his age?"

She shrugged her shoulders and turned red from the anger which was slowly rising within her and she cried out: "Ah! yes, why? So that the people will think him young under his mask; so that the women will still take him for a young dandy and whisper nasty things into his ears; so that he can rub up against all their dirty skins, with their perfumes and powders and cosmetics. Ah! it's a fine business! What a life I have had for the last forty years! But we must first get him to bed, so that he may have no ill effects. Would you mind helping me? When he is like that I can't do anything with him alone."

The old man was sitting on his bed, with a tipsy look, his long white hair falling over his face. His companion looked at him with tender yet indignant eyes. She continued: "Just see the fine head he has for his age, and yet he has to go and disguise himself in order to make people think that he is young. It's a perfect shame! Really, he has a fine head, monsieur! Wait, I'll show it to you before putting him to bed."

She went to a table on which stood the washbasin, a pitcher of water, soap, and a comb and brush. She took the brush, returned to the bed and pushed back the drunkard's tangled hair. In a few seconds she made him look like a model fit for a great painter, with his long white locks flowing on his neck. Then she stepped back in order to observe him, saying: "There! Isn't he fine for his age?"

"Very," agreed the doctor, who was beginning to be highly amused.

She added: "And if you had known him when he was twenty-five! But we must get him to bed, otherwise the liquor will make him sick. Do you mind drawing off that sleeve? Higher—like that—that's right. Now the trousers. Wait, I will take his shoes off—that's right. Now, hold him upright while I open the bed. There—let's put him in. If you think that he is going to disturb himself when it is time for me to get in, you are mistaken. I have to find a little corner anyplace I can. That doesn't bother him! Bah! You old pleasure-seeker!"

As soon as he felt himself stretched out in his sheets the old man closed his eyes, opened them, closed them again, and over his whole face appeared an energetic resolve to sleep. The doctor examined him with an ever-increasing interest and asked: "Does he go to all the fancy balls and try to be a young man?"

"To all of them, monsieur, and he comes back to me in the morning in a deplorable condition. You see, it's regret that leads him on and that makes him put a pasteboard face over his own. Yes, the regret of no longer being what he was and of no longer making any conquests!"

He was sleeping now and beginning to snore. She looked at him with a pitying expression and continued: "Oh! how many conquests that man has made! More than one could believe, monsieur, more than the finest gentlemen of the world, than all the tenors and all the generals."

"Really? What did he do?"

"Oh! it will surprise you at first, as you did not know him in his palmy days. When I met him it was also at a ball, for he has always frequented them. As soon as I saw him I was caught—caught like a fish on a hook. Ah! how handsome he was, monsieur, with his curly raven locks and black eyes as large as saucers! Indeed, he was good-looking! He took me away that evening and I never have left him since, never, not even for a day, no matter what he did to me! Oh! he has often made it hard for me!"

The doctor asked: "Are you married?"

She answered simply: "Yes, monsieur, otherwise he would have dropped me as he did the others. I have been his wife and his servant, everything, everything that he wished. How he has made me cry—tears that I did not show him; for he would tell all his adventures to me—to me, monsieur—without understanding how it hurt me to listen."

"But what was his business?"

"That's true: I forgot to tell you. He was the foreman at Martel's—a foreman such as they never had had—an artist who averaged ten francs an hour."

"Martel?—who is Martel?"

"The hairdresser, monsieur, the great hairdresser of the Opéra, who had all the actresses for customers. Yes, sir, all the smartest actresses had their hair dressed by Ambrose and they would give him tips that made a fortune for him. Ah! monsieur, all women are alike, yes, all of them: when a man tickles their fancy they offer themselves to him. It is so easy—and it hurt me so to hear about it. For he would tell me everything—he simply could not hold his tongue—it was impossible. Those things please men so much! They seem to get even more enjoyment out of telling than doing.

"When I would see him coming in the evening, a little pale, with a pleased look and a bright eye, I would say to myself: 'One more. I am sure that he has caught one more.' Then I felt a wild desire to question him and, then again, not to know, to stop his talking if he should begin. And we would look at each other.

"I knew that he would not keep still, that he would come to the point. I could feel that from his manner, which seemed to laugh and say: 'I had a fine adventure today, Madeleine.' I would pretend to notice nothing, to guess nothing; I would set the table, bring on the soup and sit down opposite him.

"At those times, monsieur, it was as if my friendship for him had been crushed in my body as with a stone. It hurt. But he did not understand; he did not know; he felt a need to tell all those things to someone, to boast, to show how much he was loved, and I was the only one he had to whom he could talk—the only one. And I would have to listen and drink it in, like poison.

"He would begin to take his soup and then he would say: 'One more, Madeleine.'

"And I would think: 'Here it comes! Goodness! What a man! Why did I ever meet him?'

"Then he would begin: 'One more! And a real beauty, too.' And it would be some little nobody from the Vaudeville or else from the Variétés, and some of the big ones, too, some of the most famous. He would tell me their names, how their apartments were furnished, everything, everything, monsieur. Heartbreaking details. And he would go over them and tell his story over again from beginning to end, so pleased with himself that I would pretend to laugh so that he would not get angry with me.

"Everything may not have been true! He liked to glorify himself and was quite capable of inventing such things! They may perhaps also have been true! On those evenings he would pretend to be tired and wish to go to bed after supper. We would take supper at eleven, monsieur, for he could never get back from work earlier.

"When he had finished telling about his adventure he would walk round the room and smoke cigarettes, and he was so handsome, with his mustache and curly hair, that I would think: 'It's true, just the same, what he is telling. Since I myself am crazy about that man, why should not others be the same?' Then I would feel like crying, shrieking, running away and jumping out of the window while I was clearing the table and he was smoking. He would yawn in order to show how tired he was, and he would say two or three times before going to bed: 'Ah! how well I shall sleep this evening!'

"I bear him no ill will, because he did not know how he was hurting me. No, he could not know! He loved to boast about the women just as a peacock loves to show his feathers. He got to the point where he thought that all of them looked at him and desired him.

"It was hard when he grew old. Oh, monsieur, when I saw his first white hair I felt a terrible shock and then a great joy—a wicked joy—but so great, so great! I said to myself: 'It's the end—it's the end.' It seemed as if I were about to be released from prison. At last I could have him to myself, all to myself, when the others would no longer want him.

"It was one morning in bed. He was still sleeping and I leaned over him to wake him up with a kiss, when I noticed in his curls, over his temple, a little thread which shone like silver. What a surprise! I should not have thought it possible! At first I thought of tearing it out so that he would not see it, but as I looked carefully I noticed another farther up. White hair! He was going to have white hair! My heart began to thump and perspiration stood out all over me, but away down at the bottom I was happy.

"It was mean to feel thus, but I did my housework with a light heart that morning, without waking him up, and, as soon as he opened his eyes of his own accord, I said to him: 'Do you know what I discovered while you were asleep?'

"'No.'

"'I found white hairs.'

"He started up as if I had tickled him and said angrily: 'It's not true!'

"'Yes, it is. There are four of them over your left temple.'

"He jumped out of bed and ran over to the mirror. He could not find them. Then I showed him the first one, the lowest, the little curly one, and I said: 'It's no wonder, after the life that you have been leading. In two years all will be over for you.'

"Well, monsieur, I had spoken true; two years later one could not recognize him. How quickly a man changes! He was still handsome, but he had lost his freshness, and the women no longer ran after him. Ah! what a life I led at that time! How he treated me! Nothing suited him. He left his trade to go into the hat business, in which he ate up all his money. Then he unsuccessfully tried to be an actor, and finally he began to frequent public balls. Fortunately, he had had common sense enough to save a little something on which we now live. It is sufficient, but it is not enormous. And to think that at one time he had almost a fortune.

"Now you see what he does. This habit holds him like a frenzy. He has to be young; he has to dance with women who smell of perfume and cosmetics. You poor old darling!"

She was looking at her old snoring husband fondly, ready to cry. Then, gently tiptoeing up to him, she kissed his hair. The physician had risen and was getting ready to leave, finding nothing to say to this strange couple. Just as he was leaving she asked:

"Would you mind giving me your address? If he should grow worse, I could go and get you."

A Ruse

The old doctor sat by the fireside, talking to his fair patient who was lying on the lounge. There was nothing much the matter with her, except that she had one of those little feminine ailments from which pretty women frequently suffer—slight anemia, a nervous attack, etc.

"No, doctor," she said; "I shall never be able to understand a woman deceiving her husband. Even allowing that she does not love him, that she pays no heed to her vows and promises, how can she give herself to another man? How can she conceal the intrigue from other people's eyes? How can it be possible to love amid lies and treason?"

The doctor smiled, and replied: "It is perfectly easy, and I can assure you that a woman does not think of all those little subtle details when she has made up her mind to go astray. As for dissimulation, all women have plenty of it on hand for such occasions, and the simplest of them are wonderful, and extricate themselves from the greatest dilemmas in a remarkable manner."

The young woman, however, seemed incredulous. "No, doctor," she said; "one never thinks until after it has happened of what one ought to have done in a critical situation, and women are certainly more liable than men to lose their head on such occasions."

The doctor raised his hands. "After it has happened, you say! Now I will tell you something that happened to one of my female patients, whom I always considered an immaculate woman.

"It happened in a provincial town, and one night when I was asleep, in that deep first sleep from which it is so difficult to rouse us, it seemed to me, in my dreams, as if the bells in the town were sounding a fire alarm, and I woke up with a start. It was my own bell, which was ringing wildly, and as my footman did not seem to be answering the door, I, in turn, pulled the bell at the head of my bed, and soon I heard a banging, and steps in the silent house, and Jean came into my room, and handed me a letter which said: 'Madame Lelievre begs Dr. Simeon to come to her immediately.'

"I thought for a few moments, and then I said to myself: 'A nervous attack, vapors; nonsense, I am too tired.' And so I replied: 'As

Dr. Simeon is not at all well, he must beg Madame Lelievre to be kind enough to call in his colleague, Monsieur Bonnet.' I put the note into an envelope and went to sleep again, but about half an hour later the street bell rang again, and Jean came to me and said: 'There is somebody downstairs; I do not quite know whether it is a man or a woman, as the individual is so wrapped up, but they wish to speak to you immediately. They say it is a matter of life and death for two people.' Whereupon I sat up in bed and told him to show the person in.

"A kind of black phantom appeared and raised her veil as soon as Jean had left the room. It was Madame Berthe Lelievre, quite a young woman, who had been married for three years to a large merchant in the town, who was said to have married the prettiest girl in the neighborhood.

"She was terribly pale, her face was contracted as the faces of insane people are, occasionally, and her hands trembled violently. Twice she tried to speak without being able to utter a sound, but at last she stammered out: 'Come—quick—quick, doctor. Come—my—friend has just died in my bedroom.' She stopped, half suffocated with emotion, and then went on: 'My husband will be coming home from the club very soon.'

"I jumped out of bed without even considering that I was only in my nightshirt, and dressed myself in a few moments, and then I said: 'Did you come a short time ago?' 'No,' she said, standing like a statue petrified with horror. 'It was my servant—she knows.' And then, after a short silence, she went on: 'I was there—by his side.' And she uttered a sort of cry of horror, and after a fit of choking, which made her gasp, she wept violently, and shook with spasmodic sobs for a minute or two. Then her tears suddenly ceased, as if by an internal fire, and with an air of tragic calmness, she said: 'We must hurry.'

"I was ready, but exclaimed: 'I quite forgot to order my carriage.'

"'I have one,' she said; 'it is his, which was waiting for him!' She wrapped herself up, so as to completely conceal her face, and we started.

"When she was by my side in the carriage she suddenly seized my hand, and crushing it in her delicate fingers, she said, with a shaking voice that proceeded from a distracted heart: 'Oh! if you only knew, if you only knew what I am suffering! I loved him, I have loved him distractedly, like a madwoman, for the last six months.'

"'Is anyone up in your house?' I asked.

"'No, nobody except those who know everything.'

"We stopped at the door, and evidently everybody was asleep. We went in without making any noise, by means of her latchkey, and walked upstairs on tiptoe. The frightened servant was sitting on the top of the stairs with a lighted candle by her side, as she was afraid to remain with the dead man, and I went into the room, which was in great disorder. Wet towels, with which they had bathed the young man's temples, were lying on the floor, by the side of a washbasin and a glass, while a strong smell of vinegar pervaded the room.

"The dead man's body was lying at full length in the middle of the room, and I went up to it, looked at it, and touched it. I opened the eyes and felt the hands, and then, turning to the two women, who were shaking as if they were freezing, I said to them: 'Help me to lift him on to the bed.' When we had laid him gently on it, I listened to his heart and put a mirror to his lips, and then said: 'It is all over.' It was a terrible sight!

"I looked at the man, and said: 'You ought to arrange his hair a little.' The girl went and brought her mistress' comb and brush, but as she was trembling, and pulling out his long, matted hair to fix it, Madame Lelievre took the comb out of her hand, and arranged his hair as if she were caressing him. She parted it, brushed his beard, rolled his mustache tips gently around her fingers, then, suddenly, letting go of his hair, she took the dead man's inert head in her hands and looked for a long time in despair at the dead face, which no longer could smile at her, and then, throwing herself on him, she clasped him in her arms and kissed him ardently. Her kisses fell like blows on his closed mouth and eyes, his forehead and temples; and then, putting her lips to his ear, as if he could still hear her, and as if she were about to whisper something to him, she said several times, in a heartrending voice: 'Good-bye, my darling!'

"Just then the clock struck twelve, and I started up. 'Twelve o'clock!' I exclaimed. 'That is the time when the club closes. Come, madame, we have not a moment to lose!' She started up, and I said: 'We must carry him into the drawing-room.' And when we had done this, I placed him on a sofa, and lit the chandeliers, and just then the front door opened and shut noisily. 'Rose, bring me the basin and the towels, and make the room look tidy. Make haste, for Heaven's sake! Monsieur Lelievre is coming in.'

"I heard his steps on the stairs, and then his hands feeling along the walls. 'Come here, my dear fellow,' I said; 'we have had an accident.'

"And the astonished husband appeared in the door with a cigar in his mouth, and said: 'What is the matter? What is the meaning of this?'

"'My dear friend,' I said, going up to him, 'you find us in great embarrassment. I had remained late, chatting with your wife and our friend, who had brought me in his carriage, when he suddenly fainted, and in spite of all we have done, he has remained unconscious for two hours. I did not like to call in strangers, and if you will now help me downstairs with him, I shall be able to attend to him better at his own house.'

"The husband, who was surprised, but quite unsuspicious, took off his hat, and then he took his rival, who would be no trouble in the future, under the arms. I got between his two legs, as if I had been a horse between the shafts, and we went downstairs, while his wife held a light for us. When we got outside I stood the body up, so as to deceive the coachman, and said: 'Come, my friend; it is nothing; you feel better already, I expect. Pluck up your courage, and make an effort. It will soon be over.' But as I felt that he was slipping out of my hands, I gave him a slap on the shoulder, which sent him forward and made him fall into the carriage, and then I got in after him. Monsieur Lelievre, who was rather alarmed, said to me: 'Do you think it is anything serious?' To which I replied: 'No,' with a smile, as I looked at his wife, who had put her arm into that of her husband, and was trying to see into the carriage.

"I shook hands with them and told my coachman to start, and during the whole drive the dead man kept falling against me. When we got to his house I said that he had become unconscious on the way home, and helped to carry him upstairs, where I certified that he was dead, and acted another comedy to his distracted family, and at last I got back to bed, not without swearing at lovers."

The doctor ceased, though he was still smiling, and the young woman, who was in a very nervous state, said: "Why have you told me that terrible story?"

He gave her a gallant bow, and replied: "So that I may offer you my services if they should be needed."

Regret

Monsieur Saval, who in Mantes was known as "Father" Saval, had just risen from bed. He was weeping. It was a dull autumn day; the leaves were falling. They fell slowly in the rain, like a heavier and slower rain. M. Saval was not in good spirits. He walked from the fireplace to the window, and from the window to the fireplace. Life has its somber days. It would no longer have any but somber days for him, for he had reached the age of sixty-two. He is alone, an old bachelor, with nobody about him. How sad it is to die alone, all alone, without anyone who is devoted to you!

He pondered over his life, so barren, so empty. He recalled former days, the days of his childhood, the home, the house of his parents; his college days, his follies; the time he studied law in Paris, his father's illness, his death. He then returned to live with his mother. They lived together very quietly, and desired nothing more. At last the mother died. How sad life is! He lived alone since then, and now, in his turn, he, too, will soon be dead. He will disappear, and that will be the end. There will be no more of Paul Saval upon the earth. What a frightful thing! Other people will love, will laugh. Yes, people will go on amusing themselves, and he will no longer exist! Is it not strange that people can laugh, amuse themselves, be joyful under that eternal certainty of death? If this death were only probable, one could then have hope; but no, it is inevitable, as inevitable as that night follows the day.

If, however, his life had been full! If he had done something; if he had had adventures, great pleasures, success, satisfaction of some kind or another. But no, nothing. He had done nothing, nothing but rise from bed, eat, at the same hours, and go to bed again. And he had gone on like that to the age of sixty-two years. He had not even taken unto himself a wife, as other men do. Why? Yes, why was it that he had not married? He might have done so, for he possessed considerable means. Had he lacked an opportunity? Perhaps! But one can create opportunities. He was indifferent; that was all. Indifference had been his greatest drawback, his defect, his vice. How many men wreck their lives through indifference! It is so difficult for some natures to get out of bed, to move about, to take long walks, to speak, to study any question.

He had not even been loved. No woman had reposed on his bosom, in a complete abandon of love. He knew nothing of the delicious anguish of expectation, the divine vibration of a hand in yours, of the ecstasy of triumphant passion.

What superhuman happiness must overflow your heart, when lips encounter lips for the first time, when the grasp of four arms makes one being of you, a being unutterably happy, two beings infatuated with one another.

M. Saval was sitting before the fire, his feet on the fender, in his dressing gown. Assuredly his life had been spoiled, completely spoiled. He had, however, loved. He had loved secretly, sadly, and indifferently, in a manner characteristic of him in everything. Yes, he had loved his old friend, Madame Sandres, the wife of his old companion, Sandres. Ah! if he had known her as a young girl! But he had met her too late; she was already married. Unquestionably, he would have asked her hand! How he had loved her, nevertheless, without respite, since the first day he set eyes on her!

He recalled his emotion every time he saw her, his grief on leaving her, the many nights that he could not sleep, because he was thinking of her.

On rising in the morning he was somewhat more rational than on the previous evening.

Why?

How pretty she was formerly, so dainty, with fair curly hair, and always laughing. Sandres was not the man she should have chosen. She was now fifty-two years of age. She seemed happy. Ah! if she had only loved him in days gone by; yes, if she had only loved him! And why should she not have loved him, he, Saval, seeing that he loved her so much, yes, she, Madame Sandres!

If only she could have guessed. Had she not guessed anything, seen anything, comprehended anything? What would she have thought? If he had spoken, what would she have answered?

And Saval asked himself a thousand other things. He reviewed his whole life, seeking to recall a multitude of details.

He recalled all the long evenings spent at the house of Sandres, when the latter's wife was young, and so charming.

He recalled many things that she had said to him, the intonations of her voice, the little significant smiles that meant so much.

He recalled their walks, the three of them together, along the banks of the Seine, their luncheon on the grass on Sundays, for Sandres was employed at the sub-prefecture. And all at once the distinct recollection came to him of an afternoon spent with her in a little wood on the banks of the river.

They had set out in the morning, carrying their provisions in baskets. It was a bright spring morning, one of those days which intoxicate one. Everything smells fresh, everything seems happy. The voices of the birds sound more joyous, and they fly more swiftly. They had luncheon on the grass, under the willow trees, quite close to the water, which glittered in the sun's rays. The air was balmy, charged with the odors of fresh vegetation; they drank it in with delight. How pleasant everything was on that day!

After lunch, Sandres went to sleep on the broad of his back. "The best nap he had in his life," said he, when he woke up.

Madame Sandres had taken the arm of Saval, and they started to walk along the riverbank.

She leaned tenderly on his arm. She laughed and said to him: "I am intoxicated, my friend, I am quite intoxicated." He looked at her, his heart going pit-a-pat. He felt himself grow pale, fearful that he might have looked too boldly at her, and that the trembling of his hand had revealed his passion.

She had made a wreath of wild flowers and water-lilies, and she asked him: "Do I look pretty like that?"

As he did not answer—for he could find nothing to say, he would have liked to go down on his knees—she burst out laughing, a sort of annoyed, displeased laugh, as she said: "You big goose, what ails you? You might at least say something."

He felt like crying, but could not even yet find a word to say.

All these things came back to him now, as vividly as on the day when they took place. Why had she said this to him, "You big goose, what ails you? You might at least say something!"

And he recalled how tenderly she had leaned on his arm. And in passing under a shady tree he had felt her ear brushing his cheek, and he had moved his head abruptly, lest she should suppose he was too familiar.

When he had said to her: "Is it not time to return?" she darted a singular look at him. "Certainly," she said, "certainly," regarding him at the same time in a curious manner. He had not thought of it at the time, but now the whole thing appeared to him quite plain.

"Just as you like, my friend. If you are tired let us go back."

And he had answered: "I am not fatigued; but Sandres may be awake now."

And she had said: "If you are afraid of my husband's being awake, that is another thing. Let us return."

On their way back she remained silent, and leaned no longer on his arm. Why?

At that time it had never occurred to him, to ask himself "why." Now he seemed to apprehend something that he had not then understood.

Could it be?

M. Saval felt himself blush, and he got up at a bound, as if he were thirty years younger and had heard Madame Sandres say, "I love you."

Was it possible? That idea which had just entered his mind tortured him. Was it possible that he had not seen, had not guessed?

Oh! if that were true, if he had let this opportunity of happiness pass without taking advantage of it!

He said to himself: "I must know. I cannot remain in this state of doubt. I must know!" He thought: "I am sixty-two years of age, she is fifty-eight; I may ask her that now without giving offense."

He started out.

The Sandres' house was situated on the other side of the street, almost directly opposite his own. He went across and knocked at the door, and a little servant opened it.

"You here at this hour, Saval! Has some accident happened to you?"

"No, my girl," he replied; "but go and tell your mistress that I want to speak to her at once."

"The fact is madame is preserving pears for the winter, and she is in the preserving room. She is not dressed for visitors, you understand."

"Yes, but go and tell her that I wish to see her on a very important matter."

The little servant went away, and Saval began to walk, with long, nervous strides, up and down the drawing-room. He did not feel in the least embarrassed, however. Oh! he was merely going to ask her something, as he would have asked her about some cooking recipe. He was sixty-two years of age!

The door opened and madame appeared. She was now a large woman, fat and round, with full cheeks and a sonorous laugh. She walked with her arms away from her sides and her sleeves tucked up, her bare arms all covered with fruit juice. She asked anxiously: "What is the matter with you, my friend? You are not ill, are you?"

"No, my dear friend; but I wish to ask you one thing, which to me is of the first importance, something which is torturing my heart, and I want you to promise that you will answer me frankly."

She laughed, "I am always frank. Ask away."

"Well, then. I have loved you from the first day I ever saw you. Can you have any doubt of this?"

She responded, laughing, with something of her former tone of voice. "You big goose! what ails you? I knew it from the very first day!"

Saval began to tremble. He stammered out: "You knew it? Then . . ." He stopped.

She asked: "Then . . . ?"

He answered: "Then—what did you think? What—what—what would you have answered?"

She broke into a peal of laughter. Some of the juice ran off the tips of her fingers on to the carpet.

"What?"

"I? Why, you did not ask me anything. It was not for me to declare myself!"

He then advanced a step toward her. "Tell me—tell me. . . . You remember the day when Sandres went to sleep on the grass after lunch . . . when we had walked together as far as the bend of the river, below. . . ."

He waited, expectantly. She had ceased to laugh, and looked at him, straight in the eyes. "Yes, certainly, I remember it."

He answered, trembling all over:

"Well—that day—if I had been—if I had been—venturesome—what would you have done?"

She began to laugh as only a happy woman can laugh, who has nothing to regret, and responded frankly, in a clear voice tinged with irony: "I would have yielded, my friend."

She then turned on her heels and went back to her jam-making.

Saval rushed into the street, cast down, as though he had met with some disaster. He walked with giant strides through the rain, straight on, until he reached the river bank, without thinking where he was going. He then turned to the right and followed the river. He walked a long time, as if urged on by some instinct. His clothes were running with water, his hat was out of shape, as soft as a rag, and dripping like a roof. He walked on, straight in front of him. At last, he came to the place where they had lunched on that day so long ago, the recollection of which tortured his heart. He sat down under the leafless trees, and wept.

The Little Keg

He was a tall man of forty or thereabout, this Jules Chicot, the inn-keeper of Spreville, with a red face and a round stomach, and said by those who knew him to be a smart businessman. He stopped his buggy in front of Mother Magloire's farmhouse and, hitching the horse to the gatepost, went in at the gate.

Chicot owned some land adjoining that of the old woman, which he had been coveting for a long while, and had tried in vain to buy a score of times, but she had always obstinately refused to part with it.

"I was born here, and I mean to die here," was all she said.

He found her peeling potatoes outside the farmhouse door. She was a woman of about seventy-two, very thin, shriveled and wrinkled, almost dried up in fact and much bent but as active and untiring as a girl. Chicot patted her on the back in a friendly fashion and then sat down by her on a stool.

"Well, mother, you are as always pretty well and hearty, I am glad to see."

"Nothing to complain of, considering, thank you. And how are you, Monsieur Chicot?"

"Oh, pretty well, thank you, except a few rheumatic pains occa-sionally; otherwise I have nothing to complain of."

"So much the better."

And she said no more, while Chicot watched her going on with her work. Her crooked, knotted fingers, hard as a lobster's claws, seized the tubers, which were lying in a pail, as if they had been a pair of pincers, and she peeled them rapidly, cutting off long strips of skin with an old knife which she held in the other hand, throwing the potatoes into the water as they were done. Three daring fowls jumped one after the other into her lap, seized a bit of peel and then ran away as fast as their legs would carry them with it in their beak.

Chicot seemed embarrassed, anxious, with something on the tip of his tongue which he could not say. At last he said hurriedly:

"Listen, Mother Magloire——"

"Well, what is it?"

"You are quite sure that you do not want to sell your land?"

"Certainly not; you may rest your mind about that. What I have said I have said, so don't refer to it again."

"Very well; only I think I know of an arrangement that might suit us both very well."

"What is it?"

"Just this. You shall sell it to me and keep it all the same. You don't understand? Very well, then follow me in what I am going to say."

The old woman left off peeling potatoes and looked at the innkeeper attentively from under her heavy eyebrows, and he went on:

"Let me explain myself. Every month I will give you a hundred and fifty francs. You understand me! Imagine! Every month I will come and bring you thirty crowns, and it will not make the slightest difference in your life—not the very slightest. You will have your own home just as you have now, need not trouble yourself about me, and will owe me nothing; all you will have to do will be to take my money. Will that arrangement suit you?"

He looked at her good-humoredly, one might almost have said benevolently, and the old woman returned his looks distrustfully, as if she suspected a trap, and said: "It seems all right as far as I am concerned, but it will not give you the farm."

"Never mind about that," he said; "you may remain here as long as it pleases God Almighty to let you live; it will be your home. Only you will sign a deed before a lawyer making it over to me after your death. You have no children, only nephews and nieces for whom you don't care a straw. Will that suit you? You will keep everything during your life, and I will give you the thirty crowns a month. It is pure gain as far as you are concerned."

The old woman was surprised, rather uneasy, but, nevertheless, very much tempted to agree, and answered: "I don't say that I will not agree to it, but I must think about it. Come back in a week, and we will talk it over again, and I will then give you my definite answer."

And Chicot went off as happy as a king who had conquered an empire.

Mother Magloire was thoughtful, and did not sleep at all that night; in fact, for four days she was in a fever of hesitation. She suspected that there was something underneath the offer which was not to her advantage; but then the thought of thirty crowns a month, of all those coins clinking in her apron, falling to her, as it were, from the skies, without her doing anything for it, aroused her covetousness.

She went to the notary and told him about it. He advised her to accept Chicot's offer, but said she ought to ask for an annuity of fifty instead of thirty, as her farm was worth sixty thousand francs at the lowest calculation.

"If you live for fifteen years longer," he said, "even then he will only have paid forty-five thousand francs for it."

The old woman trembled with joy at this prospect of getting fifty crowns a month, but she was still suspicious, fearing some trick, and she remained a long time with the lawyer asking questions without being able to make up her mind to go. At last she gave him instructions to draw up the deed and returned home with her head in a whirl, just as if she had drunk four jugs of new cider.

When Chicot came again to receive her answer, she declared, after a lot of persuading, that she could not make up her mind to agree to his proposal, though she was all the time trembling lest he should not consent to give the fifty crowns. But at last, when he grew urgent, she told him what she expected for her farm.

He looked surprised and disappointed and refused.

Then, in order to convince him, she began to talk about the probable duration of her life.

"I am certainly not likely to live more than five or six years longer. I am nearly seventy-three, and far from strong, even considering my age. The other evening I thought I was going to die, and could hardly manage to crawl into bed."

But Chicot was not going to be taken in.

"Come, come, old lady, you are as strong as the church tower, and will live till you are a hundred at least; you will no doubt see me buried first."

The whole day was spent in discussing the money, and as the old woman would not give in, the innkeeper consented to give the fifty crowns, and she insisted upon having ten crowns on top of that to seal the bargain.

Three years passed and the old woman did not seem to have grown a day older. Chicot was in despair, and it seemed to him as if he had been paying that annuity for fifty years, that he had been taken in, done in, ruined. From time to time he went to see the old lady, just as one goes in July to see when the harvest is likely to begin. She always met him with a cunning look, and one might have supposed that she was congratulating herself on the trick she had played him. Seeing how well and hearty she seemed he very soon got into his buggy again, growling to himself: "Will you never die, you old hag?"

He did not know what to do, and he felt inclined to strangle her next time he saw her. He hated her with a ferocious, cunning hatred, the hatred of a peasant who has been robbed, and began to cast about for some means of getting rid of her.

One day he came to see her again, rubbing his hands as he did the first time he proposed the bargain, and, after having chatted for a few minutes, he said: "Why do you never come and have a bit of dinner at my place when you are in Spreville? The people are talking about it, and saying we are not on friendly terms, and that pains me. You know it will cost you nothing if you come, for I don't look at the price of a dinner. Come whenever you feel inclined; I shall be very glad to see you."

Old Mother Magloire did not need to be asked twice, and the next day but one, as she had to go to the town anyway, it being market day, she let her servant drive her to Chicot's place, where the buggy was put in the barn while she went into the house to get her dinner.

The innkeeper was delighted and treated her like a lady, giving her roast fowl, black pudding, leg of mutton, and bacon and cabbage. But she ate next to nothing. She had always been a light eater, and had generally lived on a little soup and a crust of bread and butter.

Chicot was disappointed and pressed her to eat more, but she refused, and she would drink little, and declined coffee, so he asked her: "But surely you will take a little drop of brandy or liqueur?"

"Well, as to that, I don't know that I will refuse."

Whereupon he shouted out: "Rosalie, bring the superfine brandy—the special—you know."

The servant appeared, carrying a long bottle ornamented with a paper vine-leaf, and he filled two liqueur glasses.

"Just try that; you will find it first-rate."

The good woman drank it slowly in sips, so as to make the pleasure last all the longer, and when she had finished her glass, she said: "Yes, that is first-rate!"

Almost before she had said it Chicot had poured her out another glassful. She wished to refuse, but it was too late, and she drank it very slowly, as she had done the first, and he asked her to have a third. She objected, but he persisted.

"It is as mild as milk, you know; I can drink ten or a dozen glasses without any ill effects; it goes down like sugar and does not go to the head; one would think that it evaporated on the tongue: It is the most wholesome thing you can drink."

She took it, for she really enjoyed it, but she left half the glass.

Then Chicot, in an excess of generosity, said: "Look here, as it is so much to your taste, I will give you a little keg of it, just to show that you and I are still excellent friends." So she took some away with her, feeling slightly overcome by the effects of what she had drunk.

The next day the innkeeper drove into her yard and took a little iron-hooped keg out of his gig. He insisted on her tasting the contents, to make sure it was the same delicious article, and, when they had each of them drunk three more glasses, he said as he was going away: "Well, you know when it is all gone there is more left; don't be modest, for I shall not mind. The sooner it is finished the more pleased I shall be."

Four days later he came again. The old woman was outside her door cutting up the bread for her soup.

He went up to her and put his face close to hers, so that he might smell her breath; and when he smelt the alcohol he felt pleased.

"I suppose you will give me a glass of the Special?" he said. And they had three glasses each.

Soon, however, it began to be whispered abroad that Mother Magloire was in the habit of getting drunk all by herself. She was picked up in her kitchen, then in her yard, then in the roads in the neighborhood, and she was often brought home like a log.

The innkeeper did not go near her anymore, and, when people spoke to him about her, he used to say, putting on a distressed look:

"It is a great pity that she should have taken to drink at her age, but when people get old there is no remedy. It will be the death of her in the long run."

And it certainly was the death of her. She died the next winter. About Christmas time she fell down, unconscious, in the snow, and was found dead the next morning.

And when Chicot came in for the farm, he said: "It was very stupid of her; if she had not taken to drink she would probably have lived ten years longer."

Hautot and Son

1

In front of the building, half farmhouse, half manor-house, one of those rural habitations of a mixed character that were all but seigneurial, and which are at the present time occupied by large cultivators, the dogs, lashed beside the apple trees in the orchard near the house, kept barking and howling at the sight of the shooting-bags carried by the gamekeepers and the boys. In the spacious dining-room kitchen, Hautot Senior and Hautot Junior, M. Bermont, the tax-collector, and M. Mondaru, the notary, were having a bite and drinking some wine before going out to shoot, for it was the opening day.

Hautot Senior, proud of all his possessions, talked boastfully beforehand of the game that his guests were going to find on his lands. He was a big Norman, one of those powerful, ruddy, bony men who can lift wagonloads of apples on their shoulders. Half peasant, half gentleman, rich, respected, influential, invested with authority, he made his son, César, go as far as the third form at school, so that he might be an educated man, and there he had brought his studies to a stop for fear of his becoming a fine gentleman and paying no attention to the land.

César Hautot, almost as tall as his father, but thinner, was a good son, docile, content with everything, full of admiration, respect, and deference for the wishes and opinions of his sire.

M. Bermont, the tax-collector, a stout little man, who showed on his red cheeks a thin network of violet veins resembling the tributaries and the winding courses of rivers on maps, asked: "And hares—are there any hares on it?"

Hautot Senior answered: "As many as you like, especially in the Puysatier lands."

"Which direction shall we begin in?" asked the notary, a jolly notary, fat and pale, big-paunched too, and strapped up in an entirely new hunting costume bought at Rouen.

"Well, that way, through these grounds. We will drive the partridges into the plain, and we will beat there again."

And Hautot Senior rose up. They all followed his example, took their guns out of the corners, examined the locks, stamped with their feet in order to feel themselves firmer in their boots which were rather hard, not having as yet been rendered flexible by the heat of the blood. Then they went out; and the dogs, standing erect at the ends of their leashes, gave vent to piercing howls while beating the air with their paws.

They set forth for the lands referred to. These consisted of a little glen, or rather a long undulating stretch of inferior soil, which had on that account remained uncultivated, furrowed with mountain-torrents, covered with ferns, an excellent preserve for game.

The sportsmen took up their positions at some distance from each other, Hautot Senior posting himself at the right, Hautot Junior at the left, and the two guests in the middle. The keeper and those who carried the game-bags followed. It was the anxious moment when the first shot is awaited, when the heart beats a little, while the nervous finger keeps feeling at the trigger every second.

Suddenly the shot went off. Hautot Senior had fired. They all stopped, and saw a partridge breaking off from a covey which was rushing along at great speed to fall down into a ravine under a thick growth of brushwood. The sportsman, becoming excited, rushed forward with rapid strides, thrusting aside the briers which stood in his path, and disappeared in his turn into the thicket in quest of his game.

Almost at the same instant, a second shot was heard.

"Ha! ha! the rascal!" exclaimed M. Bermont, "he will unearth a hare down there."

They all waited, with their eyes riveted on the heap of branches through which their gaze failed to penetrate.

The notary, making a speaking-trumpet of his hands, shouted: "Have you got them?"

Hautot Senior made no response.

Then César, turning toward the keeper, said to him: "Just go and assist him, Joseph. We must keep walking in a straight line. We'll wait."

And Joseph, an old stump of a man, lean and knotty, all of whose joints formed protuberances, proceeded at an easy pace down the ravine, searching at every opening through which a passage could be effected with the cautiousness of a fox. Then, suddenly, he cried: "Oh! come! come! an unfortunate thing has occurred."

They all hurried forward, plunging through the briers.

The elder Hautot, who had fallen on his side, in a fainting condition, kept both his hands over his stomach, from which long streamlets of blood flowed down upon the grass through the linen vest torn by the lead. As he was laying down his gun, in order to seize the partridge within reach of him, he had let the firearm fall, and the second discharge, going off with the shock, had torn open his entrails. They drew him out of the trench; they removed his clothes and they saw a frightful wound, through which the intestines came out. Then, after having bandaged him the best way they could, they brought him back to his own house, and awaited the doctor, who had been sent for, as well as a priest.

When the doctor arrived, he gravely shook his head, and, turning toward young Hautot, who was sobbing on a chair: "My poor boy," said he, "this does not look well."

But, when the dressing was finished, the wounded man moved his fingers, opened his mouth, then his eyes, cast around him troubled, haggard glances, then appeared to search about in his memory, to recollect, to understand, and he murmured: "Ah! good God! this has done for me!"

The doctor held his hand. "Why no, why no, some days of rest merely—it will be nothing."

Hautot returned: "It has done for me! My stomach is split open! I know it well." Then, all of a sudden: "I want to talk to the son, if I have the time."

Hautot Junior, in spite of himself, shed tears, and kept repeating like a little boy: "P'pa, p'pa, poor p'pa!"

But the father, in a firmer tone: "Come! stop crying—this is not the time for it. I have to talk to you. Sit down there quite close to me. It will be quickly done, and I shall be more calm. As for the rest of you, kindly give me one minute."

They all went out, leaving the father and son face to face.

As soon as they were alone: "Listen, son! you are twenty-four; one can say things like this to you. And then there is not such mystery about these matters as we import into them. You know well that your mother has been seven years dead, isn't that so? and that I am not more than forty-five myself, seeing that I got married at nineteen? Is not that true?"

The son faltered: "Yes, it is true."

"So then, your mother has been seven years dead, and I have re-

mained a widower. Well! a man like me cannot remain without a wife
at thirty-eight, isn't that true?"

The son replied: "Yes, it is true."

The father, out of breath, quite pale, and his face contracted with
suffering, went on: "God! what pain I feel! Well, you understand.
Man is not made to live alone, but I did not want to take a successor
to your mother, since I promised her not to do so. Then—you understand?"

"Yes, father."

"So, I kept a young girl at Rouen, 18 Rue d'Eperlan, on the third
floor, the second door—I tell you all this, don't forget—but a young
girl, who has been very nice to me, loving, devoted, a true woman, eh?
You comprehend, my lad?"

"Yes, father."

"So then, if I am carried off, I owe something to her, something
substantial, that will place her in a safe position. You understand?"

"Yes, father."

"I tell you that she is an honest girl, and that, but for you, and the
remembrance of your mother, and again but for the house in which
we three lived, I would have brought her here, and then married her,
for certain—listen—listen, my lad. I might have made a will—I haven't
done so. I did not wish to do so—for it is not necessary to write down
things—things of this sort—it is too hurtful to the legitimate children—
and then it embroils everything—it ruins everyone! Look you, the
stamped paper, there's no need of it—never make use of it. If I am
rich, it is because I have not wasted what I have during my own life.
You understand, my son?"

"Yes, father."

"Listen again—listen well to me! So then, I have made no will—I did
not desire to do so—and then I knew what you were; you have a good
heart; you are not niggardly, not too cheap, in any way; I said to myself
that when my end approached I would tell you all about it, and that I
would beg of you not to forget the girl. And then listen again! When I
am gone, make your way to the place at once—and make such arrange-
ments that she may not blame my memory. You'll have plenty of money.
I leave it to you—I leave you enough. Listen! You won't find her at
home every day in the week. She works at Madame Moreau's in the
Rue Beauvoisine. Go there on a Thursday. That is the day she expects
me. It has been my day for the past six years. Poor little thing! she will
weep!—I say all this to you because I have known you so well, my son.

One does not admit these things in public either to the notary or to the priest. They happen—everyone knows that—but they are not talked about, save in cases of necessity. Then there is no outsider in the secret, nobody except the family, because the family consists of one person alone. You understand?"

"Yes, father."

"Do you promise?"

"Yes, father."

"Do you swear it?"

"Yes, father."

"I beg of you, I implore of you, so do not forget. I bind you to it."

"No, father."

"You will go yourself. I want you to make sure of everything."

"Yes, father."

"And, then, you will see—you will see what she will explain to you. As for me, I can say no more to you. You have vowed to do it."

"Yes, father."

"That's good, my son. Embrace me. Farewell. I am going to fall apart, I'm sure. Tell them they may come in."

Young Hautot embraced his father, groaning while he did so; then, always docile, he opened the door, and the priest appeared in a white surplice, carrying the holy oils.

But the dying man had closed his eyes and he refused to open them again, he refused to answer, he refused to show, even by a sign, that he understood.

He had spoken enough, this man; he could speak no more. Besides he now felt his heart calm; he wanted to die in peace. What need had he to make a confession to the deputy of God, since he had just done so to his son, who constituted his own family?

He received the last rites, was purified and absolved, in the midst of his friends and his servants on their bended knees, without any movement of his face indicating that he still lived.

He expired about midnight, after four hours' convulsive movements, which showed that he must have suffered dreadfully in his last moments.

2

It was on the following Tuesday that they buried him; the shooting had opened on Sunday. On his return home, after having accompanied his father to the cemetery, César Hautot spent the rest of the day weeping. He scarcely slept at all on the following night, and he felt so sad on awakening that he asked himself how he could go on living.

However, he kept thinking until evening that, in order to obey the last wish of his father, he ought to repair to Rouen the next day, and see this girl Catholine Donet, who resided in the Rue d'Eperlan, on the third floor, second door. He had repeated to himself in a whisper, just as a little boy repeats a prayer, this name and address a countless number of times, so that he might not forget them, and he ended by lisping them continually, without being able to stop or to think of what they were, so much were his tongue and his mind possessed by the commission.

Accordingly, on the following day, about eight o'clock, he ordered Graindorge to be yoked to the tilbury, and set forth at the quick trotting pace of the heavy Norman horse, along the highroad from Ainville to Rouen. He wore his black frock-coat, a tall silk hat on his head, and breeches with straps; and he did not, on account of the occasion, dispense with the handsome costume, the blue overalls which swelled in the wind, protecting the cloth from dust and from stains, and which was to be removed quickly the moment he jumped out of the coach.

He entered Rouen accordingly just as it was striking ten o'clock, drew up, as he had usually done, at the Hôtel des Bon-Enfants, in the Rue des Trois-Marcs, submitted to the hugs of the landlord and his wife and their five children, for they had heard the melancholy news. After that, he had to tell them all the particulars about the accident, which caused him to shed tears, to repel all the proffered attentions which they sought to thrust upon him merely because he was wealthy, and to decline even the breakfast they wanted him to partake of, thus wounding their sensibilities.

Then, having wiped the dust off his hat, brushed his coat and removed the mud stains from his boots, he set forth in search of the Rue d'Eperlan, without venturing to make inquiries from anyone, for fear of being recognized and arousing suspicions.

At length, being unable to find the place, he saw a priest passing by, and, trusting to the professional discretion which churchmen possess, he questioned the ecclesiastic.

He had only a hundred steps farther to go; it was the second street to the right.

Then he hesitated. Up to that moment, he had obeyed, like a mere animal, the expressed wish of the deceased. Now he felt quite agi-

tated, confused, humiliated, at the idea of finding himself—the son—
in the presence of this woman who had been his father's mistress. All
the morality that lies buried in our breasts, heaped up at the bottom
of our sensuous emotions by centuries of hereditary instruction, all
that he had been taught, since he had learned his catechism, about
creatures of sin, the instinctive contempt which every man entertains
for them, even though he may marry one of them, all the narrow
honesty of the peasant in his character, was stirred up within him and
held him back, making him grow red with shame.

But he said to himself: "I promised the father, I must not break my
promise."

Then he gave a push to the door of the house bearing the number
18, which stood ajar, discovered a gloomy-looking staircase, ascended
three flights, perceived a door, then a second door, came upon the
string of a bell, and pulled it. The ringing, which resounded in the
apartment before which he stood, sent a shiver through his frame.
The door was opened, and he found himself facing a young lady very
well dressed, a brunette with a fresh complexion, who gazed at him
with eyes of astonishment.

He did not know what to say to her, and she, who suspected nothing and was waiting for him to speak, did not invite him to come in.
They stood looking thus at one another for nearly half a minute, at
the end of which she said in a questioning tone: "You have something
to tell me, Monsieur?"

He falteringly replied: "I am Monsieur Hautot's son."

She gave a start, turned pale, and stammered out as if she had
known him for a long time: "Monsieur César?"

"Yes."

"And what next?"

"I have come to speak to you on the part of my father."

She articulated: "Oh, my God!"

She then drew back so that he might enter. He shut the door and
followed her into the interior. Then he saw a little boy of four or five
years playing with a cat, seated on the floor in front of a stove, from
which rose the steam of dishes which were being kept hot.

"Take a seat," she said.

He sat down.

She asked: "Well?"

He no longer ventured to speak, keeping his eyes fixed on the table that stood in the center of the room, with three covers laid on it, one of which was for a child. He glanced at the chair which had its back turned to the fire. They had been expecting his father. That was his bread he saw, and which he recognized near the fork, for the crust had been removed on account of Hautot's bad teeth. Then, raising his eyes, he noticed on the wall his father's portrait, the large photograph taken at Paris the year of the exhibition, the same as that which hung above the bed in the sleeping apartment at Ainville.

The young woman again asked: "Well, Monsieur César?"

He kept staring at her. Her face was livid with anguish; and she waited, her hands trembling with fear.

Then he took courage. "Well, Mam'zelle, papa died last Sunday, just after he had opened the shooting."

She was so much overwhelmed that she did not move. After a silence of a few seconds, she faltered in an almost inaudible tone: "Oh! it is not possible!" Then, suddenly, tears showed themselves in her eyes, and covering her face with her hands, she burst out sobbing.

At that point the little boy turned around, and, seeing his mother weeping, began to howl. Then, realizing that this sudden trouble was brought about by the stranger, he rushed at César, caught hold of his breeches with one hand and with the other hit him with all his strength on the thigh. And César remained agitated, deeply affected, with this woman mourning for his father at one side of him, and the little boy defending his mother at the other. He felt their emotion taking possession of himself, and his eyes were beginning to brim over with the same sorrow; so, to recover his self-command, he began to talk:

"Yes," he said, "the accident occurred on Sunday, at eight o'clock—"

And he told, as if she were listening to him, all the facts without forgetting a single detail, mentioning the most trivial matters with the minuteness of a country man. And the child still kept assailing him, making kicks at his ankles.

When he came to the point at which his father had spoken about her, her attention was caught by hearing her own name, and, uncovering her face, she said: "Pardon me! I was not following you; I would like to know—if you do not mind beginning over again."

He related everything at great length, with stoppages, breaks, and reflections of his own from time to time. She listened to him eagerly now perceiving with a woman's keen sensibility all the sudden changes of fortune which his narrative indicated, and trembling with horror, every now and then, exclaiming: "Oh, my God!"

The little fellow, believing that she had calmed down, ceased beating César, in order to catch his mother's hand, and he listened, too, as if he understood.

When the narrative was finished, young Hautot continued: "Now, we will settle matters together in accordance with his wishes. Listen: I am well off, he has left me plenty of money. I don't want you to have anything to complain about——"

But she quickly interrupted him:

"Oh! Monsieur César, Monsieur César, not today. I am cut to the quick—another time—another day. No, not today. If I accept, listen! 'Tis not for myself—no, no, no, I swear to you. 'Tis for the child. Besides this provision will be put to his account."

Thereupon César scared, divined the truth, and stammering: "So then—it's his—the child?"

"Why, yes," she said.

And Hautot Junior gazed at his brother with a confused emotion, intense and painful.

After a lengthened silence, for she had begun to weep afresh, César, quite embarrassed, went on: "Well, then, Mam'zelle Donet, I am going. When would you wish to talk this over with me?"

She exclaimed: "Oh! no, don't go! don't go! Don't leave me all alone with Emile. I would die of grief. I have no longer anyone, anyone but my child. Oh! what wretchedness, what wretchedness. Monsieur César! Stop! Sit down again. You will say something more to me. You will tell me what he was doing over there all week."

And César resumed his seat, accustomed to obey.

She drew over another chair for herself in front of the stove, where the dishes had all this time been simmering, took Emile upon her knees, and asked César a thousand questions about his father with reference to matters of an intimate nature, which made him feel, without reasoning on the subject, that she had loved Hautot with all the strength of her frail woman's heart.

And, by the natural concatenation of his ideas—which were rather limited in number—he returned once more to the accident, and set about telling the story over again with all the same details.

When he said: "He had a hole in his stomach—you could put your two fists into it," she gave vent to a sort of shriek, and the tears gushed forth again from her eyes.

Then, seized by the contagion of her grief, César began to weep, too, and as tears always soften the fibers of the heart, he bent over Emile whose forehead was close to his own mouth and kissed him.

The mother, recovering her breath, murmured: "Poor lad, he is an orphan now!"

"And so am I," said César.

And they ceased to talk.

But suddenly the practical instinct of the housewife, accustomed to be thoughtful about many things, revived in the young woman's breast.

"You have perhaps eaten nothing all morning, Monsieur César."

"No, Mam'zelle."

"Oh! you must be hungry. You will eat something."

"Thanks," he said, "I am not hungry; I have had too much sorrow."

She replied: "In spite of sorrow, we must live. You will not refuse to let me get something for you! And then you will remain a little longer. When you are gone I don't know what will become of me."

He yielded after some further resistance, and, sitting down with his back to the fire, facing her, he ate a plateful of tripe, which had been bubbling in the stove, and drank a glass of red wine. But he would not allow her to uncork the bottle of white wine. He several times wiped the mouth of the little boy, who had smeared all his chin with sauce.

As he was rising up to go, he asked: "When would you like me to come back to speak about this business to you, Mam'zelle Donet?"

"If it is all the same to you, say next Thursday, Monsieur César. In that way I wouldn't have to leave work, as I always have my Thursdays free."

"That will suit me—next Thursday."

"You will come to lunch. Won't you?"

"Oh! On that point I can't give you a promise."

"The reason I suggested it is that people can chat better when they are eating. One has more time, too."

"Well, be it so. About twelve o'clock, then." And he took his departure, after he had again kissed little Emile, and pressed Mademoiselle Donet's hand.

3

The week appeared long to César Hautot. He had never before found himself alone, and the isolation seemed to him insupportable. Till now, he had lived at his father's side, just like his shadow, followed him into the fields, superintended the execution of his orders, and, when they had been a short time separated, again met him at dinner. They had spent the evenings smoking their pipes, face to face with one another, chatting about horses, cows, or sheep, and the grip of their hands when they rose up in the morning might have been regarded as a manifestation of deep family affection on both sides.

Now César was alone, he went vacantly through the process of dressing the soil in autumn, every moment expecting to see the tall gesticulating silhouette of his father rising up at the end of a plain. To kill time, he entered the houses of his neighbors, told about the accident to all who had not heard of it, and sometimes repeated it to the others. Then, after he had finished his occupations and his reflections, he would sit down at the side of the road, asking himself whether this kind of life was going to last forever.

He frequently thought of Mademoiselle Donet. He liked her. He considered her thoroughly respectable, a gentle and honest young woman, as his father had said. Yes, undoubtedly she was an honest girl. He resolved to act handsomely toward her, and to give her two thousand francs a year, settling the capital on the child. He even experienced a certain pleasure in thinking that he was going to see her on the following Thursday and arrange this matter with her. And then the notion of this brother, this little chap of five, who was his father's son, plagued him, annoyed him a little, and at the same time, excited him. He had, as it were, a family in this brat, sprung from a clandestine alliance, who would never bear the name of Hautot, a family which he might take or leave, just as he pleased, but which would recall his father.

And so, when he saw himself on the road to Rouen on Thursday morning, carried along by Graindorge trotting with clattering hoofbeats, he felt his heart lighter, more at peace than he had hitherto felt it since his bereavement.

On entering Mademoiselle Donet's apartment, he saw the table set as on the previous Thursday, with the sole difference that the crust had not been removed from the bread. He pressed the young woman's

hand, kissed Emile on the cheeks, and sat down, more or less as if he
were in his own house, his heart swelling in the same way. Mademoiselle Donet seemed to him a little thinner and paler. She must have
grieved sorely. She wore now an air of constraint in his presence, as if
she understood what she had not felt the week before under the first
blow of her misfortune, and she exhibited an excessive deference toward him, a mournful humility, and made touching efforts to please
him, as if to pay him back by her attentions for the kindness he had
manifested toward her. They were a long time at lunch talking over
the business which had brought him there. She did not want so much
money. It was too much. She earned enough to live on herself, but she
only wished that Emile might find a few sous awaiting him when he
grew up. César held out, however, and even added a gift of a thousand
francs for herself for the expense of mourning.

When he had taken his coffee, she asked: "Do you smoke?"

"Yes—I have my pipe."

He felt in his pocket. Good God! He had forgotten it! He was
becoming quite woebegone about it when she offered him a pipe of
his father's that had been shut up in a cupboard. He accepted it, took
it up in his hand, recognized it, smelled it, spoke of its quality in a
tone of emotion, filled it with tobacco, and lighted it. Then he set
Emile astride on his knee, and made him play the cavalier, while she
removed the tablecloth and put the dirty dishes at one end of the
sideboard in order to wash them as soon as he was gone.

About three o'clock, he rose up with regret, quite annoyed at the
thought of having to go.

"Well! Mademoiselle Donet," he said, "I wish you good evening,
and am delighted to have found you like this."

She remained standing before him, blushing, much affected, and
gazed at him while she thought of the other.

"Shall we not see one another again?" she said.

He replied simply: "Why, yes, Mam'zelle, if it gives you pleasure."

"Certainly, Monsieur César. Will next Thursday suit you then?"

"Yes, Mademoiselle Donet."

"You will come to lunch, of course?"

"Well—if you are so kind as to invite me, I can't refuse."

"It is understood, then, Monsieur César—next Thursday, at twelve,
the same as today."

"Thursday at twelve, Mam'zelle Donet!"

Who Knows?

1

My God! My God! I am going to write down at last what has happened to me. But how can I? How dare I? The thing is so bizarre, so inexplicable, so incomprehensible, so silly!

If I were not perfectly sure of what I have seen, sure that there was not in my reasoning any defect, any error in my declarations, any lacuna in the inflexible sequence of my observations, I should believe myself to be the dupe of a simple hallucination, the sport of a singular vision. After all, who knows?

Yesterday I was in a private asylum, but I went there voluntarily, out of prudence and fear. Only one single human being knows my history, and that is the doctor of the said asylum. I am going to write to him. I really do not know why? To disembarrass myself? Yea, I feel as though weighed down by an intolerable nightmare.

Let me explain.

I have always been a recluse, a dreamer, a kind of isolated philosopher, easy-going, content with but little, harboring ill-feeling against no man, and without even a grudge against heaven. I have constantly lived alone; consequently, a kind of torture takes hold of me when I find myself in the presence of others. How is this to be explained? I do not know. I am not averse to going out into the world, to conversation, to dining with friends, but when they are near me for any length of time, even the most intimate of them, they bore me, fatigue me, enervate me, and I experience an overwhelming, torturing desire to see them get up and go, to take themselves away, and to leave me by myself.

That desire is more than a craving; it is an irresistible necessity. And if the presence of people with whom I find myself were to be continued; if I were compelled, not only to listen, but also to follow, for any length of time, their conversation, a serious accident would assuredly take place. What kind of accident? Ah! who knows? Perhaps a slight paralytic stroke? Probably!

I like solitude so much that I cannot even endure the vicinage of other beings sleeping under the same roof. I cannot live in Paris, because there I suffer the most acute agony. I lead a moral life, and am therefore tortured in body and in nerves by that immense crowd which swarms and lives even when it sleeps. Ah! the sleeping of others is more painful still than their conversation. And I can never find repose when I know and feel that on the other side of a wall several existences are undergoing these regular eclipses of reason.

Why am I thus? Who knows? The cause of it is very simple perhaps. I get tired very soon of everything that does not emanate from me. And there are many people in similar case.

We are, on earth, two distinct races. Those who have need of others, whom others amuse, engage soothe, whom solitude harasses, pains, stupefies, like the movement of a terrible glacier or the traversing of the desert; and those, on the contrary, whom others weary, tire, bore, silently torture, whom isolation calms and bathes in the repose of independency, and plunges into the humors of their own thoughts. In fine, there is here a normal, physical phenomenon. Some are constituted to live a life outside of themselves, others, to live a life within themselves. As for me, my exterior associations are abruptly and painfully short-lived, and, as they reach their limits, I experience in my whole body and in my whole intelligence an intolerable uneasiness.

As a result of this, I became attached, or rather had become much attached, to inanimate objects, which have for me the importance of beings, and my house has or had become a world in which I lived an active and solitary life, surrounded by all manner of things, furniture, familiar knickknacks, as sympathetic in my eyes as the visages of human beings. I had filled my mansion with them; little by little, I had adorned it with them, and I felt an inward content and satisfaction, was more happy than if I had been in the arms of a beloved girl, whose wonted caresses had become a soothing and delightful necessity.

I had had this house constructed in the center of a beautiful garden, which hid it from the public high-ways, and which was near the entrance to a city where I could find, on occasion, the resources of society, for which, at moments, I had a longing. All my domestics slept in a separate building, which was situated at some considerable distance from my house, at the far end of the kitchen garden, which in turn was surrounded by a high wall. The obscure envelopment of night, in the silence of my concealed habitation, buried under the leaves of great trees, was so reposeful and so delicious, that before retiring to my couch I lingered every evening for several hours in order to enjoy the solitude a little longer.

One day *Sigurd* had been performed at one of the city theaters. It was the first time that I had listened to that beautiful, musical, and fairy-like drama, and I had derived from it the liveliest pleasures.

I returned home on foot with a light step, my head full of sonorous phrases, and my mind haunted by delightful visions. It was night, the dead of night, and so dark that I could hardly distinguish the broad highway, and consequently I stumbled into the ditch more than once. From the customhouse, at the barriers, to my house, was about a mile, perhaps a little more—a leisurely walk of about twenty minutes. It was one o'clock in the morning, one o'clock or maybe half-past one; the sky had by this time cleared somewhat and the crescent appeared, the gloomy crescent of the last quarter of the moon. The crescent of the first quarter is that which rises about five or six o'clock in the evening and is clear, gay, and fretted with silver; but the one which rises after midnight is reddish, sad, and desolating—it is the true Sabbath crescent. Every prowler by night has made the same observation. The first, though slender as a thread, throws a faint, joyous light which rejoices the heart and lines the ground with distinct shadows; the last sheds hardly a dying glimmer, and is so wan that it occasions hardly any shadows.

In the distance, I perceived the somber mass of my garden, and, I know not why, was seized with a feeling of uneasiness at the idea of going inside. I slackened my pace, and walked very softly, the thick cluster of trees having the appearance of a tomb in which my house was buried.

I opened my outer gate and entered the long avenue of sycamores which ran in the direction of the house, arranged vault-wise like a high tunnel, traversing opaque masses, and winding round the turf lawns, on which baskets of flowers, in the pale darkness, could be indistinctly discerned.

While approaching the house, I was seized by a strange feeling. I could hear nothing, I stood still. Through the trees there was not even a breath of air stirring. "What is the matter with me?" I said to myself. For ten years I had entered and re-entered in the same way, without ever experiencing the least inquietude. I never had any fear at nights. The sight of a man, a marauder, or a thief would have thrown me into a fit of anger, and I would have rushed at him without any hesitation.

Moreover, I was armed—I had my revolver. But I did not touch it, for I was anxious to resist that feeling of dread with which I was seized.

What was it? Was it a presentiment—that mysterious presentiment that takes hold of the senses of men who have witnessed something that, to them, is inexplicable? Perhaps? Who knows?

In proportion as I advanced, I felt my skin quiver more and more, and when I was close to the wall, near the outhouses of my large residence, I felt that it would be necessary for me to wait a few minutes before opening the door and going inside. I sat down, then, on a bench, under the windows of my drawing-room. I rested there, a little disturbed, with my head leaning against the wall, my eyes wide open, under the shade of the foliage. For the first few minutes, I did not observe anything unusual around me; I had a humming noise in my ears, but that has happened often to me. Sometimes it seemed to me that I heard trains passing, that I heard clocks striking, that I heard a multitude on the march.

Very soon, those humming noises became more distinct, more concentrated, more determinable, I was deceiving myself. It was not the ordinary tingling of my arteries which transmitted to my ears these rumbling sounds, but it was a very distinct, though confused, noise which came, without any doubt whatever, from the interior of my house. Through the walls I distinguished this continued noise—I should rather say agitation than noise—an indistinct moving about of a pile of things, as if people were tossing about, displacing, and carrying away surreptitiously all my furniture.

I doubted, however, for some considerable time yet, the evidence of my ears. But having placed my ear against one of the outhouses, the better to discover what this strange disturbance was, inside my house, I became convinced, certain, that something was taking place in my residence which was altogether abnormal and incomprehensible. I had no fear, but I was—how shall I express it—paralyzed by astonishment. I did not draw my revolver, knowing very well that there was no need of my doing so.

I listened a long time, but could come to no resolution, my mind being quite clear, though in myself I was naturally anxious. I got up and waited, listening always to the noise, which gradually increased, and at intervals grew very loud, and which seemed to become an impatient, angry disturbance, a mysterious commotion.

Then, suddenly, ashamed of my timidity, I seized my bunch of keys. I selected the one I wanted, guided it into the lock, turned it twice, and pushing the door with all my might, sent it banging against the partition.

The collision sounded like the report of a gun, and there responded to that explosive noise, from roof to basement of my residence, a formidable tumult. It was so sudden, so terrible, so deafening, that I recoiled a few steps, and though I knew it to be wholly useless, I pulled my revolver out of its case.

I continued to listen for some time longer. I could distinguish now an extraordinary pattering upon the steps of my grand staircase, on the waxed floors, on the carpets, not of boots, or of naked feet, but of iron and wooden crutches, which resounded like cymbals. Then I suddenly discerned, on the threshold of my door, an armchair, my large reading easy-chair, which set off waddling. It went away through my garden. Others followed it, those of my drawing-room, then my sofas, dragging themselves along like crocodiles on their short paws; then all my chairs, bounding like goats, and the little foot-stools, hopping like rabbits.

Oh! what a sensation! I slunk back into a clump of bushes where I remained crouched up, watching, meanwhile, my furniture file past— for everything walked away, the one behind the other, briskly or slowly, according to its weight or size. My piano, my grand piano, bounded past with the gallop of a horse and a murmur of music in its sides; the smaller articles slid along the gravel like snails, my brushes, crystal, cups and saucers, which glistened in the moonlight. I saw my writing desk appear, a rare curiosity of the last century, which contained all the letters I had ever received, all the history of my heart, an old history from which I have suffered so much! Besides, there were inside of it a great many cherished photographs.

Suddenly—I no longer had any fear—I threw myself on it, seized it as one would seize a thief, as one would seize a wife about to run away; but it pursued its irresistible course, and despite my efforts and despite my anger, I could not even retard its pace. As I was resisting in desperation that insuperable force, I was thrown to the ground. It then rolled me over, trailed me along the gravel, and the rest of my furniture, which followed it, began to march over me, tramping on my legs and injuring them. When I loosed my hold, other articles had passed over my body, just as a charge of cavalry does over the body of a dismounted soldier.

Seized at last with terror, I succeeded in dragging myself out of the main avenue, and in concealing myself again among the shrubbery, so as to watch the disappearance of the most cherished objects, the smallest, the least striking, the least unknown which had once belonged to me.

I then heard, in the distance, noises which came from my apartments, which sounded now as if the house were empty, a loud noise of shutting of doors. They were being slammed from top to bottom of my dwelling, even the door which I had just opened myself unconsciously, and which had closed of itself, when the last thing had taken its departure. I took flight also, running toward the city, and only regained my self-composure, on reaching the boulevards, where I met belated people. I rang the bell of a hotel were I was known. I had knocked the dust off my clothes with my hands, and I told the porter that I had lost my bunch of keys, which included also that to the kitchen garden, where my servants slept in a house standing by itself, on the other side of the wall of the enclosure which protected my fruits and vegetables from the raids of marauders.

I covered myself up to the eyes in the bed which was assigned to me, but could not sleep; and I waited for the dawn listening to the throbbing of my heart. I had given orders that my servants were to be summoned to the hotel at daybreak, and my valet de chambre knocked at my door at seven o'clock in the morning.

His countenance bore a woeful look.

"A great misfortune has happened during the night, Monsieur," said he.

"What is it?"

"Somebody has stolen the whole of Monsieur's furniture, all, everything, even to the smallest articles."

This news pleased me. Why? Who knows? I was complete master of myself, bent on dissimulating, on telling no one of anything I had seen; determined on concealing and in burying in my heart of hearts a terrible secret. I responded:

"They must then be the same people who have stolen my keys. The police must be informed immediately. I am going to get up, and I will join you in a few moments."

The investigation into the circumstances under which the robbery might have been committed lasted for five months. Nothing was found, not even the smallest of my knickknacks, nor the least trace of the thieves. Good gracious! If I had only told them what I knew—If I had said—I should have been locked up—I, not the thieves—for I was the only person who had seen everything from the first.

Yes! but I knew how to keep silence. I shall never refurnish my house. That were indeed useless. The same thing would happen again. I had no desire even to re-enter the house, and I did not re-enter it; I never visited it again. I moved to Paris, to the hotel, and consulted doctors in regard to the condition of my nerves, which had disquieted me a good deal ever since that awful night.

They advised me to travel, and I followed their counsel.

2

I began by making an excursion into Italy. The sunshine did me much good. For six months I wandered about from Genoa to Venice, from Venice to Florence, from Florence to Rome, from Rome to Naples. Then I traveled over Sicily, a country celebrated for its scenery and its monuments, relics left by the Greeks and the Normans. Passing over into Africa, I traversed at my ease that immense desert, yellow and tranquil, in which camels, gazelles, and Arab vagabonds roam about— where, in the rare and transparent atmosphere, there hover no vague hauntings, where there is never any night, but always day.

I returned to France by Marseilles, and in spite of all its Provencal gaiety, the diminished clearness of the sky made me sad. I experienced, in returning to the Continent, the peculiar sensation of an illness which I believed had been cured, and a dull pain which predicted that the seeds of the disease had not been eradicated.

I then returned to Paris. At the end of a month I was very dejected. It was in the autumn, and I determined to make, before winter came, an excursion through Normandy, a country with which I was unacquainted.

I began my journey, in the best of spirits, at Rouen, and for eight days I wandered about, passive, ravished, and enthusiastic, in that ancient city, that astonishing museum of extraordinary Gothic monuments.

But one afternoon, about four o'clock, as I was sauntering slowly through a seemingly unattractive street, by which there ran a stream as black as the ink called Eau de Robec, my attention, fixed for the moment on the quaint, antique appearance of some of the houses, was suddenly attracted by the view of a series of second-hand furniture shops, which followed one another, door after door.

Ah! they had carefully chosen their locality, these sordid traffickers in antiquities, in that quaint little street, overlooking the sinister stream of water, under those tile and slate-pointed roofs on which still grinned the vanes of bygone days.

At the end of these grim storehouses you saw piled up sculptured chests, Rouen, Sèvres, and Moustier's pottery, painted statues, others of oak, Christs, Virgins, saints, church ornaments, chasubles, capes, even sacred vases, and an old gilded wooden tabernacle, where a god had hidden himself away. What singular caverns there are in those lofty houses, crowded with objects of every description, where the existence of things seems to be ended, things which have survived their original possessors, their century, their times, their fashions, in order to be bought as curiosities by new generations.

My affection for antiques was awakened in that city of antiquaries. I went from shop to shop, crossing in two strides the rotten four plank bridges thrown over the nauseous current of the Eau de Robec. Heaven protect me! What a shock! At the end of a vault, which was crowded with articles of every description and which seemed to be the entrance to the catacombs of a cemetery of ancient furniture, I suddenly spied one of my most beautiful wardrobes. I approached it, trembling in every limb, trembling to such an extent that I dared not touch it, I put forth my hand, I hesitated. Nevertheless it was indeed my wardrobe; a unique wardrobe of the time of Louis XIII, recognizable by anyone who had seen it even once. Casting my eyes suddenly a little farther, toward the more somber depths of the gallery, I perceived three of my tapestry covered chairs; and farther on still, my two Henri II tables, such rare treasures that people came all the way from Paris to see them.

Think! only think in what a state of mind I now was! I advanced, haltingly, quivering with emotion, but I advanced, for I am brave—I advanced like a knight of the dark ages.

At every step I found something that belonged to me; my brushes, my books, my tables, my silks, my arms, everything, except the bureau full of my letters, and that I could not discover.

I walked on, descending to the dark galleries, in order to ascend next to the floors above. I was alone; I called out, nobody answered, I was alone; there was no one in that house—a house as vast and tortuous as a labyrinth.

Night came on, and I was compelled to sit down in the darkness on one of my own chairs, for I had no desire to go away. From time to time I shouted, "Hallo, hallo, somebody."

I had sat there, certainly, for more than an hour when I heard steps, steps soft and slow, I knew not where. I was unable to locate them, but bracing myself up, I called out anew, whereupon I perceived a glimmer of light in the next chamber.

"Who is there?" said a voice.

"A buyer," I responded.

"It is too late to enter thus into a shop."

"I have been waiting for you for more than an hour," I answered.

"You can come back tomorrow."

"Tomorrow I must leave Rouen."

I dared not advance, and he did not come to me. I saw always the glimmer of his light, which was shining on a tapestry on which were two angels flying over the dead on a field of battle. It belonged to me also. I said: "Well, come closer."

"I am at your service," he answered.

I got up and went toward him.

Standing in the center of a large room, was a little man, very short, and very fat, phenomenally fat, a hideous phenomenon.

He had a singular straggling beard, white and yellow, and not a hair on his head—not a hair!

As he held his candle aloft at arm's length in order to see me, his cranium appeared to me to resemble a little moon, in that vast chamber encumbered with old furniture. His features were wrinkled and blown, and his eyes could not be seen.

I bought three chairs which belonged to myself, and paid at once a large sum for them, giving him merely the number of my room at the hotel. They were to be delivered the next day before nine o'clock.

I then started off. He conducted me, with much politeness, as far as the door.

I immediately repaired to the commissioner's office at the central police station, and told the commissioner of the robbery which had been perpetrated and of the discovery I had just made. He required time to communicate by telegraph with the authorities who had originally charge of the case, for information, and he begged me to wait in his office until an answer came back. An hour later, an answer came back, which was in accord with my statements.

"I am going to arrest and interrogate this man at once," he said to me, "for he may have conceived some sort of suspicion, and smuggled away out of sight what belongs to you. Will you go and dine and return in two hours? I shall then have the man here, and I shall subject him to a fresh interrogation in your presence."

"Most gladly, Monsieur. I thank you with my whole heart."

I went to dine at my hotel and I ate better than I could have believed. I was quite happy now, thinking that man was in the hands of the police.

Two hours later I returned to the office of the police functionary, who was waiting for me.

"Well, Monsieur," said he, on perceiving me, "we have not been able to find your man. My agents cannot put their hands on him."

Ah! I felt my heart sinking. "But you have at least found his house?" I asked.

"Yes, certainly; and what is more, it is now being watched and guarded until his return. As for him, he has disappeared."

"Disappeared?"

"Yes, disappeared. He ordinarily passes his evenings at the house of a female neighbor, who is also a furniture broker, a queer sort of sorceress, the widow Bidoin. She has not seen him this evening and cannot give any information in regard to him. We must wait until tomorrow."

I went away. Ah! how sinister the streets of Rouen seemed to me, now troubled and haunted!

I slept so badly that I had a fit of nightmare every time I went off to sleep.

As I did not wish to appear too restless or eager, I waited till ten o'clock the next day before reporting myself to the police.

The merchant had not reappeared. His shop remained closed.

The commissioner said to me: "I have taken all the necessary steps. The court has been made acquainted with the affair. We shall go together to that shop and have it opened, and you shall point out to me all that belongs to you."

We drove there in a cab. Police agents were stationed round the building; there was a locksmith, too, and the door of the shop was soon opened.

On entering, I could not discover my wardrobes, my chairs, my tables; I saw nothing, nothing of that which had furnished my house, no, nothing, although on the previous evening, I could not take a step without encountering something that belonged to me.

The chief commissioner, much astonished, regarded me at first with suspicion.

"My God, Monsieur," said I to him, "the disappearance of these articles of furniture coincides strangely with that of the merchant."

He laughed. "That is true. You did wrong in buying and paying for the articles that were your own property, yesterday. It was that which gave him the clue."

"What seems to me incomprehensible," I replied, "is that all the places that were occupied by my furniture are now filled by other furniture."

"Oh!" responded the commissary, "he has had all night, and has no doubt been assisted by accomplices. This house must communicate with its neighbors. But have no fear, Monsieur; I will have the affair promptly and thoroughly investigated. The brigand shall not escape us for long, seeing that we are in charge of the den."

Ah! My heart, my heart, my poor heart, how it beats!

I remained a fortnight at Rouen. The man did not return. Heavens! good heavens! That man, what was it that could have frightened and surprised him!

But, on the sixteenth day, early in the morning, I received from my gardener, now the keeper of my empty and pillaged house, the following strange letter:

Monsieur:

I have the honor to inform Monsieur that something happened, the evening before last, which nobody can understand, and the police no more than the rest of us. All of the furniture has been returned, not one piece is missing—everything is in its place, down to the very smallest article. The house is now the same in every respect as it was before the robbery took place. It is enough to make one lose one's head. The thing took place during the night Friday-Saturday. The roads are dug up as though the whole fence had been dragged from its place up to the door. The same thing was observed the day after the disappearance of the furniture.

We are anxiously expecting Monsieur, whose very humble and obedient servant, I am,

Phillipe Raudin

"Ah! no, no, ah! never, never, ah! no. I shall never return there!"
I took the letter to the commissioner of police.

"It is a very clever restitution," said he. "Let us bury the hatchet. We shall nip the man one of these days."

But he has never been nipped. No. They have not nipped him, and I am afraid of him now, as of some ferocious animal that has been let loose behind me.

Inexplicable! It is inexplicable, this chimera of a moonstruck skull! We shall never solve or comprehend it. I shall not return to my former residence. What does it matter to me? I am afraid of encountering that man again, and I shall not run the risk.

And even if he returns, if he takes possession of his shop, who can prove that my furniture was on his premises? There is only my testimony against him; and I feel that mine is not above suspicion.

Ah! no! This kind of existence has become unendurable. I have not been able to guard the secret of what I have seen. I could not continue to live like the rest of the world, with the fear upon me that those scenes might be re-enacted.

So I have come to consult the doctor who directs this lunatic asylum, and I have told him everything.

After questioning me for a long time, he said to me: "Will you consent, Monsieur, to remain here for some time?"

"Most willingly, Monsieur."

"You have the means?"

"Yes, Monsieur."

"Will you have isolated apartments?"

"Yes, Monsieur."

"Would you care to receive any friends?"

"No, Monsieur, no, nobody. The man from Rouen might take it into his head to pursue me here, to be revenged on me."

I have been alone, alone, all, all alone, for three months. I am growing tranquil by degrees. I no longer have any fears. If the antiquary should become mad . . . and if he should be brought into this asylum! Even prisons themselves are not places of security.

The Horla

MAY 8. What a lovely day! I have spent all the morning lying on the grass in front of my house, under the enormous plantain tree that covers and shades and shelters the whole of it. I like this part of the country; I am fond of living here because I am attached to it by deep roots, the profound and delicate roots which attach a man to the soil on which his ancestors were born and died, to their traditions, their usages, their food, the local expressions, the peculiar language of the peasants, the smell of the soil, the hamlets, and to the atmosphere itself.

I love the house in which I grew up. From my windows I can see the Seine, which flows by the side of my garden, on the other side of the road, almost through my grounds, the great and wide Seine, which goes to Rouen and Havre, and which is covered with boats passing to and fro.

On the left, down yonder, lies Rouen, populous Rouen with its blue roofs massing under pointed, Gothic towers. Innumerable are they, delicate or broad, dominated by the spire of the cathedral, full of bells which sound through the blue air on fine mornings, sending their sweet and distant iron clang to me, their metallic sounds, now stronger and now weaker, according as the wind is strong or light.

What a delicious morning it was! About eleven o'clock, a long line of boats drawn by a tugboat, as big a fly, and which scarcely puffed while emitting its thick smoke, passed my gate.

After two English schooners, whose red flags fluttered toward the sky, there came a magnificent Brazilian three-master; it was perfectly white and wonderfully clean and shining. I saluted it, I hardly know why, except that the sight of the vessel gave me great pleasure.

MAY 12. I have had a slight feverish attack for the last few days, and I feel ill, or rather I feel low-spirited.

Whence come those mysterious influences which change our happiness into discouragement, and our self-confidence into diffidence? One might almost say that the air, the invisible air, is full of unknowable Forces, whose mysterious presence we have to endure. I wake up in the best of spirits, with an inclination to sing in my heart. Why? I go down by the side of the water, and suddenly, after walking a short distance, I return home wretched, as if some misfortune were awaiting me there. Why? Is it a cold shiver which, passing over my skin, has upset my nerves and given me a fit of low spirits? Is it the form of the clouds, or the tints of the sky, or the colors of the surrounding objects which are so change-able, which have troubled my thoughts as they passed before my eyes? Who can tell? Everything that surrounds us, everything that we see without looking at it, everything that we touch without knowing it, everything that we handle without feeling it, everything that we meet without clearly distinguishing it, has a rapid, surprising, and inexplicable effect upon us and upon our organs, and through them on our ideas and on our being itself.

How profound that mystery of the Invisible is! We cannot fathom it with our miserable senses: our eyes are unable to perceive what is either too small or too great, too near to or too far from us; we can see neither the inhabitants of a star nor of a drop of water; our ears deceive us, for they transmit to us the vibrations of the air in sonorous notes. Our senses are fairies who work the miracle of changing that movement into noise, and by that metamorphosis give birth to music, which makes the mute agitation of nature a harmony. So with our sense of smell, which is weaker than that of a dog, and so with our sense of taste, which can scarcely distinguish the age of a wine!

Oh! If we only had other organs which could work other miracles in our favor, what a number of fresh things we might discover around us!

MAY 16. I am ill, undoubtedly! I was so well last month! I am feverish, horribly feverish, or rather I am in a state of feverish enervation, which makes my mind suffer as much as my body. I have without ceasing the horrible sensation of some danger threatening me, the apprehension of some coming misfortune or of approaching death, a presentiment which is no doubt, an attack of some illness still unnamed, which germinates in the flesh and in the blood.

MAY 18. I have just come from consulting my medical man, for I can no longer get any sleep. He found that my pulse was high, my eyes dilated, my nerves highly strung, but no alarming symptoms. I must have a course of shower baths and of bromide of potassium.

MAY 25. No change! My state is really very peculiar. As the evening comes on, an incomprehensible feeling of disquietude seizes me, just as if night concealed some terrible menace toward me. I dine quickly, and then try to read, but I do not understand the words, and can scarcely distinguish the letters. Then I walk up and down my drawing-room, oppressed by a feeling of confused and irresistible fear, a fear of sleep and a fear of my bed.

About ten o'clock I go up to my room. As soon as I have entered I lock and bolt the door. I am frightened—of what? Up till the present time I have been frightened of nothing. I open my cupboards, and look under my bed; I listen—I listen—to what? How strange it is that a simple feeling of discomfort, of impeded or heightened circulation, perhaps the irritation of a nervous center, a slight congestion, a small disturbance in the imperfect and delicate functions of our living machinery, can turn the most light-hearted of men into a melancholy one, and make a coward of the bravest? Then, I go to bed, and I wait for sleep as a man might wait for the executioner. I wait for its coming with dread, and my heart beats and my legs tremble, while my whole body shivers beneath the warmth of the bedclothes, until the moment when I suddenly fall asleep, as a man throws himself into a pool of stagnant water in order to drown. I do not feel this perfidious sleep coming over me as I used to, but a sleep which is close to me and watching me, which is going to seize me by the head, to close my eyes and annihilate me.

I sleep—a long time—two or three hours perhaps—then a dream—no—a nightmare lays hold on me. I feel that I am in bed and asleep—I feel it and I know it—and I feel also that somebody is coming close to me, is looking at me, touching me, is getting on to my bed, is kneeling on my chest, is taking my neck between his hands and squeezing it—squeezing it with all his might in order to strangle me.

I struggle, bound by that terrible powerlessness which paralyzes us in our dreams; I try to cry out—but I cannot; I want to move—I cannot; I try, with the most violent efforts and out of breath, to turn over and throw off this being which is crushing and suffocating me—I cannot!

And then suddenly I wake up, shaken and bathed in perspiration; I light a candle and find that I am alone, and after that crisis, which occurs every night, I at length fall asleep and slumber tranquilly till morning.

JUNE 2. My state has grown worse. What is the matter with me? The bromide does me no good, and the shower-baths have no effect whatever. Sometimes, in order to tire myself out, though I am fatigued enough already, I go for a walk in the forest of Roumare. I used to think at first that the fresh light and soft air, impregnated with the odor of herbs and leaves, would instill new life into my veins and impart fresh energy to my heart. One day I turned into a broad ride in the wood, and then I diverged toward La Bouille, through a narrow path, between two rows of exceedingly tall trees, which placed a thick, green, almost black roof between the sky and me.

A sudden shiver ran through me, not a cold shiver, but a shiver of agony, and so I hastened my steps, uneasy at being alone in the wood, frightened stupidly and without reason, at the profound solitude. Suddenly it seemed as if I were being followed, that somebody was walking at my heels, close, quite close to me, near enough to touch me.

I turned round suddenly, but I was alone. I saw nothing behind me except the straight, broad ride, empty and bordered by high trees, horribly empty; on the other side also it extended until it was lost in the distance, and looked just the same—terrible.

I closed my eyes. Why? And then I began to turn round on one heel very quickly, just like a top. I nearly fell down, and opened my eyes; the trees were dancing round me and the earth heaved; I was obliged to sit down. Then, ah! I no longer remembered how I had come! What a strange idea! What a strange, strange idea! I did not the least know. I started off to the right, and got back into the avenue which had led me into the middle of the forest.

JUNE 3. I have had a terrible night. I shall go away for a few weeks, for no doubt a journey will set me up again.

JULY 2. I have come back, quite cured, and have had a most delightful trip into the bargain. I have been to Mont Saint-Michel, which I had not seen before.

What a sight, when one arrives as I did, at Avranches toward the end of the day! The town stands on a hill, and I was taken into the public garden at the extremity of the town. I uttered a cry of astonishment. An extraordinarily large bay lay extended before me, as far as my eyes could reach, between two hills which were lost to sight in the mist; and in the middle of this immense yellow bay, under a clear, golden sky, a peculiar hill rose up, somber and pointed in the midst of the sand. The sun had just disappeared, and under the still flaming sky stood out the outline of that fantastic rock which bears on its summit a picturesque monument.

At daybreak I went to it. The tide was low, as it had been the night before, and I saw that wonderful abbey rise up before me as I approached it. After several hours' walking, I reached the enormous mass of rock which supports the little town, dominated by the great church. Having climbed the steep and narrow street, I entered the most wonderful Gothic building that has ever been erected to God on earth, large as a town, and full of low rooms which seem buried beneath vaulted roofs, and of lofty galleries supported by delicate columns.

I entered this gigantic granite jewel, which is as light in its effect as a bit of lace and is covered with towers, with slender belfries to which spiral staircases ascend. The flying buttresses raise strange heads that bristle with chimeras, with devils, with fantastic animals, with monstrous flowers, are joined together by finely carved arches, to the blue sky by day, and to the black sky by night.

When I had reached the summit. I said to the monk who accompanied me: "Father, how happy you must be here!" And he replied: "It is very windy, Monsieur"; and so we began to talk while watching the rising tide, which ran over the sand and covered it with a steel cuirass.

And then the monk told me stories, all the old stories belonging to the place—legends, nothing but legends.

One of them struck me forcibly. The country people, those belonging to the Mornet, declare that at night one can hear talking going on in the sand, and also that two goats bleat, one with a strong, the other with a weak voice. Incredulous people declare that it is nothing but the screaming of the sea birds, which occasionally resembles bleatings, and occasionally human lamentations; but belated fishermen swear that they have met an old shepherd, whose cloak covered head they can never see, wandering on the sand, between two tides, round the little town placed so far out of the world. They declare he is guiding and walking before a he-goat with a man's face and a she-goat with a woman's face, both with white hair, who talk incessantly, quarreling in a strange language, and then suddenly cease talking in order to bleat with all their might.

"Do you believe it?" I asked the monk. "I scarcely know," he replied; and I continued: "If there are other beings besides ourselves on this earth, how comes it that we have not known it for so long a time, or why have you not seen them? How is it that I have not seen them?"

He replied: "Do we see the hundred-thousandth part of what exists? Look here; there is the wind, which is the strongest force in nature. It knocks down men, and blows down buildings, uproots trees, raises the sea into mountains of water, destroys cliffs and casts great ships on to the breakers; it kills, it whistles, it sighs, it roars. But have you ever seen it, and can you see it? Yet it exists for all that."

I was silent before this simple reasoning. That man was a philosopher, or perhaps a fool; I could not say which exactly, so I held my tongue. What he had said had often been in my own thoughts.

JULY 3. I have slept badly; certainly there is some feverish influence here, for my coachman is suffering in the same way as I am. When I went back home yesterday, I noticed his singular paleness, and I asked him: "What is the matter with you, Jean?"

"The matter is that I never get any rest, and my nights devour my days. Since your departure, Monsieur, there has been a spell over me."

However, the other servants are all well, but I am very frightened of having another attack, myself.

JULY 4. I am decidedly taken again; for my old nightmares have returned. Last night I felt somebody leaning on me who was sucking my life from between my lips with his mouth. Yes, he was sucking it out of my neck like a leech would have done. Then he got up, satiated, and I woke up, so beaten, crushed, and annihilated that I could not move. If this continues for a few days, I shall certainly go away again.

JULY 5. Have I lost my reason? What has happened? What I saw last night is so strange that my head wanders when I think of it!

As I do now every evening, I had locked my door; then, being thirsty, I drank half a glass of water, and I accidentally noticed that the water-bottle was full up to the cut-glass stopper.

Then I went to bed and fell into one of my terrible sleeps, from which I was aroused in about two hours by a still more terrible shock.

Picture to yourself a sleeping man who is being murdered, who wakes up with a knife in his chest, a gurgling in his throat, is covered with blood, can no longer breathe, is going to die and does not understand anything at all about it—there you have it.

Having recovered my senses, I was thirsty again, so I lighted a candle and went to the table on which my water-bottle was. I lifted it up and tilted it over my glass, but nothing came out. It was empty! It was completely empty! At first I could not understand it at all; then suddenly I was seized by such a terrible feeling that I had to sit down, or rather fall into a chair! Then I sprang up with a bound to look about me; then I sat down again, overcome by astonishment and fear, in front of the transparent crystal bottle! I looked at it with fixed eyes, trying to solve the puzzle, and my hands trembled! Somebody had drunk the water, but who? I? I without any doubt. It could surely only be I? In that case I was a somnambulist—was living, without knowing it, that double, mysterious life which makes us doubt whether there are not two beings in us—whether a strange, unknowable, and invisible being does not, during our moments of mental and physical torpor, animate the inert body, forcing it to a more willing obedience than it yields to ourselves.

Oh! Who will understand my horrible agony? Who will understand the emotion of a man sound in mind, wide-awake, full of sense, who looks in horror at the disappearance of a little water while he was asleep, through the glass of a water-bottle! And I remained sitting until it was daylight, without venturing to go to bed again.

JULY 6. I am going mad. Again all the contents of my water-bottle have been drunk during the night; or rather I have drunk it!

But is it I? Is it I? Who could it be? Who? Oh! God! Am I going mad? Who will save me?

JULY 10. I have just been through some surprising ordeals. Undoubtedly I must be mad! And yet!

On July 6, before going to bed, I put some wine, milk, water, bread, and strawberries on my table. Somebody drank—I drank—all the water and a little of the milk, but neither the wine, nor the bread, nor the strawberries were touched.

On the seventh of July I renewed the same experiment, with the same results, and on July 8 I left out the water and the milk and nothing was touched.

Lastly, on July 9 I put only water and milk on my table, taking care to wrap up the bottles in white muslin and to tie down the stoppers. Then I rubbed my lips, my beard, and my hands with pencil lead, and went to bed.

Deep slumber seized me, soon followed by a terrible awakening. I had not moved, and my sheets were not marked. I rushed to the table.

The muslin round the bottles remained intact; I undid the string, trembling with fear. All the water had been drunk, and so had the milk! Ah! Great God! I must start for Paris immediately.

JULY 12. Paris. I must have lost my head during the last few days! I must be the plaything of my enervated imagination, unless I am really a somnambulist, or I have been brought under the power of one of those influences—hypnotic suggestion, for example—which are known to exist, but have hitherto been inexplicable. In any case, my mental state bordered on madness, and twenty-four hours of Paris sufficed to restore me to my equilibrium.

Yesterday after doing some business and paying some visits, which instilled fresh and invigorating mental air into me, I wound up my evening at the Théâtre Français. A drama by Alexander Dumas the Younger was being acted, and his brilliant and powerful play completed my cure. Certainly solitude is dangerous for active minds. We need men who can think and can talk, around us. When we are alone for a long time, we people space with phantoms.

I returned along the boulevards to my hotel in excellent spirits. Amid the jostling of the crowd I thought, not without irony, of my terrors and surmises of the previous week, because I believed, yes, I believed, that an invisible being lived beneath my roof. How weak our mind is; how quickly it is terrified and unbalanced as soon as we are confronted with a small, incomprehensible fact. Instead of dismissing the problem with: "We do not understand because we cannot find the cause," we immediately imagine terrible mysteries and supernatural powers.

JULY 14. Bastille Day. I walked through the streets, and the crackers and flags amused me like a child. Still, it is very foolish to make merry on a set date, by government decree. People are like a flock of sheep, now steadily patient, now in ferocious revolt. Say to it: "Amuse yourself," and it amuses itself. Say to it: "Go and fight with your neighbor," and it goes and fights. Say to it: "Vote for the Emperor," and it votes for the Emperor; then say to it: "Vote for the Republic," and it votes for the Republic.

Those who direct it are stupid, too; but instead of obeying men they obey principles, a course which can only be foolish, ineffective, and false, for the very reason that principles are ideas which are considered as certain and unchangeable, whereas in this world one is certain of nothing, since light is an illusion and noise is deception.

JULY 16. I saw some things yesterday that troubled me very much. I was dining at my cousin's, Madame Sable, whose husband is colonel of the Seventy-sixth Chasseurs at Limoges. There were two young women there, one of whom had married a medical man, Dr. Parent, who devotes himself a great deal to nervous diseases and to the extraordinary manifestations which just now experiments in hypnotism and suggestion are producing.

He related to us at some length the enormous results obtained by English scientists and the doctors of the medical school at Nancy, and the facts which he adduced appeared to me so strange, that I declared that I was altogether incredulous.

"We are," he declared, "on the point of discovering one of the most important secrets of nature, I mean to say, one of its most important secrets on this earth, for assuredly there are some up in the stars, yonder, of a different kind of importance. Ever since man has thought, since he has been able to express and write down his thoughts, he has felt himself close to a mystery which is impenetrable to his coarse and imperfect senses, and he endeavors to supplement the feeble penetration of his organs by the efforts of his intellect. As long as that intellect remained in its elementary stage, this intercourse with invisible spirits assumed forms which were commonplace though terrifying. Thence sprang the popular belief in the supernatural, the legends of wandering spirits, of fairies, of gnomes, of ghosts, I might even say the conception of God, for our ideas of the Workman-Creator, from whatever religion they may have come down to us, are certainly the most mediocre, the stupidest, and the most unacceptable inventions that ever sprang from the frightened brain of any human creature. Nothing is truer than what Voltaire says: 'If God made man in His own image, man has certainly paid Him back again.'

"But for rather more than a century, men seem to have had a presentiment of something new. Mesmer and some others have put us on an unexpected track, and within the last two or three years especially, we have arrived at results really surprising."

My cousin, who is also very incredulous, smiled, and Dr. Parent said to her: "Would you like me to try and send you to sleep, Madame?"

"Yes, certainly."

She sat down in an easy-chair, and he began to look at her fixedly, as if to fascinate her. I suddenly felt myself somewhat discomposed; my heart beat rapidly and I had a choking feeling in my throat. I saw that Madame Sable's eyes were growing heavy, her mouth twitched, and her bosom heaved, and at the end of ten minutes she was asleep.

"Go behind her," the doctor said to me; so I took a seat behind her. He put a visiting-card into her hands, and said to her: "This is a mirror; what do you see in it?"

She replied: "I see my cousin."

"What is he doing?"

"He is twisting his mustache."

"And now?"

"He is taking a photograph out of his pocket."

"Whose photograph is it?"

"His own."

That was true, for the photograph had been given me that same evening at the hotel.

"What is his attitude in this portrait?"

"He is standing up with his hat in his hand."

She saw these things in that card, in that piece of white pasteboard, as if she had seen them in a mirror.

The young women were frightened, and exclaimed: "That is quite enough! Quite, quite enough!"

But the doctor said to her authoritatively: "You will get up at eight o'clock tomorrow morning; then you will go and call on your cousin at his hotel and ask him to lend you the five thousand francs which your husband asks of you, and which he will ask for when he sets out on his coming journey."

Then he woke her up.

On returning to my hotel, I thought over this curious seance and I was assailed by doubts, not as to my cousin's absolute and undoubted good faith, for I had known her as well as if she had been my own sister ever since she was a child, but as to a possible trick on the doctor's part. Had not he, perhaps, kept a glass hidden in his hand, which he showed to the young woman in her sleep at the same time as he did the card? Professional conjurers do things which are just as singular.

However, I went to bed, and this morning, at about half past eight, I was awakened by my footman, who said to me: "Madame Sable has asked to see you immediately, Monsieur." I dressed hastily and went to her.

She sat down in some agitation, with her eyes on the floor, and without raising her veil said to me: "My dear cousin, I am going to ask a great favor of you."

"What is it, cousin?"

"I do not like to tell you, and yet I must. I am in absolute need of five thousand francs."

"What, you?"

"Yes, I, or rather my husband, who has asked me to procure them for him."

I was so stupefied that I hesitated to answer. I asked myself whether she had not really been making fun of me with Dr. Parent, if it were not merely a very well-acted farce which had been got up beforehand. On looking at her attentively, however, my doubts disappeared. She was trembling with grief, so painful was this step to her, and I was sure that her throat was full of sobs.

I knew that she was very rich and so I continued: "What! Has not your husband five thousand francs at his disposal? Come, think. Are you sure that he commissioned you to ask me for them?"

She hesitated for a few seconds, as if she were making a great effort to search her memory, and then she replied: "Yes—yes, I am quite sure of it."

"He has written to you?"

She hesitated again and reflected, and I guessed the torture of her thoughts. She did not know. She only knew that she was to borrow five thousand francs of me for her husband. So she told a lie.

"Yes, he has written to me."

"When, pray? You did not mention it to me yesterday."

"I received his letter this morning."

"Can you show it to me?"

"No; no—no—it contained private matters, things too personal to ourselves. I burned it."

"So your husband runs into debt?"

She hesitated again, and then murmured: "I do not know."

Thereupon I said bluntly: "I have not five thousand francs at my disposal at this moment, my dear cousin."

She uttered a cry, as if she were in pain; and said: "Oh! oh! I beseech you, I beseech you to get them for me."

She got excited and clasped her hands as if she were praying to me! I heard her voice change its tone; she wept and sobbed, harassed and dominated by the irresistible order that she had received.

"Oh! oh! I beg you to—if you knew what I am suffering—I want them today."

I had pity on her: "You shall have them by and by, I swear to you."

"Oh! thank you! thank you! How kind you are."

I continued: "Do you remember what took place at your house last night?"

"Yes."

"Do you remember that Dr. Parent sent you to sleep?"

"Yes."

"Oh! Very well then; he ordered you to come to me this morning to borrow five thousand francs, and at this moment you are obeying that suggestion."

She considered for a few moments, and then replied: "But as it is my husband who wants them—"

For a whole hour I tried to convince her, but could not succeed, and when she had gone I went to the doctor. He was just going out, and he listened to me with a smile, and said: "Do you believe now?"

"Yes, I cannot help it."

"Let us go to your cousin's."

She was already resting on a couch, overcome with fatigue. The doctor felt her pulse, looked at her for some time with one hand raised toward her eyes, which she closed by degrees under the irresistible power of this magnetic influence. When she was asleep, he said:

"Your husband does not require the five thousand francs any longer! You must, therefore, forget that you asked your cousin to lend them to you, and, if he speaks to you about it, you will not understand him."

Then he woke her up, and I took out a pocketbook and said: "Here is what you asked me for this morning, my dear cousin." But she was so surprised, that I did not venture to persist; nevertheless, I tried to recall the circumstance to her, but she denied it vigorously, thought that I was making fun of her, and in the end, very nearly lost her temper.

There! I have just come back, and I have not been able to eat any lunch, for this experiment has altogether upset me.

JULY 19. Many people to whom I have told the adventure have laughed at me. I no longer know what to think. The wise man says: Perhaps?

JULY 21. I dined at Bougival, and then I spent the evening at a boatmen's ball. Decidedly everything depends on place and surroundings. It would be the height of folly to believe in the supernatural on the Île de la Grenouilliere. But on the top of Mont Saint-Michel or in India, we are terribly under the influence of our surroundings. I shall return home next week.

JULY 30. I came back to my own house yesterday. Everything is going on well.

AUGUST 2. Nothing fresh; it is splendid weather, and I spend my days in watching the Seine flow past.

AUGUST 4. Quarrels among my servants. They declare that the glasses are broken in the cupboards at night. The footman accuses the cook, she accuses the needlewoman, and the latter accuses the other two. Who is the culprit? It would take a clever person to tell.

AUGUST 6. This time, I am not mad. I have seen—I have seen—I have seen!—I can doubt no longer—I have seen it!

I was walking at two o'clock among my rose trees, in the full sunlight—in the walk bordered by autumn roses that are beginning to fall. As I stopped to look at a Geant de Bataille, which had three splendid blooms, I distinctly saw the stalk of one of the roses bend close to me, as if an invisible hand had bent it, and then break, as if that hand had picked it! Then the flower raised itself, following the curve which a hand would have described in carrying it toward a mouth, and remained suspended in the transparent air, alone and motionless, a terrible red spot, three yards from my eyes. In desperation I rushed at it to take it! I found nothing; it had disappeared. Then I was seized with furious rage against myself, for it is not wholesome for a reasonable and serious man to have such hallucinations.

But was it a hallucination? I turned to look for the stalk, and I found it immediately under the bush, freshly broken, between the two other roses which remained on the branch. I returned home, then, with a much disturbed mind; for I am certain now, certain as I am of the alternation of day and night, that there exists close to me an invisible being who lives on milk and on water, who can touch objects, take them and change their places; who is, consequently, endowed with a material nature, although imperceptible to sense, and who lives as I do, under my roof—

AUGUST 7. I slept tranquilly. He drank the water out of my decanter, but did not disturb my sleep.

I ask myself whether I am mad. As I was walking just now in the sun by the riverside, doubts as to my own sanity arose in me; not vague doubts such as I have had hitherto, but precise and absolute doubts. I have seen mad people, and I have known some who were quite intelligent, lucid, even clear-sighted in every concern of life, except on one point. They could speak clearly, readily, profoundly on everything; till their thoughts were caught in the breakers of their delusions and went to pieces there, were dispersed and swamped in that furious and terrible sea of fogs and squalls that is called madness.

I certainly should think that I was mad, absolutely mad, if I were not conscious that I knew my state, if I could not fathom it and analyze it with the most complete lucidity. I should, in fact, be a reasonable man laboring under a hallucination. Some unknown disturbance must have been excited in my brain, one of those disturbances which physiologists of the present day try to note and to fix precisely, and that disturbance must have caused a profound gulf in my mind and in the order and logic of my ideas. Similar phenomena occur in dreams, and lead us through the most unlikely phantasmagoria, without causing us any surprise, because our verifying apparatus and our sense of control have gone to sleep, while our imaginative faculty wakes and works. Was it not possible that one of the imperceptible keys of the cerebral finger-board had been paralyzed in me? Some men lose the recollection of proper names, or of verbs, or of numbers, or merely of dates, in consequence of an accident. The localization of all the avenues of thought has been accomplished nowadays; what, then, would there be surprising in the fact that my faculty of controlling the unreality of certain hallucinations should be destroyed for the time being?

I thought of all this as I walked by the side of the water. The sun was shining brightly on the river and made earth delightful, while it filled me with love for life, for the swallows, whose swift agility is always delightful in my eyes, for the plants by the riverside, whose rustling is a pleasure to my ears.

By degrees, however, an inexplicable feeling of discomfort seized me. It seemed to me as if some unknown force were numbing and stopping me, were preventing me from going further and were calling me back. I felt that painful wish to return which comes on you when you have left a beloved invalid at home, and are seized by a presentiment that he is worse.

I, therefore, returned despite of myself, feeling certain that I should find some bad news awaiting me, a letter or a telegram. There was nothing, however, and I was surprised and uneasy, more so than if I had had another fantastic vision.

AUGUST 8. I spent a terrible evening, yesterday. He does not show himself anymore, but I feel that He is near me, watching me, looking at me, penetrating me, dominating me, and more terrible to me when He hides himself thus than if He were to manifest his constant and invisible presence by supernatural phenomena. However, I slept.

AUGUST 9. Nothing, but I am afraid.

AUGUST 10. Nothing; but what will happen tomorrow?

AUGUST 11. Still nothing. I cannot stop at home with this fear hanging over me and these thoughts in my mind; I shall go away.

AUGUST 12. Ten o'clock at night. All day long I have been trying to get away, and have not been able. I contemplated a simple and easy act of liberty, a carriage ride to Rouen—and I have not been able to do it. What is the reason?

AUGUST 13. When one is attacked by certain maladies, the springs of our physical being seem broken, our energies destroyed, our muscles relaxed, our bones to be as soft as our flesh, and our blood as liquid as water. I am experiencing the same in my moral being, in a strange and distressing manner. I have no longer any strength, any courage, any self-control, nor even any power to set my own will in motion. I have no power left to will anything, but someone does it for me and I obey.

AUGUST 14. I am lost! Somebody possesses my soul and governs it! Somebody orders all my acts, all my movements, all my thoughts. I am no longer master of myself, nothing except an enslaved and terrified spectator of the things which I do. I wish to go out; I cannot. He does not wish to; and so I remain, trembling and distracted in the armchair in which he keeps me sitting. I merely wish to get up and to rouse myself, so as to think that I am still master of myself: I cannot! I am riveted to my chair, and my chair adheres to the floor in such a manner that no force of mine can move us.

Then suddenly, I must, I must go to the foot of my garden to pick some strawberries and eat them—and I go there. I pick the strawberries and I eat them! Oh! my God! my God! Is there a God? If there be one, deliver me! save me! succor me! Pardon! Pity! Mercy! Save me! Oh! what sufferings! what torture! what horror!

AUGUST 15. Certainly this is the way in which my poor cousin was possessed and swayed, when she came to borrow five thousand francs of me. She was under the power of a strange will which had entered into her, like another soul, a parasitic and ruling soul. Is the world coming to an end?

But who is he, this invisible being that rules me, this unknowable being, this rover of a supernatural race?

Invisible beings exist, then! how is it, then, that since the beginning of the world they have never manifested themselves in such a manner as they do to me? I have never read anything that resembles what goes on in my house. Oh! If I could only leave it, if I could only go away and flee, and never return, I should be saved; but I cannot.

AUGUST 16. I managed to escape today for two hours, like a prisoner who finds the door of his dungeon accidentally open. I suddenly felt that I was free and that He was far away, and so I gave orders to put the horses in as quickly as possible, and I drove to Rouen. Oh! how delightful to be able to say to my coachman: "Go to Rouen!"

I made him pull up before the library, and I begged them to lend me Dr. Hermann Herestauss's treatise on the unknown inhabitants of the ancient and modern world.

Then, as I was getting into my carriage, I intended to say: "To the railway station!" but instead of this I shouted—I did not speak; but I shouted—in such a loud voice that all the passersby turned round: "Home!" and I fell back on to the cushion of my carriage, overcome by mental agony. He had found me out and regained possession of me.

AUGUST 17. Oh! What a night! what a night! And yet it seems to me that I ought to rejoice. I read until one o'clock in the morning! Herestauss, Doctor of Philosophy and Theogony, wrote the history and the manifestation of all those invisible beings which hover around man, or of whom he dreams. He describes their origin, their domains, their power; but none of them resembles the one which haunts me. One might say that man, ever since he has thought, has had a foreboding and a fear of a new being, stronger than himself, his successor in this world, and that, feeling him near, and not being able to foretell the nature of the unseen one, he has, in his terror, created the whole race of hidden beings, vague phantoms born of fear.

Having, therefore, read until one o'clock in the morning, I went and sat down at the open window, in order to cool my forehead and my thoughts in the calm night air. It was very pleasant and warm! How I should have enjoyed such a night formerly!

There was no moon, but the stars darted out their rays in the dark heavens. Who inhabits those worlds? What forms, what living beings, what animals are there yonder? Do those who are thinkers in those distant worlds know more than we do? What can they do more than we? What do they see which we do not? Will not one of them, some day or other, traversing space, appear on our earth to conquer it, just as formerly the Norsemen crossed the sea in order to subjugate nations feebler than themselves?

We are so weak, so powerless, so ignorant, so small—we who live on this particle of mud which revolves in liquid air.

I fell asleep, dreaming thus in the cool night air, and then, having slept for about three quarters of an hour, I opened my eyes without moving, awakened by an indescribably confused and strange sensation. At first I saw nothing, and then suddenly it appeared to me as if a page of the book, which had remained open on my table, turned over of its own accord. Not a breath of air had come in at my window, and I was surprised and waited. In about four minutes, I saw, I saw— yes I saw with my own eyes—another page lift itself up and fall down on the others, as if a finger had turned it over. My armchair was empty, appeared empty, but I knew that He was there, He, and sitting in my place, and that He was reading. With a furious bound, the bound of an enraged wild beast that wishes to disembowel its tamer, I crossed my room to seize him, to strangle him, to kill him! But before I could reach it, my chair fell over as if somebody had run away from me. My table rocked, my lamp fell and went out, and my window closed as if some thief had been surprised and had fled out into the night, shutting it behind him.

So He had run away; He had been afraid; He, afraid of me!

So tomorrow, or later—some day or other, I should be able to hold him in my clutches and crush him against the ground! Do not dogs occasionally bite and strangle their masters?

AUGUST 18. I have been thinking the whole day long. Oh! yes, I will obey Him, follow His impulses, fulfill all His wishes, show myself humble, submissive, a coward. He is the stronger; but an hour will come.

AUGUST 19. I know, I know, I know all! I have just read the following in the Revue du Monde Scientifique:

> A curious piece of news comes to us from Rio de Janeiro. Madness, an epidemic of madness, which may be compared to that contagious madness which attacked the people of Europe in the Middle Ages, is at this moment raging in the province of São Paulo. The frightened inhabitants are leaving their houses, deserting their villages, abandoning their land, saying that they are pursued, possessed, governed like human cattle by invisible, though tangible beings, by a species of vampire, which feeds on their life while they are asleep, and which, besides, drinks water and milk without appearing to touch any other nourishment.
>
> Professor Don Pedro Henriques, accompanied by several medical savants, has gone to the province of São Paulo, in order to study the origin and the manifestations of this surprising madness on the spot, and to propose such measures to the Emperor as may appear to him to be most fitted to restore the mad population to reason.

Ah! Ah! I remember now that fine Brazilian three-master which passed in front of my windows as it was going up the Seine, on the eighth of last May! I thought it looked so pretty, so white and bright! That Being was on board of her, coming from there, where its race sprang from. And it saw me! It saw my house, which was also white, and He sprang from the ship on to the land. Oh! Good heavens!

Now I know, I can divine. The reign of man is over, and He has come. He whom disquieted priests exorcised, whom sorcerers evoked on dark nights, without seeing him appear, He to whom the imaginations of the transient masters of the world lent all the monstrous or graceful forms of gnomes, spirits, genii, fairies, and familiar spirits. After the coarse conceptions of primitive fear, men more enlightened gave him a truer form. Mesmer divined him, and ten years ago physicians accurately discovered the nature of his power, even before He exercised it himself. They played with that weapon of their new Lord, the sway of a mysterious will over the human soul, which had become enslaved. They called it mesmerism, hypnotism, suggestion, I know not what? I have seen them diverting themselves like rash children with this horrible power! Woe to us! Woe to man! He has come, the—the—what does He call himself—the—I fancy that he is shouting out his name to me and I do not hear him—the—yes—He is shouting it out—I am listening—I cannot—repeat—it—Horla—I have heard—the Horla—it is He—the Horla—He has come!——

Ah! the vulture has eaten the pigeon, the wolf has eaten the lamb; the lion has devoured the sharp-horned buffalo; man has killed the lion with an arrow, with a spear, with gunpowder; but the Horla will make of man what man has made of the horse and of the ox: his chattel, his slave, and his food, by the mere power of his will. Woe to us!

But, nevertheless, sometimes the animal rebels and kills the man who has subjugated it. I should also like—I shall be able to—but I must know Him, touch Him, see Him! Learned men say that eyes of animals, as they differ from ours, do not distinguish as ours do. And my eye cannot distinguish this newcomer who is oppressing me.

Why? Oh! Now I remember the words of the monk at Mont Saint-Michel: "Can we see the hundred-thousandth part of what exists? Listen; there is the wind which is the strongest force in nature; it knocks men down, blows down buildings, uproots trees, raises the sea into mountains of water, destroys cliffs, and casts great ships on to the breakers; it kills, it whistles, it sighs, it roars—have you ever seen it, and can you see it? It exists for all that, however!"

And I went on thinking: my eyes are so weak, so imperfect, that they do not even distinguish hard bodies, if they are as transparent as glass! If a glass without quicksilver behind it were to bar my way, I should run into it, just like a bird which has flown into a room breaks its head against the windowpanes. A thousand things, moreover, deceive a man and lead him astray. How then is it surprising that he cannot perceive a new body which is penetrated and pervaded by the light?

A new being! Why not? It was assuredly bound to come! Why should we be the last? We do not distinguish it, like all the others created before us? The reason is, that its nature is more delicate, its body finer and more finished than ours. Our makeup is so weak, so awkwardly conceived; our body is encumbered with organs that are always tired, always being strained like locks that are too complicated; it lives like a plant and like an animal nourishing itself with difficulty on air, herbs, and flesh; it is a brute machine which is a prey to maladies, to malformations, to decay; it is broken-winded, badly regulated, simple and

eccentric, ingeniously yet badly made, a coarse and yet a delicate mecha-
nism, in brief, the outline of a being which might become intelligent
and great.

There are only a few—so few—stages of development in this world,
from the oyster up to man. Why should there not be one more, when
once that period is accomplished which separates the successive
products one from the other?

Why not one more? Why not, also, other trees with immense, splendid flowers, perfuming whole regions? Why not other elements beside fire, air, earth, and water? There are four, only four, nursing fathers
of various beings! What a pity! Why should not there be forty, four
hundred, four thousand! How poor everything is, how mean and
wretched—grudgingly given, poorly invented, clumsily made! Ah! the
elephant and the hippopotamus, what power! And the camel, what
suppleness!

But the butterfly, you will say, a flying flower! I dream of one that
should be as large as a hundred worlds, with wings whose shape, beauty,
colors, and motion I cannot even express. But I see it—it flutters from
star to star, refreshing them and perfuming them with the light and
harmonious breath of its flight! And the people up there gaze at it as
it passes in an ecstasy of delight!

What is the matter with me? It is He, the Horla who haunts me,
and who makes me think of these foolish things! He is within me, He
is becoming my soul; I shall kill him!

AUGUST 20. I shall kill Him. I have seen Him! Yesterday I sat down at
my table and pretended to write very assiduously. I knew quite well
that He would come prowling round me, quite close to me, so close
that I might perhaps be able to touch him, to seize him. And then—
then I should have the strength of desperation; I should have my hands,
my knees, my chest, my forehead, my teeth to strangle him, to crush
him, to bite him, to tear him to pieces. And I watched for him with all
my overexcited nerves.

I had lighted my two lamps and the eight wax candles on my mantelpiece, as if, by this light I should discover Him.

My bed, my old oak bed with its columns, was opposite to me; on
my right was the fireplace; on my left the door, which was carefully
closed, after I had left it open for some time, in order to attract Him;
behind me was a very high wardrobe with a mirror in it, which served

me to dress by every day, and in which I was in the habit of inspecting myself from head to foot every time I passed it.

So I pretended to be writing in order to deceive Him, for He also was watching me, and suddenly I felt, I was certain, that He was reading over my shoulder, that He was there, almost touching my ear.

I got up so quickly, with my hands extended, that I almost fell. Horror! It was as bright as at midday, but I did not see myself in the glass! It was empty, clear, profound, full of light! But my figure was not reflected in it—and I, I was opposite to it! I saw the large, clear glass from top to bottom, and I looked at it with unsteady eyes. I did not dare advance; I did not venture to make a movement; feeling certain, nevertheless, that He was there, but that He would escape me again, He whose imperceptible body had absorbed my reflection.

How frightened I was! And then suddenly I began to see myself through a mist in the depths of the mirror, in a mist as it were, or through a veil of water; and it seemed to me as if this water were flowing slowly from left to right, and making my figure clearer every moment. It was like the end of an eclipse. Whatever hid me did not appear to possess any clearly defined outlines, but was a sort of opaque transparency, which gradually grew clearer.

At last I was able to distinguish myself completely, as I do every day when I look at myself.

I had seen Him! And the horror of it remained with me, and makes me shudder even now.

AUGUST 21. How could I kill Him, since I could not get hold of Him? Poison? But He would see me mix it with the water; and then, would our poisons have any effect on His impalpable body? No—no—no doubt about the matter. Then?—then?

AUGUST 22. I sent for a blacksmith from Rouen and ordered iron shutters of him for my room, such as some private hotels in Paris have on the ground floor, for fear of thieves, and he is going to make me a similar door as well. I have made myself out a coward, but I do not care about that!

SEPTEMBER 10. Rouen, Hôtel Continental. It is done; it is done—but is He dead? My mind is thoroughly upset by what I have seen.

Well then, yesterday, the locksmith having put on the iron shutters and door, I left everything open until midnight, although it was getting cold.

Suddenly I felt that He was there, and joy, mad joy took possession of me. I got up softly, and I walked to the right and left for some time, so that He might not guess anything; then I took off my boots and put on my slippers carelessly; then I fastened the iron shutters and going back to the door quickly I double-locked it with a padlock, putting the key into my pocket.

Suddenly I noticed that He was moving restlessly round me, that in his turn He was frightened and was ordering me to let Him out. I nearly yielded, though I did not quite, but putting my back to the door, I half opened it, just enough to allow me to go out backward, and as I am very tall, my head touched the lintel. I was sure that He had not been able to escape, and I shut Him up quite alone, quite alone. What happiness! I had Him fast. Then I ran downstairs into the drawing-room which was under my bedroom. I took the two lamps and poured all the oil on to the carpet, the furniture, everywhere; then I set fire to it and made my escape, after having carefully double locked the door.

I went and hid myself at the bottom of the garden, in a clump of laurel bushes. How long it was! how long it was! Everything was dark, silent, motionless, not a breath of air and not a star, but heavy banks of clouds which one could not see, but which weighed, oh! so heavily on my soul.

I looked at my house and waited. How long it was! I already began to think that the fire had gone out of its own accord, or that He had extinguished it, when one of the lower windows gave way under the violence of the flames, and a long, soft, caressing sheet of red flame mounted up the white wall, and kissed it as high as the roof. The light fell on to the trees, the branches, and the leaves, and a shiver of fear pervaded them also! The birds awoke; a dog began to howl, and it seemed to me as if the day were breaking! Almost immediately two other windows flew into fragments, and I saw that the whole of the lower part of my house was nothing but a terrible furnace. But a cry, a horrible, shrill, heart-rending cry, a woman's cry, sounded through the night, and two garret windows were opened! I had forgotten the servants! I saw the terror-struck faces, and the frantic waving of their arms!

Then, overwhelmed with horror, I ran off to the village, shouting:

"Help! help! fire! fire!" Meeting some people who were already coming on to the scene, I went back with them to see!

By this time the house was nothing but a horrible and magnificent funeral pile, a monstrous pyre which lit up the whole country, a pyre where men were burning, and where He was burning also, He, He, my prisoner, that new Being, the new Master, the Horla!

Suddenly the whole roof fell in between the walls, and a volcano of flames darted up to the sky. Through all the windows which opened on to that furnace, I saw the flames darting, and I reflected that He was there, in that kiln, dead.

Dead? Perhaps? His body? Was not his body, which was transparent, indestructible by such means as would kill ours?

If He were not dead? Perhaps time alone has power over that Invisible and Redoubtable Being. Why this transparent, unrecognizable body, this body belonging to a spirit, if it also had to fear ills, infirmities, and premature destruction?

Premature destruction? All human terror springs from that! After man the Horla. After him who can die every day, at any hour, at any moment, by any accident, He came, He who was only to die at his own proper hour and minute, because He had touched the limits of his existence!

No—no—there is no doubt about it—He is not dead. Then—then—I suppose I must kill myself!

The text of this book is set in 11 point Goudy Old Style,
designed by American printer and typographer
Frederic W. Goudy (1865–1947).
This serif font was chosen for its readability
and beautiful characteristics.

The archival-quality, natural paper is composed of recyclable products
made from wood grown in sustainable forests;
the manufacturing processes conform to the
environmental regulations of the country of origin.
Binder's boards are made from 100% post-consumer waste.

The finished volume demonstrates the convergence of Old World
craftsmanship and modern technology that exemplifies
books manufactured by Edwards Brothers, Inc.
Established in 1893, the family-owned business is a well-respected
leader in book manufacturing, recognized the world
over for quality and attention to detail.
In addition, Ann Arbor Media Group's editorial and design services
provide full-service book publication to business partners.